S0-AFT-393

the
gates
of
evangeline

the
gates
of
evangeline

Hester Young

G. P. Putnam's Sons
New York

PUTNAM

G. P. PUTNAM'S SONS
Publishers Since 1838
An imprint of Penguin Random House LLC
375 Hudson Street
New York, New York 10014

Copyright © 2015 by Hester Young
Penguin supports copyright. Copyright fuels creativity, encourages diverse voices,
promotes free speech, and creates a vibrant culture. Thank you for buying an authorized
edition of this book and for complying with copyright laws by not reproducing, scanning,
or distributing any part of it in any form without permission. You are supporting
writers and allowing Penguin to continue to publish books for every reader.

Grateful acknowledgment is made to quote lyrics from "You Are My Sunshine" by Jimmie
Davis, © 1940 by Peer International Corporation. Used by permission. All rights reserved.

Library of Congress Cataloging-in-Publication Data

Young, Hester.
The gates of Evangeline / Hester Young.
p.   cm.
ISBN 978-0-399-17400-1
1. Women journalists—Fiction.   2. Children in dreams—Fiction.   3. Family secrets—Fiction.
4. Murder—Fiction.   5. Plantations—Fiction.   6. Louisiana—Fiction.
7. Psychological fiction.   I. Title.
PS3625.O96435G38   2015   2015019186
813'.6—dc23

International edition ISBN: 978-0-399-18358-4

Printed in the United States of America
1   3   5   7   9   10   8   6   4   2

Book design by Meighan Cavanaugh

This is a work of fiction. Names, characters, places, and incidents
either are the product of the author's imagination or are used fictitiously,
and any resemblance to actual persons, living or dead, businesses,
companies, events, or locales is entirely coincidental.

For my grandmother

Margaret Gibbons Young (1921–2009)

and her son

Robert Gibbons Young (1951–1956)

But Evangeline's heart was sustained by a vision, that faintly
Floated before her eyes, and beckoned her on through the moonlight.
It was the thought of her brain that assumed the shape of a phantom.
Through those shadowy aisles had Gabriel wandered before her,
And every stroke of the oar now brought him nearer and nearer.

—HENRY WADSWORTH LONGFELLOW, *Evangeline: A Tale of Acadie*

Prologue

I can't pinpoint the moment I cross over. It comes slowly: the seductive darkness, my face and limbs dissolving into something weightless and fuzzy. Then consciousness spreads through me like caffeine. My senses come alive.

This time there is water. A soft *shhh*, on either side of me.

I wait. Try to orient myself. Am I in a boat?

The darkness lifts, and a picture forms. Swamp. I'm in a rowboat, drifting through brown water and swirls of green scum. Around me I see dead leaves, rotted branches curling like fingers, partially submerged trees clawing their way upward. On my right, I catch a flash of movement. Watchful green eyes peer up at me. An alligator.

I drift along, trying to read the light, to get a sense of time. Morning? Evening? The swamp is sunless and dreary, offering no clues.

I feel him before I see him. Someone is with me. A small figure in a white shirt sits across from me in the boat. His face comes to me as if through mist, indistinct smudges giving way to flesh. Is it him? Is it Keegan?

Disappointment stabs me when I see the boy, not quite my son's age. He's very small, with skinny limbs. Two, maybe three years old. Pinchable cheeks and longish brown hair.

As if relieved to see me, he smiles, revealing a chipped tooth. I have the feeling that he's been waiting for me.

Who are you? I ask.

Jo-Jo, he says, as though that should suffice. When he sees my blank stare, he tries to explain. *I lived at the big white house. We had a doggie.*

I note his use of the past tense with a frown. Where *are* we? I look around for something familiar, something I might recognize, but the swampy land is foreign.

The boy's smile dissipates, and his eyes search mine. *Will you help me?* He's so young, his voice still feeling its way around each sentence.

I swallow. Somewhere he has a mother who must love him very much.

How? I ask the boy. *What do you want me to do?*

He looks down at his hands, quiet for a moment. The rhythmic swishing of the water engulfs us, an eerie lullaby. *He hurt me,* the boy says finally. *You gotta tell on him.*

Who hurt you? I press. *If someone's hurting you, you need to tell your mom.*

I can't! The boy's voice rises, tearful. *He said no tellin' or he kill Mama. He kill me, maybe, too.*

I study his eyes, brown with long lashes, and the dark hair that curls at the tips, just past his chin. I must not forget about the tooth. Front tooth, chipped. Keep every detail intact. I think I understand this vision now, and he's right, he can't tell his mother.

He's already dead.

PART I

stamford, connecticut

OCTOBER

1.

The sky is a dismal gray when I finally go to remove my son's car
seat. It's raining, a cold autumn rain that feels both cliché and
appropriate for a moment I've spent more than three months avoiding.
I stand by my Prius, peering through the rear window at the empty
booster seat, wondering for the hundredth time about the thin coating
of mystery grit Keegan always left behind. And then I do it.

I don't give myself time to think, just proceed, quickly and efficiently.
Loosen the straps. Dig into the cushions of the backseat and unhook
the metal latches. One tug, and the car seat lands with a thunk on my
driveway.

They never end, all these little ways you have to say good-bye. I turn
my face toward the drizzle.

The summer has gone, slipped away without my noticing it, and
somehow October is here, flaunting her furious reds and yellows.
Squinting, I take in the houses of my neighborhood, their wholesome
front yards: trim lawns, beds of waterlogged chrysanthemums, a couple pumpkins on doorsteps. And leaves, of course, everywhere, blazing
and brilliant, melting into the slick streets, clogging gutters.

I put my hand to my pocket, feel my keys and wallet. Blink. Try to remember what I'm doing, where I planned to go. Try not to think about the car seat lying behind me in the driveway.

I inhale deeply, wet earth and decaying leaves. It's Sunday, I remind myself. I'm going to see Grandma. I climb into the driver's seat and turn on the car, but it all feels wrong. I give myself a minute, wait to see if the anxiety will pass, before conceding that I've lost this battle. I can't drive around town with that gaping void in the backseat. Not today.

Baby steps. One thing at a time.

I exit the car abruptly and head to the garage. Find my bike. It's Sunday, and I am going to see Grandma. I will stick to the plan. I will hold it together.

Breathe, I tell myself. *Breathe.*

"GOOD GOD, Charlotte, you're soaking." Standing in the doorway of her modest apartment, my grandmother looks uncharacteristically rattled.

"I biked."

Once, Grandma would have been impatient with my running around in the rain, inviting sickness. But life is no longer ordinary. My grandmother's granite eyes register concern, compassion even, as her gnarled hand waves me inside. I step into the foyer, dripping. Wet strings of hair cling to my forehead and neck.

Grandma peels off my jacket without comment. I can feel her watching, assessing, setting aside her own sadness to make space for mine. It's a look I first saw when I was fourteen, back when my father died and she took me in. A look that has made an unfortunate resurgence in recent months.

"There's a bathrobe somewhere," Grandma says. "Want a drink? Something hot?"

We are not a demonstrative pair. We are stoic New Englanders who maintain what my ex-husband sarcastically termed "the proper Yankee distance." Feelings, in the Cates family, are more private than politics or religion. Hot tea, a mug of cocoa—this is the kind of warmth my grandmother has to offer.

"I'm okay, Grandma. I just want to sit down." To describe myself as "okay" is, of course, a brazen lie. My face tells the story: cracked lips, eyelids puffy from sudden crying spells, skin pale and sickly after a summer spent hidden from the sun.

It's obvious that I am *not* okay, but Grandma says nothing. She puts a hand on my shoulder and gently ushers me into the living room. I assume my usual post on the creaky old rocker while she arranges herself in a high-backed wooden chair. My grandmother was a beautiful woman in her day, and though she's lost most of her vanity with age, pride in her good posture has endured.

The living room is, as always, immaculate. Grandma hates knick-knacks. Her bookshelf consists largely of reference materials, although the bottom shelf holds a few guilty pleasures: some Stephen King novels, *Cold Crimes* magazine (my first steady writing gig), and old issues of *Sophisticate*, from before my promotions, back when I was a staff writer. Grandma remains a loyal reader of *Sophisticate*, although she isn't exactly the target demographic for articles like "What You Need to Know About Prenups" and "Preparing Your Baby for an Ivy League Future."

If my home is one of managed chaos, Grandma's is one of enforced order. Even my son understood this, and obediently organized his books, games, and art supplies before we left here every Sunday.

"You didn't have to come, Charlie," Grandma murmurs. "I know it's Sunday, but you didn't have to come."

"How else would I see you?" My grandmother gets around well for a woman her age, but she no longer drives, and expecting her to navigate the bus system is a little much. "Besides, it's probably good for me to get out."

"Did you leave your bike outside?" she asks. "It might rust."

I shrug. "It was Eric's bike."

My grandmother's eyes narrow at the mention of my ex-husband. "Has he called you? Even once, to see how you're doing?"

There's venom in her words. She hates Eric with a passion I can no longer muster for his hipster glasses and ever-receding hairline. *The Sperminator*, my friend Rae took to calling him after the divorce, aptly summarizing his one lasting contribution to my life.

"Eric and I have nothing to talk about," I say. "I told him not to call." I don't bring up Melissa, his new wife, but my grandmother cannot contain herself.

"I'll never understand what he sees in that woman."

My friends made similar comments after the funeral. They all knew she was the Other Woman. I suppose they expected more: good looks, big boobs, animal prints, the kind of trashiness that might have predictably turned Eric's head. But Melissa, like Eric, was unremarkable.

"He did you a favor, really," my grandmother declares. "You don't waste caviar on a man who wants corn dogs. She's exactly what he deserves."

My whole family was outraged when Eric arrived at our son's funeral with Melissa in tow. *He has to rub her face in it,* I overheard my aunt Suzie say, and maybe that was true. Maybe, in some childish way, Eric has something to prove. I didn't care about the wife. I was angry that he showed up at all. Eric had visited Keegan only once since he and Melissa moved to Chicago. What right did he have to fatherly grief?

And still, Melissa comforted him. Held him as if the loss were his. *No,* I wanted to tell them both, *that's MY son.*

"You know, she works in waste management," I inform Grandma, suddenly ready to take what cheap comfort I can.

"That explains why she loves trash," Grandma mutters.

I manage a wobbly smile. We are Yankees. These are her love words.

TWO HOURS at my grandmother's house have, more or less, the intended effect. When it becomes clear that I don't want to talk, she fills the silence. She tells me about the small fire her elderly, somewhat senile neighbor started. She comments on a recent article in *Sophisticate*, an exposé on Botox that she reacts indignantly to. It all feels familiar. Not normal, exactly, but familiar. A life I vaguely recognize as my own.

I'm picking myself up, preparing for the return to my empty, silent house, when Grandma speaks. "Is there anything I can do for you?"

It's the closest she has come to acknowledging tragedy, and it chokes me up. I swallow and shake my head. There is nothing she, or anyone else, can do.

"I wanted to ask you . . ." She gathers herself up and I can see her steeling herself, preparing to ask an unpleasant question. "The church across the street is collecting donations. They're looking for children's items, and of course, I have all these toys around . . ."

It is an entirely reasonable thing for her to ask, and yet I resent it all the same.

"Did you want to hang on to them?" Grandma asks, sensing resistance in my silence. "There's no hurry."

"No, no, donate them." I know the right words, even if I don't truly feel them. "I'm sure some kid could find a use for all that stuff."

My grandmother nods and collects my wet coat. I'm halfway out the door and headed for the elevator when she calls after me. "Charlotte?"

I turn.

"Do you dream about him?"

It's an odd question.

"I never dream," I tell her. "Ever. Do *you* dream about him?"

She shakes her head. "Sometimes I wish I did." She blows me a kiss, a gesture I find unexpectedly tender. "Be careful riding home."

THAT NIGHT, sprawled across the couch in the dark, I wait for my sleeping pills to kick in. Even before I lost Keegan, I needed pills. Now I need more. *Charlie's only off switch,* Eric used to joke, and it's true.

My body goes slack. My mind swirls. I'm on my way out.

Mom. From behind me, I swear I can hear Keegan's voice. *Mommy, are you listening?*

I try to sit up, but Ambien is pulling me under, filling my head with nothing.

You have to listen, Mommy. It's time to start listening.

The last thing I'm aware of is the sweet smell of his shampoo, his curls tickling my face. Then the drugs take me away.

2.

When my friend Rae shows up with an eggplant dish her husband made, I know exactly what play she's running. It's a move I've grown accustomed to. The food gets her inside, where she guilts me into eating *just a little, so I can tell Mason you tried it.* Then, as I dutifully pick at her husband's cooking, she tackles chores around my house.

In the beginning, her little check-ins drove me nuts. I wasn't hungry. I didn't *want* my laundry done. Dishes were beside the point. Now I realize the neighborly love behind the visits, understand the time Rae and Mason set aside each week for me, and I'm grateful—though they still drive me nuts.

Today, I don't even have time to retrieve a spoon before she's attacking my kitchen, poking a broom into the dark crevices beneath the fridge and dishwasher. I'm in no mood for it.

"Would you *stop* cleaning, damn it? The house is fine."

She sets the broom down slowly. Sighs. Sucks in her cheeks and runs a fingernail up and down her long brown throat. "Just trying to take something off your plate." Her gaze slides around my kitchen: its sticky counters, my ever-growing mound of mail, the overflowing garbage.

I know that she wants to help, wants to bring light or at least some Pine-Sol into my cave of misery, but Rae doesn't know this mess like I do. She sees smudgy sliding glass doors, and I see my son's fingerprints. She sees an old Cheerio, and I see a breakfast when he sat with me, fidgeting, complaining, dawdling.

"So what did Mason make today?" I ask, peeling back the tinfoil on her casserole dish. "It looks good."

"Eggplant rollatini."

I have an obligatory spoonful. "Tell him I like it," I say, although it tastes like nothing to me, the way everything does now. "Did Zoey help? Is she still talking about being a chef?"

"Nah, she's back to ballerina again." Rae fiddles with one of her springy Afro curls and then changes the subject, as she usually does these days when I ask about her daughter. "So, Charlie, honey," she begins, "I have to ask. Are you seeing somebody?"

I'm confused. "You mean a boyfriend?"

"I mean a therapist. A grief counselor."

I wave a hand dismissively. "I have pills, I'm fine."

Rae squints at me. "Pills are good. But maybe you need to *talk* to someone, too. You've got a lot to sort through. Most of us can't do that alone."

The thought of explaining myself to someone, giving name to my feelings—it's exhausting. "I'll figure it out."

"I know you will," she says, softening. "You're the strongest person I know. Maybe *too* strong. It's okay to be a blubbering mess for a while."

"For a while?" I give a shaky laugh. "I don't think I'll ever stop."

"Oh, sweetie." Rae crosses the room and envelops me in the kind of rib-crushing hug my grandmother and I could never exchange. "This is your low. This is your rock bottom. I don't know when and I don't know how, but you'll get through this. And you'll kick life in the balls just as hard as it's kicked you. Remember when you found out Eric was cheating?"

The question, I assume, is rhetorical. It was not the sort of moment you'd forget. Eric took me to a restaurant for a so-called date night and, shortly after our appetizers arrived, began his dramatic confession. *Charlie,* he said, gazing into the distance like a character on a soap opera, *I did something terrible.*

Two years after the fact, it still makes my blood boil. "He wanted me to make a scene," I tell Rae. "That freaking drama queen."

"Oh, I'd have punched him," Rae says. "But you didn't. You held it together. Because you're a tough-ass bitch."

I shrug. My anger that day was with myself just as much as Eric. Because I should have known, should have seen the affair coming. Our marriage had been on the rocks since Keegan's birth, and I never mistook Eric for a model of moral virtue. I just didn't think he'd get the opportunity.

We've had problems for a long time, Eric said, delivering a speech that was clearly rehearsed. *But we can get past this. For Keegan. Our son needs us.*

He expected tears, a choice between two women, but I remained calm, determined not to follow the script. *No,* I corrected him through a mouthful of crab, *our son needs* me. *I want primary custody. And if you do anything to fight me on this—anything at all—I will have you paying child support out your ass for the next sixteen years. This can be hard, or this can be easy.*

In the end, he made it easy. For me, but mostly for himself.

I want to tell Rae that I'm not tough, just dumb to have married an asshole like Eric in the first place, but I can't regret Eric. Because I could never regret my son.

"Listen," Rae says, "I better go. You hang in there, Charlie-girl. One day at a time."

She doesn't tell me that she's going to pick up Zoey, but it's Thursday. Zoey has dance on Thursdays. I haven't forgotten. As I watch her drive away, I wonder if our friendship can survive this. Can I forgive Rae? She has somewhere to go. She has a child waiting.

THAT EVENING I get a call from Bianca, my art director at *Sophisticate*. I mute the TV, some program I wasn't really watching about ancient Egyptians, and answer my cell, grateful for the distraction of work.

"Hon, how *are* you?" I'm used to Bianca enthusing over beautiful layouts and agonizing over the font and color of text. Discussing my personal life is another story.

"I'm fine," I say cautiously. "You?"

"Good, good." Bianca doesn't linger on niceties. "So listen . . . I wanted you to be the first to know." She takes a deep breath. "Dunhaven's looking to sell the mag."

The TV casts eerie blue shadows across the wall of my living room. I stare at the images of mummies and ancient tombs, trying to absorb her words. Bianca and I have never exactly been a fan of our publisher, but a sale could mean a massive, catastrophic shake-up at work. This is a big deal, a very big deal, and yet I can't quite summon the energy to get riled up.

"Huh," I say.

My response is not what Bianca anticipated. "Look," she says, "I'm not supposed to say anything, but Longview Media's already made an offer. It could be accepted as early as next week."

"You think they'll restructure?" I ask.

"I can guarantee it," she says. "I know you've been working a lot from home these last few months, but that's not gonna fly with Longview. I'm telling you this as a friend, Charlie. Starting next week, you make it to the office *every day*, okay? Because heads are going to roll. And you know how bad Tina wants your job."

"Okay," I tell her, and in some distant way I do appreciate that she's looking out for me. "Thanks for the heads-up."

After our call, I sit staring at the phone, wondering why I'm not more concerned about the job I spent most of my adult life chasing. *Twelve years*, I realize in disbelief. I began working for the magazine at twenty-six. Once I determined my stint at *Cold Crimes* magazine was going nowhere, I started freelancing for *Sophisticate* until they offered me a staff writer position. *Sophisticate* was a complete 180 from writing about old murders and advances in forensics, but it was a steady job and paycheck. Now, many years and several promotions later, I am managing editor and I have an amazing career. Right?

An amazing career and almost no social life. Hardly any family. And no son.

I wander into the bathroom, in search of my Ambien. Kick aside a heap of mildewed towels, ignoring the smell. Pry the lid off my pill bottle.

Would losing my job really be a bad thing? For years, I've dedicated myself to a magazine that promises today's affluent professional woman a life of happiness and ease. But where is *my* happiness? *My* ease?

I slip myself an extra sleeping pill. I don't want to think anymore, don't want to remember what I've lost. Don't want to ask myself where I would be without my job now, too.

DING, DING, DING.

I'm jolted from my medicated fog by the doorbell. I sit up on the couch, head pounding, stomach lurching. An Ambien hangover. That's what happens when you double the recommended dose.

The doorbell rings again, three times in quick succession. It's a sound I haven't heard in a while. Zoey. Her "secret" ring for Keegan.

In the last few months, Rae has kept her daughter's visits to a minimum, and I don't blame her. I'm still fragile, unprepared to deal with Zoey's relentless questions. How do you explain to a kindergartener that her playmate is dead when you yourself can't fully grasp the implications of that word? I consider ignoring the doorbell altogether, but I've known Zoey most of her life. I love her to pieces. She is the only child I have left in my life.

I open the front door and blink away the morning sunshine. Zoey's face tilts up toward me; she's a tiny, even more gorgeous version of Rae. Smooth coffee skin, strictly managed curls. A fashionista in training. Rae stands behind her, hesitant. I have no doubt that she's coached her daughter thoroughly, but Zoey's only five, still a bit of a wild card.

"Hi-hi!" Zoey studies me. "Are you sick?"

"Zoey." Rae's tone is a warning.

"I came to show you my new outfit." She holds out the skirt of a lime-green ensemble and spins around for me.

I kneel down to her level. "It's beautiful."

"She wanted to say hello," Rae murmurs. "I hope you don't mind."

"No, I'm glad you came by." I glance at the living room clock. "Looks like I overslept."

"We'll let you get started on your day." Rae puts a hand on Zoey's shoulder, attempting to steer her child away. "We need to go too, baby. Time for school."

Zoey glances back at me. "Hey, wanna come to my dance show? It's gonna be really good."

Her mother obviously didn't anticipate the invite. "Charlie's really busy. Maybe another time."

Is she protecting me, I wonder, or shielding Zoey? "Are you having a recital, Zo?" I ask. Even before I lost Keegan, I envied Rae for her daughter, the princess dresses, purple tutus, and glitter paint. I haven't been to either of Zoey's recitals since she started lessons.

Zoey beams at my interest. "Yeah, we're having a show. And I get a costume. It's *really* pretty."

"Wow," I say. "I'd love to go."

Zoey hugs my knees.

"Are you sure?" Rae looks dubious, like she doesn't think I can hold myself together.

"Of course."

"The recital is Sunday afternoon. I could pick you up at three."

I can tell that she's still not convinced.

"If Sunday gets here and you don't feel like it, no biggie."

I attack Zoey with tickle fingers, ignoring her mother. Zoey squeals in delight.

"I'll see you on Sunday, sweetie. I can't wait."

"Yaaay!" She does a celebratory dance, and her joy is so innocent and pure, I think my heart will break.

IN THE FORTY-EIGHT HOURS BEFORE Zoey's recital, I become strangely agoraphobic. The idea of leaving the house fills me with panic. Can I really smile and applaud as I watch other people's children on display? Fueled by my anxiety, I stop lazing around the house and start cleaning. It's time. Objects are not the same as memories, I remind myself. My son is more to me than a Ninja Turtle backpack and a hallway littered with Matchbox cars.

I put away all of Keegan's toys, stacking puzzles and games on shelves, packing blocks and Legos away in boxes. I make his bed, wash and fold his clothes, alphabetize his books. These items mean nothing now to anyone but me. I am the only one who remembers the seven thousand times we read *Moo, Baa, La La La!* and the games of Candy

Land he shamelessly cheated at. There are no new memories to be made.

When I am through, the room is neat and impersonal. Blue walls, green trim, a *Sesame Street* bedspread. It looks like an IKEA display, a room waiting to be filled by some anonymous little boy, not my little boy, but someone else's.

Afterward, I turn on the shower, step in with all my clothes on, and sit down. I cry. Cleaning has never felt this bad.

In these two days, I stop taking sleeping pills. I don't want to check out, don't want to numb myself. I need to feel. Sleep, without pharmaceutical aid, has always been elusive; now it's an impossibility. At night, I leave the TV on, letting the enthusiastic voices of infomercials keep me company. I clean out the refrigerator, attack the bathroom tiles with a toothbrush. I cringe with self-loathing as I go through past issues of *Sophisticate*, the articles on diets and plastic surgery. I think, *At least I never had a daughter to screw up.* A cold comfort indeed.

On Sunday, I sit on the couch and wait. This is it. My day to look normal, to fake it as best I can. Sunlight filters weakly through the curtains. I hear birds. Days and nights without sleep finally take their toll, and before I know it, I'm gone.

Birds, first. Crows squabbling, the light receding, then red. Red flowing, rippling, shimmering. I dip my hand in it and watch fabric spill from my fingers. Someone giggles. I peel back layers of red and Zoey emerges, sequins falling from her hair. *I'm not ready,* she sings to me, *I'm not ready for the end.* Suddenly she's dancing. Spinning, twirling, leaving me nauseous with all her circles. *I'm not ready,* she sings, *I'm not ready for the end.* I reach for her, trying to steady her, but a curtain descends. Not my green curtains, but black curtains, crushing in their weight. Now Zoey is gone, swallowed in their black folds, screaming.

Zoey! I exclaim. *Zoey!*

My ankle, she whimpers from beneath the black. *My ankle.*

I awake to Rae shaking me. "Charlie? It's time to go. You still wanna come?"

Head throbbing, I try to remember where I am. "Where's Zoey? Is she okay?"

"Mason drove her over early."

The sun has shifted, leaving the room to the afternoon's advancing shadows. "What about her ankle? Is it broken?"

"Zoey? She's fine, hon. There's nothing wrong with her ankle." Rae leans against the arm of the couch, trying not to stare at her watch. "Are *you* okay? You look like you could use some more sleep."

"Was I sleeping?"

"I think you were dreaming."

"Oh." I sit up and rub my face, though I'm more uneasy than tired. "Let's go, then."

THE RECITAL IS BEING HELD at the local elementary school, in a musty auditorium with a drooping flag. When I look at the program, I realize Zoey's class is just one of eight performing. As the youngest group, they go first, and then appear again in the finale.

Mason sees my look of consternation and tries to reassure me. "It goes fast," he promises.

I like Rae's husband, but I know bullshit when I hear it.

The first number goes as expected. The curtain opens, and Zoey and her compatriots scuttle out in red sequined leotards. Dazed by the floodlights, the children form two haphazard lines and perform a dance so jerky and out of sync they look like marionettes.

Once Zoey leaves the stage, my mind wanders. I watch restless audience members move in and out of their seats, count the number of glowing cell phones set to record. I pick at the chipped varnish on my wooden seat, trying to tune out the rustling jackets and programs. The performances drag on until finally we reach the last number, some wretched pop song about a girl resisting her boyfriend's attempts to dump her. *Boy, you got to believe that / I ain't ready for you to leave yet,* she croons.

The routine begins with older girls while the little ones line up in the wings. Rae touches my shoulder and points to Zoey, who peeks out from behind the curtain, oblivious to the fact that everyone can see her.

"Uh-oh," Rae whispers. "She's going to miss her cue!"

And it does look that way. Lips moving like she's singing, Zoey twirls and grabs a handful of curtain. She leaps up, trying to sail through the air like she's Tarzan on a vine, and—

Collapse.

A mess of black fabric crashes down, engulfing her.

Over the tinny speakers, the music reaches a dreadful crescendo. *I'm not ready,* the singer moans, *I'm not ready for the end.*

I see Rae leap to her feet. I see a woman hurry out from backstage. I see Mason push his way past unyielding laps and knees and footwear, trying to get to the stage.

The music continues, its chorus familiar and horrible, as confused dancers wonder whether or not to carry on with the show: *I'm not ready, I'm not ready for the end.* Someone has pulled Zoey from the curtain, a competent-looking man. She's crying. He talks to her patiently, touches her leg, locating the source of her pain. She points, and I feel a dark thrill of recognition at this final, inexorable detail.

Because, of course, it's her ankle.

3.

That night, I try to drown out the noise in my head with more noise. I turn up the radio, run the garbage disposal, vacuum. None of this does anything to shake my sense of foreboding, but I prefer a pounding anxiety to quiet dread. At some point after eleven, Rae appears in my living room. I switch off the vacuum, startled to see her at this hour.

"I knocked," she says. "I don't think you could hear me." She looks around the newly tidy house, eyebrows raised. "Wow. This place looks good."

"How's Zoey?"

Rae rolls her eyes. "We just got back from our whole emergency room odyssey. She'll be fine." She slumps down onto the couch, her thigh landing on Keegan's Popsicle stain from last June. "I saw your light was on, so I figured I'd stop by. Glad you made it home."

"I took a taxi. It wasn't a big deal. So . . . did Zoey get crutches?"

She nods. "She loves them. We practically had to wrestle her into bed." She leans back against the couch, peering at me sideways. "It *was* broken, by the way. Her ankle."

"I guess that's lucky. It could've been a lot worse." I don't say how much worse, and Rae isn't thinking of the son I lost, not now.

"It's weird, isn't it? How you dreamed it?" She watches me closely.

I've been a queasy bundle of nerves the last few hours, turning it over in my mind, but I don't want her to know that. Rae is completely superstitious. She believes in *everything*. Ghosts and past lives and tarot cards—all that crap. I don't want her to believe in *this*.

"It was just a dream, Rae. I don't think it means anything."

"You woke up from your nap asking if Zoey's ankle was broken," Rae persists. "That totally means something!"

"You're right," I say with an eye roll. "I'm basically one step short of Nostradamus. I'll give you a call when I start dreaming about lottery numbers, okay?"

"You get to work on that, I'm not even playing!" She stretches her legs, as if amused by my skepticism. "I better get to bed. Thanks for coming to Zoey's recital, even if it did turn out crazy."

I follow her outside, watching from my driveway to see that she arrives safely at her house. It's a cold night, the kind of cold that feels clean when you inhale it. I cross my arms, shivering. Rae waves from the brick walkway of her yard as Mason opens the front door for her. She's made it. She's safe.

I step inside and lock the door behind me. I don't usually keep things from Rae, don't want to add to the distance between us now, but I can't tell her everything. Because it wasn't just the ankle. It was the red sequins, the black curtain. That awful song. I don't know what this means, not yet, and so I stuff it somewhere deep with all the other things I'm trying not to think about and I vacuum. I dust. Wash the kitchen floor and make beds.

Some time after four a.m., I survey my house and discover that for the first time in the five years I've owned it, my home is clean. Nothing-left-to-do clean. Bianca was right. It's time to return to work.

. . .

I WORK WITH A LOT OF WOMEN. There's a handful of gay men, and presumably a straight guy buried somewhere in the ranks, but for the most part, *Sophisticate* runs on a very specific type of estrogen: bitchy, hypereducated New Yorker.

In my twenties, I loved it. That was who I aspired to be. By thirty, I had perfected the wry smile, the raised eyebrow, the long and jaded sigh. I could argue about which bagel joint on the Upper West Side was best, pay eight dollars for half an avocado without batting an eye. I jogged through Central Park and thought I was communing with nature. The city wore on me, though. One day in a restaurant I saw my reflection and thought, *I never smile. I smirk.*

I was only too ready to escape when I met Eric, my knight in shining argyle, my ticket out. We dated just five months before marrying. Three months later, I was pregnant. Stamford, Connecticut, isn't as ritzy as Greenwich or Darien, but we found a cozy three-bedroom just a few miles from my grandmother's assisted-living facility. Even after Eric left, I loved my home. I'd watch Keegan digging in the sandbox or splashing in his kiddie pool and my heart would rise up in my chest with happiness—until the morning's long commute back into Manhattan.

On this dreary Monday, I walk the dozen blocks from Grand Central, feeling too claustrophobic for the tightly packed bodies of the subway. Between hulking skyscrapers, I catch fragments of sky and swirling clouds. Hair whipping around my face, I fight my way through wind tunnels, kick away blowing trash. None of the other pedestrians look at me, and I wonder how many people I've passed, how many faces I've ignored over the years.

I'm doing the best impression that I can of Charlie Before, but the whole sideswept–bangs–to–hide–the–grow-out thing isn't working this morning and my trousers are a bit wrinkled from the month they spent dangling from a shower rod. Truth be told, I have my doubts about *Sophisticate*. After all that I've been through, can I really muster up any enthusiasm for a magazine that is, if I'm being honest, an upmarket, slightly less sex-obsessed version of *Cosmo*? We actually ran a "How Oral Sex Can Save Your Marriage" article in September's issue.

At work, only a few people mill about. It's eight forty-five. I'm early, and deadline for the printer was last week, which tends to quell the chaos for a few days. Having spent most of my waking hours in this office the last decade, I've always appreciated the chic and modern décor, but this morning the white, windowless walls and glaring chrome remind me of a hospital. I head into the break room in search of a coffee jolt and discover Lauren, my editorial assistant, pouring yesterday's sludge down the sink.

"Charlie!" Her eyes are two wide circles of black eyeliner. "Didn't know you were coming in today."

"I should be in the office full-time now." I riffle through the cabinet for a clean filter. "You look cute. I like the haircut."

"Thanks . . ." Lauren sports a new choppy bob and a pair of Miu Miu heels that, given her salary, I can't figure out how she affords. Once, we would have dished at length about the hair and shoes, but I seem to have lost my taste for superficial chitchat.

"Did the photos ever come in for that piece on Tahitian weddings?" I ask.

"Yeah, it's done. Tina dealt with everything, don't worry." She watches as I measure out coffee grounds. "I guess you heard Longview Media is buying the mag."

"I'm sure it'll be fine. So nothing pressing I need to handle?" I'm both relieved and disappointed.

"Nah." She pauses for a minute, thinking it over. "You did get a phone call on Friday, Isaac Somebody from Meyers Rowe. He said you know him."

"Meyers Rowe, the publishing house? Must be Isaac Cohen." I'm not often in touch with my old editor from *Cold Crimes* magazine, but perhaps the true-crime division of Meyers Rowe has a book they want us to review. Isaac would never hesitate to call in a favor. "Well, thanks, Lauren. Sounds like you've got everything under control." I flip on the coffeemaker, figuring our conversation is done, but Lauren hasn't moved.

She clears her throat. "It's good to see you around. We've all been thinking about you." She takes a step closer to me, and I'm afraid for a moment that she might hug me. "If you need anything . . ."

"I'll ask."

Deciding that I'm best left alone, Lauren makes a clumsy exit, but her sympathy hangs in the air like too much perfume. I feel my throat constricting, my eyes watering. I grope around for a cup. Coffee is the answer, I tell myself. Burning, acrid office coffee will get me through this day.

I SPEND THE MORNING sifting through e-mail, avoiding encounters with my coworkers. Though I leave the door to my office shut, a few people stop by to say hi. I keep things professional, remind them semi-politely of the work I have to catch up on. I immerse myself in query letters, correspondence with our various freelance writers, questions and complaints from our production editor. Somewhere in all the mess I see an e-mail from Isaac Cohen.

Hi Charlotte,

How are you faring amongst all the lipstick and designer handbags? Hope all is well. Just heard through the grapevine that Longview Media purchased your mag. Those assholes are brutal. They'll cut the best and brightest if it saves them a dime, so watch your back. If things get ugly and you need an escape hatch, give me a call. I have a job you might be interested in.

Take care,

Isaac Cohen

Senior Editor

Meyers Rowe, True Crime Division

A job offer. Unexpected, but well-timed. I feel a surge of gratitude toward Isaac for thinking of me. I haven't seen him in years, but I remember him well from our days at *Cold Crimes*. He's a few years older than I am. Lanky, hairy, incredibly strange, but an excellent editor. He didn't seem like the type to assign stories about crimes; he looked like he'd be out there committing them. I wrote several pieces for him about individual cold cases. Although I found the work engaging, the magazine was small-scale, the pay low, with no hope of advancement. I'm not surprised that Isaac has continued working in the crime genre all this time—though Meyers Rowe is a major publishing house and a marked improvement from *Cold Crimes*—but I'm not sure I have the appropriate experience for a job in that division.

Oh, what the hell, I tell myself. *It's an opportunity, even if it's a long shot. A chance to get out of here.*

I find a phone number on the bottom of his e-mail signature and grab a pen to jot it down. Somehow in the process, I knock over my cup of pens and pencils. As I'm crawling around under the desk to retrieve them, I hear people in the doorway of my office.

"It doesn't look like she's at her desk."

"Oh, well. I'll just ask Tina."

I try to place the voices. One of them sounds like Lauren. I can't identify the other. A normal person would stand up and address her visitors, but I don't. I remain on my hands and knees, not moving.

"I think Tina will be our go-to girl indefinitely." Lauren's voice, I'm sure now. She lowers it as she prepares to gossip. "When new management steps in, Charlie's gone, you watch. Did you see her this morning?"

"No, how'd she seem?"

"Out of it. Poor thing." The voices move closer and one of them drops something on my desk. "It's weird," Lauren continues, oblivious to the fact that I am just a few feet away. "You know how she is, all business, all the time. I thought she'd be pissed about Tina taking over, but I don't think she's even noticed."

"I don't blame her. If something happened to my kid . . . what did Bianca say it was, a brain aneurysm?"

"Yeah. Her son was at preschool, got a headache, and was gone before she even made it to the hospital."

"That's crazy." Their voices are moving farther away now. "My uncle had a brain aneurysm, but he's, like, sixty. And it didn't kill him. I didn't think kids got those."

"They don't. It's like a one-in-a-million thing."

My head begins to swim. I stay under the desk for a long time, face pressed to my knees. I can't work here anymore. Clinging to the familiar only highlights how much everything has changed. How much *I* have changed.

When I've calmed myself down, I call Isaac Cohen and schedule a meeting for Wednesday morning. Whatever job he has, I'll take.

THAT NIGHT, IN BED, I try to numb my mind with television. This proves surprisingly difficult, since all the local stations are running an alert for a missing child. *Nine-year-old Hannah Ramirez has been missing since three o'clock, when she left Bonner Elementary School. Distraught family members say that Hannah often made the ten-minute walk home alone and had been instructed never to talk to strangers. Authorities ask anyone with information about Hannah to call this toll-free number.*

I switch through three channels before I finally rid myself of Hannah's smiling fourth-grade photo. Something bad has happened to her, and I don't want to think about the treacherous world I live in. A world where a little girl vanishes one afternoon, and one must presume the worst. A world where blood spills into the brain of a little boy, and without warning, he dies.

Your son suffered a subarachnoid hemorrhage . . . incredibly rare in children . . . probably present from birth . . . not your fault, just very, very bad luck.

I settle for game show reruns, hours of artificial smiles and encouraging applause, until I feel myself slipping away. Sleep, or something like it. I fight my fatigue at first, but really, it's a pleasant sensation, better than the heaviness of pills. A nice, warm, floating feeling.

Then it's like waking, everything becoming sharper.

Night. I'm standing by an old inground swimming pool. No one's actually been swimming here in a while, from the look of it; the surface is covered in rotting leaves. Two diving boards, one short and one tall, extend over the fetid water. Across from the diving boards, a sagging house awaits repair. I hear a dripping sound from the shadows behind me, and my breath catches. I'm not alone.

There's a girl curled up in a broken lawn chair, watching me.

Hi, she says.

I don't know this girl, but I've seen her face before, the long dark hair, crooked bangs, and liquid black eyes.

Hannah?

She nods. The dripping sound continues in steady rhythm.

Everyone's looking for you. They all think you're missing.

I know.

I try to understand.

Are you hiding?

She shakes her head, and I see that she has small, heart-shaped earrings. A headband with a pink flower made of ribbon.

I want to go home, she says, *but I can't.*

Is that your house?

That's Laci's house. Hannah rises from the chair and joins me. *Laci's my friend from school. We're in the same class.*

The dripping noise unnerves me. I glance back at the broken chair and see a puddle forming underneath, though it's not raining. *You went to see Laci after school?*

She was home sick. I was bringing her the homework, but nobody opened the door. So I went back here where you can see her room.

It makes sense. I look at the upstairs windows of the house. In daylight, Hannah's friend could see us plainly, if she bothered to look down.

She was watching TV, Hannah says. *I waved at her. To tell her about the homework.*

Did you give it to her?

She shakes her head. *It's still in my bag.* She points to the tall diving board. For the first time, I notice a child's backpack at the bottom of the ladder. My skin begins to prickle.

She didn't see me, Hannah explains, *so I climbed up on the high board to get taller.*

The dripping sound accelerates, as if echoing my heartbeat. I look down and find myself standing in water. Is it me? Am I the one dripping?

Come on. She takes a few steps back toward the shadows, expecting me to follow.

But something doesn't feel right. My hair. There's something in my hair. I touch my head, and a slimy trail of decomposing leaves trickles down.

Hannah? The water at my feet is rising now, swelling to my knees, and I know that she's doing this somehow, taking me someplace I don't want to go. *What's happening?* I demand. *I want to leave. Make it stop.*

She reaches for my arm, drawing me in deeper, and her fingers melt like ice when they meet my skin.

Shhh, she whispers. *We're going swimming.*

4.

I sit up in bed, both sweating and freezing, hands gripping my blankets. For the first time since Keegan's death, something has penetrated my grief: fear. I glance at the windows, the open door to my room, half expecting a face, a human-shaped shadow.

It's just a nightmare, I tell myself. *A lot of people have them.*

But the fear remains, churning in my stomach, crawling up my skin. Hannah Ramirez, just nine years old, missing since yesterday afternoon. I can't stop thinking about her, those icy fingers. Can't stop thinking about her mother, lying awake all night, desperate to know where her child is. At least I knew. There was never any wondering.

Maybe they found her, I tell myself. *Maybe she's okay.*

But something in me doesn't believe that. Something in me believes in that pool.

I move through the house, turning on light after light until my home is a model of wasteful energy consumption. What is wrong with me? What is happening to my brain? I'm seeing things I should not be seeing. Is it the pills? I stopped taking them days ago. Am I going through some bizarre form of withdrawal?

I'm not going to work today, not like this. I dash off an e-mail to let my coworkers know that I'll be out for a few more days, though in truth, I'm praying I never have to go back. Tomorrow I have my meeting with Isaac, a shot at something new. Today I will visit my grandmother.

I find her in her high-backed chair, frowning at the television, a crossword puzzle in her lap. When I enter the living room, she snatches the remote and turns off the TV.

"What are you watching?" I ask.

"Just the news."

"So go ahead and watch it."

"No, no," she says. "I want to visit with you. Nothing good happens on the news." She gestures to her crossword. "A five-letter word for junction. What do you think?"

This feels like a distraction, which only annoys me further. "Really, Grandma. You think I can't handle the news?"

She sighs. "Don't get upset. It was a sad story, that's all. A little girl. Not the sort of thing you need to be thinking about right now."

"You mean the Hannah Ramirez story."

"You already saw it, then." She seems embarrassed by her attempt to protect me.

"I saw it last night."

"Oh. Well, they found her this morning." Her voice indicates the news is not good.

My stomach knots up. "Found her in the pool," I say, and it's not even a question.

"Poor girl." She toys with her pencil. "At least it was an accident, not some sick person . . ."

"It *was* a pool, right? Her friend's pool?"

She nods, and I feel dizzy. I sink down into the rocker, massaging my temples.

My grandmother misinterprets my reaction as empathy. "I'm sorry you saw that story. I suppose we could both do without the news for a while."

I look up. This is not something I can keep to myself. "I didn't see it on TV," I tell her softly. "I dreamed it."

"Dreamed what?" She enters a word into her crossword, then checks off the clue.

"About Hannah. Where they found her."

"You dreamed it last night?"

"Yeah."

Grandma pencils in another word. "They didn't find her until this morning."

"I know."

She pauses. Regards me closely. "Charlotte, you told me you don't dream."

"I didn't. But then I stopped taking sleeping pills."

"And you dreamed about that missing girl? You dreamed she was in a pool?"

I nod and watch her reaction.

She stares at me for a long time, thinking. Splinters of light dance across her hands, and the daylight makes my words all the more ridiculous.

"Just say it," I tell her. "You think I'm crazy."

"No." But she won't look at me now. Her eyes are on the crossword, the rows of empty boxes.

"It's okay." I bite my lip. "I saw a dead girl. Talking to me. That is crazy."

"No, honey, no. That's not what I'm thinking."

"Then what?" My voice is rising. "This isn't the first weird dream, Grandma. I had another one, too, something that came true, and it's starting to scare me."

She raises her head. Sets her puzzle down on the coffee table. "I don't think you're crazy," she says. "I think you're like me."

THE SUMMER BEFORE I began high school, my father drove his car into a tree. The coroner estimated that his blood alcohol level at the time of death was .22, about three times the legal limit. If he hadn't died, he would've been in jail. That was when I went to live with my grandmother.

I'd visited my father's mother occasionally over the years, but I wasn't particularly close to her when she decided to take me in. I liked her because she never asked me to talk about my feelings and because she was honest, something the adults in my life had never been. "James is dead because he was a drunk," she told me. "We can love him, but we don't have to forgive him." Or, on the subject of my mother: "She was nineteen and stupid. I'm sorry you don't have a mother, but I'm glad you don't have *her*."

Sometimes her plainspoken words have hurt me, but they are always true. For twenty-four years, I've respected my grandmother for giving me the facts as she knows them, for setting aside unpleasant emotions and carrying on, for allowing me my privacy. I always thought I was the one with secrets. It never occurred to me that she had her own.

I study my grandmother, her steely eyes and short, wavy hair. Though I'm green-eyed and much paler, our features are similar: oval face, sharp chin, high cheekbones. People say we look alike, and I suppose our personalities are similar, too. But that's not what she means now when she says that I am like her.

"Grandma," I say, "do you have creepy dreams, too?"

"I used to." She rises slowly to her feet. "I'd like something to drink. Can I get you anything?"

"No thanks." My mind is not on liquid as I follow her into the little galley kitchen. "So . . . did they happen? The things you dreamed about?"

She pours some cider into a pot and turns on a burner. "They aren't dreams. It just seems that way in the beginning." Grandma rummages through a cabinet, selecting ingredients. "Dreams move quickly, change suddenly. They don't make sense. I used to *see* things. Really see them."

"What do you call them, then? Visions?"

"That sounds so hocus-pocus." She stirs some brown sugar into the pot. "I always thought of them as—pictures. It didn't happen often, but when I saw pictures . . . well, I knew what was coming."

"What did you see?"

She thinks it over. "The first one came after I married your grandfather. It was about my friend Alice."

I've heard about Alice before, mainly that she was a tremendous flirt, and six different men proposed to her during the war. My grandmother wraps her spices up in cheesecloth, drops them in the pot, and tells me the story.

"Alice had been dating a soldier. He wanted to get married, she didn't. Well, they sent him off to Europe somewhere, and about two months later, Alice came to me, very worried. She was afraid that she was pregnant."

"That was the picture you saw?" I ask.

"No," my grandmother tells me, "that was real. The night after she told me, I saw a picture. A baby, a little transparent baby. It was Alice's. And it turned to blood. Then I saw Alice, wearing a blue dress soaked in blood. I asked if she was all right, and she laughed and spun around in her bloody dress."

I lean against the worn Formica countertop, frowning. "That *is* creepy. Did she lose the baby?"

"The next time I saw her, she was wearing that blue dress. She took me aside, so happy. 'Forget everything I said,' she told me. 'I'm fine, there's no baby.'"

"So she was never even pregnant . . . ?" I suggest.

"I think she was."

"But how do you know?" I want her to be wrong. I want these pictures—hers *and* mine—to mean nothing.

"I *don't* know," Grandma admits, "but years later when Alice did get married, she tried to have a child. And she couldn't. She got pregnant four different times, but she always miscarried."

The story leaves me with mixed emotions. On the one hand, perhaps I'm not so deranged, after all. On the other, the Hannah dream may only be the beginning. A whole parade of scary visions could be lurking in the ether, waiting for me to go to bed each night. It's an awful thought. "Do you still see things?"

"Not in many, many years."

The cider is heating up now, steam rising from the pot. It smells like autumn, and suddenly I'm thirsty, an amazingly normal sensation. "What's the last one you had? Do you remember?"

She nods, suddenly mute.

She doesn't want to tell me.

"Someone who died?"

She nods again, and I hold my breath.

Maybe she knew and said nothing.

"Grandma," I say sharply. "Who was it?"

But her answer is not what I expect. "Your father," she says. "I saw your father."

"What did you see?" We've talked about my father—her son—many times over the years, and she's never said a word about this.

"It was the night he died." She runs her tongue over her dry lips. "I saw James standing by his car. The green one."

I know the car she means. It smelled like vomit, from the days when I got motion sickness.

"It was dark, and the car was smashed against a tree." She squints, as if the scene is laid out there in the tiny kitchen. "I was upset about the car at first. I thought he'd ask me for money. But he told me no, this was worse than just a totaled car. He kept saying 'sorry.'"

"Sounds like Dad. 'Sorry' was his favorite word." Grandma seems to have forgotten about the cider, so I switch off the burner and let it cool. "That was it? He apologized for being a screw-up?"

"And he asked me for a favor."

"Naturally."

"I made a promise to your father and I'd like to think I've kept it." Grandma fetches two mugs from the cabinet and hands me one. "I've taken care of you, haven't I?" There is a real question in her voice, a need for validation I've never heard before.

"That was your promise? That's why you took me?"

She meets my eyes. "He was thinking of you. He knew he'd let you down."

I turn away. I rarely get upset with my grandmother, but the whole story sounds like some made-up tale to comfort the bereaved. Why tell it now, when I've moved past that particular loss?

"You would've taken me anyway, right?" I fix my gaze on the empty mug in my hands.

"Oh, Charlie. I don't know. Your mother's family was ready to take you. If I hadn't been convinced it was what James wanted . . ." She shrugs. "Your aunt was younger and more energetic. She had children your age. I really wrestled with the decision."

"Aunt Suzie?" I grimace. "*That would've* been horrible."

"Then I did the right thing."

"Yeah," I tell her, "you did."

We don't mention my father or the dream-pictures again. For the next hour, we sit in the living room sipping Grandma's mulled cider. At some point I realize that Keegan's box of toys is gone. My grandmother must have donated them to the church. My chest tightens at this discovery. How did I fail to notice that before? How was I so oblivious? If I truly love my son, how could I ever think of anything else?

There is nothing more unnatural than losing your child. Not even talking to the dead.

5.

As I enter Isaac Cohen's office on Wednesday morning, I determine that he has changed very little in the twelve years since I left *Cold Crimes*. His beard could use a trimming, and his olive suit doesn't quite fit his long frame. Although he's gained some weight and lost some hair, he's the same eccentric man I remember.

"Charlotte!" Isaac flaps an arm at the chair beside him. "Come in, come in!"

The small office is made even smaller by all the clutter. I worm my way around teetering piles of manuscripts, boxes of newly printed books, and a scraggly potted plant. As I sit down, a framed black-and-white photograph on his desk gives me pause. I stare at the empty-eyed man from another era, not sure why I find him so disconcerting.

"A Victorian death portrait," Isaac says with relish. "Welcome to my lair."

He's joking, of course, but "lair" is in fact an apt word for his office. Isaac has plastered the walls with book jackets much in the way a serial killer might cover his walls with souvenirs of his victims. On the right side, I see titles like *Heist!* and *Encyclopedia of Gangsters*. The opposite wall is more grim: *Green River Grave* and *Dinner with Dahmer*.

"Serial killers are in this season," I observe.

Isaac chuckles. "They never go out of style, believe me."

I'm already wondering if this is a mistake. Somehow in my rush to escape *Sophisticate*, I've overlooked the subject matter of my work at *Cold Crimes*. Murder. Sick and twisted people doing sick and twisted things. It didn't bother me in my twenties, but that was before I became a mother, back when the only life I thought of was my own.

"So." Isaac sucks on his teeth. "Always nice to see a face from the past."

"I'm flattered you thought of me. It's been a while."

"Well, this project came up. I think it would be a good fit for you."

My eyes narrow at the word "project." That doesn't sound like a job—it sounds like freelance.

Isaac grabs a tissue and blows his nose. "The Meyers Rowe crime division is working on a series of books right now called *Greatest Mysteries of the Twentieth Century*." He blows again and dabs delicately at the resulting strand of snot. "Each book features a high-profile unsolved crime. We're doing one book per decade. The Black Dahlia for the forties, Dan Cooper in the seventies, JonBenét Ramsey for the nineties. You get the picture."

"Who's Dan Cooper?"

"D. B. Cooper." He waits for the name to register with me, but it doesn't. "Hijacked a plane, got two hundred thousand dollars, parachuted out. Never seen again."

"Cooper didn't kill anyone?"

"No, no. Not all the books are about murder." He gives his nose a final scouring and discards the tissue. "What I have in mind for you is our crime of the eighties. You're familiar with the Deveau family?"

Of course I know the name. They're like the Hilton family, only the granddaughter is better behaved, and their upscale hotel chain was founded with Old South plantation money. Rae, who often travels to the Gulf Coast for business, has always boycotted them. Apart from a history of slave owning, the Deveau family has been mixed up with only one major crime.

"The Deveau kidnapping?" Now that I understand where Isaac is going with this, I'm disgusted. "That's hardly one of the greatest mysteries of the century. Or even that decade."

"Do you know the case?"

"Not well," I concede. "I was only nine when the kid went missing."

"Then you'll need this." He thrusts a folder into my hands. "Gabriel Deveau. Two years old. That's an overview to get you started."

I glance inside the folder and see a couple of photocopied articles that I don't intend to read. "I know the basics. They never found him. One ransom note, no body, no criminal. Not much of a story, Isaac." Privately, I wonder how the hell another missing child has stumbled into my lap.

"Next August will be the thirty-year anniversary, and local law enforcement recently reopened the case. There could be a major break." He drums his fingers on the desk. "I reread that piece you did for *Cold Crimes* on the Lindbergh kidnapping. Brilliant."

"The Lindbergh baby turned up dead," I point out. "Hauptmann was convicted and executed for the crime. That's a pretty crucial difference." I rub my temples, trying to swallow my disappointment. "So this is the job? A book deal?"

"Beats unemployment," he says. "Maybe you'd like a change of pace."

I'd been so hopeful, so ready to start something new. But this? "I appreciate you contacting me," I tell him, "but I don't think it's the opportunity I'm looking for."

"I haven't told you the best part."

I stand up, eager to get out of Isaac's ghastly office.

"The Deveau family approached *us*. They *want* to do this book." A slow grin spreads across his face. He has beautiful white teeth, which I find alarming. "You'll receive unprecedented access to their documents and exclusive interviews. Plus, they're offering three months' room and board at Evangeline, their Louisiana estate. You'd literally be working at the scene of the crime."

That stops me in my tracks. "It's an authorized family biography?"

Isaac sees that he's got me curious and his grin broadens. "Neville Deveau has always been tight-lipped with the press, but he died last winter, and his wife has cancer. It's the twin daughters, Sydney and Brigitte, who came to us. They want someone to write a history of their family."

"A book about the kidnapping isn't exactly—"

"I've assured them their family history is necessary to provide context for the kidnapping. We can meet both goals here. They're excited to proceed."

"Brigitte married into the Caldwell family, right?" I rack my brain for tabloid headlines I've seen about them, but it's been a while. They're old news. "And there's a brother, too. Andre Deveau."

"Yeah, he's the CEO of Deveau Hotels."

"I interviewed him once for an article." It was years ago, I remember, an article on luxury hotels. His assistant allotted me five minutes to get a couple sound bites for the magazine; Andre gave me half an hour and bought me a twenty-two-dollar mojito. One of the few times in my life that I, the child of an alcoholic, have actually permitted myself to drink. Andre Deveau was a pleasant, surprisingly low-key man. We had a nice conversation, first about his hotel chain and then about travel more generally. I recognized a quality in him that I possessed too at the time: the loneliness of the chronically overworked.

"So you've already got a connection here!" Isaac jumps on the slightest sign of my interest, the semi-maniacal smile never leaving his face. "How serendipitous!"

I have no desire to immerse myself in another family's tragedy when I'm already struggling with my own. "Thank you," I tell Isaac, moving toward the door again, "but I can't leave my day job for a short-term project. Have you tried Derek Santana? He's good at these—"

"Yeah, I tried him." He rakes a hand through his beard. "I won't lie to you. I've approached several people. Brigitte Caldwell has been a nightmare to deal with. She refused to work with the last writer we sent her."

I shake my head. "Why bother? You're a great editor, Isaac. You've got to know this project is crap."

He sighs. "Sydney and Brigitte have promised to throw their weight behind this. They have connections. Think book signings, radio interviews, TV. You can't buy publicity like that."

"Profiting off their missing brother seems a little desperate. They can't be hurting for cash."

Isaac shrugs. "Who knows? Hotels and properties along the Gulf Coast have lost business, what with Katrina and the oil spill. And I get the sense the sisters like attention. They have a lot of . . . family pride." He makes his final pitch. "I need a writer who can speak their language, and the twins are big fans of *Sophisticate*—"

I'm too tired to hold this remark against him. "Good luck, okay?"

Before I can make a full escape, Isaac leaps after me with the folder of articles. "Don't forget your info packet."

I grab the folder and hurry out into the maze of Meyers Rowe cubicles. One more metaphorical door closing. Give me a window and I might jump out.

WHEN I GET HOME that afternoon, my yard is curiously devoid of leaves. Someone has raked. Mason, possibly, or else my retired neighbor across the street. There's also a pumpkin on my front steps, and I remember that Halloween is approaching. I sit out on the stoop for a while, holding the pumpkin in my lap like a cat. They want me to keep fighting, all these people in my life. To carry on, day after day after day. But for what? A job I've grown weary of and may very well lose? A house so quiet and full of objects from another time that it feels like a museum? Sometimes these things aren't enough to fight for.

When the sun goes down, I head inside. Go through the motions of living. Shoes on the mat, coat in the closet. Heat up a pizza and force myself to eat. Slip into my pajamas, brush my teeth. And then I enter Keegan's room.

It's abnormally clean, but the smell is almost right, the light from his airplane lamp warm and sleepy and inviting. He doesn't seem so far away tonight.

Maybe I can bring him closer.

From the toy box, I select his three favorite stuffed animals—Dinosaur, Fat Teddy, and Ringo the Rhino—and arrange them around his pillow. I peel back the blankets and untuck them at the corners, forming a little cocoon in the middle just big enough for a four-year-old to snuggle inside. I flip off the lights. Sit down on the edge of his bed. Watch swirls of glow-in-the-dark adhesive stars appear on the walls around me.

"Shall we sing a bedtime song? *You are my sunshine, my only sunshine.*" My voice is low, half song, half whisper. "*You make me happy when skies are gray. You'll never know, dear, how much I love you . . .*" I don't sing the final line. "Mommy used to sing that to you when you were a baby."

The stuffed animals stare at me, stiff and unblinking.

I sing another song, one of Keegan's favorites from school that I mangle the words to. He would've hated that. My inability to remember lyrics correctly always drove him nuts.

But I won't let myself think in the past tense right now.

"Time for bed, buddy," I say, patting the covers. "Should we do a monster check?" I get down on my hands and knees and look under the bed. "Nope, nothing there. Looks good. Now we'll check the closet." I slide open the closet door. "Hmm, any monsters in here?" I peer into the dark space, push aside a few hangers. "Just clothes, I think we're—"

Behind me, a sound.

I stop, my head still in the closet, and listen.

A stirring of sheets from the bed. A child sighing, as if in sleep.

He's there, I think, not daring to breathe. *This is real.*

I turn around very, very slowly and face his bed.

It's empty.

"Keegan?"

I wait, but there's no answer. No movement, no sound, just the three stuffed animals huddled around the pillow in the exact same positions where I left them. Is my mind playing tricks on me? But I have to trust myself, have to believe in my own senses. I felt something. Still feel it. An electricity in my body. Hope crackling through my veins.

"I'm right here, baby. Mama's right here."

Still nothing. The quiet is crazy-making. I heard him, didn't I? Heard *something.*

I plant myself next to his bed, eyes sweeping around the room for anything out of place, any sign that I'm not alone in here. Because I don't want to be alone in here.

"Okay, Kee," I murmur. "I'll just wait. I'm not going anywhere, I promise."

I sit. I listen. I keep waiting.

My eyes flicker open. I'm curled up on the floor of my son's bedroom, cheek pressed to the carpet. Outside, the sky is just starting to lighten with the purple-gray beginnings of morning. I realize that I was dreaming. Or whatever it's called.

A swamp. Swishing water.

I roll on my side, get my bearings. There was a boy in my dream, although not my son. A boy in a boat.

Somewhere outside a mourning dove coos, soft and plaintive. I pick myself up, roll my neck a few times to ease out a crick. I'm not scared this time, the way I was with Hannah, just focused. He was speaking to me, this boy. He told me things. I shouldn't forget them.

Downstairs, I find a notebook and pen on the kitchen counter. I jot down a few notes, barely able to make out my own handwriting in the dark.

Place: Boat in swamp. Trees, brush, alligator.
Boy: 3ish. "Jo-Jo." Dark eyes, longish hair, chipped tooth. Dead?
Told me: Lived in big white house. Had doggie. Hurt (killed?) by male.
*   Afraid to tell mother.*
Guesses: Abuse. Physical? Sexual? Possible family member?

I'm about to close the notebook when I think of one more thing. *Asked me to help*, I scribble, and the words send little chills down my spine. What happened to this child? What could I possibly do for him?

I settle in for a breakfast of lumpy instant oatmeal and work through the picture. Was he a local kid, like Hannah? I try to recall any nearby swampland but draw a blank. And alligators don't inhabit the Northeast. I do a quick search on my phone for "alligator habitat." The closest alligators, it would appear, are in North Carolina, but most alligators within the United States live in Florida and Louisiana.

The connection lodges itself in my stomach, sharp and heavy. Louisiana.

In my office, I dig out the info packet Isaac gave me yesterday. I flip through the pages, searching for a picture of the missing Deveau boy. The only one I find is too small and fuzzy to be sure. He has dark hair, that much is accurate. Not quite as long as the boy's hair in my dream, but who knows when this photograph of the kid was taken. I also discover a picture of Evangeline, the Deveaus' beautiful antebellum mansion. The photo isn't in color, but the giant, pillared home looks white.

I lived at the big white house.

It makes sense. Louisiana is filled with swamps. But I need more. Something concrete. I skim through the packet, trying to confirm my hunch.

Gabriel was last seen on the fourteenth of August, the night of Sydney and Brigitte's sweet sixteen party in New Orleans. His parents, Hettie and Neville, left him at Evangeline in the care of his nanny while they attended the ball. I read further and find mention of their brother Andre. At the time of the kidnapping, Andre was eighteen, even older than the twins. According to the packet, Gabriel was a month shy of three when he went missing. But why such an age gap between children? Maybe Gabriel was an "oops" baby.

I sink into my office chair, drawn in despite myself, and breeze through a summary of the investigation. Gabriel's nanny, Madeleine Lauchlin, said she'd put him to bed at eight o'clock the night of August 14. As was her custom, she locked his door from the outside to prevent him from leaving his room in the night. When she went to wake him the following morning at seven, the door was still locked. Lauchlin realized she didn't have her key with her and asked Danelle Martin, the cook, to unlock the door with her spare. The two women entered the room together and found Gabriel missing from his bed. The room had only one other entrance, through Hettie and Neville's adjoining bedroom, but that door was latched on both sides. The windows, too, were locked. Gabriel could not have left the room unassisted.

By the time authorities arrived, frantic staff members had thoroughly contaminated the crime scene. Several sets of fingerprints were lifted, but all were consistent with people known to have entered the room. Police had no leads or promising suspects, until Hettie Deveau found a ransom note tucked under the pillow of her bed. Written in ballpoint pen, the note demanded

ONE MILLION DOLLARS FOR YOUR BOY

in capital letters. The handwriting was extremely sloppy. Analysts believe the author of the note was writing left-handed to disguise his or her handwriting. The note didn't contain details about delivery of the money, and no additional notes followed. No one has ever conclusively determined whether the note was from Gabriel's abductor or just a hoax.

The FBI, working with local and state police, quickly focused on Roi Duchesne, a groundskeeper whom Neville Deveau had recently fired. Duchesne later proved to have an ironclad alibi for the night of Gabriel's disappearance and could not be linked to the crime. Hettie and Neville Deveau, seen at three a.m. in their New Orleans hotel after the birthday party, were ultimately dismissed as viable suspects, as was Andre, who had spent the night in the city with a friend. Twin sisters Sydney and Brigitte received little scrutiny, as they'd both passed out drunk in their hotel room following a lively after-party—a fact that Neville later raged at the media for reporting.

The last page in the packet outlines some of the major theories people have about the kidnapping.

One part jumps out at me:

> Investigators noted that the family dog, who usually slept in Gabriel's room, did not alert staff to any intruders and was found wandering the grounds later that morning. This supported the widespread belief that a staff member, or even a member of the family itself, was responsible for Gabriel's disappearance.

It's him. Has to be. The boy in the boat.

I had a doggie.

There's just one piece bothering me. The name. Why would a child named Gabriel call himself Jo-Jo? Nothing Isaac has given me explains that.

I switch on my computer and search "Gabriel Deveau" and "Jo-Jo." No results. A search for "Gabriel Deveau," on the other hand, turns up about six hundred thousand results. I wade through some of the mess. Mostly sites about the kidnapping and images no more helpful than the picture I got from Isaac. I think the boy I saw is Gabriel, but plenty of little boys have dark hair, dark eyes, and a nondescript nose. Gabriel never appears smiling in the photos, so I can't see if his tooth is chipped. And maybe his tooth was chipped during the abduction.

I lean back in my chair, now wrestling with doubt. I've heard various things about the Deveau kidnapping over the years, and just because I don't consciously remember them doesn't mean they weren't floating around my subconscious, turning up in my dream. It's possible my brain just strung together details I picked up somewhere. The house, the dog, Gabriel's age and appearance—all of that is widely known.

The name "Jo-Jo" is different. It's personal. If I can confirm the nickname, then I'll know, really know.

I scroll through a couple of pages of search results, clicking on several sites, but there's no mention of a Jo-Jo. Finally, with a certain amount of self-disgust, I open the Wikipedia entry on Gabriel. With its questionable crowd-sourcing, I consider Wikipedia only one step up from the *National Enquirer*. All my notions of journalistic integrity vanish, however, when I read the first line:

Gabriel Joseph Deveau (born September 22, 1979, missing since August 15, 1982) was the youngest son of Neville and Henriette Lessard Deveau.

It's that easy. "Joseph." A middle name that no other site bothered to include.

I wander around my house. Chew a fingernail. Sort my thoughts. Obsessively plan. It's a little past seven; I'll call Isaac in a couple of hours. In the meantime, I can work on my resignation letter. That will feel good.

Of course I'll have to rent out the house. With renters, I should get by financially, at least for a little while. Rae will help me with the property. She'll want me to get away, think that it's healthy. And Grandma will understand, although I'm not sure I understand it myself.

Will you help me? the boy asked, and truthfully, I'm not sure. Can I help a boy who has been dead for nearly thirty years? But there is nothing else for me. So why not try?

I stand by the kitchen window, watch the sun claim the sky. Misguided though it may be, I have a purpose now.

I'm going to Louisiana.

PART II

chicory, louisiana

JANUARY

6.

On the third day of the new year, I arrive in Chicory, Louisiana. The WELCOME TO CHICORY sign puts the population at 24,032. Not exactly a booming metropolis, but hardly the boonies. I pass a wrecking lot, a Dollar Store, Popeyes, a few gas stations, and a sketchy-looking establishment called Cajun Canteen. On Main Street, I discover rows of brick storefronts, many empty. Tangles of Christmas lights still dangle from the streetlights, and a large plastic Santa Claus grins in the window of a shoe store. Behind all the buildings, I see the bayou. Once the lifeline to this town, the river now appears brown and unspectacular.

I've been driving for three days, pausing only for food, gas, and a few hours of sleep at a pair of no-name motels. I've liked reading maps, selecting odd detours. I've liked the feeling of a dark road, seeing only as far as my headlights allow. When day broke this morning, I was in Mississippi, meandering along a country road my GPS would never have chosen. Against the peach-dusted sky, I saw the silhouettes of trees, cows, and a little farmhouse in a paint-by-numbers landscape made real. Traveling has agreed with me, but now I'm here and the real work begins.

It's a sunny fifty-four degrees out, and not even noon yet—hardly the kind of January I'm accustomed to. I park in a municipal lot and think about how to kill an hour. Jules Sicard, the estate manager at Evangeline, isn't expecting me until the afternoon. Neither Sydney nor Brigitte will be at the home, but their mother, Hettie Deveau, has been living there year-round since her cancer diagnosis. Of all the players in this drama, she's the one I'm most curious to meet. Her husband, Neville, was always terribly combative with news media, threatening several lawsuits over the years, and even winning one against a tabloid. Now that he's dead, Hettie may be ready to speak more candidly.

I step out of my car and stretch my legs, fielding curious glances when passersby notice my Connecticut plates. Across the street, there's a sign for the Chicory Public Library. You can tell a lot about an area from its library, and I'd never discount the usefulness of town archives. They're a good way to kill an hour.

Inside, I find hideous orange carpeting, cheap furniture, and pretty decent stacks. I make my way over to the reference desk, where a gray-haired woman of about sixty watches a maintenance worker patch a wet and rotted section of ceiling.

It takes her a moment to notice me. "I'm sorry, can I help you with something?"

"I'm looking for information about Neville and Henriette Deveau." I don't mention the kidnapping. I don't want to look like some crude Northerner drawn by celebrity and an unsolved crime, even if I am.

"The Deveau family, hmm?" The librarian points to a shelf a few aisles down. "I'd start with the Local History section right over yonder. Periodicals'll have plenty for you, too. And you might try the Abe and Thomas Brennan Photo Collection."

I inquire about the collection, and she explains that a local photographer for the newspaper donated fourteen thousand photographs he and his father took of the town, its events and people. "The pictures capture Chicory from 1922 to 1991," she says, her gaze drifting back up to the maintenance man's work on the ceiling.

Sifting through a photo collection is a bigger research project than I can tackle in an hour, but another day, maybe. "So, how did the town get its name?" I ask. "Chicory's a plant, right?"

The librarian nods. "Part of our French heritage. Some of the finest restaurants in New Orleans add a little chicory to the coffee."

"You grind up the roots, bake 'em, and they've got a real nice flavor," the maintenance man calls from his ladder as he removes a stained plaster tile.

"I'll have to try that."

"Poor folk sometimes used chicory in the place a coffee," the maintenance man adds, his gloved hand full of chunks of crumbling ceiling. "When times were tough, like durin' the Depression or the War a Northern Aggression."

I blink, trying not to convey my horror. War of Northern Aggression? Is that what they call the Civil War down here?

The librarian sees my consternation and purses her lips, embarrassed. "The War Between the States, he means."

She smiles apologetically, and I have the sudden sneaking suspicion that, despite my travels to London, Paris, Hawaii, and even Hong Kong, I am now farther from home than I have ever been.

As I turn down the road to the Deveau estate, I wait for Evangeline to appear dramatically on the horizon. I'm expecting to be dazzled, maybe even a little appalled. Trees on either side of the winding road bend inward, scattering the sun amongst the leaves and branches in tiny diamonds of light. When I come to one sharp turn, I think I must be close. Instead, I find a fork in the road and no signs. Jules Sicard did not mention this in his directions.

I opt for left, and at first, it's promising. The trees thicken, forming a dense canopy. Spanish moss drapes down, gloomy and majestic. As the pavement narrows and becomes gravel, I begin to have doubts. I catch glimpses of water off to my left, bayou or some swampy off-shoot. I can only imagine what a few days' rain would do to this road. Why would anyone build a home out here?

The swamp creeps closer and closer as I ease my Prius down the path. I know that I've chosen the wrong way, but I want to see where this takes me. Eventually the road opens into a large circular parking area. To the left, I can make out a boat ramp and dock. Beyond it, swamp. That's when everything begins to shake.

It isn't coming from the ground, or the sky, or the car, I realize. It's me. I'm quaking.

I hit the brake and take a few short, panicked breaths before the tremor passes. This place scares me in a way I can't explain. Is this it? The swamp where I saw the boy in the boat? I step gingerly from my vehicle. No sign of any human but myself: no tire tracks or cigarette butts or soda cans. No voices. Quiet, except for the crunch of gravel beneath my feet.

The silence is, to a city dweller, unearthly. No birds, no rushing water. Only stillness. I walk out onto the dock and gaze at the green-brown water. There's a smell I don't like, a dank and almost moldy odor, like someone's leaky basement. The decaying leaves remind me of Hannah Ramirez and that dirty old pool.

Are you there, Gabriel?

I haven't seen him, or been spooked by any children, since I decided to do the book. The more time has passed, the more impossible it seems. How can I believe so absolutely in one vision? How can I give up my career for some half-baked project? But as I stand at the edge of the swamp now, my skin prickles with recognition. The boy feels close. He was here once. We're separated only by time.

They dragged the swamp, of course, after Gabriel went missing, but even I can see the margin for error in that. Too big. All that muck. Alligators. Such a little boy. And now I admit it to myself: I think he's out there, hidden within these murky waters. Why else would I have seen him in a boat, drifting through the swamp? Why else would this place affect me so immediately and so viscerally? This must be where he died—or at least where he ended up. A dump site.

The thought turns my stomach.

My gut hypothesis following my dream was that a male family member, probably his father, had somehow been involved. But Neville Deveau had an alibi. And he's dead. Gabriel's older brother, Andre, was also cleared by police. Is it possible that authorities missed something? I try to picture the boy I saw, but more than two months have passed. He's a vague memory now, dark hair and a chipped tooth.

Talk to me, I think. *You want my help, so talk to me.*

As if in reply, I feel a crack to the back of my head. I whirl around, dizzy. There's nothing there, but I have a splitting headache. I close my eyes, holding my head. A wave of nausea hits. It's like the dock is moving, drifting through the water, and my stomach is bobbing up and down. I feel seasick. My eyes flicker open and a coldness creeps up my spine. These sensations may not be my own.

Gabriel? Is that you?

Suddenly I can't breathe. Panic. I'm inhaling air, but I can't breathe, can't breathe, can't—

"Stop."

The sound of my own voice snaps me back into myself. I dig my fingers into my palms to make sure I'm in control of my body. The pain in my head is gone, but that warm, wet swamp smell has become overpowering. I step away from the dock and do a quick sanity check. I feel normal. But what was that? Some sleep-deprived hallucination, or a message?

He hit you in the head.

He put you in a boat.

You couldn't breathe. Did you drown?

From somewhere in the swamp, a motorboat tries to start. The engine growls a few times before settling into a low, steady purr. The sound jars me into action. I glance at my watch and hurry back to my car, already late for my first meeting at the Deveau home.

I SPOT THE FENCE FIRST, its black metal pickets flashing through the trees. The winding road suddenly straightens, and there before me, between two massive stone pillars, are the gates of Evangeline.

Standing at least twelve feet tall, the gates are both beautiful and foreboding, with wrought iron that rises in a flourish of curlicues and then dives into sharp latticework. A relatively recent addition to the property, the fencing was erected in the aftermath of Gabriel's disappearance—one of many measures, I've heard, that Neville Deveau took to ensure the subsequent safety of his family. Through the thin bars, I can see the house waiting at the end of the drive, lovely and white, half shielded by trees. An elegant, expectant ghost of a home.

As I approach in my car, movement in a nearby branch catches my eye. I look up and spot a camera. I'm being watched.

I pull up slowly to the gate, where a man in a beige uniform steps from a small wooden guard shack. "You got ID?" he asks, and proceeds to inspect my license and quiz me about the purpose of my visit like a customs official.

Thankfully, Jules Sicard warned me about all of this. I'm prepared for a little Deveau paranoia. What I'm not prepared for is Jules himself.

The estate manager, I quickly discover, is handsome. Too handsome. The kind of handsome you're afraid to look directly at because it might leave you flustered and tongue-tied. I expected Evangeline's beauty, its precise symmetry: the white pillars, the row of French windows opening onto the second-floor balcony, the sculpted hedges and stone cherub perched atop the fountain out back. Although the home seems a bit misplaced in an area so remote—who exactly are they showing off for?—it's as picturesque as I've imagined. Jules, on the other hand, is entirely unexpected. When he greets me on the front steps, all I can think is, *Where did they find YOU?*

He's thirtyish, tall, and dressed impeccably in a slim-fitting brown suit. Clean-shaven, with brown-blond hair that has been strategically tousled to counterbalance the formality of the suit. Not my type—too pretty, too groomed—but intimidating in his physical perfection. I can't meet his eyes. I think they're hazel.

"Welcome to Evangeline." Coming from anyone else, the oh-so-French pronunciation of "Evangeline" would be pretentious. "I'm Jules Sicard, the estate manager. Pleasure to meet you." He lacks any trace of a Southern accent.

"Charlotte Cates. Thank you for having me." Already I can feel my brain vaporizing. This always happens to me around really attractive men. An instinctive response left over from junior high, I guess.

Jules, thankfully, barely registers my existence. "This way, please." He moves briskly up the stone steps and to the door, which he holds open for me. There's no gallantry in the gesture, just businesslike efficiency.

Jules doesn't bother to flip on the lights as I enter the expansive foyer, which feels surprisingly drafty for a home that surely has central heating. An intricate plaster frieze painted in gold leaf draws the eye upward to a dizzying crystal chandelier. Otherwise, the tasteful furnishings show both sophistication and restraint: a grandfather clock, a mirror, and two matching wine-colored settees. Gold-framed paintings depict a battle scene, a bird standing in tall grass, and a very serious, bearded soldier. As I move through the shadowy room, I have the odd sensation of wandering through not a home but a showroom.

Four rooms adjoin the foyer through large, embellished archways, and a staircase leads to the upper floor. I follow Jules into a room on the right. Light streams in through two massive windows, illuminating dark wood furniture, a fireplace, a desk, and an impressive liquor cabinet and serving area. For a moment I feel like I'm in a game of Clue. Charlie Cates, in the study, with a—

"Sit," Jules says. "There are some things we should discuss straight off."

I sit on a green armchair that is more fashionable than comfortable and fight the urge to fiddle with my hair.

"First off, security." He seats himself opposite me, legs crossed, lacing the tops of his fingers. "Obviously you saw the guard station as you came in."

I nod. If I didn't know what happened to Gabriel, all the security measures would've appeared downright pathological.

"There are cameras throughout the grounds," Jules informs me. "We have an on-site guard who monitors the cameras and patrols the area. I've notified our team that you'll be here, but you'll want to introduce yourself."

"Of course," I murmur.

"If for some reason you need to bring a guest to the estate, please inform our security personnel so that they can be logged in. And make sure they have appropriate identification." From the look on Jules's face, I understand that guests are discouraged.

Not a problem, I want to tell him. I didn't come here to improve my social life.

"Now let's clarify the terms of your project." He cocks his head to one side.

Here it comes. I knew there would be strings attached.

"Brigitte informed me that you'll be writing a history of the Deveau family."

"I wouldn't call it a history," I say, finally looking him in the eye. "You and I talked about this on the phone. The book is primarily about their brother's disappearance."

Jules continues as if I said nothing at all. "Of course they intend to provide you with complete access to the family genealogical archives. I think you'll find many fascinating stories about the Deveaus over the last two centuries."

I can only assume he's representing the wishes of the sisters with this genealogy business, which sets off alarm bells. I sincerely hope this doesn't turn into an ugly tug-of-war, Isaac pressing for a dramatic true-crime tale on one hand, the Deveau twins expecting some storied family chronicle on the other.

"You promised me interviews," I remind Jules, already getting a headache. "They'll be crucial to the book's success."

"Certainly. Sydney and Brigitte are eager to speak with you."

I wait for the catch; he delivers it.

"The sisters do have one stipulation. I'll need some assurance of your cooperation." He glances at the doorway and lowers his voice. "You know, of course, that their mother is very ill."

"Yes, I'd heard that. Is she . . . lucid?"

"For the time being. But given her condition, her daughters are asking that you not discuss the book and its subject matter with her. They see no need to upset her at this stage."

I lean forward in my chair, incredulous. "You mean Hettie doesn't know I'm here?"

"Oh, Mrs. Deveau is expecting you."

"Then what exactly am I hiding?"

"Her daughters told her that you're writing a book about plantation

homes. I think we can agree there's no reason to tell her otherwise."
His tone has a smooth politician quality that rubs me the wrong way.
I'm no longer awed by the pretty face.

"Plantation homes? I don't know the first thing—"

"She's ill, Ms. Cates. Dying. I don't think the subject will come up,
and if it does, I trust that you're equipped to handle it gracefully." He
sees me about to protest and adds, "This really isn't negotiable. Brigitte
made their wishes very clear."

"So I can't interview Hettie about Gabriel?"

He shakes his head. Good-looking or not, this guy is seriously
starting to piss me off. I'm tempted to ask who he works for, anyway.
Neville Deveau must have left his estate to his wife. As estate manager,
Jules should be answering to Hettie, not her daughters. Obviously he's
decided to ingratiate himself with the women who will be in charge
once Hettie dies. Job security.

I gnaw on a fingernail. Jules may be a traitor, but what about Sydney
and Brigitte? Hettie's own daughters, scheming behind her back. I have
no doubt she would nix the project if she knew anything about it.
Gabriel was her son, not some trashy, sensationalist piece of journalism. Her son.

Don't make this about you.

I take a deep breath. "Hettie Deveau is the single best resource I
have going into this project, Jules, and you're telling me she's not on
board."

He stiffens when I address him by his first name. "Hettie Deveau
won't live to see the summer," he says. "We're all trying to make her
final days as pleasant as possible."

"The story of Gabriel's kidnapping is *her* story. She has the right to
know what's going on."

"If you have an ethical objection, we can contact Meyers Rowe and
find another writer," Jules tells me evenly. "Otherwise, work around

it." He stands up to signal that our chat has ended. "Would you like to see the grounds?"

I've invested too much to just walk away now. I bite my lip and nod, but the expression on my face plainly says, *Prick*.

For the first time since I've met him, Jules smiles. The smirk is short-lived, though. He smoothes a lock of hair back in place and his face becomes expressionless, plastic, yet still so infuriatingly handsome I want to punch him.

7.

"Charlie?" Rae picks up on the second ring. "I'm so glad you called!" She really does sound glad, and I miss her suddenly, her gossip and her sass. It's half past five, and I'm sitting cross-legged on a pastel bedspread, hoping someone can convince me this book thing was not a mistake. "Hey, you," I greet Rae with more pep than I feel. The sun is gone, and the radiator hasn't quite kicked in yet. "Is now a good time?"

"I'm on my commute. Now's perfect. So . . . wow, are you in Louisiana?"

"I'm here," I confirm.

"How was your drive down? No, wait—" Rae interrupts herself before I can reply. "I want to hear about the house first. Is it insane?"

I climb under the quilted bedspread to get warm. The mattress squishes beneath me, promising a long and uncomfortable night. "Evangeline is—what you'd imagine. Very elegant." That much is true. Every room that Jules showed me was exquisite, and with the exception of the well-equipped contemporary kitchen, each retained its Old South charm.

"How many rooms?"

I grilled Jules for this kind of information on our brief tour, taking notes as he dispensed factoids about the estate. "Sixteen rooms total," I recite. "The place was built in the 1840s, but the family has made a number of additions and updates."

"Dang. Do they have a cook and a butler and all that?"

"No butler," I report, "but an estate manager. And definitely a cook. I met her today." Her name is Leeann and she looks impossibly young to know her way around all those gorgeous stainless steel appliances. A plump, pink-faced girl, Leeann strikes me as someone who probably still rises with breathless delight at five a.m. on Christmas morning. "I think she cooks more for the staff than the family," I explain to Rae. "She said they have a chef come on weekends and for guests or parties."

"You don't count as a guest?"

From my crater in the squishy mattress, I eye my ugly pastel room. "Uh, no. I think I'm on par with the hired help." I don't tell her that Jules explicitly urged me to eat meals with the staff. In some weird way, I find it embarrassing.

"How many people does it take to run a place that big, anyway?" Rae asks.

I try to remember everyone that Jules mentioned. A housekeeper, groundskeeper, part-time landscaping crew. Security. Nurses for Hettie. The cook, a chef, and of course, Jules himself. "I'm guessing they have about fifteen people who work here full- or part-time," I say. "And the mom, Hettie, is the only one who lives here. Her kids and granddaughter just stop by for visits."

Rae sighs, out of envy or disapproval or maybe both. "Is it crazy gorgeous?"

"I only got to see the downstairs, but yes."

"Wait, your room is downstairs?"

I laugh dryly. "More like in the backyard."

"Say what?" I figured Rae wouldn't be thrilled by this development, and in point of fact, neither am I. Before I left, Rae spent hours selecting a wardrobe for me that she deemed appropriate mansion-wear, and now I'm not even living in Evangeline. In fact, the house gets alarmed at eight p.m. each night to keep me and all the other employees out.

"It isn't *that* bad," I say, picking at a square on the quilt. "They put me in a guest cottage. I have a mini kitchen and a bathroom." I omit the details of the flowered wallpaper, lace curtains, and excessive use of lavender. I think they were going for homey, but the space reminds me of a giant girly Easter egg.

"So the guest cottage is a separate house out back?" Rae asks.

I try to describe it for her. "You walk five minutes from the main house and there are four little cottages, where some of the staff live. They used to be slave quarters, like from plantation days." I know that will get her going.

"Are you *kidding* me? They invite you over and stick you in a slave house?" She whoops indignantly. "That's disrespectful to you and all the black folk who were enslaved on that plantation. Seriously, that's like making a motel out of Auschwitz."

According to Jules, the original slave housing was demolished early in the twentieth century. The cottages as they stand now were built about fifteen years ago. They're modern to the point of having key-coded doors, but I don't tell Rae that. I find her outrage oddly comforting.

"Evangeline actually has Confederate memorabilia in the sitting room," I offer.

Rae whistles. "You really gonna stick this out for three months, Charlie-girl?"

"Gonna try." Three months sounds like a long time right now, so I change the subject. "Did my renter show up?" For a while, it didn't look like I'd be able to find a short-term renter, but a couple of weeks before I left, a divorced mom whose home had been damaged in a fire materialized.

"She moved in yesterday," Rae says. "She's got two daughters. Teen-agers."

"Oooh, our dream come true. Babysitters!"

The second the words leave my mouth, I'm shocked. *You forgot*, I realize. *For a minute, you actually forgot.*

"Maybe they can sit for Zoey," I add lamely, but the empty space in my chest is already burning. Guilt blazes through me in a quick fire. *How could you forget your child, forget he's gone?*

Rae and I talk for a few more minutes, but I'm guarded now. I hold my loss close, pressing it against my chest, my lungs, until it hurts to breathe. Maybe I'm punishing myself. Maybe I'm protecting myself, from forgetting and having to remember all over again. Either way, my absent little boy hovers between us. Without him, what do Rae and I really have in common?

Finally her train pulls into the Stamford station, and we say a quick good-bye.

"Take care of yourself," Rae tells me. "Make sure you eat, promise?"

"Promise."

After we hang up, I don't know what to do with myself. I can't just lie here sinking into this monstrous bed, so I do something useful and look up the contact Isaac gave me in local law enforcement: Detective Remy Minot. Although Gabriel's abduction was originally handled by local, state, and federal law enforcement agencies, the cold case has fallen to the parish sheriff's department—a solid indication the investi-gation is dead in the water. If there were anything promising to go on, I have no doubt the FBI would be all over it. Still, Detective Minot will have access to files from the original investigation. He's worth talking to.

I call the Bonnefoi Parish sheriff's department and am quickly trans-ferred to Detective Minot's voice mail. I leave a message, knowing the chances of this guy returning my call are slim. Cops like journalists when a cold case needs exposure, but the one thing Gabriel's kidnapping never lacked was publicity.

It's six o'clock. Leeann, the cook, said she puts out a spread for the staff every weeknight between six and seven. If I want to eat tonight, it's that or drive back to town in the dark. There are definite advantages to meeting the staff. Maybe there will be some old, faithful caretaker who has been working for the family thirty-some years and remembers Gabriel. At the very least, I can get quotes for the book—an insider's view of the family.

I slip on a jacket and step into the night. The moon is just a sliver as I follow the dirt path back toward Evangeline's distant lights. *Why couldn't Hettie spring for some outdoor lighting?* The garden, with its tall and spindly shrubbery, has become a jungle of strange shapes and unidentifiable shadows, and the solemn cherub who presides over the empty fountain looks better suited to a headstone. I can feel the swamp not so far away, ready to swallow up anything, anyone. I quicken my step. Whoever took Gabriel probably stood in this very garden, watching the house that night, waiting. That person could still be out there. Could still be close.

I weave along the path, eyes darting around for some unknown danger, and jump when a low-lying plant brushes my ankle. At the height of my paranoia, I hear something. A male voice, almost immediately to my right.

"Do you know how long I've been waiting for you?"

I freeze. There's a figure, partially obscured, standing on the other side of a hedge. I think that my heart will fly out of my chest. *Who the hell—*

"Three weeks. It's been almost three weeks now. So don't tell me to be patient." It's Jules, I realize. Jules is talking, but not to me. He must be on a cell phone. "Yes, I am aware of your busy schedule, thank you. You reminded me of it both times you canceled our plans last week.

Are you aware of the sacrifices I make to keep our relationship even remotely functional?"

I'm about to continue walking when he steps into the path ahead of me, still absorbed in his conversation. I stand in the darkness of the hedge, not six feet behind him, debating whether or not to reveal my position. Will it look like I've been spying on him if I burst suddenly from a bush? Is it worse to *look* like I was eavesdropping or to actually eavesdrop?

"No, you listen. I lie for you, I sneak around like some guilty teenager, I change my plans for you at a moment's notice—" Jules paces around, tilting his chin up to the sky so I get a good look at his perfectly proportioned silhouette. If he turned around, he'd see me lingering in the bushes. But he doesn't.

"So you'll be here? That's a promise?" His voice sweetens when it appears he will get his way. "Good. Don't forget my cuff links this time. They should still be on your dresser." He pauses. "No, the Louis Vuittons. They're black." He pauses again, then chuckles as if the caller has said something amusing. I wonder what kind of joke one can make about designer cuff links. "Right. I'll see you this weekend, then." He takes off for the house, too pleased with his domestic victory to notice me, thank goodness.

I give him a couple of minutes, idly imagining what kind of beautiful, high-powered woman has chosen to tolerate Jules—a married one, if they're sneaking around—and then head for the warm glow of the kitchen.

Through large French doors, I can see a young black family seated in the breakfast nook. Employees of the estate, I guess, since they aren't being served in the dining room. It hadn't occurred to me that families might live on the premises, but there they are: a mother, a father, and a small girl on bent knees who frowns suspiciously at her food. I hesitate for a moment, not wanting to interrupt the scene, but Leeann, the cook, spots me and hurries over to let me in. A large, old, rust-colored dog follows on her heels, waiting for handouts.

"Well, hey there! I was wondrin' if you were goin' to stop by." She's a hefty, fair, apple-cheeked girl who barely fits into her massive chef's shirt, and she's even friendlier now than when I met her with Jules. Again I'm struck by how young she looks. If I saw her on the street, I'd put her at twenty.

"Hi, Leeann." I return her toothy grin and stoop to pet the dog. "This place smells heavenly." Although I've never been a fan of Country French décor, the whitewashed cupboards, cart of potted herbs, and hanging rack of copper pots provide the room with a homey sweetness. On the wooden island, Leeann has laid out a plate of fish, along with half-empty bowls of collards and something orange. I help myself and join the young family at the table.

"This is the lady from New York I was tellin' y'all about," Leeann informs them. "Charlotte, right?"

"I go by Charlie." I wave at the little girl. Her father, a long-limbed young man who doesn't look much older than Leeann, leans over her plate cutting her fish into pieces. Beside him, the mother shifts in her chair and regards me neutrally. I see now that she is very pregnant.

"Charlie, this is Paulette." Leeann puts her hands on the pregnant woman's shoulders. "She's the housekeepa. Well, for a couple more months, anyway. She and Benny here got a baby boy comin' March first."

"Congratulations," I say, but the word feels awkward in my mouth. *Of course there would be kids here. And a pregnant woman.* I don't know why this surprises me.

I turn to Paulette's husband, forcing myself to be pleasant. "Do you work here too, Benny?"

He nods. "I look afta da cars, drive Mrs. Deveau around, fix stuff what breaks."

Their daughter eyes me as she shovels chunks of fish into her mouth with her fingers. In a few years, she will be a homely child, but for now her wide-apart eyes and big forehead are still cute.

"Bailey, use a fork." Benny hands her one. The dog makes an astute canine calculation and plops himself down by Bailey, who continues studying me.

"I'm tree years old," she announces loudly. "Ma name is Bailey Thomas. You should wear makeup."

"Bailey!" Paulette exclaims. "You act right!" She looks at me, apologetic. "I'm sorry. We still workin' on manners."

"No problem. She probably has a point." It's embarrassing to have a three-year-old tell me I'm not keeping up my appearance, but Bailey is right. I've let myself go. If I'm going to run with the Deveaus, I need to look like money.

"Don't you mind Bailey. She the li'l princess around here, ain'tcha, mamzelle?" Leeann coos.

Bailey swallows her food down with a gulp of milk. "I'm tree years old," she reminds me, a bit aggressively, as if I might accuse her of being two.

I put on an impressed face. "Three is pretty old." Older than Gabriel ever got to be.

"It's not that old." Bailey frowns. "On ma next birthdee, I'm gone be four."

"She the same age as ma li'l man," Leeann tells me.

I can't conceal my surprise at that one. I knew I was an older mother, but seriously? How can Leeann have a three-year-old?

"You look too young," I say.

"I'm twen'y-three."

I bet she didn't even mean to have him. I bet he was an accident and yet there she was, popping out a baby before she could even legally drink. Why does she get to have a child and I don't?

"Does your son live here, too?" I ask. If I have to watch him frolicking about every day, I might have a breakdown.

"Not anymore." Leeann looks awfully proud of herself. "We live in town now, with ma boyfriend. Those cottages get a li'l cramped."

"For true," Benny agrees. "I dunno how we all gone fit."

"So, Charlie, you a writa?" Paulette asks with polite interest.

I do my best to sell the plantation-home story. Fortunately, the subject is dry enough to kill any further lines of questioning. Leeann switches the topic to New York City, which she has a small-town-girl crush on. Bailey, no longer the center of attention, begins playing with the cushion on her bench, singing noisily, and accidentally-on-purpose dropping food for the dog. Her parents exchange The Look, excuse themselves, and haul their daughter out of the kitchen.

Time alone with Leeann is not without potential benefits. She's a talker by nature, the perfect candidate to say something indiscreet. I let her interrogate me about Broadway, the cost of rent in Manhattan, and subway safety. I inquire about her job at Evangeline, which she says she's had for two years now.

"My daddy owns a diner in town called Crawdaddy's," she explains. "I used to cook there, and then Mr. D liked my food so much he offered me the job."

"Mr. D? You mean Neville Deveau?"

She nods. "I heard he was a mean'un when he was young, but he was always sweet as pie to me. When he passed, I cried and cried."

I take my final bite of perfectly seasoned catfish. "So now Hettie's your boss?"

"I guess technically Jules is." Leeann rolls her eyes. Exactly the opening I'm looking for.

"What's he like?"

She giggles. "Well, you met him."

I smile. "I thought maybe he was having a bad day. It sounded like he was having girlfriend issues earlier."

Leeann gives me a long look. "Jules got issues, fo'shore, but girl-friends ain't one."

As soon as she says it, I can't believe I didn't put it together before. The hair, the clothes, the painstaking enunciation of every syllable, the fussy mannerisms—all glaring stereotypes I missed. I mean, Louis Vuitton cuff links? Where was my gaydar? Somehow I just didn't imagine gay men as part of the conservative Louisiana landscape. *Jesus, Charlie. And you mock Southerners for their prejudices.*

I ask Leeann about the rest of the help, who has been at Evangeline the longest.

She shrugs. "Deacon and Zeke are olda. Maybe ma daddy's age. They work security. I dunno how long they been here."

I'm about to pursue it further when Leeann exclaims, "Oh no!" She's looking over my shoulder, where a small elderly woman stands in the doorway, propped up against a nurse. No more than five feet tall, she's a gaunt, bony thing with wispy white hair and skin you can see the blue of her veins through. She looks to be my grandmother's age, although I know she's about fifteen years younger. The old dog rises to its feet, tail wagging furiously at the sight of her.

Leeann clamps her hand to her mouth, horrified. "Oh ma gosh, Mrs. D! I'm so sorry! I forgot to send you food on up." She scrambles to grab a plate.

"Leeann, darling, don't worry." Hettie's voice belies her frail exterior. "I'm not a bit hungry, but Rose here is insisting I eat something." She pats the hand of her nurse and then shifts her gaze to me. "I don't believe we've met."

I rise from the table and approach her nervously. "Charlotte Cates, ma'am. I'm with Meyers Rowe—"

"Oh!" Her eyes light up. "The writer! Jules didn't tell me you'd arrived. When did you get in?"

"This afternoon."

"Marvelous." Her thin lips stretch into a genuine smile. "I think we've got quite a treat for you."

"What's that?"

Even ill and unable to walk without her nurse, she still possesses a stately dignity. "We're entertaining some friends and family this weekend. I hope you'll join us for dinner on Saturday."

This is a far cry from the attitude Jules gave me. "That sounds wonderful."

"There's someone you'll want to meet. *Raleigh Winn.*" Hettie pronounces the name as if I'm a preteen receiving news of her favorite boy band.

"Raleigh Winn," I repeat. I really, really wish I knew who that was. "Well . . . wow."

"I assume you'll include a chapter about Fairview Manor in your book," she says, "and Raleigh takes such pride in the restoration work he's done. He'll be thrilled to speak with an expert in the field."

I'm dying to hunt down Jules and Brigitte and kick their conniving little asses. There is no way I can keep up this plantation-book charade, not if I'm paraded in front of people who actually have a clue about the topic. But what can I do, having already accepted her invitation?

"Mrs. Deveau," I say, smiling until it hurts, "I can't wait."

8.

Smoky eyes, perfectly arched eyebrows, and a mouth like a fresh red gash. The woman in the mirror is one I haven't seen in a long time. I've taken Bailey's advice: I'm wearing makeup. Dinner starts in twenty minutes, and I have yet to choose my dress. There are two options. The safe choice, a modest black number, won't turn any heads. My other possibility, a cobalt Elie Saab with a plunge-neck bodice, will leave an impression, but the right kind? Do I want to be ignored or stared at? I'm not sure.

The last few days at Evangeline, I've accomplished little. I've met most of the staff, but no one's warmed to me like Leeann. They see me for what I am, a college-educated woman from the Northeast out for dirt on the rich people they serve. Why would they trust me? Yesterday I finally met Zeke, one of the older security guards Leeann mentioned, but he was not exactly friendly, offering one-word answers to my questions with a barely suppressed scowl.

Jules, for the most part, avoids me. I pulled him aside yesterday to air my grievances about the Raleigh situation, but his response was a shrug and a "Run with it." Thus far, his sole contribution to my project has been sending Benny over to my cottage this afternoon with a dozen

boxes of the family "archives." When I told Jules that I needed something better than old genealogical records to write this book, I wasn't
expecting unsorted junk from Evangeline's attic. Junk, however, is
what I've received. Loose photos, cards, toys, a daily planner from
1991—I haven't gone through most of it yet. But who knows. Something interesting could turn up.

I stare again at my two dresses. There's only one chance to make a
first impression, and Sydney and Brigitte arrived last night. Their older
brother, Andre, should be getting in today. I'll be meeting them all
for the first time at this dinner. I can be a little nobody in black, or I
can make my presence known. An old article from *Sophisticate* flashes
through my head: *Dress like the woman you want to be.* I know the person
I want to be, and I can dress like her.

With a little time to spare, I sort through one of the Deveau boxes,
the contents of which belong primarily to Andre. I find copies of the
Economist from 1981. A notebook from a high school physics class, for-
mulas and problems copied in painstakingly neat handwriting. Yearbooks from what appears to be a prestigious prep school. I flip through
the pages of the 1981–82 edition and find Andre's senior photo. He's
clean-cut and unsmiling, his face forgettable. Listed, unsurprisingly, as
an officer of the Future Business Leaders of America. I feel sorry for
him. As the oldest, and ultimately the only boy, did he ever have a
choice about who to be?

I dig a little deeper into the box and discover a book of Shakespearean
sonnets with a barely legible inscription: *For Andre on his 18th birthday.
Hope you enjoy these as much as I did.—Sean.* Scraps of paper bookmark
various sonnets throughout, and I gather that, despite his sensible ex-
tracurricular activities, Andre had a more sensitive side. There are also
loose photos. Andre and some boys from school, dressed in tuxedoes.
His smile is thin-lipped, restrained. In another photo, he stands with his
date, a plump blonde with a generous bosom. Finally, on the bottom of

the box, I see it. An invitation to Sydney and Brigitte's sweet sixteen bash on the evening of August 14, 1982. A shiver runs through me. That was the night Gabriel went missing. I trace the silver edges with my finger.

Your mommy and daddy were in New Orleans with the twins that night. What about you, Gabriel? Who unlocked your door?

I hold the invitation in my hands, close my eyes, let my mind go blank. He communicated with me at the swamp. Maybe I can summon him now.

Show me that night. Show me what happened.

Nothing. The room is absolutely still. My eyes flutter open and I realize I'd better check the time. Already past eight. Shit.

I give myself a quick look in the mirror and begin to doubt my choice of outfits. The dress accentuates all the right parts, making my boobs look bigger, giving shape to my butt, and cinching in at the waist, but it's a little . . . sexy. I vacillate. The black dress lies on my bedspread, shapeless, an invitation to be blah. I can't do it.

Be bold. Own this.

At eight fifteen I dash out of the cottage, black clutch in hand, and stumble through the dark in my heels. The moon is out tonight, so I can see somewhat, but it's cold. I wish immediately that I'd grabbed a throw. Oh well. No time to turn back.

Upon entering the lavish dining room, I come to an unfortunate realization: there's no such thing as fashionably late to a Deveau dinner. Ten people are already sipping glasses of wine around the exquisitely set table. A man dressed in a server's uniform helps me to my seat, which happens to be beside Sydney Deveau. Cheeks flaming, I murmur apologies to everyone.

The server takes my wineglass. "Red or white, ma'am?"

"Just water, thank you."

"Well," says Hettie, "here she is! Our writer!" She doesn't say my name, probably because she's forgotten. I'm not particularly keen on anyone knowing my name right now anyway because I've just made my second unfortunate discovery.

My dress is very, very wrong.

The other women at the table, and there are five, all look prepared to join a convent. Drab, dark colors. High necklines. Long sleeves. I, in comparison, belong on a street corner. I stare at my place setting—crystal glassware, whitework embroidered linen, polished and monogrammed silver cutlery—afraid to look up, afraid to see who is watching me. A moment later, the server returns with plates of salad. They must have been waiting on me to start eating.

Only when everyone is occupied with their food and an ardent discussion of Belgian endives is under way do I finally dare to peek at the other guests. At the head of the table, Hettie Deveau presides, so bright-eyed and beaming I'd never guess that she was terminally ill. I recognize her daughters, too, from television and gossip pages. Although the two women are identical twins, Sydney and Brigitte are easy to tell apart. Sydney, seated to my right, wears her hair short and dark. Brigitte, opposite me, wears hers long with blond highlights. At forty-five, both women are overweight, with expanding cheeks and chins that call to mind a pair of greedy hamsters.

Their brother, Andre, must have begged out of this dinner, as the only other person I recognize is Jules, even more spruced up than usual, though looking a bit sulky. I don't blame him. I don't know how he got roped into this, but exchanging banal pleasantries with the wealthy friends of his employers must be a far cry from the weekend with his boyfriend that he'd been planning.

"Where is Andre?" Brigitte asks, as if reading my mind. "I thought he was coming tonight. He *has* to meet Ginny over there. She's single. She'd be perfect for him."

"His flight was delayed," Jules reports dutifully. "He's still hoping to be here for dessert."

"He always does this," Brigitte complains. "I swear, I don't even bother to count on him for my dinners anymore. He throws off my numbers."

From her end of the table, Hettie leaps to her firstborn's defense. "Well, he has a company to run, doesn't he? I think we're very lucky he takes his responsibilities so seriously. And speaking of absentees, where's my granddaughter?"

Brigitte falls into a stony silence, leaving the man I assume is her husband to tactfully explain that their daughter is with her friends on a cruise to Mexico.

"*Mexico?*" I don't hear the rest of Hettie's scandalized response because Sydney gives my hand a little tap.

"Mama hasn't been asking too many questions about your book, has she?" she murmurs.

"Not yet," I tell her.

She nods, relieved. "Good. She's lively tonight, but this may be her final dinner party. Another month and I doubt she'll know what's going on."

The comment is delivered so matter-of-factly I can't tell what's behind it, regret or resignation or—I cringe at the possibility—impatience. I'm about to express gentle dismay at the lie she and Brigitte are asking me to perpetrate when the guest to my left addresses me.

"So, young lady, I hear you're writing a book about plantations." He's older, red-faced with just a few strands of greasy gray hair, and his thick, phlegmy voice sets my teeth on edge. He doesn't introduce himself, just smiles smugly as if I ought to know him already.

This must be the famous Raleigh Winn. Ew.

Since Hettie's invitation, I've been studying up on Fairview Manor, hoping to develop a few intelligent questions for the much-anticipated Mr. Winn. It soon becomes apparent, however, that this was unnecessary. I ask about his home, and off he goes. Construction. Materials. Previous owners. His purchase. Experts consulted. Brilliant refurbishing decisions and their rationale. All this delivered in a voice that makes me want to scream, *Clear your throat!* I suffer through his not-so-subtle glances at my chest, wishing that I'd covered up.

As Raleigh delivers his incessant monologue, I keep an idle eye on the other guests. It's not a young crowd, and for rich people, they're decidedly unattractive. Most of the men are, like Raleigh, some combination of balding, wrinkled, and overfed. The women are plump, too, and overly generous in their use of makeup, although tonight I'm not really one to condemn excessive cosmetics.

Over at her end of the table, Hettie sits beside the only guest who looks younger than me. He's pleasant-looking, probably in his midthirties, and I feel an immediate kinship with him because he's made a fashion faux pas even graver than my own: he sports jeans and a plaid shirt. Hettie doesn't seem to care. She asks him questions, laughs, smiles and nods at his replies. *A family member?* He retains an expression of vague unease throughout dinner that makes me wonder. I don't think he's used to running in these circles. To add to the intrigue, Sydney and Brigitte have it in for him. They cast him several contemptuous glances, exchange eye rolls with one another, and avoid Hettie's attempts to engage them in her conversation with the man.

Who is this guy? He's hardly stop-in-your-tracks handsome, but he has a nice smile and the way he listens attentively to Hettie puts her daughters to shame. With his deep tan and close-cropped, almost military dark hair, he looks like more of a construction-worker type than someone who'd be running with the Deveaus. I wish I could hear what he and Hettie are talking about, but Raleigh's booming voice has rendered that impossible.

"Now, in the original home," Raleigh says, shaking a meaty finger at me, "the kitchen was outdoors to avoid fires. Expandin' the house while preservin' the flow a the space was, a course, a challenge."

Having finished our salads, we are now staring down the main course: roast duck. Over the course of a half hour, Raleigh manages to both speak and ingest more than the average person would in a day. Once or twice, Brigitte asks me a few questions to be polite, but otherwise I'm at Raleigh's mercy. Maybe Hettie knew what she was doing inviting me. Maybe I was the sacrificial lamb, there to protect the other guests from his pompous, long-winded lectures on plantation shutters.

"See, it wasn't until the Victorian era that we put shutters outside the house," Raleigh explains, pausing to empty another wineglass. "Used to keep 'em on the interior, which kept out sunlight, but also, I think, aesthetically speakin' . . ."

I get a brief reprieve when Andre Deveau arrives. As a server quickly sets a place for him at the foot of the table, Andre makes his rounds, greeting guests and pausing to kiss the top of his mother's head. He looks a bit puzzled by the casually dressed man beside her, but Hettie is too busy asking her son about his trip to make the introduction. When Brigitte waves Andre over and whispers something in his ear, I think at first that she's briefing him on the mystery man in jeans. Then I see Andre glancing in my direction, nodding.

"So you're our writer," he says to me with a smile. "Welcome." He looks as I remember him from our *Sophisticate* interview years ago, only older. "Prince Charmin' with gray hair," Leeann declared when I asked her about Andre, and although he's not exactly handsome, I can see what she means. The silvery hair and crinkly eyes suit him, make him look distinguished. In his blue eyes and high forehead, I detect traces of Hettie.

Andre finishes making nice and slides into his chair near Jules. "I have something for you," he tells Jules. "Before I forget." He reaches into his breast pocket and drops two black cuff links onto the center of the table. There's no mistaking the interlocking-L-and-V design: Louis Vuitton. "I found these lying around. I assume they're yours."

"Ah, yes. Thank you." Jules doesn't bat an eye, but I can barely keep my jaw from hitting the floor. Was Jules speaking to Andre Deveau on the phone the other night when he asked his seemingly overscheduled boyfriend to bring these exact cuff links? Are these two an item?

The more I think about it, the more it makes sense. Jules is young and hot; Andre has money, power, and pedigree. It's an old recipe for attraction, really. Their professional relationship could make things a bit sticky, I suppose, but the real obstacle here is that Andre is not gay . . . to anyone's knowledge. I don't necessarily blame him for his silence on the subject. As the CEO and owner of a South-based hotel chain, he would find his homosexuality a professional liability. And maybe it's an unfair Northern stereotype, but the conservative, Confederacy-loving Deveaus don't strike me as terribly gay-friendly. I doubt anyone in this family has a clue.

Not five minutes later, Brigitte's attempts to matchmake for her brother confirm her ignorance. "Andre," she calls, coming over to fetch him before he's had even three bites of dinner, "did you meet Ginny over here? She's the woman I've been telling you about." There's no mistaking her intentions as she drags Andre to the other end of the table. "I *really* think you two would get along."

Beside me, Sydney glowers at her sister. "Just because she's married, she thinks everyone else has to be." She spears a piece of asparagus, and I remember reading something about a nasty divorce or two in Sydney's past. "Being single is not a disease," she mumbles to no one in particular, and I almost feel sorry for her.

My pity proves extraordinarily short-lived because at that moment Raleigh leans over and places his hand on my thigh. "I've been thinkin'," he says. "Seein' as you're so interested in houses, maybe you'd like to come by after dinner for a visit. Whattaya say? I'll give ya the full tour a my domain."

That's it. I can think of no place I wish to tour less than Raleigh Winn's domain. I grab my clutch and excuse myself to the restroom, leaving him to interpret my look of nausea as he likes.

IN THE BATHROOM, I turn on the sink and let the water run, my fingers pressed to the cold, white marble. I don't belong here. Any idiot can see that. I dab a tissue with water and attempt to clean up my smudgy eyes. Did I really think I was going to help Gabriel? How, exactly, does my attending a stuffy dinner party further this objective? As far as the Deveaus are concerned, I'm just some no-name hoochie for Raleigh to paw at, and I'll never get any useful information if I'm stuck playing Little Miss Plantation Journalist.

I pop open my clutch and check my phone, hoping for an update from home. Two voice mails, but the reception is too spotty to access them. Now I know why Jules was out in the garden talking to Andre. I sneak out through the kitchen door and listen to my messages in the dark. The first is a greeting from my grandmother, who assures me that she's doing fine and hopes I am enjoying my brush with high society. The second message contains the only good piece of news I've had all day. "This is Detective Remy Minot from the Bonnefoi Parish sheriff's department. Just returning your call. There's not much to discuss about the Deveau case, but you're welcome to come by the station tomorrow morning, say, nine o'clock. You have a good evening, ma'am."

Finally. Someone knowledgeable to talk to. Odds are he wasn't on the force when Gabriel went missing, but in a community like this, you never know. He could potentially get me in touch with the cops who *were* involved. Or old witnesses even. I make a mental wish list. Madeleine Lauchlin, the nanny. Danelle Martin, the cook. Roi Duchesne, the recently fired groundskeeper who was originally of interest to police. I rub my arms, wishing again I'd brought a jacket.

I'm trying, Gabriel. I'm trying to help you.

As I head back toward the house, I come across the man in jeans who Hettie's been talking to all night. He's lighting up a cigarette, in no particular hurry, and I'm struck by how relaxed he appears. Relaxed, despite the cold, despite the stink-eye Sydney and Brigitte have been giving him, despite showing up to dinner in jeans and—I see now—cowboy boots. For the first time in ages, I feel pangs of regret that I quit smoking. I want some of that peace. I remember going to parties in college, parties where I didn't know a single person and it didn't matter. If I sat on the front step with a cigarette, people joined me, bummed a smoke off me, started talking. It's been fifteen years since I quit, but suddenly I'm jonesing hard.

The man takes his first long drag, eyes half-closed as he savors it. My gaze travels down his fingers and settles on the glowing end of his cigarette.

"You lustin' for me or my Marlboro?"

I look up, totally busted.

He's smiling. "You want one?"

"You don't know how bad. But I better not."

He nods. "Bad habit, I know. I quit for ages, but then . . . had a rough year." His voice is twangy, not the flat Cajun accent I've been hearing the past few days.

"Texas?" I guess.

"You're good." He looks me over, but not in a creepy way. "I'm gonna say New York."

"Uh-oh." Looking like you're from New York is probably not a good thing. "What tipped you off?"

He grins. "Heard you tell Brigitte durin' dinner. Congrats on your escape, by the way. Tough crowd."

I'm glad we're on the same page about that torturous meal. "It wasn't easy. You saw what I was up against."

He chuckles. "Yeah, that old guy was workin' you pretty hard."

By now, I'm really, really cold, but I don't want to go back indoors. There's something about this guy, an easiness I like. And I'm curious. I want to get his story. I take a few steps in his direction. "We were never properly introduced."

He extends a hand. "Noah."

"Charlie," I tell him. His hand is large and rough when I shake it, like he's someone who could change his own tire or repair a leaky roof. But warm. Very warm.

"Charlie," he repeats. "That's cute."

"So what brings you to dinner tonight?" I ask.

"I'm out here doin' some work for Hettie."

Now I'm really confused. Is he some kind of laborer, and if so, why was he at dinner?

"What kind of work?" I'm bordering on nosy, but I might not get another chance to ask.

"Landscapin'."

Huh? Hettie is palling around with the gardener? "Do you . . . like it?"

"I started my company when I was nineteen." He shrugs. "It's what I know."

"Nineteen, wow. Contract work can be so hard. Hard to get enough jobs, I mean."

Noah senses where I'm going with this. "Not too hard," he says. "I got enough to keep forty guys busy full-time. Got a contract with parks and rec back home." He smiles at me, his eyes crinkling at the corners like all my caste-sniffing amuses rather than offends him. "Look, I know what you're thinkin'. I've known Hettie just about all my life. She's an old family friend. Sweetest woman alive. Knew my grandparents."

"I wasn't judging," I protest. "I just figured—"

"You figured I don't go to these kinda dinners much." Noah looks down at his jeans and laughs. "And you'd be right."

"Yeah, well . . ." I point to my low neckline. "You can tell I don't either."

He casts a quick glance at my cleavage and then virtuously averts his eyes. "I think every woman in that room would like to have some a what you got." Then he adds as an afterthought, "The guys too."

"Thanks." I don't know whether he's counting himself as one of the guys, but I kind of hope so. I take a few steps back toward the house. "I better go say a proper good-bye."

"You'll never get out again."

Actually, I'm afraid of that. I don't think Raleigh will let me slip away so easily next time, and I'm not sure how to defend myself from future awkward gropes without making a scene. But I've already screwed up enough tonight, etiquette-wise. "I've got to thank the hostess," I tell Noah. "Aren't you going to?"

"Nope. Told Hettie I was turnin' in for the night. Just got in today, so I played the tired-from-travelin' card."

"Good call." I sigh.

"Hey, if you don't wanna go back, then don't. Tomorrow you can just say you got sick."

I think it over.

"You really think any a them care if you're there? Besides the grabby guy, I mean."

"No," I say. "I don't." It's tempting. And I did say I was going to the bathroom. If they assume I got the shits and ran off, it's not any worse than the rest of the evening.

He sees me wavering. "You stayin' in one a the guest cottages?"

"Yeah."

"Me too. I'll walk you back."

And just like that, we ditch dinner. The garden is considerably less frightening when I have an escort. Shrubs look like shrubs; I can sensibly attribute the soft rustling sounds to wind and leaves. Only the temperature spoils an otherwise lovely stroll. My teeth start chattering.

"Wish I had a coat for you," Noah says apologetically. "I'll give you an arm if that doesn't seem too bold."

Too bold. I can't help but smile. "Sure, I'll take an arm." I latch on to him. With my heels on, I'm about the same height as he is, but his arm is like two of mine. I wonder if he's a gym rat or bulked up on the job.

"So what got you smoking again?" I ask. "You said you had a rough year."

"Oh." He rubs his forehead like it gives him a headache. "Lost my granddaddy. Got a divorce."

"Ah. The first year is bad, but it gets better," I promise. "I got divorced a couple years ago."

"Yeah? What happened?"

"He was cheating." For a brief second I'm oddly grateful to Eric for making me sound so blameless. "How about you?"

"Nothin' like that." He steadies me when I trip on a tree root. "I guess when we got married, we were on the same page about kids, but . . . I changed my mind." Noah takes another pull off his cigarette. "There's no real compromise for that one. You can't push someone into havin' a kid they don't want. So we went our own ways."

I feel fleeting sympathy for his ex-wife, probably in her midthirties now and stuck searching for a man to father her child. My sympathy is quickly eclipsed by relief, however. This guy won't be pulling out photos of his adorable children, thank God.

We're standing outside my guest cottage now, and though I could leave, could end the night here, I don't. I watch as Noah stamps out his cigarette. The embers die beneath his boot, but I still smell it on him, the fresh smoke. He reads the hunger on my face and pulls out a pack from his pocket. "I got more. All you gotta do is ask."

"I'd be *such* a hypocrite."

"I won't tell." He holds up three fingers. "Scout's honor."

I wince. "Okay, fine. You've sold me. Light me up."

He removes a cigarette from the pack and places it in my mouth. Apparently rekindling an old addiction is like riding a bicycle, because the sensation is instantly familiar. I cradle the Marlboro between my index and middle fingers, enjoying the weight, the shape. Noah retrieves the lighter from his back pocket, and with a quick movement of his thumb, the flame springs up. I lean toward him, into the flickering, pale orange light, and inhale deeply.

Maybe it's the hint of his aftershave or the way his arm feels when I huddle against it. Solid. And safe. Maybe it's his broad shoulders, or those dark eyes I can just make out in the moonlight, trying to figure me out, letting me make the next move. Maybe it's just the heady feeling of nicotine spreading through my bloodstream, hitting my brain, asking me, *Why the hell not?* I look up into the clear, starry sky and blow a small ring of smoke.

"Hey," I ask, "do you wanna come in?"

9.

My mouth tastes like an ashtray. It's the second thing I notice when I wake, the first, of course, being the naked man in my bed. Both my mind and heart race. I go from a disoriented state of just-woke-up to full-blown panic in a matter of milliseconds.

Shit, shit, SHIT.

He's still crashed out, thank goodness, a mound of skin and shadow and bedsheets splayed beside me. A butt cheek peeks out where he ran out of blanket. It is a very, very nice butt, which leaves me even more rattled. I don't even know this man. I should not be assessing the cuteness of his butt.

Plan. You need a plan. First step: locate clothing.

I've never been the one-night-stand type. I'm too picky. And being naked in front of a stranger has always seemed more stressful than sexy. Yes, I made a couple of bad decisions in college, but who hasn't? There was Kurt, the German guy I slept with the night of his going-home party. Predictable outcome: he went home. And Justin Shanley, a crush I jumped into bed with, hoping it might go some-where. Predictable outcome: it didn't. I thought I'd learned something from my youthful stupidity, but here's Noah, proof that I can be as dumb at thirty-eight as I was at twenty.

I slip on a bra and fresh underwear, but I still reek of cigarettes. I need a shower. I look back at Noah and cringe. Every awkward moment of the previous night comes flooding back. It was like we were seventeen one minute, all misplaced elbows and knees, clueless about the gentle choreography of lovemaking, then seventy the next, too slow and careful with each other for the breathless, animal encounter you're supposed to have in these situations. *Is this okay?* he kept asking. *Are you sure?*

But I was sure—at least I was at the time. I could smell the aftershave on his jaw, his neck, and he smelled so *good*.

I head into the bathroom and frown at my reflection. Dark smudges of mascara have gathered under my eyes, and my hair spikes out in bizarre directions like a manga character's, minus the cute. I wash my face, brush my teeth. There's no fixing my hair until it gets a good washing.

Do I wake him? Let him sleep? Bump loudly around the cottage until he gets up? I'm not used to men anymore, I realize. The space they occupy, the little snorts of their sleep-breathing, their big man feet and hairy, crooked toes.

Any way you slice it, Noah's an unpredictable choice. I'm an over-educated, liberal New Yorker. Noah doesn't even have a college degree. He's from Texas. He wears cowboy boots and probably owns guns. Ten to one he's a Republican. And he's clearly rebounding from a rough divorce. Wrong time, wrong place, wrong person. So why, why, why?

Right now, all I know is that I wanted to. Just thinking about it makes my cheeks burn, my stomach do wild flip-flops. I've got to get him out of my place, sort myself out.

I peer at him from the bathroom doorway. He's rolled over and his eyes are at half-mast.

"Hey." He stretches. "You're up. What time is it?"

"Almost seven." I spot his jeans and briefs in a pile by the bed and collect them.

He rubs his face. "You sleep okay?"

I nod, and now that I think about it, I did. I got more than five hours of uninterrupted sleep. For me, that is a pretty big accomplishment. I hand him his clothes, careful not to look at his body.

"How 'bout we both shower and get dressed, and I'll come back here in half an hour," Noah suggests. "I'll take ya to breakfast."

"You don't have to do that."

He still hasn't put on his briefs. "I'd like to. If that's all right."

I fall silent, still in flight mode, trying to figure out the best strategy to extricate myself. He must see it on my face because doubt creeps into his voice. "Did I do somethin' wrong?"

"No, no." And he didn't. The wrongness is all me, thinking I could handle this.

"Look, I don't know anything about datin' anymore. I hope I didn't—disappoint you."

I look the other way as he slips into his clothing.

"I was with the same woman for twelve years," Noah says. "I'm kinda learnin' everything all over. And I wasn't expectin' . . . I mean, you took me by surprise." I have no idea what he's getting at until he says, "Gimme some time. I'll figure out how you work, how to make you feel good."

Oh God, the poor thing. He's afraid he sucked in bed. I want to tell him there's blame enough to go around, but at this stage, that might be a little too much honesty.

"You were fine," I assure him, and then, realizing no guy wants his sexual performance to be just "fine," I add, "It was nice." My weak attempts at sensitivity are probably negated by my handing him his boots immediately after.

He finishes dressing in silence; I do nothing more to encourage him. We walk together toward the cottage door and he pauses, runs a hand over his buzz cut. His eyes meet mine, questioning, and we both understand this is my call. If I open the door, he won't bother me again. When we see each other around the estate, he'll be personable, but he'll keep his distance. Privately, though, he'll worry. He'll play the night over in his head, asking himself, *What did I do?*

Your move, Charlie.

In the end, I have to accept facts. I'm not a frat boy out for conquests. I'm a woman, endowed with empathy, and I don't want to leave some basically good guy freaking out about his penis size or whatever it is that men freak out about when they're rejected. One meal. I can survive one meal.

"I hear there's a good diner in town," I say.

His relief palpable, Noah smiles and gives my hand a quick squeeze. "I'll see you in half an hour."

WE'RE EARLY ENOUGH that Crawdaddy's Diner isn't crowded yet. Leeann told me her dad's place is a madhouse on Sundays after church gets out, but it's barely eight. Most of the patrons are older or look like they were out all night drinking. Our waitress, a puffy-eyed teenager in the latter category, leads us to a booth and doles out menus with an anemic smile.

The diner is a worn little joint with an off-white and avocado color scheme, but it's clean and smells pleasantly greasy. Noah and I study our options quietly until our waitress returns a couple of minutes later with a pot of coffee and a notepad. Noah gets a crawfish omelet. I'm not in the mood for anything adventurous. I need comfort food.

He seems content for us to sip our coffee in silence, but the not talking unnerves me. We should get to know each other, right? I reach

for some stock question—*What are your hobbies? Do you have any pets?*—
but something else tumbles out.

"Do you own a gun?"

He raises his eyebrows. "That's a funny question."

Well, yes. But I play it off. "I'm just curious. Do you?"

"Sure. Couple a huntin' rifles and a nine-millimeter."

"You hunt?" There's a sinking feeling in my stomach.

"Mostly deer. My buddies and I do a huntin' trip every year."

I picture his living room walls, rows of mounted deer heads. "So
you just—kill animals? For fun?"

"For sport and for meat," he says. "I eat what I can of 'em. Why?
You think it's cruel?"

"Yeah, I do. Isn't killing animals for fun pretty much the definition
of animal cruelty?"

He rolls his eyes. "You gotta control the deer population somehow.
And how do you have a leg to stand on talkin' 'bout animal cruelty?
You just ordered bacon, didn't you?" He swallows the last of his coffee.
"You really think that pig you're gonna eat had a better quality a life
than the deer I shoot?"

That shuts me up. I still think he's a bloodthirsty hick, but at least
he's not a pushover. Eric was always so reluctant to disagree with me—
so placating. I'm dying to get a read on Noah politically, to see what
kind of fireworks that produces, but figure I should probably back off.
What do our differences really matter, anyway?

"So how big is your job at Evangeline?"

"Not sure 'til I get the plans drawn up, but pretty big." He holds out
his empty cup to a passing waitress, who promptly refills it. "Hettie
wants the garden to look like it did in the 1920s. I've got some photos
to work with, and my designer should be comin' in a week or so."

"That seems like a strange project for Hettie to start when she's so
sick," I point out.

He twists his napkin around a finger. "She wants to leave the home behind in a certain condition."

"Why? Her kids won't care. They're hardly ever there." I know that he is close to Hettie, but maybe he doesn't realize how poor her health is. "From what I hear, she doesn't have a lot of time, Noah."

"I know. That's why we've got to do it now."

His answers don't sit well with me. I find the project increasingly suspicious. "Whose idea was this whole garden renovation, anyway? Hers or yours?"

He heaves a deep sigh. "Hettie called *me*, okay? I'm not some asshole tryin' to screw over a dyin' woman here." He hesitates. Gazes at me appraisingly. "Can I trust you?"

"Yes . . ."

We're interrupted by the arrival of our breakfast. Little Miss Hangover plops our plates on the table, looking nauseous. I look at Noah, expectant, but he's already stuffed his mouth full of egg, and now I have to wait for him to finish chewing.

"So you can't tell *anyone* this." He wipes his mouth.

"Okay." I wrap both hands around my mug.

"Hettie's not leavin' the estate to her kids."

"*What?!*" This is better than I thought. "Do they know?"

"Hell no. She says Andre won't care. He's got no love for Evangeline. But the daughters . . ."

"They'll pitch a fit," I predict. "What's happening to the property, then?"

He shovels another chunk of omelet into his mouth. "She's donatin' the place to the Louisiana Historical Association. Should generate some tourism for Chicory. That's real important to her, takin' care a the folks in town."

Impressive, really, the deception that goes on between Hettie and her daughters. I knew the twins were sneaky bitches, but Hettie's treachery surprises me. "Who knows about this, besides you?"

"Just her lawyer, I guess, since he drew up the will. And you. That's probably it."

Something about this situation doesn't smell right. "Why would she tell *you* something like that? No offense, but that's big stuff."

"Well, I needed to know for the job, to get the place historically accurate and tourist-ready. And Hettie likes me." He sees my skepticism and gets defensive. "She does. She's really looked out for me over the years. Gave me the seed money to start my business."

This baffles me. "She must've been really close to your grandparents."

He nods. "They worked at Evangeline for, oh, thirty years, I think. I used to visit when I was small."

And then suddenly I get it. "How old are you, Noah?"

"Thirty-two."

He's younger than I first thought, and now it makes perfect sense. "You're the same age her son would've been," I say softly. "He would've turned thirty-two last September."

"Gabriel? Yeah. We used to play together."

An odd little shiver runs up my back. Something about seeing this adult man in front of me—a real, physical being with stubble and eyelashes and ears that stick slightly out—drives it home for me. This is what Hettie lost. Not just the child, but the man. Can it really be pure chance that the man I fell into bed with last night is connected to Gabriel? I don't *think* I was drawn to Noah by inexplicable supernatural forces, but at this point, I'm not ruling anything out.

"You remember him?" I ask.

"Charlie, I was only three when he went missin'."

"Hettie must think of you as a son," I say. "She must think of him every time she looks at you."

And then it hits me. Noah is her Zoey. Her son's playmate, loved to pieces, but always a reminder. I try to imagine how I'll feel looking at Zoey ten, twenty years from now, seeing what Keegan never had a chance to be. I pick at the food on my plate, no longer hungry.

Noah looks uncomfortable. He dumps a package of creamer into his cup. "She's been good to me, whatever the reason."

"So your grandparents—" I suddenly remember his telling me last night that his grandfather died recently. "Your grandmother," I correct myself, "is she still alive?"

"Died my senior year a high school." He loads up a forkful of hash browns, not meeting my eye. "She and my granddaddy raised me."

"I'm sorry," I tell him. "You're like an orphan, then." My sympathy is, of course, mixed with disappointment. His grandparents would've made for some excellent interviews. "What happened to your mom?"

"Died when I was a baby. And my dad went AWOL, so. Just me, Nanny, and Daddy Jack."

"You mean your father just took off on you?" Parent Ditches Child is familiar territory with me.

"I mean he was in the military and he literally went AWOL. Was supposed to get sent overseas somewhere, and he disappeared. We never saw or heard from him again." He shrugs, like this is no big deal. "I was little. I don't even remember him."

"That sounds a lot like my family," I say, "if you switch the genders." I wasn't planning to get personal with Noah, but the similarities to my own life are eerie. "My mom was the one who ran off, and my dad died. I was older, though, when I lost him. Fourteen. My grandmother took me in."

"Weird." Noah studies me. "Shitty thing to have in common." Our waitress trudges over to top off our coffee. She has a faraway look, like she's mentally composing a suicide note. "Don't know what she got up to," he says after she's dragged herself to the next table, "but I'm pretty sure we had the better night."

Oh God, last night. Now I'm thinking about him naked again. I can feel a blush coming, so I abruptly change the subject. "What did your grandparents do at Evangeline? Is landscaping a family thing?"

"Kinda. Daddy Jack was a caretaker and Nanny was . . . well, a nanny. She took care a the twins and Andre when they were little, and years later, Gabriel."

The nanny. My God. His family was in deep with this. "Madeleine Lauchlin," I murmur. One of the witnesses on my wish list, and she's dead.

"Everyone called her Maddie, but yeah." He peers at me. "You know a lot about Gabriel."

This is my cue to spill my guts about the book, but I can't do it. He's too close to Hettie. "I used to write for *Cold Crimes* magazine," I say. It's not a lie, anyway.

He wrinkles his brow. "And then suddenly you started writing about plantations?"

"Even weirder. I started working at a women's magazine. *Sophisticate.* For rich women who need the latest scoop on collagen injections or, I don't know, the dangers of wearing high heels in icy weather."

Noah busts out laughing.

"It isn't funny. I worked there for twelve years. It was soul-killing." I've never admitted this before.

He tries to take a sip of coffee, still laughing, and chokes. "My wife reads that magazine," he says when he's finished coughing. "Ex-wife, I mean."

That throws me. I'm about to completely reevaluate my ideas on Noah, his lifestyle, and the women he goes for, when I remember something. The voice mail I got last night.

"Oh no, I have to be somewhere . . ." Detective Minot invited me to stop by this morning to chat about the case, and I completely forgot. "Any chance you could drop me off at the police station?"

Noah squints at me. "Something I should know about you?" He's only half-kidding.

I can't tell him the real purpose of my visit, so I stare at my lap, face flushing as I deliver the first stupid lie that comes to me. "Just, you know, trying to fix a parking ticket."

He chuckles. "I'll take you over, but I wouldn't hold your breath on that."

"Yeah, well. You never know. I can be pretty persuasive."

His eyes flicker over me, and he smiles slightly. "I bet you can."

10.

Though seated in Chicory, the sheriff's department serves all the towns in Bonnefoi Parish, and it's not as podunk as I'd imagined. Like the surrounding municipal buildings, it's an ugly brick structure with unexpectedly grand white columns. The sprawling grounds boast oak trees that must be at least a couple hundred years old, and in the background, a dark ribbon of bayou weaves by.

I climb out of Noah's truck, my brain shifting to Gabriel mode. "Thanks for the ride. And breakfast."

"Let me give you my cell number," he says. "I'll pick you up."

I try to protest, but Noah assures me he's got nothing better to do. I program his number into my phone, well aware that chauffeuring me around town is dangerously boyfriendlike behavior.

Once inside, I'm surprised by how clean and well-lit the building is. I follow signs to the Bureau of Investigations, where a receptionist tries to calm two very distraught women. I study a community board while I wait, reading a flyer for a women's handgun safety class and marveling at news of a Bonnefoi Parish sheriff's department mobile app that boasts instant access to the parish sex offender registry. I'm imagining the kind of resident who might avail herself of these two resources when a middle-aged officer comes up behind me.

"You lookin' for someone, ma'am?" He smiles at me from under a rather large mustache.

"I'm here to see Detective Minot."

"You gotta be the journalist, right? I'm Officer Kinney. Heard you might be droppin' by." He places his hand on the small of my back, a gesture I find overly friendly. "Remy's in a meetin', should be just a minute." Officer Kinney steers me through the reception area and past a few cubicles. In one, three men wearing button-down shirts and badges stand around having a discussion and drinking coffee. In another, a woman fills out a report on her computer. For a Sunday, the place is dishearteningly busy.

We stop at a tidy desk fringed with yellow Post-it notes. The reminders, I see, are both personal and professional: *Pick up Rx* and *Toussaint Testimony, Thurs 10 a.m.* On the computer, a photograph of a little red-haired girl bounces around as the screen saver. Detective Minot's daughter, I guess, or maybe granddaughter. She looks about five or six.

"You want somethin' while you wait, ma'am?" Officer Kinney asks.

"No thanks." I sit down, expecting him to leave, but he lingers.

"So you writin' a book?" It's a good-natured question; not suspicious, just curious.

"Hopefully." I go into journalist mode. The guy clearly wants to chat. "Do you know much about the Deveau case?"

He chuckles, running a finger across his mustache. "I know that case ain't gonna get solved."

"Why do you say that?"

"No evidence." He shrugs. "Been thirty years. I don't see things goin' anywhere unless someone walks in one day an' confesses. Or if a body turns up, I guess that'd be a start."

"Why did they reopen the case if it's so hopeless?"

He rolls his eyes. "Those Deveau sisters started makin' a fuss some months back, after they found out Old Missus had cancer. Said she gone die without peace a mind and it's time to start runnin' DNA tests. Like somebody got DNA just settin' around a drawer someplace." He shakes his head. "The FBI and state police, they got better things to do than chase their own tails, I promise you. So they sent the case our way."

"What about the ransom note? Wouldn't that have DNA?" It's been bugging me.

"At this point you prob'ly got DNA from thirty people on that note. Won't prove a thing. And there's no sayin' for sure it was the kidnapper even wrote that."

"But the case was still reopened?"

"Politics," he says. "Those folks own this town. I bet halfa Chicory's worked for that family at some time or other." He looks about to say more when a tall, lean man approaches.

"Look at you, Kinney. Running off at the mouth again." The man gives us a crooked smile.

Officer Kinney straightens up. "We were just waitin' for you, Remy."

He's not wearing a badge, so it takes me a second to realize this is Detective Minot. He doesn't look like the stereotype of a cop I had in my head. Pale eyes, shaggy salt-and-pepper hair, and a complexion that's been beat up by the sun. Forties? Fiftyish? I'm not sure. His face is drawn and tired, and he's too thin.

"Glad to meet you, ma'am." He nods at me. "Al, I can take it from here." Officer Kinney drifts away, disappointed. Detective Minot settles down at his desk and regards me dubiously. "Miss Cates, is it? So tell me, is this book *your* idea?"

Great, I think. *Even the guy with the criminal justice degree can see this is a stupid move.*

"The publisher approached me," I say. "I'm fully aware this project has some limitations."

"So you're in it for the paycheck."

"Something like that."

"Well, you got some sense, then." He turns to his computer and checks his inbox. "Ask me whatever you like, but understand this case is colder than a cast-iron commode on the shady side of an iceberg."

I smile. "I guess that's my first question. On a case this old, how can you make headway?"

He deletes a few e-mails. "All I can do is follow up with good, old-fashioned police work, ma'am." I get the sense he's fielded this before, maybe from Sydney or Brigitte. "Chat with the original investigators. Go back to the files, review statements, see if there's anything we might've missed. Reinterview witnesses, see if anybody's story has changed. Cross-reference names of all the folks who worked at Evangeline to see if any have a criminal record now."

"Has anything turned up?"

"Well, sure. A few DUIs, tax evasion, possession and sale of a controlled dangerous substance. But nothing in particular that raises a red flag."

"What would raise a red flag?"

Minot looks up from the computer and ticks things off on his fingers. "Anything illegal involving a minor. Extortion, what with the ransom note. Larceny, breaking and entering. Violent behavior."

Across the hall from us, a trim detective leads a sluggish boy in baggy pants into a conference room. I wonder if the boy is a witness, perp, or victim. It bothers me that I can't tell, that a predator can look no different from its prey.

"Have you reinterviewed many people?" I ask Detective Minot, hoping he might throw a few names and addresses my way.

"Many of the key players in the Deveau case have passed away," he replies. "Gabriel's father, Neville, had a heart attack last year. Maddie Lauchlin, the nanny, has been gone a good fifteen years, and her hus-

band, Jack, the caretaker, passed not so long ago. There was a housekeeper named Della who died, too. And tracking down the ones still
living can be a real pain in the rear."

I wish he'd stop fooling around on his damn computer. I know I'm
not exactly a priority, but following some basic rules of conversational
etiquette would be nice. "Can I ask your opinion on something, Detective Minot?"

"Can't guarantee an answer."

"Do you think Gabriel's dead?"

He picks up a pen, studies it a moment, then looks at me long and
hard. "You do my job awhile, Miss Cates, and you don't think highly of
your fellow man. What else could've happened to him? Not quite three
years old. Nobody takes a kid that young with anything good in mind."

"No, I guess not." I think of the dream I had, Gabriel's words: *He
hurt me. You gotta tell on him.* If only I could confirm that I'm on the
right track.

"Was there any indication that Gabriel was being abused?"

He shakes his head. "Nobody reported anything. He'd never been to
a hospital. According to statements made by the Deveau help, he never
had more cuts and bruises than your average toddler."

"What about sexual abuse?"

"Again, nothing reported. But without a body, no one could exam-
ine him."

"Okay, but his *behavior* could indicate a problem. How did people
describe him? Was he withdrawn? Fearful? Did he have any sleep dis-
turbances?"

Detective Minot scribbles something on a Post-it. I can't tell if it's
related to our discussion or a reminder to pick up milk. "Folks said he
was a handful. Very attached to his mother and his nanny."

"Did he have contact with anyone else on the estate?"

"The whole staff knew him, of course. Neville was there some, but he was in New Orleans during the week and he traveled a lot. Andre and the twins, when they were home from boarding school. And whatever other visitors the family had." He makes another note. I'm starting to suspect it's a grocery list.

"So not a lot of people had unsupervised access to him."

"From the reports, no, not during the day. At night and during his nap times, hard to tell."

I shudder. If I'd encountered this case a year ago, I'd probably never have let Keegan sleep alone again. "How long have you been a cop?"

"Twenty-four years."

"You get a lot of homicides in the parish?"

"Some. Drug-related or domestic violence, mostly."

I butter him up a little. "With all your experience, you must have good instincts. What does your gut tell you about the Deveau case?" I'm hoping his "gut instinct" will be based on information that hasn't been made public, and I want to see if it jibes with my visions of Gabriel.

Detective Minot looks at me and for the first time there's a spark of something. "I've got no doubt you've done your research, that you're familiar with the details of this case."

"I know what's been released," I say cautiously.

"You're a smart lady, I can tell that."

"Thanks." Suddenly he's buttering *me* up. What's he after?

"Let's have an honest conversation about this, off the record. Put on your detective cap and tell me what *you* see in this case." I have his full attention now. He's testing me, getting a feel for how I think.

I have a vague feeling that Detective Minot is much smarter than I've been giving him credit for. "Um. Well, Gabriel's abductor was in the house. He knew where to go. He picked a night when Gabriel's parents were gone. And the family dog didn't make a fuss when he entered the room. So I'd say the abductor wasn't a stranger." This is a run-of-the-mill analysis you could read on hundreds of websites, but it's all I've got.

"You say 'he.' You think the abductor is male?" Detective Minot leans back in his chair.

I think my answer has disappointed him. "Yeah, I do."

"Why's that?"

"Just . . . a hunch."

"You got kids?" he asks, as if that would explain my inability to consider a woman a suspect.

The question hangs in the air for a few ugly seconds before I respond.

"Not anymore."

Something flickers in his gaze. He doesn't pursue it, but I can feel him softening, perhaps thinking of the red-haired girl on his computer as he wonders about my loss. "All right," he says, "you think it was a man. What else?"

"Well, two possibilities." I take a deep breath. "One, somebody had been watching that kid a long time, learning about the family routines, the locked door at night. Somebody who people, and the dog, trusted. He took Gabriel, maybe with an accomplice from the inside, hoping to get ransom money. He left the note in Neville and Hettie's bedroom. But something went wrong and whether accidentally or intentionally, Gabriel ended up dead."

"Or? What's your second possibility?" His face betrays no emotion.

"The ransom note was bullshit, left to throw off police. Gabriel's abductor was someone he knew who . . . hurt him. The guy had probably been doing it for a while, but Gabriel was getting old enough to talk. Maybe the guy got scared. So he killed Gabriel to hide what he'd been doing."

Detective Minot doesn't comment on my theories. Instead, he folds his arms behind his head. "You're staying at Evangeline, aren't you?"

I nod, wondering how he knows. Some of Evangeline's employees live in town. They must talk.

"You met the family yet?"

"I met Andre and the twins last night. And I've met Hettie a couple times, briefly."

"What do you think of her?"

What is he getting at?

"She was . . . polite. She had more snap-crackle-pop than you'd expect from somebody who's dying."

"What kind of mother do you take her for?" His tone remains casual, but I'm taken aback.

"Excuse me?"

"Devoted? Distant? Overprotective? What's your read?"

I think about her giving Noah the money to start his business, all her motherly affection projected onto someone else's kid because hers was gone. And then I think about her giving away the entire estate without informing her daughters. "I don't know," I admit. "She's a tough read."

Detective Minot leans toward me, his blue eyes suddenly intense. "You've been a mother, Miss Cates. Let me ask you. If someone took your child, would you ever stop searching for who?"

I say nothing. Of course I wouldn't. No one took my child, and I'm *still* searching for who. Still unable to believe that something was wrong with Keegan's brain, that no one was at fault. I want to know where this is going. "Have you talked to Hettie?"

"Oh, I talked to her." Someone at the front of the building seems to be yelling at the receptionist, but Detective Minot is now completely focused on me. "After we reopened the case, I went to see Hettie Deveau. Usually families like to know you're still working for them, and I thought I'd interview her again, seeing as she was sick and likely to decline. You know what she said?"

The shouting over at the reception desk continues, and I hear male voices attempting to calm the screamer down.

Detective Minot is too caught up in his story to notice. "She said there was no sense dredging up the past because God knew the truth and He would judge. Said she appreciated that I was doing my job, but I probably had more important things to do." He stares at me. "More important things to do. From Gabriel's *mother*."

It's a weird reaction, and I get why it doesn't sit well with Detective Minot. "Well," I say doubtfully, "she'd just found out she was dying, right?"

Detective Minot taps his pen on his desk. "You know, statistically speaking, who's usually responsible when a kid gets killed."

"The parents," I acknowledge. "But Neville and Hettie Deveau both had an alibi. They were in New Orleans at the twins' sweet sixteen party until ten forty-five on the fourteenth. And some guy from their hotel confirmed seeing them at three a.m. that morning, didn't he? When he brought them aspirin?"

"New Orleans isn't exactly cross-country. It's a two-and-a-half-hour drive. Their entire alibi hinges upon that one witness."

"You think they paid him off? You think Neville went back that night—" I'm a little breathless. I've thought from the beginning that Gabriel was sexually abused by a family member. It would fit.

Detective Minot holds up a hand. "Now, I'm not saying that. It could've been a legit kidnapping, an employee or someone connected to the family. Hell, could've been multiple people involved. But in an unsolved case, you gotta start from square one. To me, that means an alibi's gotta be more solid than just some kid from room service."

"So you consider Neville a serious suspect," I murmur.

He shrugs. "Mothers are just as likely to kill a child as fathers. Unlike you, I'm not ruling out a woman."

I can't imagine tiny Hettie hurting anyone, let alone her own child, but I can definitely imagine her covering up for her husband. The thought sickens me. If she knew—if she even suspected yet continued to live with Neville right up to the very end—she is every bit the monster he was.

Detective Minot stands up, satisfied that he's planted this disturbing idea in my head, and hands me a business card. "You're not a cop," he says, "and people talk differently to women. You hear anything interesting, you call me, all right?"

I thank him and leave the building, my mind running in circles. The cool morning air fills my lungs and clears my head. I dig my cell phone out of my purse and call my ride.

"How'd it go with your ticket?" Noah asks.

"I took care of it," I say, and leave it at that.

As I wait for Noah to arrive, I try to figure out my next move. I've got to find a way to talk to Hettie, preferably without Jules and the twins finding out. If I can spend some time with her, maybe I can get a sense of what makes her tick. Is she a grieving mother who has suffered thirty years not knowing the fate of her youngest child? Or is she somehow complicit in his disappearance? My stomach clenches up like a fist. Can I even handle the answer?

The truth could be so ugly.

11.

Back at Evangeline, Noah and I stand by his truck, trying to figure out where to leave things. The sun has emerged at last, lighting up the house and grounds in blinding Technicolor. I shade my eyes with one hand and remark on the good weather, but the conversation is about to run out and a decision will have to be made. Do we like each other as human beings? Is there any purpose in pursuing this?

"So . . . ," Noah says, scratching the back of his neck. "You got plans for this week?"

This is my opportunity to tell him how busy I am, to gently shut off any future possibilities between us, and I should take it. The man is a dead end, a detour at best. There are bigger issues in my life, issues that require my full attention. I *know* this.

But his smell. Fresh laundry, cologne, a dash of pheromones—I'm off my game.

I'm halfheartedly racking my brain for something I can say to make a clean break when Jules bursts from the house and strides toward us. Andre's arrival yesterday does not seem to have improved his mood any, so who knows what kind of drama has transpired between them. Or perhaps Jules has realized that he looks best when broody and ill-tempered, like a lovely and petulant Ralph Lauren model. I wonder if Andre sees more in him than the fabulous jawline and full, pouty lips. I don't.

"Where have you been?" Jules demands. He doesn't give Noah a second glance. "I heard you disappeared last night."

"I wasn't feeling well," I say, and Noah smiles slightly.

"Well, Sydney and Brigitte want to speak with you."

"Speak with me about what?" Can they really be that offended by my leaving their party early?

Jules glares at me. "About your book. You wanted an interview, didn't you?" He smoothes his hair, plainly irritated by all this running around. "They're returning to New Orleans shortly, but you can meet with them in the study in five minutes." Having delivered the message, he heads back for the house, nose tilted an inch or two higher than necessary.

Noah turns to me, smelling a rat. "What's goin' on with this book a yours, anyway?"

I give him a wide-eyed look and feign ignorance, but he's having none of it.

"Sydney and Brigitte don't know the first thing about architecture," he presses. "And I don't think you were dealin' with any parkin' ticket this mornin'." He leans against the bed of his truck assessing me with quizzical eyes. "Plantation homes, my ass. You even really a writer?"

I'm caught, no way out but the truth. "I'm not writing about houses," I say. "I'm writing about Gabriel."

He snorts. "I shoulda known. Another Gabriel groupie." He kicks at the dirt with the toe of his boot, and I feel myself dissolving in guilt. "I wish you knew what my poor Nanny went through. I wish you coulda seen how scared she was a reporters, journalists, all you folks that go sticking your nose in other people's business. And I can't even imagine how it's been for Hettie."

"Look, it's not a topic I chose." I make only a weak attempt at defending myself because part of me thinks that Noah is right. "The publisher offered me a contract. It's a job, okay?"

"If you got no problem with what you're doin', then why're you keepin' it a big secret?"

I see no point in dishonesty now. "Sydney and Brigitte came up with the whole plantation-home thing. They don't want their mom to know about the book."

Noah's face clouds over as his allegiance to Hettie takes hold. "You serious? You're workin' for *those* two?" His eyes flash, and I'm scared for a second that he's going to break something. "I know this may be *inconvenient* for y'all, but Hettie isn't dead yet. It's bad enough how her daughters act, but you, you're a guest! She's got a right to know what people stayin' in her home are up to, especially if they're fishin' around her personal affairs."

"And I agree with you, Noah! But as you're aware, Hettie and her daughters have some problems in the communication department. I got caught in the middle of it all; is that really *my* fault?" I'm nearly shouting at him now, not what I intended at all. I lower my voice. "You told me this morning about Hettie donating the house, and I won't tell anyone. I'd appreciate if you could return the favor."

Bringing up the secret he shared only pisses him off further. "That's the difference between us," he spits out. "I *told* you."

I search for a good response, but he's already walking away, hands curled into fists. *That's what you wanted,* I remind myself. *For him to leave you alone.* But as I watch him trudge away, I have the sneaking suspicion this isn't what I wanted at all.

I FIND SYDNEY LOUNGING in the study's oversized armchair, one leg kicked over the side, while Brigitte complains to Jules about one of the nurses. Although Brigitte is certainly the louder twin, Sydney is the more fashionable of the two. Her short dark haircut makes her blue eyes pop, and a good tailor has made the best of her difficult figure. Brigitte's fluffy blond mane, on the other hand, looks like a throwback to the eighties, and her white sweater calls to mind a lumpy snowman. Both women have broad shoulders and big hips, but Brigitte has at least thirty pounds on her sister. Marriage, I guess. No one to impress.

And impress me she does not.

"We pay these people entirely too much to tolerate any attitude from them," Brigitte says, in the midst of her nurse rant. "I know my mama, and when I ask the help to do something, I am not looking for their *professional opinion* on why they shouldn't do it. You need to replace her, Jules."

"I apologize, and I'll speak to her about it," he promises as he gathers some folders off the desk in the corner. "Rose *is* your mother's favorite caregiver, however. It would be premature to let her go." Jules knows his way around high-maintenance women.

"Just tell her Rose quit," Sydney pipes up from her chair. "Mama won't notice."

I cough lightly, and all heads swivel toward me. Brigitte adopts a large and welcoming smile, but her eyes dart around, calculating exactly how much I heard and what level of blabbermouth I might be.

"There you are," Sydney yawns. "Feeling better, I see." Jules must've passed along my sick excuse. "Bridgie and I have to be getting back to the city soon, but we thought we could give you an hour, anyway."

Brigitte shoots her sister a look that seems to chastise Sydney for her lack of warmth and enthusiasm. "Charlotte, was it? I'm sorry we didn't get the chance to speak much yesterday, but with Mama there . . ." She turns to Jules. "Would you please draw the drapes? I can't stand this awful little man cave of yours."

Jules pulls back the drapes obediently, but the study's dark and somber furnishings expertly fend off natural light. It is a room for migraine-ridden women, scholars burning the midnight oil, grave old white men weighing matters of political and economic import.

"Raleigh seemed to be enjoying your company last night," Sydney tells me with a laugh, though I can't tell if she's amused by Raleigh's lechery or my falling victim to it.

"Oh yes," Brigitte agrees, "he was very taken with you. After you left, he kept asking where you'd gone. He was really concerned."

"It was an interesting evening," I manage.

Brigitte plops herself down on an antique cream-colored love seat with carved wooden detail on the back. She folds her dimpled hands in her lap, left over right, so the enormous diamond on her wedding ring is displayed to its best advantage. "Isaac told us that you work for *Sophisticate*. I want you to know, your magazine ran an article on personal organizers that transformed my life. I'm so happy to be working with you. You wouldn't *believe* some of the people Isaac tried to send our way."

I thank her and politely suggest we make use of our limited time together. I pull out a recording device and do a quick sound check while Jules slips out of the room, giving us some privacy.

"Okay, let's get started," I smile, though every minute spent with these women seems to confirm Noah's ill opinion. "Could you tell me a bit about your family before Gabriel went missing?"

"Of course." Brigitte leans forward in the love seat, genuinely eager to share. "It all began in 1846, when our great-great-great-grandfather Pierre Deveau built Evangeline for his new wife, Cherisse." I get the feeling that she's told this story before. "*He* was a wealthy New Orleans merchant, and *she* was the youngest daughter of the Adrepont family. You've probably heard of the Adreponts. They ran a very successful sugar plantation until the war, which left them just *destitute*."

She charges ahead, and I realize I'm about to receive two hundred years of Deveaus. Time for an intervention—but how to steer her back to the topic of Gabriel without inviting a debate on the subject of my book? "Now, the Deveaus fared very well in the war," Brigitte continues. "Our fortune wasn't entirely dependent on sugar, you see. Our ancestors had the foresight to maintain many diverse sources of income—"

"Like selling supplies to the Union Army," Sydney says.

"No, Syd. No, the Union Army *commandeered*—"

"It's not commandeering when they pay you," Sydney argues, and from the outrage on Brigitte's face, another Civil War may erupt right here in the study. I take advantage of the opening.

"Of course I'll be researching all of this," I say. "But what I'd really like to focus on for the moment is *your* family, the family you grew up in."

The twins glance at each other. Brigitte shrugs, a bit grumpy. "There's not much to say. We were a regular sort of family."

"Our father was gone a lot on business," Sydney elaborates. "We three kids were off at boarding school. And Mama stayed here or in the New Orleans house. By herself and then with Gabriel."

"Did you spend much time together as a family?" I ask, suddenly wondering if they ever really knew their little brother.

"Oh, sure," Sydney says, "we had summers and vacations, usually on the water. Daddy would hire a crew and we'd sail the Virgin Islands, the Greek isles."

"Your average, all-American family, would you say?" Somehow I keep a straight face.

"Definitely," Brigitte replies, "until we lost Gabriel. Our poor mama, she . . . went through a hard time." She turns to her sister. "Do you remember, Syd, Thanksgiving break after he went missing?"

Sydney shakes her head at the memory. "Oh, it was awful. She just looked . . . well, she didn't dress herself very nicely, I'll just leave it at that. She was . . ."

"Completely mismatched," Brigitte supplies. "And her hair . . ." She shudders. "Mama had this awful pink robe," she tells me. "Morning, noon, and night, she wouldn't take it off. She just kind of wandered around the house like someone's doddering old granny. It felt like we'd lost her right along with Gabriel."

"And how did your dad take it?" I ask, ready to assume the worst of the late Neville Deveau.

"You've seen the security measures around here, haven't you?" Sydney says. "That's how he took it. Also, I think he punched a few reporters."

"*One* reporter," Brigitte corrects, "and that man said something nasty about Mama. Daddy was grieving as much as she was, Syd. He just didn't show it the same. You know he had such high hopes for Gabriel."

I jump on this. "What kind of high hopes?"

"Just—doing the things a father does with a son. Sports, fishing, sailing," Brigitte explains.

"Did your father do those things with Andre?"

Sydney wrinkles her nose and stretches. "Andre isn't that type. He was more interested in school."

"He was a good student," Brigitte adds. "All A's. Unlike us!" She giggles.

Until this moment, I never knew how annoying a middle-aged woman's giggle could be.

The image of Neville as a would-be involved father bothers me. It doesn't mesh with my preconceptions of a child-molester-turned-killer. And the lack of interest in Andre, Neville's not-stereotypically-masculine-enough firstborn, seems so . . . normal. Sad and ignorant, but normal. *He hurt me,* Gabriel told me in the dream, and my gut instinct has been telling me he meant his dad. Now I'm not sure.

I try to direct the twins back to their little brother. "How would you describe Gabriel?"

"He was only two when he disappeared. And we didn't see all that much of him." Sydney sits up in her chair and checks her watch.

My time is running out.

"He was a happy kid," Brigitte volunteers. "He couldn't sit still. Tired Nanny right out."

I ask them as many questions as I can about family dynamics and the night that Gabriel disappeared, but the only thing either woman has much to say about is their sweet sixteen party. Brigitte, I learn, still harbors resentment toward Andre for not attending and isn't shy about voicing her complaints.

"He had a *date*," Sydney tells her, trying to calm her down. "Probably the first date of his life. You know how shy he used to be with girls. Cut him some slack."

"It wasn't a date," Brigitte declares, "it was some boy Andre knew. He should've been at our party, there was no excuse."

Poor Andre, I think. *No wonder you're living in the closet. They don't want to know.*

Sydney climbs off her perch on the chair and stretches. "Bridgie, we should get going."

"Just one more question." I can't let them get away without giving me *something,* anything. "You had a lot of different people working at Evangeline over the years. Did any stand out to you as strange or overly interested in Gabriel?"

"Roi Duchesne," says Sydney automatically, "that man they arrested at first. He was shady."

"But he didn't do it," Brigitte protests. "They proved that."

"She asked about weird people and Roi *was.*"

"I assume you were both questioned several times, too," I say. "That must have been exhausting."

"Oh, it was *endless.*" Brigitte clutches her chest as if the very thought is too much for her poor nerves. "And then all that business about us passing out drunk—I had *one* glass of champagne that night. *One.*"

"Bridgie." Sydney turns sharply to her. "Don't."

My ears perk up. From what I understand, Sydney and Brigitte's alibi that evening has always hinged upon their supposed intoxication, a night spent unconscious and sick in the hotel.

"Oh, what does it matter?" Brigitte brushes off her sister's worries with a toss of her hair. "You think they'd come bothering us now? It's been thirty years."

"I think you're forgetting what it was like dealing with a bunch of rabid journalists out to make a name for themselves," Sydney says through clenched teeth.

But Brigitte has already moved on. She casts her sister a dreamy look. "You know who I was wondering about the other day? Sean Lauchlin."

Sydney frowns. "Nanny and Daddy Jack's son? You thought *he* was suspicious?"

Could this be Noah's father, the guy who went AWOL?

Brigitte twirls a strand of hair around her finger. "He was around Gabriel sometimes when he visited."

Sydney bursts out laughing. "Honey, Sean Lauchlin was not overly interested in Gabriel. *You* were overly interested in *him*."

"I know I had a little crush," Brigitte admits, "but think about it. He wasn't around a lot, and then he'd come back and just hang around the house all day with Mama and Gabriel or Andre or us. He could've done anything, and nobody would've thought twice."

"He was in the army, sweetie, visiting Nanny and Daddy Jack on leave." Sydney pats her sister on the shoulder. "He wasn't even around when Gabriel disappeared. Now we'd really better go." Her expression indicates she finds the Sean Lauchlin hypothesis both childish and sad.

I disagree. "Do you remember the last time you saw Sean?" It's a long shot, but Brigitte does not disappoint me.

"June," she answers immediately. "Right after we got out of school.

He had some kind of fight with his folks, and he left. I always wondered what happened to him."

"Stalker," Sydney sighs, and grabs Brigitte by the hand, pulling her to her feet. "Lovely to see you again. Can't wait to read your book," she tells me as she marches Brigitte out.

I flip off my recorder and stand alone in the study, listening to them call for their suitcases. What was Sean fighting with Maddie and Jack about? I wonder. And if Sean Lauchlin ditched Noah, his own son, in June, why come back for Gabriel two months later? Money, I'd assume. I'll have to ask Detective Minot if anyone ever looked at him as a suspect.

As I stand there in the study surrounded by expensive objects, all I can think of is Keegan, what he would have done to this room as a toddler. Climb the desk. Shimmy up the drapes. Track dirt on the upholstery. I wonder if this room was always so beautiful, so impersonal. Was this ever a house that *wanted* children, or did it just tolerate them until they were old enough to send off to boarding school?

Who would Gabriel have been, had he lived? A superficial socialite like his sisters? An uptight businessman ashamed of his true self like his brother? Someone even worse, even sadder?

I'm losing my way. Allowing morbidity to overwhelm my sense of purpose. I step into the hallway and shut the study door firmly behind me. If only death were something you could lock away in a single room. If only grief, like a kid in a long game of hide-and-seek, would grow bored, give up, go home.

THAT NIGHT, for the first time in months, it happens. The sweet dark. The fading out. A message coming through.

I must have been asleep at some point, but now I'm dimly aware of my body. Blankets, pillows, the squishy mattress in my guest cottage. I shed these physical sensations one by one. Step past them into what's waiting.

Then I'm so alert it hurts. My head rings like someone's turned the volume button all the way up. I blink away the noise. Allow myself to calibrate.

Pay attention. You're going to see something important.

A long hallway. I'm making my way down a red-and-white-tiled floor. Blue lockers line the walls, and the sickly fluorescent lighting makes the colors unnaturally bright and jarring. *A school.*

The hall ends abruptly with a white concrete wall, blank except for a large round clock. Beneath it, a girl with shoulder-length red hair stands, as if waiting for an appointment. Fifth, sixth grade, maybe? She looks young but carries herself like a much older child, glancing at the clock, the floor, then back at the clock again with a very adult anxiety.

I try to get her attention.

Hello?

She looks up, and for a moment our eyes meet. She's wearing lip gloss, and her nose and cheeks have a smattering of freckles. Her mouth opens, as if she wants to tell me something. From somewhere in the bowels of the school, a bell begins to ring, loudly and insistently, almost like an alarm.

The girl covers her mouth, suddenly looking ill, and makes a bee-line for a door marked GIRLS. I follow her inside, concerned, and find a restroom with three stalls, a sink, and a mirror. I catch a whiff of lemon-scented toilet cleaner and notes of old urine.

Are you okay? I ask, but the stalls are empty. The girl is gone.

Suddenly my stomach begins to churn. I'm going to be sick. I step into one of the stalls and drop to my knees, vomiting. I gag, heave, spit. When I look into the toilet bowl, I see long red hair floating in a slow, ominous circle.

As I back out of the stall, eyes on the swirling hair, I feel someone behind me. I spin around, realize it's the mirror. My own reflection gazes back at me, bald. My scalp is smooth as an egg.

I gasp. Hold my head for a moment. Stare at my hands. Fistfuls of red hair spill from my fingers, littering the floor. *No, no, no,* I say. *No.*

It'll be okay soon. Someone is patting my back, consoling me. *It's almost over.*

The girl is with me. She's the one who has lost her hair, not me. No hair, no eyelashes, and just a trace of eyebrows. I recognize her only by the lip gloss and the faded sprinkling of freckles on her nose. She pats my back again, but her big eyes against that pale, alien-looking skull are anything but comforting.

And the setting has changed. We're in a dim pink room now, standing beside a neatly made hospital bed. Nearby, an IV drip adds an air of menace. I don't think it's an actual hospital, judging from the whimsical balloon bedspread, the ballet-shoes lamp, or the shelves of teddy bears. Her bedroom, maybe.

Are you dead? I whisper.

She shakes her head. *I'm sick.*

Are you going to get better?

She shakes her head again, and she looks so old, so tired. *I'm not strong enough. I've been sick too long.* She sighs heavily. *My mama and daddy are sad all the time 'cause a me.*

Her voice, I note, sounds local. Is she from Chicory?

It's not your fault, I murmur. *Sometimes people just get sick.*

Like your li'l boy, she says, and I freeze.

You know him? You know Keegan?

She climbs into the hospital bed, ignoring my question, and settles herself under the covers. *I don't have much time. Will you tell them? My mama and daddy? They're gonna wanna be here.*

But I'm not ready to do her any favors, not without an answer. *Do you know my son?*

She leans back against the pillow and closes her eyes. *You wish you coulda been with him, don't you? You wish you coulda said good-bye.*

Where is he? I grip her shoulder harder than I mean to. The bone is heartbreakingly tiny. *Have you seen Keegan? Please, I want to speak to him.*

She doesn't open her eyes again. Her voice is sleepy, distant. *One more day. I'm gonna give them one more day. Then I can go.*

The light in the room turns inky and thick. I can feel myself rising out of the moment, moving away even as I try to hold on. All that remains is the sound of her, soft and faraway. *Tell my daddy, would you? Tell him four sixteen.*

"Who?" I ask. "Who do I tell?"

My voice echoes throughout the dark cottage. I sit up, momentarily disoriented by the configuration of furniture, so unlike my bedroom in Stamford. My toes feel half-frozen, but my forehead and bangs are damp with sweat. Another disturbing dream of children. Another message. And the girl in my dream knew about Keegan.

Hope, wild and desperate, takes root within my chest. If I do what she wants, can she help me talk to him? Can I finally see my son? But I lost the picture before she could give me something concrete. I don't have a clue who the girl is, don't know how I'm supposed to track down her father. And even if I did, what would I say? *Hi, I'm Charlotte Cates. Your daughter came to me in a dream and told me she's going to die tomorrow. And do the numbers four and sixteen mean anything to you?*

One thing's for sure: I can't sleep. I flip on the lights and power up my laptop, figuring I might as well do some work. That's when I notice the clock on my bedside table: 4:17.

When she said one more day, she meant to the minute.

12.

First stop in tracking down the dying girl: Evangeline's kitchen. Chicory's not small, but Leeann strikes me as the kind who knows people. I head over before breakfast and am instantly met with the smell of brewing coffee and Leeann's megawatt smile.

"Just in time!" She looks up from watering a pot of rosemary. "I'm fixin' to fry us up some beignets this morning. You had beignets before?"

"I don't think so. Are those a Louisiana thing?"

"Mm-hmm. You fry 'em up, sprinkle powdered sugar on top." Her eyes roll up in her head. "Little piece a heaven."

"So they're basically just fried dough? Like a funnel cake?"

"Oh no. Betta. You'll see. I got some chilled dough in the fridge all ready to go." As she scurries about the kitchen gathering up her pre-made dough, powdered sugar, and cookware, I take the opportunity to pick her brain.

"Hey, so somebody told me a sad story about this sick little girl," I say. "She's local, a redhead. I think it was cancer. She lost all her hair. I was thinking I'd like to help, but I forget her name." I wander over to the herb cart and pinch off a chive to chew on as I wait for Leeann to identify my mystery child.

"Cancer, huh?" She dumps an insane amount of vegetable oil into the fryer. "Could be Lila Monroe. She died last year, left behind a whole house of chilren."

"No, this was a kid." I grope for more information, but there's not much to offer. "She's been through chemo, but it sounds like she just took a turn for the worse."

Leeann sprinkles flour on a cutting board. "Sick kids break my heart. I dunno *what* I'd do if ma baby got sick." She rolls the dough out until it's thin and begins cutting squares. "You know, Dr. Pinaro's girl got sick a few years back. There was a church benefit, I rememba. Don't recall if it was cancer. But I know they still got nurses goin' ova the house."

That would explain why the girl was in a bedroom, not a hospital. Maybe she's in some kind of hospice program.

"Does Dr. Pinaro have a practice here in town?" I ask. "Where could I find him?"

Leeann laughs and drops pieces of dough in the sizzling oil. "Not that kinda docta. An' Dr. Pinaro's a lady. The superintendent of schools."

"How old's her daughter?"

"Gosh, I dunno. Ten? Twelve?"

The age sounds about right. There's just one more thing. I'm not sure it matters, but the girl in my vision told me to speak to her dad, not her mom. "Is Dr. Pinaro married?"

"I think so," Leeann says, eyeing the beignets, "but it's kinda confusin'. She's one a dem never took her husband's name."

As another one of those who never took her husband's name, I like Dr. Pinaro already. I didn't figure you'd find any maiden-namers around Chicory, but superintendent of schools? Not too shabby. I press Leeann for more details but get nothing. She doesn't remember anything about the husband or where they live or even what Dr. Pinaro's first name is. I'm itching to go track her down, but for PR reasons I stick around long enough to eat some beignets.

As anticipated, they taste no different than fried dough, but I sing their praises for a full two minutes and Leeann nearly bursts with pride.

GIVEN DR. PINARO'S JOB in the public sector, I don't expect her to be hard to locate. Straight off, I find a photo of her on the town's web page: Dr. Justine Pinaro, a handsome woman, fiftyish, with short auburn hair. The red hair seems promising.

I call the superintendent's office, but the secretary informs me that Dr. Pinaro is on a leave of absence and they don't share employee information. No phone numbers for her online. She could have an unlisted number, or a number listed under her husband's name, or no landline at all. No e-mail addresses beyond her work e-mail, which bounces back with an automated reply. I search for her on various social networking sites, but she has no visible accounts. Archives from the local newspaper contain more than a dozen articles that include her name, but her comments on district decisions reveal nothing personal.

I need an address or phone number, or at least the name of her husband. What if Justine Pinaro isn't even the mom I'm looking for?

I try a people-finder website that searches public records. A Justine Pinaro does show up. Forty-nine years old; previous residences in Maylee, Georgia, and Eunice, Louisiana; relatives in Wyoming. To access any more information, I have to pay a fifty-dollar sign-up fee. Right as I'm breaking out my credit card, my computer freezes. When I reboot, I get an OBJECT CANNOT BE FOUND error message. Every subsequent reboot yields the same result.

"Goddamn it!" If I had a sledgehammer, my laptop would now be lying in mangled pieces.

I try to use my phone, but I'm barely getting a signal, and after fifteen minutes, the site still won't load. I head up to the house to beg Internet access off Jules.

The office door is closed. I knock lightly and press my ear to the door. He's in there, speaking in a tone that clearly indicates he's upset, but the only words I can make out are "too damn busy."

"Lookin' for Mista Sicard?"

I whirl around and see the housekeeper, Paulette, watching me intently, one hand resting on her pregnant belly.

"I just need the Internet for a few minutes. My computer's down."

Paulette's face is entirely unreadable. "Mista Sicard's takin' a personal call. Could be a bit."

He must be fighting with Andre.

"You don't have Wi-Fi in your cottage, do you, Paulette?" I ask. "I'm in a bind here."

She shakes her head, and I'm not sure that she knows what Wi-Fi is.

I start over. "Listen, I need to get in touch with the superintendent of schools."

Paulette doesn't blink an eye or question me further; working for the Deveau family has taught her that much. "Aks Deacon 'bout it," she suggests. "His daughta works ova dere."

"At the superintendent's office?"

She nods, still poker-faced, like this is not an amazing and lucky coincidence.

"Okay, so—where do I find Deacon?" I seem to recall that he is one of the older employees Leeann mentioned, but I'm not sure I've ever actually seen him.

"He's night security. Gets in at eight."

Eight is later than I'd like, but it's a lead and I have until roughly four a.m. if I'm to understand the girl in my vision and help her. I thank Paulette and hope that she doesn't spread around the fact that I listen outside doors. There's just one more thing I have to ask her while I know Jules is safely occupied.

"Is Hettie upstairs?" I'm hoping I can sneak in to talk to her, but Paulette's report is not encouraging.

"She sleepin' now. Nurse said she had a rough mornin'. Prob'ly all dem guests dis weekend. Every time she see her daughtas, I swear she take a turn for da worse." She raises her hand to her mouth, realizing that last part could be construed as a complaint about her employers.

I smile. "I hear Sydney and Brigitte have that effect on people."

Paulette drops her eyes. "I betta go pass da mop."

AFTER DEPOSITING MY COMPUTER at a repair shop, I have nothing to do with my day but work. I break out a stack of legal pads, hole up in the cottage, and write the old-fashioned way. For hours, I immerse myself in the story of the Deveau family, trying to draw a picture of their lifestyle, set the scene. Eventually it gets dark and my hand gets a cramp, but I pace the room, brainstorm, work out the book's structure.

At eight o'clock, I go searching for Deacon. I find him walking along the side of the house with a giant high-powered flashlight. He has the kind of wild white hair that tends to connote genius or lunacy, and I'm not sure anyone can successfully evoke Einstein while patrolling the grounds of a century-and-a-half-old Southern plantation at night. He casts his beam in my direction, momentarily blinding me, and looks me over. Evidently I pass inspection, because he quickly lowers his flashlight, the caution on his pink and jowly face giving way to cheer. "Evenin', ma'am! Cold nuff fo' ya?"

In my winter jacket, it's actually not bad. "Deacon, right?" I ask, and he nods. "I'm Charlotte. I heard you might be able to help me. I'm trying to track down Dr. Pinaro, the superintendent of schools. Paulette told me your daughter works at that office."

He puffs up at the mention of his daughter. "Yeah, Prissy been workin' dere, oh, ten year maybe. She smart one, dat. But she workin' for Mr. Robicheaux now." He scratches the corner of his eye with a dirty fingernail. "Dr. Pinaro had to leave on account of 'er li'l girl."

His accent is so thick I have to concentrate to keep up. "Do you happen to know where Dr. Pinaro lives? Or maybe have her phone number?"

"Ah bet Prissy do. Ah can call 'er, if ya lak." He pulls out a cell phone and punches at some glowing buttons with a knotty finger, but I'm out of luck. The line just keeps on ringing. "She prob'ly puttin' da chilren to bed," Deacon tells me. "It some kinda 'mergency?"

"It's about Dr. Pinaro's daughter."

"Ah, Didi. Dat po' li'l ting."

At the sound of the girl's name, I get goose bumps. "Yeah, Didi. Little redhead, right?"

He nods vigorously. "Dem folks been tru hell and back gettin' 'er treatment. Evertime dey tink she got a prayer, dat cancer come on back."

This has to be the right girl. I rack my brain for some other tactic. "You don't know the name of Dr. Pinaro's husband, do you? Maybe his number is listed."

"You could try 'im at work," Deacon suggests. "He wit da sheriff's department, Ah tink."

As soon as he says the word "sheriff," I understand. Why this girl came to me. Why she asked me to tell her father, not her mom. Why Detective Minot looked so thin, so haggard. *You didn't choose me at random, did you, Didi?* I remember Minot's computer, the photograph of the healthy little red-haired girl bouncing about the screen, and I realize with a pang how long ago that photo must have been taken.

"Remy Minot," I murmur, "that's Dr. Pinaro's husband?"

"Minot, dat's right." He thinks it over. "Yep, Remy."

"Then I've already got his number. Thanks, Deacon!" I sprint back to the cottage, wondering how I will tackle my next challenge: relaying Didi's message without sounding certifiable.

I SIT CROSS-LEGGED on the bed, Detective Minot's business card in front of me. I'm not afraid of being wrong. I'm afraid of being right. Afraid of knowing this is real, that I can never be normal again.

When he answers, I say it like I've rehearsed it in my head. "This is Charlotte Cates. We met yesterday morning."

He takes a second to place me. "Oh, Miss Cates. Everything okay?" I can't tell if he's at work or at home.

"I have something I need to tell you. Not about the Deveau case. Something personal."

"Personal?" He sounds guarded, like I'm about to ask him on a date.

I spit it out as fast as I can. "I know this sounds crazy, but I think I have a message for you. From your daughter." I grab a fistful of blanket and hold my breath.

There's a silence and then he says flatly, "My daughter's been unconscious for two days. She's not giving anyone any messages."

I can sense he's about to hang up. "Wait." I hold the image of Didi in my mind, her bald head and bony shoulder. "Detective Minot, I need to tell you this. If not for you, then for me. Because I know what it's like to lose a child."

"If this is some speech about accepting Christ as my savior, you can save it. I don't care if Justine put you up to it. The whole bunch of you can take your—"

"No, no," I interrupt, "it's not a God thing. I'm the last person who'd preach at you."

"Then what do you want?"

"I know it's nuts, but I had a dream. About Didi." I rush to get it out before he can end the call. "She told me a time, four sixteen a.m. Tomorrow. She thought—well, that you and your wife would want to be there." I can't bring myself to say *when she dies*. "Look, I know it's just a dream, maybe it means nothing. But my son died. And I wasn't there for him when it happened." I can barely hold it together after that. "He died in a hospital, in a room full of strangers, without his mom. I would give anything to have been there. So even if it's a long shot . . ."

"I don't know how you heard about my daughter, but I'll tell you right now I've got no interest in 'heavenly visions.' Not yours or anyone else's."

"I understand." I try to swallow my disappointment, but really, what's the point of seeing things if I can't change them? "I apologize for bothering you. Sometimes my dreams are . . . pretty accurate. I just wouldn't have felt right, not saying anything."

"Well, you said it." He sounds more tired than mad now. "And, Miss Cates?" His tone softens somewhat. "I'm sorry about your son."

Too choked up to manage a simple thank-you, I hang up. Wrap my arms around a pillow. Bury my face in it.

13.

One advantage of insomnia is that you get to see a lot of sunrises. Standing on the banks of the bayou the next morning, I try to focus on the spectacular scenery instead of dwelling on my failures. A thin layer of mist hovers above the water like breath. For these few minutes, I let myself enjoy the retreating shadows, the golden light. Day is unyielding. It always comes. A comforting or an exhausting thought, depending on my mood, which is currently trending toward melancholy.

When a call comes from an unknown number, my first panicked thought is of Grandma's assisted-living facility. *Something's happened. I never should've come here, it's too far, she's too old, how will I—*

But it's Detective Minot, and his news isn't really news at all. "Didi's gone," he says. "I don't know how you knew, but it was this morning. Four sixteen."

"I'm sorry." I lean back against a tree, feeling guilty at the brief surge of relief his words bring me. "Were you with her?"

"Yeah. After we hung up last night, I told my wife about your call. She insisted we stay up. Just in case." His voice is surprisingly steady for someone whose daughter just died, but then he's probably been bracing himself for months, dreading and preparing for this day. "We knew she didn't have a lot of time left," he says. "The nurses told us she'd probably never regain consciousness. But . . . four sixteen. She stopped breathing that exact minute."

The bayou and sky seem to glow, both suffused with the same dusty orange. Behind me, Evangeline is quiet. Except for Detective Minot's voice in my ear, I feel like the only person left living. "I hope being with Didi at the end brought you and your wife . . . I don't know. Some peace."

"We were holding her hands," he says. "We were all three there when she came into this world, and all three together when she left it." His voice cracks, and I think how peculiar it is that I should be privy to this man's grief.

"You should go," I say gently. "Go be with your wife."

"I will. But I had to ask you." He takes a second to formulate the thought. "See, I haven't believed in God in a long time, Miss Cates. Maybe it's my job, seeing what people do to other people. To kids, even. And some of it's Didi, of course, watching her sick for three years. But from what I've seen, there's no one out there manning the store."

I wait for the question. Across the bayou, I see a flash of white. A bird. A big one, wading at the edge of the water.

"You said you had a dream about Didi. Well, Justine thinks it was God's message to me. To renew my faith. Yesterday I would've told you that was horseshit, but . . . I've got no other explanation. So I want to know what you think."

I never expected to land in the middle of a bereaved couple's religious debate. I've never attributed my dreams to God, but I don't have any better answers for Detective Minot. And maybe it doesn't matter. This man has watched his daughter fight a losing battle for three years, and now she's dead. Won't faith feel better than skepticism?

"I don't know where my dreams come from," I tell him. "But maybe your wife is right."

"You've had others?"

"Just a few. They started after my son died."

"But you see things? In the future?" He seems somewhere between intrigued and freaked out.

"Not always the future. Sometimes it's already happened." The white bird dips its head in the water.

"Like what kinds of things?" Detective Minot wants to know.

"They're always bad and they're always kids." So far he sounds like he believes me, so I plunge ahead and hope for the best. "I wasn't being totally straight with you the other day when I told you why I came to Chicory. It wasn't the book that brought me here. It was Gabriel."

The bird lifts its head suddenly and gazes at me across the water. I swear it's listening as I lay bare my secret.

"I saw him," I say. "I saw Gabriel Deveau."

I DON'T KNOW EXACTLY what kind of response I was expecting, but Detective Minot's long, noisy exhale is not it. I wait.

"I don't believe it," he mutters.

"I'm not lying, I really—"

"No. I mean, I don't believe that after all this time, we could finally solve this case."

"He didn't give me any names," I say, not wanting to get the detective's hopes up. "Just a few details."

I hear a woman's voice in the background, presumably Dr. Pinaro. "Listen, I better go," Detective Minot says reluctantly. "We have preparations to make for the funeral. Don't tell anyone what you've just told me, okay? I'll be in touch with you in a few days."

There's a lightness, an almost soaring feeling in my chest when I hang up. I tilt my face toward the newly risen sun. I don't know what feels better: the fact that I helped Didi's parents, or the fact that Detective Minot believes in me.

Leeann is pulling a pan of banana bread from the oven when I show up for breakfast. "Mornin', Charlie," she calls cheerily.

"Morning," I reply. "How's it going, Leeann?"

There's no one else eating yet, just the old red dog splayed by the French doors. Leeann sets down her pan, eager to talk. "You won't believe what ma *boug* is doin'." From the pocket of her apron, she produces a napkin with letters on it. "Right here. He wrote 'MOM,' see that?"

I remember that sweet mama high, remember it well. I want to tell her about Keegan, how he loved writing with "grown-up pens" and once put Sharpie on the wall, but that would change everything. Leeann has assumed that I am childless, and if I mentioned him, I'd have to tell the ending. And then she'd apologize too many times and feel guilty, like she couldn't mention her own son or coo over Paulette's big belly in front of me. So I smile at Leeann's napkin, its squiggly letters, and say, "He's a smarty."

I'm on the verge of getting sentimental and weepy when I spot Noah coming up the path outside. I didn't run into him yesterday. Was he avoiding me or just busy? Part of me wants to apologize for not being more up front about the book, but who am I kidding? I can't tell him about the dreams, the things I've been seeing. I can't tell him that I have my suspicions about Hettie, maybe even about his father. Our relationship will always involve my holding something back. So what's the point in pursuing it?

Still, I can't resist greeting him as he enters the kitchen. "Hi." I lift my fingers in a tentative wave.

He looks over in my direction. He's wearing jeans, a close-fitting thermal, and a windbreaker. Mr. Casual. I can't read his expression when he sees me, but I think it's a smile. A cautious smile. "I thought I saw you over by the water earlier," he says. "Great sunrise." He leans down to pet the dog.

"Noah, have you met Leeann?"

Leeann seems delighted to have someone new to chat with and cuts us both slices of warm banana bread. She then proceeds to interview Noah about his life in Texas while frying up eggs and sausage. From her questions, I learn that Noah's ex-wife is Mexican-American, that he speaks Spanish fairly fluently, and that the hardest part of their splitting up was losing the dog.

"Don't you fret," Leeann says sympathetically. "Life can get betta in a hurry." She slaps down sausages one by one on a plate. "Four years ago, I was nineteen and pregnant by a lyin', no-good boy who I come to find was engaged to somebody else. I was livin' with ma folks, workin' at ma daddy's diner, not a hope in the world."

Getting pep talks from a twenty-three-year-old doesn't seem to annoy Noah the way it would me. He watches her, chin in hand, waiting for the happy ending.

"Now I got ma own place with the most carin' man alive who loves ma son like his own," she concludes. "Still haven't got ma ring yet, but we'll get there! Ma mama always says trust in God, and I do. Life'll turn sweet."

Noah smiles at her. "Well, your bread just made mine sweeter." He turns to me, probably to avoid further talk of personal hardship. "You been workin' on your book, Charlie?"

A sore subject, although he doesn't *sound* hostile. His dark eyes hold mine for a second. Accusing? Apologetic? Probing? I can't read them, but all that eye contact makes me blush.

"Yeah, I've been working," I say. "I'm going to hit up the library today, do some research."

He deposits his plate over by the sink. "If you see any old pictures a the garden, let me know."

"They open at nine," I tell him, surprising myself. "Come along."

THE GRAY-HAIRED WOMAN at the reference desk sits cataloging film reels when we arrive. She wears a purple turtleneck with a garish studded snowflake pin that only a teacher, librarian, or grandmother would find attractive. On the ceiling above her, an amorphous brown spot hovers, presumably some type of water damage. I remember the maintenance man trying to patch it up the last time I was here; his efforts have obviously failed.

The woman recognizes me immediately. "You're back! Still looking for materials on the Deveau family?"

"Good memory. And today I've brought a friend." I gesture to Noah.

"The more the merrier," she beams. "You know, I never did ask where you're from."

"Connecticut."

"That's quite a distance. Welcome!" She looks over at Noah. "Are you from Connecticut as well?"

"Nah, my family's from Chicory. Just—visiting for a while."

Her face lights up. "You doin' genealogical research? That's my specialty. What's your family name?"

He glances at me, hesitating. I shrug. "My grandfather was Jack Lauchlin," he says. "L-A-U-C—"

"Lauchlin? Don't tell me you're related to Sean."

"My father." Noah looks uncomfortable.

Given what he told me about his dad taking off on him, I can understand that. My mother has never been my favorite topic of discussion either.

Oblivious, the librarian jumps all over the family connection. "You kiddin' me? I went to high school with Sean Lauchlin way back when. I had no idea he had children. He never seemed interested in the girls around here. What happened to him, anyway? Left town ages ago, right?"

"Yeah," says Noah, "he didn't stick around."

"Nice-looking boy, your daddy. I had English with him, you know. I bet he never told you this, but when we did poetry, Mr. LaValle always asked him to read. Your father had such a lovely speaking voice." She smiles at the memory. "What can I do for you today?"

Noah explains his quest to restore the gardens of Evangeline and his search for historic photos, which leaves the woman nearly breathless with delight. "Oh, you've got to see the Abe and Thomas Brennan Photo Collection. Abe Brennan just *loved* to photograph gardens."

She hustles him down a lonely little hallway to the viewing room. I browse periodicals and leaf through a book called *Dynasty: The Louisiana Deveaus* and learn that Maurice Deveau once shot himself in the foot while drunk; that Dulcie Deveau became a suffragette, much to the horror of her family; and that Neville's grandfather developed polio and required an iron lung. Maybe the twins are right. A little family history could jazz up my book.

I pace the stacks for a while, dip into various volumes and inhale that nice, fusty old-book smell before joining Noah in the viewing room. Inside, he pages through an album of black-and-white photos. Etched on the spine are the words *Abe and Thomas Brennan Photo Collection, 1924*. Beside him, I see two large carts of similar albums, each labeled with a different year. The reference librarian returns shortly, dragging a third.

"I'll be back at my desk if you need anything," she tells Noah. "Remember, don't touch the photos. If you'd like to reproduce any images, we've got to submit a request to the Brennan family."

She closes the door behind her and waves good-bye to us through the little glass window. I take an album from 1963, the year Neville and Hettie married. Maybe I can find wedding photos. Noah and I sit quietly together for about half an hour, absorbed in these glimpses of the town and its inhabitants. I don't find the Deveau wedding, but I'm drawn in by other stories on display: a first communion, a town fair, a family portrait with four generations of black folks smiling proudly.

Noah's the one to eventually break the silence. "Hey, Charlie?"

I look up. "Hmm?"

"I didn't mean to go off on you the other day about your book. I know you gotta work, like everyone else."

"I understand why you were upset," I say. "I wasn't thrilled with the whole arrangement myself."

He nods, and we leave it there. I'm pretty sure we're okay again. I forget about him and continue looking through the photo albums, eventually locating a 1965 picture of Hettie on a parade float, baby Andre on her lap. She's so young, about Leeann's age. Fresh-faced and eager as she faces the crowd. Neville, sitting beside her, already looks like a bloated stick-in-the-mud.

I take a quick bathroom break, Deveau family dynamics dancing through my head. Hettie was twenty, maybe twenty-one when she got married. She and Neville had met less than two years earlier at a polo game, according to books. He was six years her senior, wealthy, from one of *the* eminent Southern families. She was pretty, well mannered, from a solidly upper-class family. Neville must have looked at her and seen a blank slate. Was their marriage about love or a mutually advantageous social contract?

I'm about to head back into the viewing room when something gives me pause. Through the door's small glass window, I see Noah sliding one of the pictures out of its protective case. I can't make out the image, but I can definitely see some people. He rolls up the photo and stuffs it into the zippered pocket of his windbreaker.

I play dumb when I enter, wondering if he'll tell me about the photo, but he's closed the album. Without a word, he replaces it on the cart, spine pointed outward: *1982.*

Adrenaline surges through me. The year Gabriel vanished.

This is definitely not part of your garden renovation project, Noah.

I say nothing, although the curiosity is killing me. What exactly is he after? I need to see the picture he stole. Sooner or later he'll leave his jacket unguarded, and when he does, I expect to learn something very interesting about Noah Lauchlin.

I GET MY CHANCE when we stop for gas on the ride home. Noah goes inside to buy a pack of cigarettes, leaving his windbreaker behind. The moment he's safely inside, I reach into his pocket and remove the rolled-up photograph.

Two figures stand in front of a massive tree trunk, their smiles circumspect. The husky, middle-aged woman has her arm around a tall young man in military fatigues. He's handsome in a sort of piercing and intense way. It takes me a second to notice the tiny boy near the bottom of the frame, his head buried in the woman's legs. I read the label: *Homecoming. Maddie and Sean Lauchlin, June 1982.* I remember what Brigitte said about last seeing Sean in June.

Something moves above me, and I jump.

Noah's watching me through the passenger window.

"My God, don't creep up on me like that." I drop the picture back onto the seat as he ducks back into the car.

"Sorry." His hand closes around the photograph.

We face each other, embarrassed.

"I guess you're wonderin' why I took that."

Actually, I'm feeling ridiculous for thinking he was wrapped up in the Gabriel mystery. Noah was only three back then, barely out of diapers. I point to the young man in the photo. "Is that your father?" I can see similarities in their nose, broad shoulders, and buzz cuts if I use my imagination a bit, but Sean is, objectively, far better-looking. Now I understand why Brigitte used to crush over him, why the librarian gushed at his name.

"That's him," Noah confirms. "I know I shouldn'a run off with it, but . . . well, I don't have any pictures of him."

"None?"

He shakes his head. "Nanny always said what's past is past. We never had pictures of anything." He reaches for his seat belt but never actually fastens it, just plays with the buckle absently. "She didn't like to talk about sad stuff, so I never heard much about my dad. And even less about my mother."

"What was your mother's name?"

"Violet," he says. "Violet Johnson. I only know from my birth certificate. She died in a car accident when I was a year old, and that's pretty much all I know." He shakes his head again. "I don't think my Nanny liked her."

I remember all the years I spent poring over albums at my aunt Suzie's, learning who my mother was through pictures. I watched her evolve from a gawky grade-schooler to a too-cool, frizzy-haired adolescent to a sullen, pregnant teen, to a washed-out girl with a baby. I could see, in photos, her transformation while Aunt Suzie narrated it for me. *That was right after she met your dad* or *That was a few weeks before she left. Look at her, I bet she was high.* I haven't forgiven my mother for who she is—I only assume she's alive because no one's ever told me otherwise—but at least I have some idea where I came from. If I didn't know about her, how could I ever really feel sure of who *I* am?

"I don't know why I took this thing." Noah leans back in his seat and stares at the picture of his dad. "Stupid."

"No, that's your past," I tell him. "It means more to you than anyone else who will ever look through that collection."

He doesn't reply.

"Is that you, hiding behind your nanny's legs right there?"

"Nah, look at that outfit." He gestures to the little boy, who seems to be wearing a polo shirt with the collar turned up. I squint at the kid's footwear. Are those boat shoes? On a toddler? Ultra preppy. "They wouldn'a dressed me like that," Noah says. "It's probably Gabriel." He tucks the picture back in his pocket.

Are we getting too emotionally charged for him?

June 1982, the photo read. The last time Sean Lauchlin would ever visit Evangeline. Two months later, the little boy hugging Maddie's legs would also be gone. I don't place too much stock in Brigitte's opinions, but I can't help but wonder if she was onto something when she brought up Sean. He knew Gabriel. As Maddie's son, he would've had plenty of access to him, and to the house. I think of Maddie going to Gabriel's room on the morning of August 15, how she couldn't find her key and had to use the cook's. Was the key missing because her son took it?

And if Sean hurt little kids, sexually or physically or otherwise—did that mean he hurt Noah? It occurs to me that maybe Sean didn't actually skip out on his child. Maybe Maddie and Jack took their grandson from him. Maybe Sean ended up in prison. Could I blame Noah's grandparents if they'd tried to spare him the knowledge that his father was a criminal and a pervert?

I look over at the man in the seat beside me. He's gazing out the window, tapping his just-purchased pack of cigarettes against his thigh. He must have wondered about his father, Sean Lauchlin, so many times. What the man looked like, what they had in common. What

Sean would think of him. I know how it feels to have a parent leave. I understand that beneath all the self-sufficiency and drive is a layer of *Who could really want me?* It's a weird experience, seeing myself in someone else, and suddenly I want to hold Noah.

I reach across the seat and take his hand. There's something in my chest, a feeling absent that whole night we spent together, that rises up now. He doesn't speak, but I feel his fingers tighten around mine, warm and rough.

He doesn't let go. I don't want him to.

14.

For the next few nights, Noah sleeps in my bed. We talk when we feel like it, and we're quiet when we don't. He rubs my feet and sings half-remembered country tunes in a voice that's intentionally off-key until I hit him with a pillow. I surrender my long-held position at the center of the bed and grant him the left half. We sleep back-to-back, joined at the spine. At some point during the night he flips over on his stomach into a bizarre face-smothering posture. No, his light snores aren't romantic or sexy, but they relax me. He's like a magic talisman, there to guard me from the darkness.

The first couple of nights, we don't have sex. I get used to his shape beside me, his breathing sounds, his faintly smoky scent. I watch him wake in the morning, watch his smile fade in and out as he sees me and then drifts back to sleep. Later, I watch him brush his teeth and shave, not sure why I find these simple domestic acts so titillating. One morning, as he stands around drinking coffee in his briefs, I can't help myself.

"God, you have a nice butt."

He grins. Strikes a *GQ* pose, coffee in hand. "For your viewin' pleasure."

"Oh no. Don't tell me this is an eyes-only establishment."

Noah raises an eyebrow. "Whoa. That an invitation?"

"Yeah," I tell him. "I think it is."

He sets down his coffee so fast that some spills.

I'm nervous, but not *too* nervous this time. We smile as we kiss. Fall into bed laughing. We're still clumsy and fumbling and figuring it all out, but it's okay. Because I *like* him.

I stop trying to understand why. I can't explain how someone who fails to meet even the most basic requirements on my usual relationship checklist is, right now, the one I need. But he is. I can't explain how a man who I've known only days can calm me, shut down my mind, and let me rest. But he can. I certainly can't explain how my body, dead for months to even the most basic needs—hunger, thirst—can feel again, can want. But it does.

Am I happy? I don't know. My concept of happiness has changed without Keegan, but I think I'm happy now. I'm not consumed by a delirious teenage-style lust. And I'm not filled with the hopeful, heart-singing love that makes you call everyone you know to spew bliss—not that I've ever really been that type. Instead, I feel content, my days spent on the book, my nights spent with this man.

On Saturday evening, he tells me he's going to drop by to see Hettie. It's raining, a chilly January rain. He stands outside my cottage in his windbreaker, a bowl of flower bulbs in one hand.

"I'll be by a bit later tonight," he tells me. "Just didn't want to leave you wonderin'."

"Are those for Hettie?" I point to the bulbs.

"Yeah. Thought some paperwhites might cheer her up. Nice to have growin' things around." He doesn't mention she might not live to see them bloom.

"Can I come with you?" I brace myself for a comment about vulture journalists, but he runs a hand across his damp head, considering it.

"You can't interview her, if that's what you're after," he says.

"I know." It's not the book I'm thinking of now. "I've just read so much about Hettie, it would be nice to spend some genuine time with her. To get a sense of her, you know?"

Noah touches the green shoots of the flower bulbs and shrugs. "Fine. Just behave yourself."

I toss on a raincoat and we trudge up to Evangeline through the dark and drizzle. On the way over we pass Zeke, the security patrolman, who's outfitted in some heavy-duty rain gear. Inside, the house is still. Most of the help have gone for the weekend.

I'm sort of amazed that no one stops us when Noah and I start up the large staircase. Somehow I always had a feeling that sirens would go off and guards would come running if I went upstairs uninvited. The reality is an eerie quiet. A series of gold sconces bathe the hallway in their drowsy light. Every door is closed.

Noah stops at the end of the hallway, raps on the door. Waits. Knocks again, a bit louder.

"Must be the guy with the iPod," he mutters. He opens the door a little and gives an exaggerated wave, trying to get the nurse's attention. Sure enough, a guilty redhead in scrubs peeks out a minute later, earbuds dangling around his neck. He seems to recognize Noah and ushers us in.

Hettie's in a standard hospital bed, sterile white sheets and all. Something about that awful bed in the middle of this beautifully decorated room hits me. I've been picturing her wasting tragically away, and the looming pieces of mahogany furniture and mauve drapes are about right. But I forgot the *ugliness* of dying. How slow it can be. How degrading. Whether you're Didi Minot or Hettie Deveau, cancer is cancer. Hettie's a sad sight: three children living, yet no one but hired help here to care for her.

"Hettie," the nurse murmurs, "you have visitors."

She's propped up in bed, eyes closed though she's awake, wincing.

She looks even thinner than she was at last weekend's dinner. Has she stopped eating these past few days?

At the sound of the nurse's voice, Hettie's eyes flicker open, and the naked, undisguised pain on her face is quickly replaced with a strained smile. "Well, hello," she says to Noah in a hoarse voice. "I was hoping you'd stop in, honey."

"Promised you, didn't I?" He sets down the bowl of bulbs on a table by her bed. "Have your nurses take good care a these, okay? They're paperwhite narcissus. Should be out by Valentine's Day."

"A Valentine gift?" Her blue eyes bulge from her gaunt face, but she's still smiling. "I'm not sure I care to make it that long."

Noah nods, not shocked. "Nobody would fault you any for lettin' go."

Her hand is milky white and veiny when she points a shaky index finger at him. "You're a good boy. Always were." With some effort, she turns her head in my direction. "That your girlfriend?"

I've met her twice now, and she still doesn't remember me. Given my embarrassing performance at dinner the other night, I'm relieved.

"Yeah, that's my girl," Noah says with a smile.

I don't read too much into that one. It's a more polite introduction than I probably merit, but simpler, too. "Good to meet you," I tell Hettie.

"You two better start having babies soon," she says, and I marvel at that total disregard for manners that only young children and the elderly can get away with. "You're not getting any younger."

Noah holds up a hand. "Let's not go there." He doesn't mention his divorce or his burning desire to avoid kids. And he doesn't even know about the baggage I'm carrying. "So how you feelin', Hettie? Heard you hit a rough patch this last week. I stopped by, but they told me you were restin'."

"I wish you wouldn't call me Hettie," she complains.

"What should I call you?"

"You used to call me Mama."

My heart squeezes up when I see her mistake. Noah appears less disturbed.

"Hettie," he says, taking both her hands and looking directly into her eyes. "Do you know who I am?"

The nurse, who has been sitting quietly in the corner with a *Men's Health* magazine, is now following their conversation carefully. *Put your iPod back in, dude,* I want to tell him.

Hettie meets Noah's gaze and her eyes fill with tears. "You're my boy."

"No, I'm Noah," he says firmly. "Do you remember me? Noah."

She stares at him, wide-eyed, and a tear spills onto her cheek. I wish he wouldn't argue with her, wish he'd just let Hettie believe what she needs to believe, but Noah persists.

"I'm Sean Lauchlin's boy, do you remember him? My mother's name was Violet, but she died. Remember Maddie and Jack? Those were my grandparents."

Now she's weeping openly. "I want my baby back." Her voice is so small and pitiful that I wish I could cradle her in my arms, tell her *shhhh,* offer Noah up as the substitute Gabriel. But she scares me, too. Will I be calling for Keegan on my deathbed, ready to turn any man who fits the part into my lost son?

Noah can't watch her anymore. He turns to the nurse, shaken. "How long has she been like this?"

The guy puts down his magazine. "I dunno. I haven't seen her get confused like that before, but it's been a hard few days. She hasn't been talkin' much."

"Is it permanent?"

"Gotta wait and see." There's sympathy in his voice. "She's been declinin', then fightin' back."

They both stare at Hettie, who clutches her sheet, still crying for her son. Noah takes a deep breath and kneels beside her. Very, very quietly, he says something in her ear. I can't make out the words, but she stops her weeping and regards him with big eyes. He touches her cheek.

"I gotta go now," he says. "I'll check on you soon." He points at the nurse. "Give her somethin' to help her sleep. She's hurtin'."

I hurry after him into the hallway, trying to get a sense of whether or not he wants to talk. Above us, rain falls loudly against the roof. In the distance, thunder rumbles. Noah stops walking.

"We're gonna get soaked," he says.

"Probably. You okay?"

"I'm tired a watchin' people get old and sick." He leans against the wall for a moment, hooking his thumbs into the pockets of his jeans. "My granddaddy was sick a long while, too."

I think of my grandmother and pray that she'll die peacefully in her sleep, or else suddenly, with minimal pain. Mostly I just hope she'll be there when I get back to Stamford.

"What did you tell Hettie?" I ask. "At the end, before we left?"

He sighs. "Told her Gabriel was comin' for her. That he'd be there when she passed."

"You believe that?" It's not just his religious views I'm feeling out with this question. I want to know if he believes in spirits. If my visions might make sense to him.

"I just wanted her to feel better," he says wearily. "I mean, I believe in God, but I don't claim to know how He works. Although . . ." He cocks his head to the side. "Every now and then I'd swear my Daddy Jack's still keepin' an eye on things. When I'm alone sometimes, you know? I just feel him." He gives a self-conscious laugh. "Sorry, that's weird."

"No. It isn't." I slide my arm around his. "Come on. Let's go get wet."

We do. We get very, very wet. We arrive at my cottage drenched and shivering. Kick off our shoes, throw our jackets in a heap by the door. Peel articles of soaking clothing from each other, one by one. Our skin is cold and damp, but our mouths are warm. Outside, lightning flashes. Thunder rolls through. I wrap my arms around Noah's neck and enjoy the storm.

ON SUNDAY MORNING it all begins to unravel. We stop by Noah's cottage to get him fresh clothes, and as I'm rummaging through his sock drawer, my hand hits metal. I brush aside a pair of socks and find a handgun. Heart pounding, I turn to face him.

"What the hell is that?"

He doesn't even have the grace to be apologetic. "I told you I had a nine-millimeter. Quit worryin', it's not loaded unless I'm wearin' it."

That hardly eases my mind. "Jesus, Noah! Why do you have a gun with you at *all*? Is that even legal?"

He rolls his eyes. "Sure it's legal. I carry it with me when I go to town. Had it at the diner with us the other mornin'."

His loose-fitting shirts become suddenly sinister.

"They let you carry a concealed weapon?"

"I got a permit in Texas," he says. "They got reciprocity in Louisiana. We don't have all your East Coast rules out here, baby."

Of course I've known, intellectually, about these laws. To have been out with a man I didn't even realize was armed, though—that's something else. I thought killing animals was bad, but he could kill people. Himself, if he's not careful. I try not to think of all the other widely divergent views we probably hold. *This relationship does not have a long shelf life,* I remind myself. *You've always known that.*

I take a few steps back from the drawer. "Put it away. I don't want to see it."

Noah makes a big production out of closing his sock drawer. "I'm not the only person who carries a gun in these parts," he says. "You might as well get used to it."

Okay, I think, gritting my teeth. *Things are different here. I'm not on my home turf, so I'll just bite the bullet. Hopefully not literally.* In a matter of minutes, though, the morning gets much, much worse. As we're walking through the fog to my car, Noah gets a phone call. He glances at the caller ID and quickly carries his phone out of earshot. I watch him pace across the grass, patches of fog wrapping around his ankles like some detestable white cat. I can already sense that our plans to grab breakfast won't survive this conversation.

When he returns minutes later, Noah's all business. "That was my landscape designer," he says, rubbing his neck. "She's outside Houston, on her way over. Should be here this afternoon." He hasn't mentioned this woman much, but I don't think it's a big deal until he tells me, "I'll be really busy while she's here. I won't be able to hang out."

"Okay," I say, although it strikes me as a bit odd. "How long's she in town?"

"A week, maybe." He scratches his head, clearly uncomfortable. "Don't take this the wrong way, but . . . it's probably better if you two don't meet. I don't wanna mix my personal life with work, ya know?"

What does he think I'm going to do? Try to make out with him in front of his coworker?

He takes a few steps back toward the cottages. "I better skip breakfast. I got some stuff to get ready." He sees the skeptical look on my face and tries to smile. "Soon's I got time, I'll come see you."

And then he's gone, leaving me with growing misgivings.

I can't focus. My mind spins in anxious circles. *Who is this woman coming? Why is Noah acting so sketchy? What's he hiding?* I drive into town, hoping a change of scene will help. The temperature is in the high forties, unusually chilly, I'm told, and not the best weather for a jaunt, but I walk up and down the historic district of Main Street, hands in my pockets.

I should've just asked Noah straight up what was going on. Now it's too late.

I stop and read a couple plaques about historic homes, admire the wraparound porches. The houses on this side of the street open up to the bayou in the back. I see a few boats in driveways and imagine the days when people hopped into their vessels and sailed all the way to the Mississippi.

On the opposite side of the road, nicely dressed families start to trickle out of a local church. I continue walking, still ruminating about Noah's weird behavior, and then pause. Did someone just say my name?

"Charlotte!"

Detective Minot is waving at me from across the street. I raise a hand to greet him just as his wife, Dr. Pinaro, reaches me. I recognize her from all my Internet stalking. She's a short but sturdy woman who could probably rock a pantsuit, though at present her cheeks are flushed with cold and her short auburn hair windswept.

"Sorry to chase you down like this," she pants. "I'm Justine Pinaro. I just really wanted to meet you." Despite all her degrees, she has a sweet, down-home voice that has probably served her well career-wise. I try to shake her hand, but she engulfs me in a quick, clumsy hug. "No, no. You aren't a stranger to us. Not after everything."

"I'm so sorry about Didi," I tell her, and she shakes her head.

"She's in God's hands now. And I had my good-bye with her. I couldn't have asked for more." She manages a weak smile. "To be honest, it's still hard to believe it's over." She motions for her husband to join us. "I don't know if Remy told you, but the funeral was yesterday."

"No, he didn't. I wish I'd known, I would've—"

"It's fine. There were too many people anyway."

Detective Minot joins us on our patch of sidewalk. Unlike the first time I saw him, he's dressed up, slacks and a tie, a classy-looking trench coat. But still haggard. He lays a hand on his wife's shoulder. "You all right?"

She nods. "I just wanted to thank Charlotte here. And I was going to—" A plump woman walking by us pauses to offer her condolences. Dr. Pinaro's face immediately slips into public-figure mode, sad but gracious. "We appreciate your prayers, Maggie, we really do. And the lasagna you left the other night was wonderful. Thank you."

Detective Minot shifts his weight from one side to the other. He doesn't like people talking about his personal business in the middle of a busy sidewalk; go figure.

"Listen," Dr. Pinaro says as soon as her well-wisher has gone, "I don't want to waste your time, Charlotte—may I call you Charlotte? I bet you have things to do. I just wanted to tell you, I think you have a very special gift. And I feel fortunate you and God brought that gift to my family."

I glance at her husband to see how he's taking the God talk, but he's staring at the pavement. "I'm . . . just glad if I helped."

"Remy said you might be able to help him with a case. I hope you will."

"I'll try."

She moves closer to me. Her mouth, coated in a plum shade of lipstick, is just inches from my ear. "Before today, my husband hadn't been to Sunday service in ten years. There are no accidents, I know this." Her voice is low and assured. "You," she whispers, squeezing my hand, "are an instrument of God."

It's not the unblinking intensity of her eyes that terrifies me, or even the gross violation of my personal space. It's the fact that, with all my years of spiritual ambivalence, I can't be sure she's wrong.

Detective Minot swoops in and expertly steers his wife away from me. "You better get going, Justine. The Pellerins invited us for lunch today, remember?" He looks back at me. "You got some time now, we could talk. I'm not a big fan of the Pellerins."

I check to make sure Dr. Pinaro won't be upset, but she's nodding enthusiastically like, *Oh yes, God would approve of his ditching this lunch date.*

"All right," I say slowly, because an idea is just occurring to me. "Why don't you come with me? I'll take you to Evangeline."

15.

On the drive back, I tell Detective Minot about my Gabriel dream. Having told only my grandmother up to this point, I'm hesitant, but Detective Minot makes it easy. He doesn't seem surprised or incredulous, just repeats back the salient details like he's planning on filing a report.

"Okay, so chipped tooth. He lived at the big white house and had a dog. And he said that a man had been hurting him."

"Right," I confirm. "He said the man threatened to kill him and his mom if he told her. I'm thinking sexual abuse." We come to a yellow traffic light. With a cop in the car, I actually stop instead of breezing through.

"Threats to Mom does sound like sexual abuse," Detective Minot agrees. "Anything else?"

I rack my brain for details. "Gabriel had a white shirt on. Dark eyes, dark hair. Oh, and we were in a swamp. A rowboat in the swamp."

"You think that's where he ended up? The swamp?"

"Yeah. But I don't know how you'd ever prove it." We're not far from the fork in the road where I took a wrong turn my first day in Chicory. On impulse, I make a decision. "There's a place I need to show you," I tell him. "Before we go to the house." Maybe he knows something about that boat launch.

With the recent rainfall, the gravel path is partially flooded. My Prius creeps through puddle after cloudy brown puddle, and I can hear the tires spin out a few times, floundering for solid ground. Ignoring Detective Minot's dubious looks, I successfully coax my little car down to the circular parking lot. The minute we step outside, I regret coming. The feeling is so strong it's almost physical, like hands pulling me somewhere I don't want to go. Sweaty, dirty hands.

Detective Minot heads over to the wooden dock, squinting, trying to determine exactly where we are. "Is this part of the Deveau property?"

"I don't know." I trail behind him, the sensation of grimy fingers becoming unbearable. I push up my sleeve, half convinced I'll find something unpleasant coating my skin. Nothing. Just the hairs of my arm standing on end.

"Is this the place you dreamed about?"

"Not exactly. But Gabriel's been here."

Detective Minot studies me with cool blue eyes. "How do you know?"

"I just . . . feel it . . ." I want to leave. Right now. I want this disgusting place to stop touching me. "Actually, this was a mistake. Can we go?"

As I turn back toward the car, I swear I feel someone grab at my hip.

Detective Minot watches me from the dock, much too far to have touched me. "You okay?"

The short answer is no. "Something bad happened here." My voice is shaky.

Detective Minot glances at the boat launch and then out at the murky water. I don't wait around for him. I hurry back to the car and shut myself inside. Wrap my arms around my chest. Fight back a wave of nausea.

He gives me a couple minutes to compose myself, getting the lay of the land before he joins me. "Want me to drive?"

I shake my head. "I'm all right." But I don't start the car. I want to make sure all the Gabriel feelings are gone, that it's just me now.

"Did you . . . see something?"

If only it were that simple, Gabriel speaking to me in pictures. But it's not. "He's making me feel it like he did." I'm almost whispering. "It happened the last time I came to this place, too." I close my eyes, remembering the headache I got, that seasick feeling, my inability to breathe. "I think the guy brought him here. He hit Gabriel on the head, then took him out on a boat. The guy threw him in the water, but Gabriel wasn't dead, not then. I think he drowned."

Detective Minot's eyes widen. "Jesus." It's more of a prayer than a curse. He holds his head and massages his temples. "Okay. And you're sure they left from this boat launch?"

"Yeah. They left from here. And one other thing." There's only one explanation for the way I felt here, the sense of violation, the unseen hands. "We're definitely dealing with sexual abuse. This guy was a frigging pervert." I brush away a few tears, hoping Detective Minot doesn't notice.

A blood vessel bursting in the brain of a four-year-old should be the worst thing that could happen, the absolute worst. But it's not.

AFTER THE EXPERIENCE at the boat launch, I'm no longer eager to explore the upstairs of Evangeline. Who knows what I'll feel when I step inside that child's bedroom? Detective Minot sees the shift in my mood and gives me a chance to bow out, but I refuse. Gabriel has waited long enough.

The time is right. I wouldn't go roaming through the house on my own, but with a cop at my side, I feel bold. And Detective Minot would never barge into the Deveau home without an invite, but I've provided him with one, sort of. It's Sunday. No pesky twins, Jules is gone, and Hettie hasn't exactly been up and at 'em lately. There's no one to get in our way.

"So . . . have you seen his room before?" I ask as we catch our first glimpse of Evangeline through the trees. "I haven't been in yet."

"Me neither," he replies, "just seen photographs and diagrams in the case files. Hettie wasn't exactly cooperative when I approached her."

I stop at the gate to let the guard get a look at Detective Minot. "This is Remy Minot," I say. "He's visiting me today."

It's one of the young guards. "I'll have to log it. You got ID?"

I feel kind of cool when the gate opens, like a girl who just got her big brother into an exclusive club. Then, in the staff parking area, I spot an unfamiliar red SUV with Texas plates that read HUNNY B. *Really, Noah? She has cutesy misspelled vanity plates?* Noah and his designer are nowhere in sight, so I do my best to focus on the task at hand.

"Let's start with the exterior," Detective Minot suggests, bringing me back. I didn't realize before how badly he wanted to get onto the property, how frustrated he was by Hettie's stonewalling. Now that he's here, he doesn't waste a minute. "The original investigators believed that the kidnapper walked right into the home," he tells me, heading toward the rear of the house, "but I'd still like to see the windows."

I scramble to keep up with him. "I thought the windows were locked. You don't really think the guy climbed in a second-story window and then hauled Gabriel out with him, do you?"

"No," he concedes, "but if a window was the point of entry and exit, it would explain how Gabriel's door was still locked the next morning, and how the adjoining door to his parents' room was still latched from both sides. The only other explanation is someone with a key to Gabriel's bedroom."

We're standing by the fountain at the back end of Evangeline. Ordinarily the stone cherub centerpiece would joyfully spew water from his lips, but the fountain has been turned off for winter. Now the cherub stands on one foot, face tilted upward and mouth agape as if in shock.

"Is that the ballroom?" Detective Minot points to the two sets of French doors.

"Yeah," I tell him. "They don't use it much anymore."

He studies the second floor and its balcony. "So that's the master bedroom where Neville and Hettie slept." He draws a line with his finger. "And Gabriel's room adjoined theirs off to the left."

We turn the corner of the house and inspect the upper level. "Right there." He points. "Those windows would've been Gabriel's."

Assuming there haven't been major changes to the house in the last thirty years, I have to agree with the original investigators. There's no obvious access through the windows. The balcony doesn't extend nearly far enough to reach them, and there aren't any trees or overhangs to help someone get inside.

"*Maybe* you could make it with a ladder," I say, "but the windows would have to be open, and it would be hard to go down with a toddler." That was what Bruno Hauptmann attempted when he kidnapped the Lindbergh baby—and his ladder broke.

"There was never any sign of a ladder," Detective Minot muses. "And the windows were locked, at least by the time police showed up."

"And then there's the dog," I remind him.

"Yeah. Someone from the inside *had* to be involved, at least as an accomplice." He sighs. "I sure wish we coulda talked to that nanny. See if her story stayed consistent."

I feel an irrational surge of anger at the whole Lauchlin family. Maddie and Jack for dying. Sean for disappearing. And Noah for being too young to be useful. Thinking of the Lauchlins does prompt a question, though. "Did anyone ever look at Maddie's son as a suspect? Sean Lauchlin?"

We're making our way to the front of the house, but the mention of Sean's name stops Detective Minot in his tracks. "How'd *he* turn up on your radar?"

"Brigitte mentioned him last week." I find his reaction more interesting than my question. "I take it investigators had an eye on him?"

Detective Minot glances around, despite the fact that there is absolutely no one here. "This isn't the place to discuss it," he says. "Let's check out the room first and get outta here."

I resolve to grill him later. We enter the house and hurry up the staircase, its thick carpeting absorbing the sounds of our footsteps. Strands of daylight make the second-floor hallway much less sinister today, but my heart is banging at my rib cage anyway. *Will I have to feel every horrible thing that happened to that poor child?* Detective Minot stops at a door on the right and gestures for me to enter first.

I put a hand on the knob and recoil sharply when a door opens behind us. I whirl around and see a hefty black woman helping Hettie with a walker.

"Hey there," the nurse greets us cheerily. "I was just gonna take Miss Hettie out to the garden for a bit a fresh air. Y'all comin' by for a visit?"

I bank on the old woman's dementia and run with it. "We were, but we can wait," I say. "You two take advantage of the day while it's not raining."

Hettie examines us both with intelligent eyes. She looks better than she did the last time I saw her. Still thin, but more alert. Not exactly a good thing at this particular moment. Beside me, Detective Minot rubs his palms together and stares at the floor. If she recognizes him, we could be in trouble.

"Come with us to the garden," the nurse suggests.

I rack my brain for plausible excuses. "No, I have allergies. We'll come back."

The nurse is too polite to point out that it's January, hardly allergy season. She shrugs. "That suit ya, Miss Hettie?"

Hettie moves slowly, peering at me like a turtle. "It's kind of you to drop by again," she says. "I trust your book is going well."

I freeze. *She knows. She knows everything.*

But her face still says benevolent hostess, and there's no sign she remembers Detective Minot whatsoever. "Has Jules been telling you all about the history of the house?" she asks, and I realize that she remembers me as the plantation-home writer. I can make this work.

"He's told me some," I say, "but I was hoping to chat with *you*, too. And do you mind if I explore the house? I'd love to see the design choices you've made, but I don't want to intrude."

"We wouldn't have invited you if it were any intrusion. You treat Evangeline as your home." She grips the handles of her walker, struggling to hold herself up. "I told Jules he ought to put you and Gabriel in the house, but he thought you two'd prefer a little privacy, even if those cottages are small."

Oh. My. Hettie's brain is completely scrambled.

The nurse eventually convinces her they'd better continue on to the garden, and Detective Minot helps her safely down the stairs.

He returns shaking his head in amazement. "I don't get it. She didn't even ask who I was. And what was that about Gabriel?"

The last thing I'm going to do is tell him about Noah. If he finds out I've been sleeping with the son of Sean Lauchlin, I'll never get the info I want. "Hettie's been a little confused lately," I say. "But you heard her. She gave us the run of the house." So what if that permission was predicated on her belief that I'm a potential daughter-in-law? Before I can reconsider, I open the door to Gabriel's room and step inside.

. . .

I DIDN'T REALIZE IT BEFORE, but all this time I've been picturing his room a certain way. Blue walls, green trim. A *Sesame Street* bedspread. A big comfy armchair in the corner where he could sit in his mother's lap and read bedtime stories. Somehow, in my mind, Gabriel's room was Keegan's.

It's a little unsettling to walk into a space so different from what I imagined. Gabriel's room looks nothing like my son's, or any other child's. Above the white chair-rail molding, the walls are sage green and decorated with antique prints of rosemary, wild chives, and chicory. The Deveau family has transformed the space into a guest room.

What did you want them to do? Leave it forever, like some creepy mausoleum? They had to let go, Charlie. And sooner or later, so will you.

I walk around the room opening drawers, touching blankets and furniture, picking up objects: a small clock, a lace cloth, a glass of potpourri. I search for some lingering hint of Gabriel, but there's nothing. I approach the windows at the far side of the room, stand in the waning light, and wait. Part of me has already given up. I didn't have to *try* to feel something at the boat launch. It just happened. Maybe Gabriel has communicated with me enough for one day.

My last hope is the door that adjoins the master bedroom. Thirty years ago, investigators found it still latched from the inside; today, the small metal latch has been replaced by a sizable dead bolt. I twist back the dead bolt and turn the doorknob, expecting to see the room that Neville and Hettie once shared on the other side. Instead, I find a huge, sparkling bathroom.

"They remodeled." I have to admit defeat now.

Detective Minot takes a few tentative steps toward me. "Did you get anything? Any . . . messages?"

"No."

"Is it because they changed the room around or . . . you think noth-ing significant occurred here?"

I feel like a complete and utter failure. "I don't know how it works. I'm sorry."

"We'll try some other rooms. We're here anyway."

We do a quick survey of the upstairs. With each new room, Detec-tive Minot glances hopefully at me, and I shrug, unable to meet his eyes. At the end of our expedition, the only thing he's gained is that self-consciousness you get from being around people with more money than you.

"And I thought *my* house was pretty nice," he jokes.

I can sympathize. When I first began writing for *Sophisticate*, I felt that way all the time: intimidated by the high-end events I had to attend, both repelled by and drawn to my readers' lavish lifestyles. Gradually, I came to appreciate my position as a writer. I could be an observer, a know-it-all, the Woman with the Answers who was never really one of them. And once I had Keegan, I didn't waste time pining over designer clothes or gourmet restaurants anyway.

Detective Minot, however, hasn't yet reconciled himself to being around artwork worth more than his annual salary. He shifts around, trying to conceal his discomfort.

"Let's go. I'll take you home," I say.

We've been driving all of two minutes when I broach the issue I'm really curious about. "So. Sean Lauchlin. What's the deal?"

Detective Minot sighs, and I can tell he was hoping I'd forget. "That information is part of a confidential investigation. I can't get into it."

I don't give up that easily. "I'm trying to help you."

"I know." He pulls out his cell phone and begins texting someone. Dr. Pinaro, I imagine. "All I can say is nothing we currently know about Sean suggests that he's responsible for Gabriel's disappearance."

"Then why was he a person of interest?" I persist.

"During the original investigation, some . . . irregularities were discovered." He doesn't look up from his phone.

"Damn it, Remy, just tell me what you know." I pull the car over to a shoulder of muddy road so we can have this out. "I'm not gonna put it in my stupid book, if that's what you're afraid of. The book was just an excuse to get here, don't you understand? I'm doing this for the same reasons you are."

"It's not the same," he tells me, not remotely rattled. But of course, that's part of being a cop. Staying in control, even when crazy New Yorkers drive you off the road and yell at you. "I appreciate that you want to help, but Gabriel isn't your job."

"Oh, please. This isn't just about your job." An old pickup speeds by us, the driver glancing over to make sure we don't need assistance. "It bothers you on a personal level, doesn't it? That little boy vanishing, not even a proper burial. It bothers me, too. You know why?" I realize the answer only as I speak it. "Because it's not like leukemia or a brain aneurysm. It wasn't just random, shitty luck. Somebody is responsible. Somebody should be punished."

Detective Minot's voice is still measured, toneless, but his jaw is tighter. "And that's what I'm trying to do."

"Gabriel came to *me*. Not you." I let that sit with him a moment before whispering the thing that scares us both. "What if I'm the only one who can help you?"

He's silent for a long time. He wants to let me in. He's tired of doing it alone. "I could be fired."

"I won't repeat a word you tell me. I swear."

"Fine. Just . . . fine. What does it matter anyway? It's a job, not a life." He wipes away the fog forming on my windshield with his fist and begins. "In June 1982, Sergeant Sean Lauchlin received an honorable discharge after serving six years in the army."

"I thought he went AWOL." That was the story Noah told me, although his grandparents could've lied to him.

"No, he completed his service," Detective Minot says. "And then he went home to visit his parents, Maddie and Jack."

I nod. That fits with what Brigitte told me.

"According to his parents, the three of them had a falling-out about some woman Sean was involved with, and then he left. He told them he was heading for Mexico. On June twenty-fourth, he emptied his bank account. As far as we know, that's the last anyone saw or heard of him."

"Okay . . ." I fail to understand all the buildup. "He took his money and went to Mexico to start a new life with his lady. What's the big deal?"

"The big deal is the money, Charlotte." Detective Minot runs a finger over his clean-shaven chin. "He had almost half a million dollars in that account."

16.

Half a million dollars," I repeat. It's not an unthinkable sum even in 1982, but it's a hell of a lot to have stashed away for a handful of years in the military. "How'd Sean get it?"

"Unclear. The account was opened in April of 1979 with an initial deposit of forty thousand. Every month after that, a twelve-thousand-dollar deposit was made from an offshore account. By the time he withdrew the money, he had four hundred ninety-six thousand dollars."

My eyes widen. "Does the military know? He could've been—"

"Selling information? The FBI was all over that. As far as I know, the US government has never linked him to any crimes against the state. Apparently his work in the army didn't have him handling particularly sensitive material anyway."

"Do you think there's any connection to Gabriel?" Maybe I'm missing the obvious, but I don't see it. "I mean, that account was created before Gabriel was even born, right?"

Detective Minot sighs. "We've never established any connection between Sean Lauchlin and the kidnapping. The money is the only thing we have on him. Could've been drugs, or maybe he was connected to some other kind of organized crime, I don't know. The FBI probably pursued it further, but I don't have access to that investigation."

"But they never found him?"

"No. If he's alive, he's gone completely off the grid."

"What about the woman? The one he fought with his parents over?" Could this have been Noah's mother, Violet Johnson? Noah told me his mother died when he was little, but that may have been another lie his grandparents told him. His entire knowledge of his parents came from two people who gave him, at best, a sanitized version of the truth.

"We don't know the woman's name," Detective Minot says, "but Jack and Maddie said their son kept talking about making a fresh start with her. He felt he'd have to leave the country to do that."

No wonder Noah was stealing photos at the library, searching for something concrete. For all anyone knows, his parents could both be living as Mexican crime lords. At least Sean's mysterious lady love is an argument against his being a pedophile—if the woman truly does exist.

Something else occurs to me. "What about blackmail? What if Sean Lauchlin knew something about the Deveau family? That could've been hush money."

"I've got no doubt that Neville Deveau had a lot of offshore accounts to protect his assets, but we couldn't trace anything to him." He shrugs. "You think Neville stopped paying Sean and then the guy got mad and snatched his kid?"

I could buy this theory, except that it doesn't fit with the sexual abuse angle, and I know what I felt out there at the swamp today.

"I'm not sure what to think just yet," I admit, "but if I see anything, you're the first person I'll call." I start the car back up and flip off my hazard lights. Dr. Pinaro will be wondering where he is, and she's been more than generous about lending out her husband for the afternoon.

Back at his house, Detective Minot thanks me for the ride. I wait for him to get out, but he has one more question for me.

"What are you doing Thursday afternoon?"

"I don't know . . ." I'm immediately on guard. Surely he can't be hitting on me?

His face reddens when he sees my discomfort. "I've got a meeting," he explains. "I'm driving up to Lafayette to speak with Danelle Martin."

"The cook?" My voice comes out an excited squeak. Now, *that* is a different story. I've been hoping to track down Danelle Martin, who was with Maddie Lauchlin when she discovered Gabriel was missing. The way the case has been going, I'm thrilled that Danelle's even still alive. "Can I go with you?"

"I think you should." He chuckles a little. "I get the impression this woman is a real handful, and she doesn't like cops, that's for sure. Maybe you two will hit it off."

I have a feeling there's a hidden insult in that statement, but I don't care. I just want to be there. Before I can ask him for more details, the rain that's been threatening most of the day arrives with a vengeance. Detective Minot hops out of my car and salutes me.

"One o'clock on Thursday. I'll come get you."

You should be happy, I think as I drive back to Evangeline, much too fast now that I'm no longer chauffeuring law enforcement. *He trusts you. He's telling you things you could never find out on your own. That's good, isn't it?*

But I can't stop myself from stressing about Noah. Something is off with this female visitor, I can feel it. He isn't being honest with me, and it's not hard to imagine why.

The sky continues to pour, already flooding the roads. I steer directly into a puddle. The skid warning lights up as the Prius struggles to regain traction. With a child in the backseat, I used to be so cautious. Now it doesn't matter. Now it's just me.

· · ·

THE NEXT DAY, Monday, I get my first glimpse of Noah's mysterious designer. She's Latina, as far as I can tell, like his ex-wife. Short but curvy in a fitted red leather jacket, and boobs that are disproportionately big for her little frame. She's at *least* ten years younger than me. She stands in the garden chatting animatedly to Noah about an arbor, which raises my hopes. Maybe it truly is an innocent work relationship. But why does she have to be so damn pretty?

"I know you like the classics, but wood is too cutesy," she's telling Noah. "When you come into the estate, those gates are intense. I say we build off that look and go with wrought iron."

I'm about fifteen feet away from them, on my way to the kitchen to beg a late breakfast off Leeann. Noah glances at me and then looks away. Whatever faith I might've had in him dies as I watch him quickly steer the woman out of my path. There's no mistaking it. He's avoiding me. I dig my fingernails into the palm of my left hand and swallow. It hurts more than I expected.

After that, the two of them turn up everywhere. First, they're wandering the grounds, then examining the trees that line the driveway, then discussing the front entrance of the home with frowns and knit eyebrows. Noah follows her around, half-listening, nodding or gently disagreeing, and I have a flash of the kind of husband he must have been: the one playing with his cell phone outside the women's dressing room who says, "It looks good," or "I like it," without fully looking up.

That evening, as I walk along the bayou, I come across the two of them yet again. I search for a detour—if he doesn't want to see me, I don't want to see him, either—but the woman has already spotted me and begins waving.

"Hi there! We keep seeing you around." She greets me with a perky grin. "I thought I should say hello. I'm Cristina Paredes, the landscape designer."

"Charlotte Cates." I fail to match her enthusiasm. Standing beside her, Noah looks rather constipated.

"Do you work here?" she asks.

"Charlotte's a writer," Noah informs her, apparently not ready to totally disown me. "She's from New York."

"Oh, really? I *love* New York." Cristina puts a hand on her hip and runs the other through her hair. "How are you holding up out here, poor thing? This place must be such a yawn for you."

"Actually, it's a welcome change of pace." Being near her makes me feel a little sick, and it's not just the cloud of perfume hanging over her. *He's going to smell like her tonight,* I think. "Well, I'm sure you have a lot to do," I say. "Nice to meet you, Cristina. Have a . . . productive visit."

Maybe she can tell he's edgy. Maybe she sees the way I refuse to look at him. *Something* must tip her off, because her fake-friendly expression melts away and she falls silent, examining Noah with narrowed eyes.

"See you, Charlie," he mutters, and the nickname can only solidify her suspicion. I hurry off into the dusk, toward the silvery line of water. I hope she lets him have it.

THE WEEK DRAGS ON, and Cristina makes no more friendly overtures. All I can do is wait her out. The repair shop calls and confirms that my laptop cannot be resuscitated, although they did manage to rescue the files off my hard drive. I suck it up, buy a cheap replacement, and begin typing all the handwritten pages I've produced since the disaster. It's enough material for a couple of chapters, which I e-mail to Isaac. He'll let me know if I'm on the right track.

Jules shows up at my cottage Wednesday morning and throws a hissy fit, having somehow heard about my visits to Hettie. Note to self: one of the nurses has a big damn mouth. I assure him there was no discussion of Gabriel or the book, but Jules threatens to contact Sydney and Brigitte if it happens again. The prospect of getting kicked off the estate isn't financially appealing. I figure I'd better lie low for a little while and avoid Hettie. Thinking about her reminds me of my own grandmother and her precarious health, so I call home to check in.

"I'm doing just fine," Grandma insists. "The staff stop by every morning to help with my medicine, and I go for a walk with Helga in the afternoon. Quit your worrying." She changes the subject before I can press her further. "What about you? Are you missing home?"

"No," I say truthfully. Everything about my life in Stamford was tied to Keegan, and the farther I get from *Sophisticate*, the more I question all the years I devoted to it. "It's different here," I concede, "but it feels like I have . . . a purpose."

"You mean the book?"

"I mean Gabriel Deveau."

"Charlotte." There's a warning in the way she says my name. "Thinking about that child all the time and Keegan, too—well, it doesn't sound like the healthiest frame of mind."

She's right, of course. And I haven't even told her about the experiences I had by the swamp, or about Didi. She'd just worry, and why do that to her when she can't stop me? "It's something I have to do, Grandma," I tell her simply. "I'm sorry, I just do."

"I trust you," she says, as if I've given her a choice.

An hour later, my old life comes knocking again with a text from Rae: *Biz trip to NOLA soon!! We can hang. Call me, xoxo.* Rae's been to New Orleans for business before, so it isn't totally surprising. While I don't relish the thought of Rae in Chicory—my existence here is a lot less glamorous than the two of us had imagined, and she's likely to sniff out the Noah situation—the idea of spending a few days with her in New Orleans does lift my spirits.

By night, though, my nerves are acting up again. Tomorrow is Thursday. Tomorrow Detective Minot and I meet Danelle Martin. One casual remark could open up a new line of questioning, could be the breakthrough. You never know what will be the game-changer.

It could be *me*.

THE NEXT DAY, on the hour-long drive to Lafayette, Detective Minot briefs me on Danelle Martin. A black woman originally from Shreveport, she was about thirty-five when the kidnapping occurred. She'd worked as the Deveau family cook for almost ten years at the time and continued on with them for another six afterward. Martin's loyalty to the family and her reluctance to speak about their private lives infuriated police from the get-go. A vocal critic of the investigation, she complained to several media outlets that too much attention had been focused on Roi Duchesne in the early stages, allowing the real culprit to escape and jeopardizing Gabriel's life. Possibly in retaliation for her big mouth, Martin became a person of interest in the case and was called in repeatedly for questioning. She hired a big-gun lawyer—likely paid for by the Deveaus—who threatened to sue the Bonnefoi Parish sheriff's department, the state police, and the FBI for harassment. Without any evidence to implicate her, investigators were forced to back off. By then, however, the damage had been done, and Martin's interest in helping law enforcement was nil.

"You weren't kidding when you said she disliked cops," I observe. I'm starting to understand the strategic decision to bring me along and realizing it will benefit Detective Minot far more than me.

"She wasn't too happy about this meeting," he says. "I figure if things go south, you're my best shot. A woman outside the system might grease the wheels a bit."

I check myself in the passenger-side mirror, trying to see myself as she will. On the phone, Detective Minot instructed me to look approachable. I opted for jeans, a tailored shirt, and red slip-ons, hair flipped out. Now I'm regretting my choice of dress. I look like a suburban white woman in a cleaning product commercial. *I* wouldn't trust me.

Lafayette is supposedly one of Louisiana's biggest cities, but most of our drive takes us along winding country routes. I can't figure out what the people here do for a living; few of the local businesses seem to be thriving. A dingy old gas station is boarded up, and a food mart and breakfast joint don't look as though they see a lot of customers.

Eventually, we start to see some signs of real industry. The road converges with a major route and suddenly there are pharmacies, restaurants, major hotel chains, even a place advertising drive-through daiquiris. We end up in a so-so residential neighborhood with small, boxy, one-story homes. Danelle Martin's place is no bigger than the others, but her well-maintained yard and dark purple shutters set it apart from the weedy properties with chipping paint.

As Detective Minot and I step from his vehicle—an unmarked Impala issued by the sheriff's department—I see a pair of young black males eyeing us suspiciously from their porch. I wonder if they can sense that Detective Minot's a cop, or if it's just the fact that we're white. We walk up to Danelle's front door, and he rings the doorbell. There's barking inside, then someone muttering about putting the dog out. Detective Minot holds his badge up to the peephole. Finally the door opens and Danelle Martin stands, arms crossed, staring us down. She's a trim, formidable-looking woman in her sixties. She has dark skin, close-cropped gray hair, and a pointy chin. She reminds me of a resistance poet, some warrior woman from the civil rights movement, but when I glance at her chest, I realize she's a veteran of an altogether different battle. On the left side is a normal, slightly drooping breast. On the right, nothing.

"Got one boob left," she says, and I'm embarrassed that she caught me looking. "You ask me, that's still one too many. Even more people starin' at my chest now than when I had the two." She shoos us into a tidy little living room.

"I'm so sorry." I don't know if I'm apologizing for gawking or for the loss of her breast.

"Lost a boob, saved my life. Pretty good trade." She sits down on an old, pet-scratched recliner.

Detective Minot and I hover for a moment before realizing we aren't going to get any invitations. We sit on opposite ends of the couch, and I do my best to tactfully ignore the thin layer of dog hair coating it.

"So you the writer, I guess," Danelle says, addressing me. "Been wonderin' about you, how you gonna make a book with a whole lotta nothin'. Those fools never turned up head or tail of that chile. Why you wanna make a book on this, anyhow?"

I could tell her about my dream, which sounds more than a little crazy, or about Keegan, but she has no apparent use for sentiment. "It's an interesting case, and this is the job they offered me," I say. "I have to earn a living."

Wrong move. "You best watch what you do for money, girl," Danelle advises me. "There's more than one kinda whore."

Detective Minot purses his lips, but I can't tell if he's suppressing a laugh or getting frustrated that I'm not doing a better job at winning Danelle over. "I'm sure Miss Cates will try to tell Gabriel's story respectfully and accurately," he says, taking over. "Thank you for seeing us today. You mind if I record our conversation?"

Straight off, there's trouble. "Yes, I mind. I don't want you people messin' with my words, pullin' sound bites that make it look like one thing when I meant another."

"It'll be a more accurate reflection of the conversation if I tape it," Detective Minot warns. "And I write slow."

"Suits me fine," she retorts. "I'm retired anyhow."

And so they begin, both old pros at navigating Q & As.

I don't know why I thought this would be interesting. It's not. Detective Minot walks Danelle through a long series of questions she must have answered a hundred times before about her employment with the Deveaus, the routines of the house, and the night of August 14. He pauses periodically to jot things down, and I inwardly curse Danelle's mistrust of recording devices. Even worse, half of his questions concern seemingly pointless minutiae. I don't blame her when she rolls her eyes at "Can you tell me what you made for dinner that night?" and "Walk me through the steps of that recipe, would you?" I'm guessing that Detective Minot is establishing a timeline, but I hear nothing promising in her replies.

According to Danelle, Gabriel was getting ready for his bath when she left for the evening. It was roughly half past seven. The last time she saw him, he was running naked down the hallway while Maddie Lauchlin chased after him. Danelle spent the rest of the night in her cottage and noticed nothing unusual. The next morning, around seven o'clock, she headed back to Evangeline to make breakfast. Despite all the starts and stops, I'm listening anxiously now to her narrative, waiting for the inevitable discovery. Unlike the first time I learned the details of the case, I can picture it all now. I've *been* there.

"I was makin' waffles when Maddie came in, lookin' upset," Danelle continues. "She said she'd misplaced the key to Gabriel's room and needed mine. So I went upstairs with her to unlock the—"

"Why'd you go with her?" Detective Minot asks. "Why didn't you just give her the key?" There's no change in his tone or demeanor, but I find it a compelling question.

"I tried," Danelle tells him, "but Maddie said she was bein' so scatterbrained, she'd probably just go and lose mine, too. So I went with her."

I glance at Detective Minot to see if that explanation sounds as flimsy to him as it does to me. There's no getting around the fact that, without Danelle present to see the door still locked that morning, Maddie would've been the first person blamed for Gabriel's disappearance. Nobody would've been talking kidnapping. The assumption would've been that Maddie forgot to lock the door and Gabriel ran out into the night and got himself killed. Having Danelle there as a corroborating witness was certainly convenient.

Detective Minot flexes his writing hand a few times, tired of note-taking. "Was that typical of Maddie? Being scatterbrained?"

Danelle hesitates. "Maddie'd had a bad few months. Used to be she ran a tight ship, but she was dealin' with some family business and sometimes things got away from her."

Like locking the door? I wonder. Maybe there was no murder here at all, just a terrible accident that Maddie tried to cover up to save her own skin. With the bayou situated directly outside Evangeline's front door, it's not hard to imagine something horrible happening to a rambunctious two-year-old. But that wouldn't explain the absence of a body, or the dream I had about Gabriel.

"You said she was upset when she came into the kitchen," says Detective Minot, still pursuing the Maddie angle. "What did you mean by that?"

Danelle is cautious, and I can see that she and Maddie must have been friends. "Just . . . upset."

"A little bothered, would you say, or extremely distraught?"

"I wouldn't know, I was thinkin' about waffles, wasn't I?" She leans forward in her chair and stabs the air with her pointed finger. "Look, if you gonna try to pin somethin' on Maddie, I got nothin' else to say 'cause you're a damn fool. Maddie loved that li'l boy more than her own son. She loved all those kids, even Andre and those yappity girls. She raised every one of 'em."

"I've heard nothing but good things about her," Detective Minot assures her. "I'm sure it was hard for everyone when she and Jack left Evangeline." He doesn't bring up the circumstances of their leaving, but even I know the Lauchlins' departure—just two weeks after Gabriel went missing—caused quite a stir in the media. DEVEAU BLAMES NANNY, one paper speculated, reflecting the widespread belief that they'd been fired.

Danelle scowls, well aware of public perception. "Nobody made 'em go," she says, "if that's what you're thinkin'. Maddie and Jack left 'cause they wanted to. She couldn't stand the place no more. Had nightmares. And with the baby gone, she had no job left anyhow."

"Where did she and Jack go?" Detective Minot asks.

"They had some family things to attend to, I don't recall where."

For the first time since our awkward introduction, I jump in. "You mean their son? Do you know what happened to him?" If Danelle's got information about Sean, I want to hear it.

"I think it was Maddie's sister." Danelle regards me probingly, and I realize I have loudly broadcast our special interest in Sean.

Just as I'm resolving to keep my stupid mouth shut, Detective Minot stands and tucks his notebook under his arm. "Mind if I use your restroom, Ms. Martin?"

She grunts her assent. "First door on the right."

From the look he gives me on his way out, Detective Minot doesn't need the bathroom at all. This is it. My chance to be alone with Danelle, woman to woman. To establish a rapport. But how? I'm afraid she'll skewer me for any subject I bring up.

"So . . . were you and Gabriel close?" I expect some smart-ass answer, but she only shrugs.

"I never was a fan a little ones. Always got on better with Andre. He was old enough to have some sense."

Ah, I think, *the ever-elusive Andre.* Now that I'm acquainted with his sisters, mother, and boyfriend—not to mention the time I've spent going through his personal items—it's starting to feel ridiculous that I haven't talked more to the sole surviving Deveau male. The fact that he's Danelle-approved makes me even more curious. "I take it Andre was a good kid?"

"Sure." Danelle isn't going to make this easy.

"The twins said he never got on well with Neville."

"Andre and his daddy were different, that's all."

"And Hettie? Was she more accepting of Andre's . . . differences?"

Danelle meets my gaze with a steely look, annoyed by my pussyfooting. "He's a homosexual. How easy do *you* think he's had it?" She clucks her tongue in disapproval. "Come on, now, you writin' a book or a gossip column?"

I have to admire her loyalty. Danelle Martin is a decent human being, and it's her decency, her respect for privacy, that makes her a hard nut to crack.

I don't want to leap to unfair conclusions, but Andre *is* a male relative who surely had access to his little brother. "Did Andre show an interest in Gabriel? Did he spend much time alone with him?"

The question comes out more pointed than I intended.

Danelle knows exactly what I'm getting at, and she doesn't like it. Her hand twitches as if she's fighting the urge to slap me. "Andre may have liked men," she says with cold fury, "but he did *not* like little boys, and he certainly wasn't after his own brother."

"How do you know?"

"Because he had crushes on *older* men, not younger."

I pry further. "Older men like who?"

Danelle doesn't look happy to be having this discussion, but my insinuations of incest and pedophilia are too much to ignore. "Fellas in their late twenties, mostly," she says reluctantly. "Andre took a shine to one a the drivers when he was twelve. And when he got older, I'd say he had special feelings for Maddie's boy, Sean. That's all I know about it, and I'm done talkin', you understand?"

I half-smile at the mention of Sean. *Not you again. Those Deveau kids couldn't get enough of you.* It occurs to me that in 1982 Sean was about the same age that Jules is now. Perhaps Andre has always been attracted to men of that age. That gets me wondering: Could Sean Lauchlin have been more than just a crush? Could he and Andre have actually been involved? I study Danelle, seeking the answer in her face, but she's tapping her fingers, waiting for Detective Minot to return so she can hustle us out.

There's no evidence that Sean was gay. He fathered a child, and he was making plans to leave the country with a woman. On the other hand, maybe it *wasn't* a woman he was running away with. Maybe that's why Maddie and Jack disapproved, why they never told Noah much about his dad. I can only imagine the fireworks if Maddie discovered that Sean, her almost-thirty-year-old son, was having a relationship with the barely legal Andre. I remember what the librarian said, how Sean read poetry in English class and never seemed interested in the girls around town. I'd assumed he was just a sensitive type who didn't fit in. Now I see another interpretation.

However compelling this theory is, it does nothing to explain Gabriel's disappearance or Sean's abnormally large bank account. And how does Noah's mother fit into all this?

I throw it out there, just in case. "Did you ever see Sean Lauchlin with a woman named Violet?"

Danelle doesn't miss a beat. "Violet Johnson? Never saw 'em togetha, but she mighta known Sean. Got the impression she knew a lot a men."

Aha. That could explain why Maddie Lauchlin was not a big fan of Noah's mother.

"Who was she?" I ask.

"Violet was a cleanin' girl at Evangeline. Pretty li'l thing, and she knew it." Danelle rolls her eyes, unimpressed by pretty little things. "That who you askin' 'bout?"

"I think so. When did she work there?"

Danelle thinks it over. "She wasn't there long. Woulda been '75, '76."

Noah was born in 1979, leaving several years unaccounted for, but at least I have some idea now how his parents met.

"What happened to her? Why'd she leave?"

Danelle answers with her characteristic warmth and affection. "Never knew, never cared."

Detective Minot has no visible reaction when he returns to find us sitting in awkward silence, but I gather he is disappointed. I can't blame him. Part of me was really expecting to blow the lid off everything today, to succeed where hundreds of trained professionals failed. I'm forced to admit that things are not moving in that direction.

For another half hour or so, Detective Minot continues with his slow, plodding questions. Both Danelle and I are squirming in our seats by the time he wraps it up.

"Well, this is a good start," he tells her. "I'll be in touch with you in the next few weeks and we can arrange a time for a written statement."

She makes a sound somewhere between a laugh and a snort. Detective Minot rises to his feet and holds out a hand. She folds her arms, leaving him stranded.

"Y'all still in the dark, same as you always was," she declares. "Thirty years, and you back to where you started."

Detective Minot doesn't dignify the remark with an answer, just thanks her and heads out.

I don't follow. I'm not done with Danelle. "So that's it?"

"I answered every damn question you folks asked, didn't I?"

I don't believe for a moment that she's given us the whole story. "I don't get you."

"Nobody asked you to."

"You *know* something." I can't let it go. "You know something, and you're holding back."

"I know a lotta things," she retorts, "and I tell you one. We done here."

"I admire your loyalty, I really do." I shake my head. "But at this point, who is it you're protecting?"

Danelle stares stonily back at me but doesn't say a word.

"Thirty years ago, Ms. Martin, I could understand. But there's no one left, don't you know that?" Maybe she *doesn't* know. She hasn't worked for the family in a couple of decades. I decide to do a quick update. "Neville is dead, Maddie and Jack are dead, and Hettie's brain is so fried she thinks the gardener is her son."

Some of her hardness melts away at this news. "Jack died?"

"Last year."

"He was a good man."

"They're all gone now," I say quietly. "There's no one left for you to hurt." For a moment, I think I've got her.

Doubt flickers across her face, but it's quickly replaced by attitude. She puts a hand on her hip and looks to the door. "Your cop friend is waitin' on you, and I got things to do. You better skedaddle."

Fail.

Outside, Detective Minot has started up the Impala.

I climb into the passenger seat, defeated. I tell him about my conversation with Danelle and slump back, sure that he regrets bringing me.

"Why the long face?" His cheery tone surprises me. "I think it went all right."

"We got *nothing*. This was our chance."

Detective Minot keeps his eyes on the road, but I know he sees me pouting. "Most of these old cases never get solved, Charlotte, and that's just how it is." He's so stoic, so resigned to inaction. "Anyway, I wouldn't give up on Danelle Martin just yet. Give her a few days."

"A few days for *what*?"

"Let her sit with it." He pulls out into an intersection and I see that traffic has picked up. "She might come up with something interesting."

Is he stupidly optimistic or trying to make me feel better? "I think she'd rather lose her other boob than tell us shit," I say.

"All right, you think. But I think deep down that woman's itching to talk." He gives me a rare smile. "Fifty bucks, what do you say? Give her a week."

"Easiest money I ever made."

But Minot's confidence rekindles my hope a little.

17.

I'm not sure why, but the meeting with Danelle fires me up. Back in my guest cottage, I attack the boxes of Deveau miscellanea with renewed vigor. I know it's just a bunch of old crap that's been lying around in storage, but no one has ever properly sorted it. Why stress out over what Danelle does or doesn't say when I've got real, uncensored artifacts all around me?

I set aside the box of Andre items I've already gone through and choose another, laying out its contents on the bed. Children's items, for the most part, that must have belonged to the twins. Dolls, a pink diary with only two pages filled in, a bottle of sparkly purple nail polish. I pull out a third-place ribbon for an equestrian competition, flip through a sketchbook with pencil drawings of badly proportioned horses. On the bottom of the box, there are some 1978 issues of *Teen*. The twins have marked their answers to a "What Type of Guy Do You Go For?" quiz in green ink. I learn that twelve-year-old Brigitte had a thing for jocks, while Sydney preferred bad boys. Actually, Sydney may not have outgrown that. I think I saw something in a tabloid once about her ex-husband being a sex addict.

The one good find is a scrapbook that Brigitte tried to keep. Like the diary, the pages are mostly blank, but over the years she sporadically pasted things in it. Movie stubs and airplane tickets, playbills, concert programs, Polaroids with friends. What thrills me, though, are a couple of baby photos of Gabriel. It's been hard to find any pictures of him at all, and these aren't bad. He's probably just a few weeks old, a shapeless blob in Brigitte's teenage arms. In the other, taken maybe a month or two later, he lies on his back, flashing a gummy smile at the camera. Looking at it, I feel a sense of recognition, a strange rush of love for this child that I never knew and will never know.

He was so small. Vulnerable. And someone took advantage. I remember the feeling of fingers over by the swamp, the violation. I don't know what that poor little body was subjected to, but there must have been signs. Signs that something was wrong. Signs people missed.

What room do I have to judge? I know all about missing signs.

I've searched my mind a thousand times, and I still can't recall anything unusual about the day Keegan died. I was in a rush that morning, like always, and he was taking his sweet time. He fussed about the cereal I gave him, stirring it around until it got soggy. That was nothing new—he was a picky eater. But maybe that morning was different. Maybe he wasn't feeling well. Maybe he already had a headache. I never asked how he was feeling, just packed him into the car and hightailed it out of the house. I don't even remember the last thing I said to him when I dropped him off at day care. *Have a good day at school,* maybe. *I love you,* perhaps. But it could just as easily have been a reminder to behave himself. He'd been a handful for the teachers lately.

How could you forget those last words?

I wonder if Hettie went through this, too. Did she remember the last thing she said to her son? Did she comb through every memory, searching for something a little off? Was she like me, certain in her heart of hearts that, ultimately, the fault was her own? She must have regretted attending that sweet sixteen party every day of her life since.

It takes a couple of hours, but I make it through four more boxes and confirm they're all junk. When I find a brown leather Bible in box number five, I almost ignore it. But it's lying amongst items from the early eighties, and there's a bookmark inside, so I open to the marked page just to see.

I skim the section briefly: the Judgment of Solomon. I'm not much of a biblical scholar, but even I remember the two women fighting over a baby from the children's Bible my aunt Suzie gave me. The story is supposed to contain a great lesson on wisdom, I guess, to inspire the reader with Solomon's brilliant deductive powers.

Who in the Deveau family was drawn to this story? And why? I flip to the first page of the Bible to see if there's a name or inscription and find a sheet of yellow stationery covered in big, loopy cursive. Not Andre's handwriting—I remember the tight, neat numbers and letters in his old physics notebook. This looks female and it doesn't match what I've seen of the twins, so my money's on Hettie.

I unfold the paper and realize that it's a list of Bible passages.

Isaiah 64:6. We have all become like one who is unclean,
and all our righteous deeds are like a polluted garment.
We all fade like a leaf,
and our iniquities, like the wind, take us away.

This strikes me as a pretty bleak worldview, but I keep reading.

1 Corinthians 6:18. Flee from sexual immorality. Every other sin a person commits is outside the body, but the sexually immoral person sins against his own body.

This gets my attention. Was Hettie considering sexually immoral acts? Was she worried for someone else she deemed immoral? There's no date on the paper, so I can only imagine when this might have been written.

> 1 Corinthians 10:13. No temptation has overtaken you
> that is not common to man. God is faithful, and he will
> not let you be tempted beyond your ability.

I can't help but think of Andre as I read. These seem like passages that a religious mom might dig up after learning that her son was gay. Could Hettie have been trying to offer him spiritual guidance? Or was she seeking help for her own reasons?

> 1 Thessalonians 4:3–5. For this is the will of God, your
> sanctification: that you abstain from sexual immorality;
> that each one of you know how to control his own body in
> holiness and honor, not in the passion of lust . . .

The reverse side of the paper has two more passages, a little less grim:

> 1 Corinthians 13:7. Love bears all things, believes all
> things, hopes all things, endures all things.

> 1 Peter 4:8. Above all, keep loving one another earnestly,
> since love covers a multitude of sins.

I look for a common thread in the Solomon story and these Bible verses, but the lessons in each don't strike me as similar. I could ask Leeann what she thinks—she's pretty churchy. I don't have much confidence in her capacity for theological analysis, however. Maybe Dr. Pinaro could shed some light.

I put the Bible on the table by my bed and work through the remaining boxes. By the time I'm done, it's past midnight and I've got nothing more of interest. The Deveau clan may be fancy folk, but their twelve boxes of attic junk wouldn't fetch fifty dollars at a yard sale. The day has not been all I hoped. I slip into my PJs, turn on the TV, and go to bed. For some people, going to bed means going to sleep. I am not one of them.

I DON'T LEAVE THE COTTAGE the next morning. It's Friday, and if Cristina Paredes has a purely working relationship with Noah, she should be heading home today—not that her leaving would prove his innocence. There's *something* funky going on with them. At this point it's just degrees of bad. Still, I open the curtains enough to keep an eye on what's happening outside.

In the late morning, Isaac calls to discuss the chapters I sent him. "This is risky," he mutters, almost to himself. "You've got kind of a nonfiction novel going. It's not what we discussed. I can't use it for the *Greatest Mysteries* series."

"Do you want me to change it?"

He exhales. "Not yet. Give me a few more chapters. I like the sociological aspect, the class differences between the staff and the family. But, Charlotte?" He's quick to temper his praise with reality. "Not a lot of writers can pull off the whole *Midnight in the Garden of Good and Evil* thing. Be prepared for a rewrite."

After our talk, I sit down and map out where I'm going with the book in more detail. Around two o'clock, I'm distracted by voices outside. Peering from behind the curtains again, I see Noah hauling two obscenely large purple suitcases. Cristina follows in a pair of poured-on jeans and heels. I don't see which cottage they came out of, so I can't tell if she was staying with Noah or had her own place. But she's leaving.

It's embarrassing how fast my heart beats when there is a knock on the cottage door about fifteen minutes later. I'm tempted to leap to my feet and fling open the door. Instead, I catch myself, count to ten, make him wait. If I could survive Eric cheating on me after four years, surely I can muster up some cool when my one-week fling doesn't work out.

But it's hard, seeing the way Noah's face lights up at the sight of me. His grin seems like the worst kind of lie.

"Hey! Been too long."

"I take it you've been tied up." I speak in a voice that's neither nasty nor friendly, just to see how he'll play it.

"Work stuff." He shrugs. "I missed you, though." He leans in the doorway toward me, waiting for me to step aside and let him in.

I don't budge, don't smile.

Uncertainty sets in. "Is it a bad time? You busy?"

"No," I tell him, "I'm just . . . not sure why you're here."

"To see you . . . ?" He trails off as he puts it together. "You're upset." He studies me. "Because of my job? Because I haven't been around? I told you 'bout that . . ." He gets a wounded look, like a dog who's been unfairly scolded.

"It's not because you haven't been around. It's because you *have*."

His eyes widen. The "uh-oh, I'm in trouble" look.

"Let's be real, Noah. You chose not to see me." I look directly into his mournful-dog eyes and lay it on the line as clearly as I can. "I'm not gonna pretend I have any claim on you, okay? I don't. But it's a little ballsy of you to show up like this after avoiding me for a week."

"It was work," he says. "I told you."

"Work," I repeat. "Do you even know how sketchy you were acting? You practically broke out in hives whenever I came near you and Cristina." His mouth opens and then closes again. "I guess I'm curious." I cross my arms, still blocking the doorway. "How exactly were you expecting me to react? Just give you a big hug, ask no questions, and jump into bed with you?"

I wait for a string of excuses or indignant replies, but Noah just shoves his hands in his pockets and stares at the ground.

"All right," he says, nodding. "I'm man enough to admit I made a bad call with this—this whole Cristina visit." He exhales. "I wanted to keep things from gettin' weird, but they're probably even worse now. I'm sorry, Charlie. I am."

It's a great performance, oozing with remorse, but totally lacking an explanation. I stare at him.

"I get why you'd think . . . there was somethin' goin' on," he says slowly. "I guess there was, kinda."

"Is Cristina your girlfriend? Are you sleeping with her or—"

"No, no." He looks alarmed at the prospect. "God, no. She really is my designer. I put her through school and all. But I shoulda told you, she's Carmen's sister."

"Who's Carmen?"

"My ex-wife."

This is the best news I could have expected to hear. "Wait, Cristina is your sister-in-law? And you work with her?" It's a huge and amazing relief, if it's true. Although that would mean that his ex-wife shares genetic material with that woman, which is intimidating.

"She was my sister-in-law, yeah. Couple of Carmen's cousins work for me, too. You can see how messy my divorce got."

As much as I'd like to believe this story, there are some holes. "Why didn't you just tell me that? Why'd you have to ignore me? What were you afraid I'd see?"

"It's not what you'd see. It's what she'd see." Having figured out he's not getting into my cottage, he sits down on the edge of the front step. "I've known Cristina since she was in the ninth grade. She was maid of honor in our wedding. I just thought it would be weird for her, seein' me with somebody else. Seein' how happy I was." He leans his head back and sighs. "And then she'd have to decide whether or not to tell Carmen, and . . . well, it all seemed real complicated."

I'm getting the sense that their divorce was not quite as amicable as I first thought, which is kind of comforting. I'm not alone in my dysfunction. But his dating someone else should not be that big a deal unless . . .

"Noah, when exactly did you get divorced?"

"December first."

Not even two months ago.

"Oh Jesus."

He holds up his hands. "Hey, I wasn't lookin' to start somethin' right off. I took this job with Hettie 'cause I wanted to get my head on straight. I didn't expect some good-lookin' Yankee to haul me off to bed first thing."

I smile, because this isn't a wholly inaccurate version of events. I think I believe him now. He could've handled this far better, and I'm not thrilled to know his ex-wife's family is still in the picture, but at least he's not a cheating bastard. He's just a gun-toting, deer-hunting son of a potential criminal. Somehow I can live with that.

I sit down beside him on the porch. "I need a smoke."

He laces his fingers through mine and kisses my hand before breaking out the pack of Marlboros. "Baby," he tells me, "I got what you need."

THAT NIGHT, as he snores lightly beside me, I find myself facing a whole new set of worries. Getting attached to someone right now is the last thing I need, and my reaction to Cristina has already proven I care more than I want to about someone I don't really know. I'm supposed to be gathering material for my book and helping Gabriel. No-where on this list does it say "falling for Texan with potentially awkward family connections to the case." Come April, I'll be back in Stamford, and Noah may be leaving even sooner. Haven't I lost enough? Why give myself someone else to miss?

Noah rolls over into his pillow, mumbling incoherently in his sleep. His broad shoulders are bare and tempting, but I resist the urge to touch him. There must be some way to enjoy his company without risking anything, some way to maintain a safe emotional distance. Men do it all the time, don't they? Noah is probably not overly invested in me. I'm the one with the problem.

Perhaps it's a sign of weakness, but I can't take another night of brooding. I take an Ambien and hope that this isn't the night Gabriel intends to reveal all.

By morning, the pill has left me feeling hungover and apathetic. I'm not enthusiastic when Noah suggests we get out and see the area, but I go, and as the Ambien fog lifts, I'm glad I did. We spend the weekend exploring the local scene: strolling City Park, eating bad Chinese take-out, catching a movie at the second-string theater. We get chicory-flavored coffee at a bakery near the center of town and I almost gag. It tastes like dirt, but Noah pronounces the flavor "nice and sort of woody" and drinks both his cup and mine.

On Sunday we hike a four-mile nature trail and devour fried catfish and dirty rice at a little hole-in-the-wall. Back at the estate, Noah flips on a basketball game and flops onto my bed, totally content.

"Been a good weekend," he says.

I don't tell him this is the best weekend I've had in months. I don't thank him for this brush with happiness, however brief it ends up being. He doesn't know the dark place I'm coming from, and I want to keep it that way.

I watch him shout at the muscled giants on the television, mystified that a sloppy turnover should inspire such passion. My dad was a sports fan, but I've never dated one before. Eric was the kind of guy who, even as an adult, became bitter if you mentioned high school gym.

"You gettin' sick of me yet?" Noah asks during a commercial. "I don't wanna overstay."

I shrug. "Do you want a night to yourself?"

"Nope." He strokes my knee absently. "I don't like sleeping alone."

I could be offended. The fact is, though, I don't like to sleep alone either. For the rest of the night, he talks more to the TV than he does to me. I don't mind. I call Rae back and arrange to spend a few days with her while she's in town, then settle in with a pint of ice cream and a few sudokus. This arrangement feels like the nice part about being married. The day-to-day togetherness.

Not that Noah is anything like Eric. I rushed into things with Eric because he was the means to an end I desperately wanted, part of a plan. Live together, get married, buy a house, get pregnant, have a baby. His involvement ended there. I can't blame Eric for finding someone else. From the moment our son was born, my husband was no longer part of the equation.

You wanted him to leave.

It's a strange realization that comes right as Noah throws a pillow and starts screaming, "That's bullshit! That call was bullshit! He was out-of-bounds! Are you *blind?*"

I smile. Somehow I don't want this guy to leave, and that is even stranger.

A COUPLE OF NIGHTS LATER I'm getting a pretty hot foot massage when my cell rings. Noah pauses, his thumbs still deep in the arches of my left foot. I hate to interrupt, but it could be Grandma. He sighs as I snatch my phone from the bedside table.

I don't recognize the number, but it's a local area code, so probably work-related. I scramble to answer. "Charlotte Cates."

"Hey there," says a familiar female voice. "Got your number from that detective fella. This is Danelle. Danelle Martin." She sounds like she has misgivings about making this call.

I shake my head in admiration. *Remy, you son of a bitch, you nailed it.* I have never been so happy to lose fifty dollars.

18.

I was kind of hoping that Danelle would drop an earth-shattering nugget of information over the phone and we'd be done with it, but instead she wants to come speak with me at Evangeline.

"Hettie there?" she asks.

"She's here," I say. "You want to see her?"

Beside me, Noah wrinkles his brow, trying to figure who I'm talking to and what about.

"You said she's sick," Danelle says. "Figured I might pay my respects. I never did get to thank Mr. Deveau before he passed. Be nice to see the place again. They still got the cameras and guards?"

"I can get you in." This, of course, is what she's counting on. I've no doubt it's why she wanted to speak to me and not Detective Minot. I just hope she has something worthwhile to say.

"Tomorrow morning, then." Danelle doesn't bother asking if that's convenient for me. "I'll speak my piece and that's that. I don't want my name in any book, and I don't want any more policemen knockin' on my door, understand?"

It's not a promise I can make, not if she tells me something of real value. "I'll do my best."

When I get off the phone, Noah wants to know who it was. I hesitate. I'm sure he'd love to meet Danelle, a woman who knew his grandparents and his mystery dad—probably even him, when he was little. But I can't let them know about each other just yet. If Danelle has anything interesting to say about Maddie, Jack, or Sean Lauchlin, I don't want concern for the surviving Lauchlin holding her back.

"It's for my book," I tell Noah. "I'm just following up on something."

"Oh yeah? What's that?" My answer has only made him more curious.

"Nothing important." I place my feet in his lap. "I believe you were working on these before we were so rudely interrupted."

He rolls his eyes. Takes my left foot and gives it a halfhearted rub. "You can talk to me about your work, ya know. I'm not too dumb to understand."

"It has nothing to do with your intelligence," I protest. "You just have this weird family connection to everything I'm writing about."

His face grows deadly serious and I can tell my arches are getting no more love tonight. "What's it matter who my family is? Unless you think they did somethin' wrong."

"I'm not worried about your grandparents," I say, although it isn't exactly true, "but even you have to admit that your father is a big question mark."

"You're lookin' at him?"

The moment Sean enters the equation I can feel a wall go up in him, although I don't know if it's for me or the man he feels rejected by. Either way, I'm sure Noah would like some insight into the bum who fathered him. Unfortunately, I made a promise to Detective Minot—a promise I intend to keep.

"I'm not looking at anyone," I say. "I'm not the police. Just trying to tell this story, and your dad's a piece of it." Something occurs to me. "If he did turn up, would you want to know? I mean . . . would you get in touch with him?"

"No," he says quickly. But he's brooding now, working it over in his mind. "He's probably dead anyhow."

A charitable explanation, I think, for Sean's failure to contact his son or parents at any point in the last thirty years. Actually, death is probably the *only* acceptable excuse. Even a stupid death, like driving your car off the road and into a tree because you're too damn drunk to operate a vehicle, is still better than outright abandonment.

"You're probably right," I agree. "I bet he died a long time ago. What about your mom? Violet Johnson. Would you like to know more about her?"

He's dismissive. "She's dead."

I don't point out his grandparents could've lied about that. "Someone named Violet Johnson worked at Evangeline in the midseventies," I tell him. "She was a housekeeper. I'm guessing that's how she met your father."

"A housekeeper, huh?" Noah's face is unreadable.

I wish I knew what was going on in that head of his. "It's a common last name, but I bet you could find her records if you tried."

"Yeah," he says. "Prob'ly could."

Maybe he's afraid of what he'd find. Maybe he genuinely doesn't care. Maybe he's just a guy, disinclined to share his feelings with me.

"You got somethin' to eat?" he asks. "I'm starvin'."

ALL OF DANELLE MARTIN'S ATTITUDE and self-assurance seems to shrink when she enters her former place of employment. I meet her on the steps around nine o'clock the next morning. She has spruced herself up with a long black dress, earrings, a string of rectangular glass beads, and a colorful scarf. "Good to see you, Ms. Martin," I greet her.

Her gaze sweeps past me, over the great oak trees and along the bayou, traveling up to the shining white house. I wish I knew what memories the place evokes for her. "Always was such a purty home," she says. "Hard to think of somethin' ugly happenin' inside."

"Do you want to look around? I bet a lot has changed." I'm hoping a tour might prompt some stories, but as I lead her through the house and outdoors, she offers only terse remarks about changes to the property.

"New cabinets," she says of the kitchen. "They took down the gazebo," she tells me in the garden. She has a quick walk and her sharp eyes remind me of a predatory bird scanning the horizon for food, trained to any flash of movement. When Danelle sees the remodeled cottages, she is scornful. "No character," she pronounces.

Eventually I'm done with all the small talk. We've seen enough. Either she trusts me or she doesn't.

"Well?" I sit back on a garden bench in front of the old fountain and take in the crisp sunshine, no longer caring about good manners. "You came here to talk to me, didn't you?"

She places her hands on her hips. "You think I know what happened."

"Do you?"

She scowls. "Got no damn clue."

"Then what are you doing here?"

Her mouth pinches into a pink knot. "I came 'cause there's things I oughta set straight. I been carryin' around that family's business long enough. Got my own life to get on with." She puts a hand to what remains of her breast and stares at the blank-eyed cherub on the fountain. "Sometimes doin' the right thing means tellin' a lie, and thirty years ago when the FBI and them was askin' all those questions . . . well, I guess I told a few."

I'm not sure she realizes the seriousness of what she's admitting here. I let her go on.

"That family was goin' through a hard enough time havin' lost their baby boy." She doesn't sit beside me on the bench but stands, stolid, drawing up her small frame as tall as it will go. Her eyes are fixed on some point directly ahead of us. "Alla sudden they got every cop on the planet breathin' down their necks tryin' to say they done it. I'll tell you certain as I'm standin' here that Neville and Hettie Deveau didn't hurt Gabriel. They had their faults—don't get me started—but they wouldn'a harmed a hair on that boy's head, and that's God's honest truth. If I'd a said all I knew to the police, I'd a made it worse for them."

"You wanted to help," I say, trying to coax it out of her. "The truth can be complicated."

She gives me an exasperated look that indicates my conciliatory tone is transparent and unnecessary. "Neville had a lady. I told 'em I didn't know about it, but he did. More'n one, over the years."

"He was having an affair?" I try not to show her what a letdown this is, but frankly, it would be more surprising if Neville Deveau had been faithful to his wife. I can't see why Danelle considers this such a bombshell. Of course it would have humiliated Hettie if her husband's infidelities got out, but why would the FBI care? I suppose one of Neville's lovers could've kidnapped Gabriel, but why? And that doesn't fit with the sexual-abuse angle.

"Neville wasn't a bad man," Danelle tells me. "I hope you say that in your book. He had the money and position to turn heads, and he was weak-willed. Nothin' more to it. But he didn't honor his marriage vows the way he shoulda. Never did."

"Did Hettie know?" *She can't have been that naïve*, I think. The twins mentioned how frequently their father was gone on business trips.

"Oh, she knew," Danelle confirms. "First time she found out, Neville made nice, swore he'd behave. Then a couple years before Gabriel came along, some other lady turned up. It was an ugly scene. They had some words one night."

"What did she say?" I'm trying to understand how Hettie went from being devastated by Neville's philandering to pregnant with his child a few years later. What happened in between? Did he make promises to change? Did she reach some kind of grudging acceptance? I remember the Bible I found, its passages about sexual immorality and sin. Maybe she put her faith in divine justice, believed that in the end her husband would answer to God.

Danelle cocks her head to the side, remembering. The light catches one of her earrings. "Somethin' just snapped in her. Never heard her yell like that before. She told him she'd wasted her life tryin' to be a good wife, and for no good purpose. Said her life had no purpose at all. I'm not much for head shrinkin', but I think Hettie was depressed. She didn't know what she was gettin' into with this kinda life." Danelle glances over her shoulder at the house, and I know what she means. I can't imagine regularly enduring dinner parties like the one I was subjected to here.

"But she stayed with him. She could've taken him to the cleaners with a divorce settlement. Why didn't she leave?"

"And cut Neville loose? That wasn't her way. She was gone make him sweat it." Danelle toys with her string of beads, thumb and forefinger closing on a jagged blue one. "She talked about leavin', mind you. Had him beggin'. But she was real mad. Said if he wanted to continue on with his whores, then fine, but the least he could do was find her a nice pool boy." Danelle purses her lips, as if she thinks Hettie went too far.

Maybe Jules is just one in a long line of family pool boys, I think. "How'd Neville react to that?"

Danelle looks me square in the eye. "He hit her."

I inhale sharply. "You saw this?"

"I heard 'em. He said she ever touched another man, he'd kill her, and—well, she went crashin' into a table."

"Did he hurt her?"

She nods. "Bloodied her nose. She came by the kitchen later askin' for ice."

Now I realize Danelle's big secret wasn't the infidelity at all. Any whiff of domestic violence when Gabriel went missing, and that would've been the end for Neville Deveau. Guilty or innocent, he would have been buried alive in a sea of salivating investigators, immediately convicted in the court of public opinion.

"Look," Danelle says, "Neville had a temper an' I don't pretend otherwise. But I don't believe he ever hurt anyone but that once. He never lifted a finger against any a those children, that I know. That's why I didn't go spreadin' it around. Woulda just confused things, see?"

I do see. It's hard to be objective about a guy who cheats on his wife and then pops her in the face for threatening him with a dose of his own medicine. *I'm* struggling with it, anyway. "So after he hit her, what happened?"

"Hettie went to their New Orleans house, lived there a few months while they sorted things out. The kids were away at school, but she went back to Evangeline when they came home, so they never even knew she was gone."

"And all of that was before Gabriel."

"Yeah. Couple years before. He'd taken up with some new lady by the time Gabriel was born."

It troubles me that Hettie had another child with this asshole. Was she stupid enough to think a baby could fix things? Or perhaps she was simply a good Christian woman who believed it her duty to yield to her husband's desires. "Was Neville happy when she got pregnant?" I ask Danelle.

She nods emphatically. "Pleased as punch. Hettie was the one who didn't want that baby. She came around later, I guess, but . . ." Danelle trails off, declining to speculate further. "All I know is, nobody took it harder than Neville when Gabriel went missin'." She shakes her head, and her obvious empathy for this man angers me. "Even after he put in them cameras and guards and all, he never had peace a mind. But he wouldn't get rid of this place either, no matter how many times Hettie tried to make him sell it."

"Why not?" I think of the house in Stamford, all the memories of my son that it holds. I realize now that there is no future in that house for me, only past.

Danelle considers my question. "Sounds crazy, but I think he was hopin' Gabriel'd come back one day." She studies my face, and for the first time, I detect something resembling anxiety in her. "I hope I did right tellin' you this. I know it sounds bad for Neville, but I believe in my heart he did nothin' wrong. He shouldn'a done what he did to Hettie, a course, but there's a long way between gettin' rough with a woman once and wipin' your baby offa this earth." Her eyes dart to the looming white house behind us and then back to me. "Whatchu thinkin'?"

"I'm thinking you're right," I tell her. "I don't think Neville was involved." And it's true. What Danelle just told me doesn't, in my mind, implicate Neville. If he hit Hettie, isolated her from the world, and cheated on her, then it's Hettie who had the motive. To rid herself of a child she never wanted. To bring pain to the man who hurt her.

It's possible, isn't it? The twins' birthday party ended around eleven, and Room Service Boy said both Neville and Hettie were present when he delivered aspirin at three a.m. If he was lying, though, if he was paid off, as Detective Minot suspects . . . she could've done it. She could've driven back to Evangeline, spent several hours there, and still made it back by eight o'clock when they got the phone call from Maddie that Gabriel was missing.

File this one under "Things I Won't Be Mentioning to Noah."

Danelle and I walk back to Evangeline, both clearly absorbed in our own thoughts. Suddenly the history of this place seems oppressive. For a moment, I can feel it all: the despair and drudgery of the hired help and the slaves before them, the listlessness and tedium of so many Deveau wives, the stress and pressure of being the owner of this estate. Sickness, injury, abuse—terrible things must have happened here, though they didn't all make headlines. In truth, Gabriel Deveau is just another name in more than a hundred and sixty years of pain and sadness at Evangeline.

"Is Hettie upstairs?" Danelle asks, bringing me back to the present. We're at the front door, stepping into the shadowy foyer.

"Yeah," I say, trying to shrug off the bad vibes. "End of the hall." I haven't told the nursing staff to expect her, so I'm not sure what type of reception she'll get. I linger at the foot of the staircase, listening. A quiet exchange of words, and then Danelle comes back down the stairs.

"She's sleepin'."

"Would you like to wait?" I have no idea how to entertain Danelle in the meantime, but it seems polite to offer.

"I guess not," she tells me, and I wonder if unburdening herself was the real purpose of this visit all along. "You said Hettie's been confused in her mind anyhow. I saw the place. Maybe that's enough." She casts another glance around the large, airy foyer and up at the chandelier, almost mournful. Does she miss her life here? I imagine her presiding over the kitchen like a magistrate, handing out plates to the staff like some kind of judgment. But it's not nostalgia on her face, I decide. It's pity. Compassion. She feels sorry for them.

I can't let her leave without asking one more thing. There's been no delicate way to work it into our conversation today, to make it appear anything other than pointed and suspicious, but I have to know. "Ms. Martin, do you know if Maddie Lauchlin's son spent time with Gabriel?"

"Sean?" She eyes me shrewdly. "When he came to visit his folks, his mama was usually lookin' after Gabriel. So yeah, they spent some time together." She lowers her voice. "You got a special interest in Sean?"

I don't play this close to the chest, not after the way Danelle opened up to me earlier. "Kind of," I admit. "I don't know much, but the guy seems shady as hell to me."

I wait for her to leap to his defense as she did with Maddie, Neville, and Andre. She only nods and studies one of the gold-framed paintings. "I got no love for Sean myself."

"No? Why not?"

Danelle weighs this a couple seconds before delivering a heavy edict. "Sean Lauchlin got above himself. He spent so much time around fine folks, he started struttin' 'round like he was one of 'em." Her mouth twists in disapproval. "The family was awful fond of him. Made him worse."

I'm startled to hear Danelle upholding class divides, particularly when she seemed so open-minded about Andre's sexuality. On the other hand, she's confiding in me. Maybe we can get somewhere. "I heard Sean had a big fight with his parents a couple months before Gabriel went missing. Did Maddie ever say why?"

Danelle shakes her head. "She and Jack were pretty tight-lipped about it. Sean'd been worryin' them for years doin' I dunno what. Poor Maddie just about went to pieces when he left."

I remember Noah said he used to play with Gabriel when he was little, and I have to ask. "Did you know Maddie and Jack's grandson?"

She looks surprised. "No. Never heard Maddie talk about him but once."

"What did she say?"

"I dunno. Just slipped out one day when she was upset, somethin' 'bout her grandbaby. Didn't even know she had one 'til that minute.

When I asked her, she clammed right up." Danelle sees my bemused expression and offers an explanation. "Maddie was real religious, and I guess Sean didn't marry the girl. She musta been embarrassed. She was that kind."

I'd love to continue with the conversation, but Jules pops his head out of the study and gives us both an icy stare.

"Can I help you?" he asks Danelle in a voice that is anything but helpful.

"No," she says, unmoved by some pretty boy less than half her age. "I'm on my way out, thank you." She pats my shoulder, the friendliest gesture I've received from her to date. "You have a good day."

Jules waits for Danelle to leave and then turns to me. "It really isn't appropriate for you to bring personal guests onto the property."

"She was here to see Hettie," I say evenly. "But I'll certainly keep that in mind."

I need to get away from this damn house. The fencing and cameras and guards are making me feel very mental patient. Besides, I want to pass everything Danelle told me today on to Detective Minot. The fifty dollars I lost in our bet is a small price to pay for escape.

I don't know how Hettie stayed at Evangeline all these years— largely alone, from the sound of it—without losing her mind. Maybe she didn't.

19.

I f I find Detective Minot comfortable to be around because he shares my rather cynical worldview, I find Leeann comforting because she does not. I spend my Wednesday afternoon engaged in grim but ultimately unproductive conjecture with Minot, and my Thursday writing about it. By Friday, I'm ready for a little kitchen gossip.

I have to give Leeann credit: there's just no earthly way to dislike her. With her big, toothy smiles and rambling tales of folks around town, I can see how she charmed old Neville Deveau into hiring her two years ago. I could pretend that my frequent kitchen visits are about research for the book or even her cooking—and in fact, I value Leeann for both of these reasons—but the simple truth is that I feel happy in her presence.

Six months ago I would have had nothing but disdain for Leeann. She is an overweight, uneducated twenty-three-year-old unwed mother who has lived her entire life in Chicory, Louisiana. She's never been out of state, and her only goals in life are to marry her hard-to-pin-down boyfriend and have more children. To the elitist Manhattanite, Leeann's not much, but she's kind, something I'm learning to appreciate.

Historically, I've always avoided "nice" people whose niceness is their primary quality. I pitied them. I spent my time with snarky intellectuals, basking in our superiority, our finely tuned sense of irony. Leeann wouldn't recognize sarcasm if it paraded by with a banner and a bullhorn, but any sign of sadness or stress in one of her coworkers, and she's all over it, offering to help. When she babbles about some drama unfolding within her church congregation or earnestly recounts a scene she saw on *Real Housewives*, I feel grateful to hear about a world not tinged by evil or tragedy.

"So . . ." Leeann smiles as she scrubs a copper pot from lunch. "How much you like 'im?"

I know without asking that she means Noah. I shouldn't be here, of course, shouldn't be indulging in some middle-school discussion of "boys." Rae is flying in tomorrow night, and I ought to be banging out a chapter so I'll have time to hang out the next few days. Really, though, this is more fun.

"I like him enough," I say, returning Leeann's smile.

"Nuff for what?" Leeann presses. "Do you 'happily eva afta' like 'im? Or just 'have a li'l fun 'til you get back to New York' like 'im?"

"He just got divorced," I tell her. "And I . . . haven't dated in a while. A little fun is all I can handle." I approach the farmer's sink, where she's working, and grab a green-checked dishrag. "Here, let me dry for you."

Leeann hands me her pot, smirking. "You best watch out, Charlie. God might have more in store for you than fun." I think she's trying to tease me, but it sounds ominous given all the other things that God or Fate or Chance has dumped on me recently.

"I know you believe in God and Jesus, Leeann, but . . . do you believe in other things? Things you can't explain?" I didn't intend to have this conversation, but I can't help myself.

I'm not making a whole lot of sense, but she responds confidently anyway.

"When you believe in God, you got an explanation for everything." She's so certain, those mild blue eyes totally untroubled. I find myself inexplicably infuriated. *An explanation for everything? Like why my son is dead?* But I hold it in.

I remind myself that Leeann is only twenty-three. She hasn't lost anything she loved enough to hate the idea of God. She hasn't seen enough of the world to make it complicated.

"What about ghosts?" I ask. "Do you believe in spirits?"

Leeann sets down her last pan on the counter and wipes her soapy hands on a free dishrag. "I believe the Lord has His messengers," she says, "and sometimes He sends His angels to us."

"Angels," I repeat. Not exactly the word that pops into my mind when I think of my visions of Gabriel Deveau, Hannah Ramirez, and Didi Minot.

Leeann nods. "There's heavenly visitations in the Bible. And my son saw one."

"Your son saw an angel?" The fact that I'm only 90 percent skeptical of this claim alarms me.

"He's seen her a few times," Leeann says with perfect seriousness, as if one can trust absolutely a three-year-old's reports of an angelic presence.

"How did he know it was an angel?" I realize it's pathetic that I'm looking to a preschooler for tips, but what else do I have to go by?

"He just knew," Leeann says. "Maybe she had wings. Anyway, that's what I believe in. Messengers from heaven, not ghosts."

I still don't see the distinction, but before I can pursue the matter, the pocket of Leeann's pants starts to vibrate. She fishes out an ancient, scratched-up cell phone. "It's Mike." She frowns, and I gather that's her boyfriend. "I hope there's not trouble at home." She presses the button with her thumb. "Hello?"

A pause. Her face knits up into a worried frown. *"Qui ça dit?* Why you on Mike's phone, sha?"

I haven't heard Leeann break into Cajun French before, but I gather from her tender tone that it's her son, the Angel Spotter. I can just make out a tearful little voice on the other end, and it fills me with a stabbing sense of loss. I would give anything to be inconvenienced by my child at work.

"Okay, sha, s'okay." Leeann soothes him. "Mike just come in? Put 'im on da phone."

A low male voice replaces the little-kid whine.

"What's goin' on ova dere, boo?" Leeann listens intently. *"Mais,* he says he sick. Says he got *mal au ventre."* Mike doesn't sound too happy, and soon Leeann is stuck soothing him as well. "I know you could handle it, but he's pretty worked up. Chilren always want dere mama when dey feel bad."

I stare at the wood floor. She's right. Kids do want their mama. But I wasn't there for my son when he needed his mama most.

Even if I'd left work when Keegan's teacher first called to say he had a headache, I wouldn't have made it back in time. But I didn't leave after that first call. I told her that he could have some Children's Tylenol and resumed composing an angry e-mail to our web page designer. I could've asked to speak with Keegan, could've told him I loved him, but I didn't. I went back to work because, like Leeann, I thought work mattered. Fifteen minutes later, when they called to say he'd been rushed to the ER, I knew that it didn't.

I watch Leeann, the lump in my throat growing bigger and bigger.

"All right," Leeann says, ending her call, "you tell T-man I gone be home soon. *Lâche pas la patate.* Hang in dere, beb. Love you." She stuffs her phone back into her pants, too anxious to see how shaken I am.

"Do you need to be with your little boy?"

"I dunno." Leeann chews on her lip. "He's cryin' for me, sayin' he sick. I haven't seen Jules today, but if he comes by and I'm gone . . ." She doesn't have to finish that sentence. We've both seen the mood Jules has been in lately. "I mean, Mike's there, but . . ." She trails off, consumed by motherly guilt. I get it. Mommy's boyfriend, however good he may be with kids, is no substitute for Mommy.

"Don't worry about Jules," I urge her. "We can feed ourselves for a night. You go be with him."

"You think?"

It's not that I'm afraid Leeann's kid will drop dead of a brain aneurysm before she makes it home. That sort of thing doesn't happen to other people. But one day, probably soon, she won't have this job anymore and she'll have to remember every pointless sacrifice she made for it at her child's expense.

"Trust me," I say, "your son is more important than dinner."

I don't have to tell her twice. She's off, ready to administer whatever hugs and kisses and cuddles her child requires.

Now alone in the kitchen, I feel a quiet depression creeping up on me. I remove an apple from a fruit bowl on the counter and rotate it absently in my hand. Through the kitchen window, I can see Noah taking measurements of some kind. I don't know how he stays so focused on this whole garden job. He's the only one who cares about the project anymore. But I suppose it's his way of honoring Hettie: leaving something beautiful behind that others can enjoy.

I'm not sure how long I stand there toying with the apple, but when I turn away from the kitchen window, there's a man in the doorway.

Andre Deveau.

He wears a navy suit and his short gray hair is parted and brushed back at an angle, the grown-up version of prep school fashion. I'm not sure whether he recognizes me from the dinner party or is just used to seeing strangers in his kitchen, but Andre makes no attempt at establishing my identity. "Has Jules been in today?" he asks, frowning at his phone. "I didn't see his car."

Of course. He's here to settle their lovers' quarrel. Or maybe fire Jules, which would make my life a lot easier.

"I haven't seen him, sorry."

Andre nods, about to leave, and then changes his mind. "I should eat. A snack, something low fat, please."

He thinks I work here. I hesitate. I could tell him I'm not the cook, but I don't want Leeann to get in trouble for skipping out early. "Uhh . . ." I pluck something from the air. "How about a parfait?" It's the only quasi-healthy thing I've ever seen Leeann serve and will require no cooking on my part.

"Sure. I'll be in the study."

He leaves without a thank-you, not bothering to learn my name.

It takes fifteen minutes to locate and combine the items necessary for a parfait, and the final product dismays me with its blobs and lumps and lopsided layers. Maybe Andre won't notice? I find the study door ajar, a fire crackling in the fireplace. Andre, now reclining on the love seat and glued to his iPad, wears a look that conveys murderous intent.

"Your parfait."

"Oh. Thank you." He peers at my sad rendition of a parfait and then at me, suddenly registering something's amiss. "I'm sorry, are you new? I should've introduced myself before. I'm Andre."

"Charlotte," I tell him. "We met at your mother's dinner party a few weeks ago."

He stares at me a second before making the connection. "Oh God, that book thing Syd and Bridgie are doing. I'm sorry, you look different without the blue dress." His forehead creases. "But—why are you making me snacks? Aren't you a guest?"

"The cook had to leave unexpectedly. Her son was sick, and Jules wasn't around . . . I just didn't want you to get upset."

He puts a hand up. "Despite all appearances, Charlotte, I'm not a complete asshole." He shakes his head. "I can't believe I mistook you for the cook. You must think I'm so spoiled, marching into the kitchen and barking out orders at whoever happens to be there." He stands up and heads for the liquor cabinet on the opposite wall, his hand hovering over two bottles of amber-colored liquid. "Please. Have a drink with me and tell me about your book—not that plantation-home nonsense Bridgie's been feeding my mother."

Andre selects one of the bottles and pours us each half a glass. Brandy? Scotch, maybe. Whatever he's got, it's bound to make him talkative. I recall the mojito he bought me when I interviewed him for *Sophisticate* years ago—not that he'd remember—and figure I can make a strategic exception to my no-alcohol policy.

"Thank you." I accept the proffered glass and have a seat. "I've been wanting to talk to you."

"I take it my sisters haven't been fountains of useful information? Well, no surprise there. They barely knew Gabriel." He gives me a crooked smile. "To tell you the truth, I don't think they've ever forgiven him for overshadowing their birthday party."

"I'm sure it was inconvenient for them," I say carefully.

"Quite. They were expecting a nice little article in the society pages and he took the front page of every paper. They sulked about it for a few decades, and now thirty years later they're converting my mother's pain into a source of revenue. A bit mercenary, don't you think?"

Good, I think. *He's under no illusions about who his sisters are.* If this is Andre pre-alcohol, I can't wait to chat when he's knocked a few back.

"I didn't intend to step on any toes with this book," I tell him. "I took the assignment under the impression that your whole family supported the project."

He shrugs. "I don't waste my time telling Syd and Bridgie what to do. Let them have their book." He settles back down on the love seat and kicks his feet up on the ottoman. "So . . ." He shifts the conversation to me. "You've been here a few weeks. Are you enjoying the train wreck that is my family?"

I smile. "All things considered, yes. Your family's quite . . . interesting."

"To train wrecks, then." He holds out his glass in a wry toast.

I raise mine in return and force down a sip of whatever's in there. My throat burns and it's all I can do not to gag. Andre, on the other hand, takes a long, unflinching drink. He leans back and stares at the ceiling like the weight of it all—the struggling hotel business, his crazy family, the secret of his homosexuality, the drama with Jules—is dangling precipitously above him.

"All right," he murmurs, "ask me anything. I might even give you an honest answer."

I raise my eyebrows in mock surprise. "Honesty? I hadn't dared to hope."

"I said 'might.'" He flashes me a tired smile. "It all depends on what you ask."

ANDRE CAN TALK, and he can talk well. His voice is rich and expressive, his words well chosen. His faint Southern accent sounds intelligent and gentlemanly without suggesting snobbishness. Somewhere in the course of our conversation, I realize that the CEO of Deveau Hotels does not entirely owe his position to nepotism. He knows how to work a listener. As he relates countless stories of his family to me— some cringe-worthy, some heartbreaking, some funny—I find myself drawn in, sympathetic toward this younger, more vulnerable version of him.

When he tells me his happiest memory of his father, I can picture it:

Andre at age ten, his hair windblown after a ride in the convertible, attending the racetrack with his dad for the first time. Neville wasn't much for gambling—"he respected money too much to just throw it away," Andre explains—but he wanted his son to admire the horses, and he let Andre place a few small bets. "I won eighty-six dollars," Andre says, pride still lighting up his face.

I wish I had my tape recorder to capture each detail, but that would ruin the intimacy, destroy the charade that we are two equals engaged in friendly conversation, acquaintances by choice and not circumstance.

"I can't imagine being Neville Deveau's son," I say. "I used to be so embarrassed by my father. I thought everyone was looking at him, judging anything he said or did or wore in public. I was being a paranoid teenager, but in your case . . . well, it was probably a legitimate fear."

Andre considers this. "He wasn't the most visible figure in the circles we ran in. I'd say he was much better in public than private, actually."

"You didn't get along at home?"

He shakes his head. "My father was a blowhard with a bad temper. I avoided him when possible. You could probably count our positive interactions on one hand." He rises to refill his glass and realizes that mine is nearly untouched. "You don't like it?" he says, part disbelieving, part crestfallen, like a parent who has just received a negative report about his child.

"Just pacing myself."

"This is good stuff, I promise you. Glenlivet Twenty-Five. A twenty-five-year-old single-malt whiskey with two years of finishing in sherry casks." He takes a sip and closes his eyes, savoring it.

I make some agreeable reply and take a few more sips, but this is strictly social drinking. I want to minimize the alcohol, maximize the schmoozing, and remain as clearheaded as possible. Already, I can feel my book sprouting up around Andre's stories, feel the sad portrait of this family that I need to paint.

I ask him about family holidays, and he tells me about the lavish Mardi Gras parties his parents used to throw. Maddie Lauchlin—Nanny, he calls her—would spend a full month decorating the house. She erected a huge tree in the foyer and draped it in green, purple, and gold. She set up elaborate displays on every mantelpiece, decked out the front door with masks and beads and sparkling ribbons. She had doubloons made with Evangeline's image imprinted on them. I know little about Mardi Gras traditions, despite the fact that it's only about three weeks away, but the idea of Noah's grandmother pimping out the home in all kinds of tacky makes me smile.

"When did they stop with the parties?" I ask.

"After we lost Gabriel," he says. "My father didn't feel we could maintain proper security with so many people around. I never cared. I'd rather spend Mardi Gras in the city, anyway."

"Is that where you live now?"

Andre nods. "I have a condo in the French Quarter. But I'm not home much. Our family owns a place on St. Charles, though, right along several parade routes. Bridgie and her husband are planning quite the party there this year. Have you been to Mardi Gras?"

I shake my head, a little self-conscious.

"It's like spring break for kids *and* grown-ups. Hard to beat if you like alcohol." He glances at my half-full glass. "Although maybe you don't."

"I'm not much of a drinker," I admit. "Shirley Temples are probably more my speed. Just plain old ginger ale and grenadine."

He chuckles. "That's not the Louisiana way, honey. We work a little, play a lot, and don't stop drinking 'til we're unconscious."

"Even your mother?"

"My mother's not from Louisiana. But I hear she had a good time back in the day."

"Were you closer to her than your dad?" His mother has been a shadowy figure in his family stories thus far. Andre has no problem with portraying his father as a bastard, his sisters as superficial airheads, or himself as clueless and bewildered. But Hettie—she's largely absent.

Andre must sense my curiosity because he stares at the fire for a moment. "She's my mother," he says at last, "so it's complicated, isn't it? I love her more than anyone on this earth. She's made her share of mistakes, but she'd do anything for me."

Someday, like Hettie, I will be old and near the end. But my son will not be there to tell people about our complicated relationship, to reflect on what I did right and how I screwed up. I wonder if the stinging injustice of this will ever go away.

"Your mother's entitled to a few mistakes, right?" I say lightly. "But lay it on me. Where'd she go wrong?"

"Well, marrying my father comes to mind. And you can put that in your book, I don't care who knows it."

"She was unhappy?"

Andre shrugs. "She wanted love. He wanted a uterus. You see the mismatch." He gets up to stoke the fire. "My father mellowed out some toward the end, but it was a hard road for her. When he died, I thought she might finally get a few good years without him. She deserved that. But then they found the cancer. Which reminds me . . . I haven't been to see her since I got in today."

Evidently Andre's visit was more about Jules. I wait for him to excuse himself, but he doesn't budge.

"I'll tell you a secret, Charlotte. Sick people scare the bejeezus out of me." Andre shudders. "I don't want to see her . . . wasting away."

I nod, but inside I'm raging. *Your mother is* dying . . . *Who cares what you want?* Of course I'm hardly qualified to join the "honor thy father and thy mother" police. If I learned that my own mother was dying, I wouldn't visit, wouldn't call, wouldn't care.

"Have you seen her recently?" Andre asks me. "How bad is it?"

"She's very thin," I tell him. "And the last time I spoke with her she seemed . . . confused."

"How so?"

"She was talking about Gabriel a lot. She didn't seem to know that he was gone."

He frowns. "She *never* talks about him. What did she say?"

"She was just talking like he was alive and all grown up. Like he never went missing."

He exhales. "Oh God. This isn't—she's not well." Andre presses a hand to his temple. "Someone should've told me. I had no idea she'd declined to that point." He downs the last of his Glenlivet and sets his glass on the table so hard I'm afraid it will break. "I've got to go see her."

Southern hospitality and good manners prevail.

"Charlotte." He takes my right hand in both of his and gives me his best sincere CEO smile. "It's been a pleasure. Next time I'll have that Shirley Temple for you."

20.

The chat with Andre gets me writing. I record the stories he told me as faithfully as possible, then work these anecdotes into the existing structure of my book. Noah pops in at some point, but I wave him off, too engrossed to offer any explanation beyond furious typing. He nods like he gets it and quietly retreats. By the time I have the new material down and reach a stopping point, it's half past one in the morning.

Entirely awake and alert, I find myself unable—or maybe unwilling—to go to bed. I try to resume working, but the spell is broken, my focus and drive dissipated. Two a.m. What to do? It occurs to me that I'm not the only one up at this hour. Deacon should be working security tonight, and I haven't spoken much with him since he helped me track down Dr. Pinaro.

I throw on a coat and step into the chilly night air, using the light of my cell phone to guide me. I'll walk to the house, I decide, and if I don't see Deacon, I'll come straight back. Yet as many times as I've made this trek, there's something especially nerve-racking about doing it alone at this hour. The light of my phone telegraphs my where-abouts and renders me blind to anything outside its small, glowing sphere. Beyond this dim circle, there's a blackness deeper than I've ever seen.

Thankfully, as soon as I near the house, Deacon intercepts me. All that high-tech security must've alerted him to the presence of some bumbling stranger. He examines me warily from behind the beam of his high-powered flashlight, much less friendly than he was our last encounter. Understandable. At this hour, criminal intent or mental illness are the only sensible explanations.

"I couldn't sleep," I tell him, doing my best to look both sane and apologetic. "I was just trying to clear my head. Sorry for setting off the cameras."

Having realized I am not an armed intruder, Deacon is magnanimous. "Aw, dat's awright. Ah had a few of dose nights maself. Sometimes yuh mind just gets da best of yuh . . ." He is peering at me.

"Charlotte," I remind him.

"Well, now, Shalit, Ah'd be real careful ramblin' 'round at night when yuh dis close to da bayou. Neva know when a *cocodrie*'s gone go fo' a ramble of 'is own."

"You mean a gator?" I glance around the ground by my feet, but Deacon remains cheerful.

"You stain in a guest 'ohm? I'll walk you ovadaddy."

I can't go back, not if I'm going to pick his brain. "Please. I'm going a little stir-crazy. Is there somewhere I could go sit a bit? To calm down?"

He scratches his frizzy white head and then makes the offer I'm looking for. "Guess you could come back wit me to da carriage house if you lak. Nuttin goin' on, just me keepin' an eye on da cam'ras. But Ah got a pot of coffee an' some doughnuts, if you hungry."

I wonder if it's the smartest move to be following some old man I don't even know to a place no one would ever think to look for me if

I went missing. And at two a.m.! Remnants of my former self—clearly a much more responsible Charlie—berate me for my stupidity. But I do it anyway.

From the outside, the carriage house resembles a four-car garage, but as Deacon leads me through the side door, I see only one car parked here. The rest of the structure houses a variety of tools, bicycles, fitness equipment, and other odds and ends. This is probably all the storage space Evangeline has, I realize. With all the homes in Chicory standing just a dozen feet or so above sea level, I'd wager basements are unheard of.

The carriage-house clutter is actually a reassuring contrast to Evangeline's immaculate interior until I spot the desk and panel of TV screens in the corner. A series of green night-vision images flicker on and off. Cameras blink on at the movement of scurrying animals, tracking them in the dark. It gives me the willies to think of all the times I've appeared on these screens while someone sat bored, observing me.

Deacon hits a few buttons to make sure he hasn't missed anything and then grabs a box of doughnuts off his desk. "Wan one?"

I select something jelly-filled. "So how long have you been working here?" I ask through a mouthful.

"Six yeeahs. Ah did security at da university in Lafayette, but ma daughta lives ova heah."

Six years isn't long enough to know much about the family, let alone the case. This expedition has been a waste. I wander around the carriage house, glancing at flowerpots, a stepladder, some old cans of paint. *Just put in a few minutes of chitchat, then you can get out of here.*

"You like Chicory?"

"Ah lak it well nuff. Worked heah at da mill some yeeahs afta I finished high school, met ma wife heah."

"What mill did you work for?" From the corner of my eye, I watch one of the TV screens, where a fat, unidentifiable animal creeps around.

"Da sugah mill," Deacon says. "Deveau family owned dat, too, but she wasn't makin' nuff money and dey closed 'er down."

I don't remember hearing about a sugar mill before. "When was that?"

"Long time ago." He chugs some coffee from a Styrofoam cup. "Late seventies, maybe? Neville neva did sell da land. Dem buildins still dere. Ah heah da teenajas go drinkin' dere at nights, get chockay."

Before I can pursue this, my eyes fall on something large and wooden propped up behind a treadmill. The hairs on the back of my neck begin to rise. I take a few steps closer, hardly daring to breathe, and confirm my suspicion.

A long, thin rowboat. One I think I've seen before.

"How old's that thing?" I point at it, trying to keep both my voice and my hand steady.

"Dat dere?" Deacon shrugs. "Dunno. Been 'round since Ah rememba. You lookin' to take 'er for a spin?"

I shudder. "No. It—probably leaks."

"Nah," he says, "she's a good'un. Took 'er out in da swamp a couple yeeahs ago. Sometimes yuh wanna boat lak dat, small and quiet. Got right up close to a heron."

Can this really be the boat I dreamed about? The one I sat in with Gabriel? Instinctively, I run my hand over the wooden side, follow the contours of the boat with my fingertips. I feel a faint crackling sensation, a charge that spreads to the palm of my hand. *He's going to show me,* I think. *Somehow he's going to show me.* And he does.

I'm pushing the boat into the water. Trying to hold it steady.

I'm peering over the side. Searching.

Water. Murky. So cold.

Panic.

I withdraw my hand quickly and glance back at Deacon, afraid that my face will betray my shock. He's adjusting one of the cameras, oblivious. I have to talk to Detective Minot, have to tell him what I've found.

This boat. This exact boat, in that swampy area by the dock. And the brown-eyed boy with dark hair and a chipped tooth. Jo-Jo. Gabriel Joseph Deveau. I can feel this object, this place, this person all linked together, a blazing triangle in my mind. And the evil. I can feel the evil, calculated and predatory, seizing me in the guts.

"I want to go home now," I tell Deacon, and then I throw up.

I REFRAIN FROM CALLING Detective Minot until six a.m. He sounds so alert when he answers, I wonder why I bothered waiting.

"Charlotte! I've been thinking about you. I had a big break yesterday." He's speaking so fast I can barely understand him. "Now, you can't use this in the book, you can't breathe a word of it, but—"

"A break? What kind of break?"

"A break in the case!" He's practically shouting. "This could be big. It *is* big. It's major."

"Remy, what happened?" He sounds like an overexcited five-year-old.

"I spoke to Rob Schaffer yesterday, one of the lead FBI agents involved in Gabriel's kidnapping."

"Okay . . ." The name is familiar. Agent Schaffer was quoted in some articles I've read about the case.

"He's in his seventies now. Wife is dead, no kids, lives on an oxygen tank."

I sink down into my mattress, hands jittery with anticipation. "Let me guess. Schaffer suddenly felt the need to confess his sins?"

"He didn't seek me out. I don't think he had a guilty conscience. He just . . . didn't care enough to lie anymore."

I'm getting impatient. "So what did he tell you, exactly?"

"The alibis. I've been telling you all along I thought Neville paid some people off, haven't I?" He breathes a long sigh of satisfaction. "Well, Schaffer was one of them. He fabricated a witness. Neville paid him twenty-five thousand dollars."

Suddenly the exhaustion of the last twenty-four hours I've spent awake evaporates. "Jesus. He just . . . told you this? Over the phone?"

"He lives near Baton Rouge. I went to see him yesterday."

I'm oddly hurt that Detective Minot didn't invite me along. We were just hashing things out together on Wednesday—he could've asked. And I thought I did a pretty good job with Danelle, all things considered. But of course a retired FBI agent would respond better to Detective Minot than to me. I remind myself that I have no real official role in this investigation.

"Wow," I say. "They faked a witness? That is big. Was it the guy who delivered aspirin to Neville and Hettie in their hotel? Because then their alibis—"

"No, the room service guy is a real person," Detective Minot clarifies. "I've got his Social. They could've paid him off, too, I don't know. But he exists. So far Neville and Hettie are still in the clear."

"Then who are we—"

"Andre." Detective Minot pronounces the name with relish. "Agent Schaffer was covering for Andre."

Maybe it's because I just met Andre and liked him or maybe some deeper intuition is at work, but I can't bring myself to believe that Andre killed his little brother. Deceptive, sure. An outright liar? Maybe. But a pedophile and a child killer? No.

If I can trust the sensations I experienced by the dock, then sexual abuse played a part in Gabriel's disappearance. What Danelle said sticks with me. Andre didn't like boys; he liked men. Handsome broody men of about thirty, to be precise. Crushing over Sean Lauchlin and sneaking around with Jules are pretty normal behaviors for a gay man, a far cry from molesting one's two-year-old sibling. And if I'm wrong about the sexual-abuse angle? Andre makes even less sense. He didn't need a million dollars of ransom money, not with the bottomless financial support his parents offered. If Detective Minot is going to sell me on Andre as a suspect, I need something more compelling to go on.

"So Neville paid Schaffer off," I say. "Does that really prove that Andre is guilty?"

"That's a lot of money to shell out if you think your kid is innocent," Detective Minot contends. "Anyway, I didn't tell you Schaffer's explanation. Supposedly, Andre's spent-the-night-with-a-friend story wasn't far from the truth. He says Andre was with a woman that night. A prostitute. That's why Neville wanted to hush it up."

"How would Schaffer know who Andre was with?" I demand.

"Well, that's the story Andre told him, at any rate. That he bailed on the twins' birthday party so he could have a night with a hooker. And Schaffer bought it. He thought he was doing the kid a favor, saving him from embarrassment. He figured if it was a prostitute, they'd have trouble locating the woman for questioning anyway. So he made up a 'friend' to corroborate Andre's whereabouts."

"Maybe Andre *was* with a prostitute that night," I say. "Why are you skeptical?"

"You told me he doesn't even like women."

"He was only eighteen!" It irritates me that Andre's sexuality is being used against him this way. "Maybe he was trying to figure things out, act straight, I don't know."

"I thought you'd be a little more excited." I can tell from Detective Minot's tone that he's starting to agree with me. "I thought we had something . . ."

"Maybe we do." I tell him about the boat I saw in the carriage house, how certain I am that it's connected to Gabriel.

He mulls it over. "The boat's been sitting there for thirty years?"

"No, it's still a working boat."

"So even if we found any physical evidence, which is doubtful, we couldn't prove when or how it got there." Detective Minot lets out a long sigh. "Damn. All these dead ends."

I feign optimism. "Well, you've established that Neville could buy off law enforcement. I still say you should work on that room service guy and see if his story about the aspirin changes any."

"Maybe we're overly focused on the parents. Maybe I need to . . . look at the hired help again." He sounds like he's given up.

Inwardly I curse myself for being so quick to tear apart his theory. I try to pull something from the ashes. "Whoever took Gabriel out on that boat had to have access to the carriage house, right? And familiarity with its contents. That might narrow it down."

"Assuming the boat was stored there in 1982."

"Let's assume it was." I press forward. "Just a hunch, but I don't think a member of the family would've used that rowboat. Not in the dark. So let's look at former employees whose jobs centered around the carriage house. See if we can find someone who dealt with boats, someone who knew the swamps. Groundskeepers, a handyman, whoever." I don't like the idea, but Noah's grandfather would most certainly have had access to both that boat and, given his wife's position, Gabriel. "Maybe we should focus more on Jack Lauchlin."

"Okay. Fine." Detective Minot still reeks of defeat.

"Hey, don't let this get you down. We're close. I really feel we're close."

"That's what's driving me crazy," he says. "I feel like we've got all the pieces. We're just putting them together wrong."

21.

Thank goodness Rae is coming tonight. Amidst all these dead ends, our trip to New Orleans is a bright spot on my horizon. Perhaps a new city and an old friend will get me in a better headspace.

Rain moves in late morning and lingers. Noah and I lounge around his drafty cottage all afternoon, indulging our inner sloths. We're eating grilled cheese and tomato soup when Rae calls from JFK airport to let me know her flight's showing on time. Good news that goes bad within seconds, as I realize we have widely divergent views on our visit.

"I booked a hotel about five miles out of Chicory," Rae informs me, "so I figure we'll get breakfast tomorrow and then you can give me the grand tour of Evangeline."

"Chicory? I thought we were going to New Orleans."

She dismisses our previous plans with maddening carelessness. "I've been to New Orleans a hundred times. You've gotta show me the *real* Louisiana. Seriously, Charlie, I'm psyched to see this house."

It requires incredible restraint to keep from snapping at her. "I just got a lecture from the estate manager this week about not bringing my personal acquaintances on the grounds. If you'd asked me, I would've told you—"

Noah, who has been following my end of the conversation, inter-venes. "I can get her in," he offers.

I can just picture Rae's ears perking up at the sound of a male voice. "Who's that?" she wants to know. "Is someone with you?"

I scramble for an innocuous answer. I haven't told her about Noah yet, and I'm not about to do it with him sitting right here at the table. "The landscaper," I say.

"Listen," Noah tells me, loud enough that Rae can hear, "if your friend wants to visit, I'll talk to security, tell them she works for me."

Rae cheers. "Woo-hoo! See, I knew you had connections."

I glare at Noah. "I thought you were leaving for Texas tomorrow morning. You said you had business stuff to catch up on."

"I'll leave a little later," he says. "No problem."

"Perfect! This is working out!" Rae chirps.

Before I can protest, the PA system begins blaring in the airport. "Looks like we're boarding," she announces. "See you tomorrow, hon!"

I scowl at my phone and then at Noah. He slurps a spoonful of to-mato soup, and I'm not sure if he fails to see my annoyance or is choos-ing to ignore it. "Cool," he says. "I get to meet your friend."

I pick apart my sandwich, still grumpy. "Maybe I don't want you to meet her."

"Why?" he asks. "I'd *like* to meet one of your friends."

"Rae's nosy. She's going to ask a lot of questions about you."

"So?"

"So I don't know what to tell her." I wasn't intending to launch a State of Our Relationship discussion, but that seems to be where we're headed.

"Tell her I'm great in bed," Noah says with a grin, deftly avoiding the issue.

"That's actually more than she needs to know."

"But true, right?" His confidence has come a long way from that first morning when he was so worried about his performance. I guess I've given him enough positive reinforcement at this point.

"Yes." I roll my eyes. "You rock my world."

He smiles and gulps down the last of his soup. "How 'bout you tell her the truth?"

"Which is?"

"You like me, right?"

"Yeah."

"You're happy, right?"

"Yeah."

"I'm happy, too." Noah leans over and nuzzles my neck. I figure we're done talking, and that's fine by me. His breath, his lips, the feeling of his teeth on my ear—they give me goose bumps. The good kind.

He gives my earlobe one final kiss and then settles back in his chair. "You know, I should probably ask, seein' as Carmen and I never worked this one out." His tone is so casual, I'm expecting a throwaway, not the ridiculously monumental question he lays on me. "Where do you stand on the whole kids thing?" From the way he's slung back in his chair polishing off his third sandwich, you'd think the issue was no big deal.

I want to shake him. I want to tell him that children are, in fact, a very big deal. That my child was a big deal.

I know what I'm supposed to say. He told me the night we met that he and his wife of ten years divorced because he changed his mind about having children. If I want to take our relationship to the next level, all I have to do is say, *Kids? I don't want kids.* Which is true. I have no love left to lavish on some small, fragile person who could be here one day and then, without warning, gone the next.

But Keegan matters. Losing Keegan matters. My four years as his mother will define me, at least in part, for the rest of my life, and Noah will never understand.

"Looks like I threw you off a bit there," he observes. "Sorry. I'm gettin' ahead a myself."

"Way ahead." I fold my arms, not allowing myself to cry. I can't explain about my son. Won't even try. "At this stage, Noah, maybe let's talk about our plans for the weekend, not the rest of our lives. We're only three weeks in."

He calculates quickly on his fingers. "Damn, you're right. Feels longer."

"Well, it's not. It's three weeks." I don't know why I'm getting snippy with him. I dated Eric about a month before deciding I wanted to marry him, and we discussed having children the second date. It's not the speed Noah's moving at but the territory he's trying to cover. "I'm going back to my place for a bit." I'm already moving toward the door. "I should wrap up a chapter before I see Rae tomorrow."

Noah furrows his brow. "You okay? Didn't mean to freak you out."

"I'm fine." My hand is on the doorknob.

"You want me to come by later?"

What began as a drizzle has now turned to a full-fledged downpour. Still, the rain remains more appealing than hanging around Noah's apartment while I'm on the brink of a breakdown. "I'll call you," I promise before sprinting off.

But I don't.

I MEET RAE at a Waffle House (her guilty vacation pleasure) the next morning and we exchange all the customary hugs and greetings. Rae's a good-looking woman anywhere, but the suede jacket, leather boots, and perfectly coiffed curls attract more than the average amount of attention in a southern Louisiana Waffle House. From the looks of more than one patron, waffles aren't the only mouthwatering items in the restaurant today.

"A month here, and you already look better," Rae tells me, ignoring the leers. "Less scary skinny. You came to the right state to fatten up."

I slide into one of the booths. "How's Zoey?"

"She misses you. Asks about you all the time."

Given how long I've known Zoey, my sudden absence from her life feels inexcusable. I should've called. At least sent a postcard. Before I can apologize, though, Rae drops the question she's doubtless been dying to ask since we talked yesterday.

"So who's this landscaper guy?" Really, the woman should work for the *National Enquirer* or TMZ. She has an uncanny ability to sniff out a story.

I'm a terrible liar, but I do my best to play it off. "You mean Noah? He's doing work at Evangeline."

"Is he cute?"

I deliberately misinterpret her. "This is Louisiana, not Vegas. You're married, remember?"

"Yes, happily and boringly married." She laughs. "I've gotta live vicariously. So is he cute or is he, like, a hundred years old?"

In a more reputable establishment, a waitress would come to get our orders. The lone Waffle House waitress, however, is speaking in hushed tones with one of the cooks. She's large and blocky with the kind of sour, world-weary expression normally reserved for mug shots. I don't dare wave her over.

"He's okay, nothing special." I shrug. "Not really your type."

"So he's young," Rae says. "Are you guys, what, friends? You hang out?"

"I guess. You're making it sound way more exciting than it is." I'm doing an amazing job at appearing blasé, but then Rae pulls her signature game-ending move, the Long Stare.

After about a minute, I start to squirm. "What? Why are you looking at me like that?"

She doesn't answer, just looks.

"Jesus, Rae, it's just a guy! Why are you so stuck on him?"

I don't know what in this whole exchange gives me away, but her mouth drops open and she stares at me in shocked delight. "You *bitch!*" She shakes a finger at me. "You slept with him, didn't you?"

Poor Zoey, I think. *I can only imagine what your teenage years will be like living with this.* I glance around at the other Waffle House customers, but no one else seems to care who I've been sleeping with.

Rae's rocking back and forth, half-covering her grin with one hand. I can't remember the last time I saw her this happy. "Well, hallelujah, Charlotte Cates, you've been making it with the gardener. God is good." She thumps the table with her fist. "That's like a porno, hooking up with the hired help."

"I'm the hired help, too, remember? And maybe you can lower your voice."

Rae discounts this last plea entirely and stands up, flagging down our ex-con waitress. "When you get a minute, can I buy this lady some breakfast?" she calls, and casts one quick, beaming glance back at me. "We've got a lot to celebrate this morning."

I'M HOPING THAT Evangeline's security will give Rae a hard time, but the guy barely looks at her driver's license. Noah must have got to him. It's the best kind of morning, sun streaming through the trees, everything a vibrant green after yesterday's rain, air rich with the smell of the bayou. Not bad for end-of-January weather. Rae hops out of the car, already gushing about the beauty of the home.

I'm a little nervous. Jules wouldn't normally be around on a Sunday, yet with Andre home and the state of their relationship seemingly in flux, all bets are off. Andre seemed quite personable, but I don't know if that extends to my traipsing through his home with my Northeastern acquaintances. Before I can explain these complexities to Rae, Isaac calls. He must've received the chapters I sent him last night.

"I have to take this call from my editor," I tell Rae. "Feel free to look around the garden."

She wanders off and I catch up with Isaac, who, to my enormous relief, wants me to continue with my hybrid nonfictional fiction approach. He still has some misgivings, he tells me, and it will never fit into the *Greatest Mysteries* series. Nevertheless, he advises me to follow my instincts. We hash through some of my chapters, and when I eventually end the call, I discover that a full half hour has elapsed.

As I mentally craft an apology to Rae, I catch sight of something frightening in the garden. It's Rae. Chatting animatedly. With Noah.

Not good.

I hurry over, trying to assess from their faces the level of damage control I need to do. How long have they been talking, and what exactly has she let slip? Has she mentioned Keegan?

"Hey." My smile is more flustered than friendly. "I take it you two introduced yourselves?"

"Quit sweating bullets," Rae says. "We've been having a nice little chat. Don't worry. I didn't tell him what you look like without your makeup on."

"She didn't," Noah affirms, although he has seen me without makeup plenty of times by now. "I was just telling her about the garden." He studies me, uncertain, and I remember with a guilty twinge that I did blow him off last night.

"Your boy's got big plans," Rae says. "This place will really be something." Her use of "your boy" doesn't escape me, but I let it slide. Perhaps I am compartmentalizing a wee bit much if a conversation between my best friend and boyfriend-ish person sets me into such a tailspin.

"Glad I got to meet you, Rae," Noah says. "I'm gonna hit the road now. Probably won't be back until Thursday." He leans close to me for a hug and whispers, "Sorry 'bout yesterday. That was my bad."

Then he's Texas-bound. I turn to Rae, suddenly anxious for her approval. He isn't much, not by the metrics she and I have always used. I think of the guys she set me up with after my divorce: Tom, a stockbroker who retired in his midthirties, and Elliott, whose uncanny resemblance to Richard Gere rendered me tongue-tied and blushy for the entirety of our one date. I want her to like Noah, but I can't help but see the college degree he never earned, the gun he keeps in his sock drawer, his failure to enunciate words ending in -*ing*.

Rae, however, proves a kinder judge than I. "That is a nice man," she declares. "And that cute little Texas accent, my God. Does he wear a cowboy hat to bed?"

I OPT NOT TO GO inside Evangeline. There's been enough drama for one day—why invite more by setting up a potential Jules confrontation? Rae, surprisingly, doesn't argue. The tiny glimpse into my sex life was probably more exciting for her than a bunch of antique furniture, anyway. I do show her my cottage, and we bask in the awfulness of the lavender color scheme. Then it's off to town, where we tour Main Street and scarf down some jambalaya and shrimp étouffée at a price that wouldn't buy you a bowl of oatmeal in Manhattan. Running low on ideas, I suggest the Rail and River Museum. Rae, at last satisfied that Chicory is as boring as I've been telling her, whips out her iPhone and books us a hotel in the French Quarter.

The drive is peaceful, miles upon miles of highway through areas that vary mainly in their degree of swampiness. Sometimes the trees are tall and scraggly. Sometimes the land is flat and watery. We cross the occasional bridge, pass dilapidated shacks and rotting docks. I tell

Rae about the people I've met, doing my best approximation of Deacon's thick Cajun accent. She chatters about the incredible food in New Orleans.

Through it all, like a persistent and annoying hum, thoughts of Gabriel linger. Detective Minot is right. We have the pieces of this puzzle. We're just coming at it from the wrong angle. The boy. The swamp. The boat. If I put these three things together, who do they point to? By the time we make it to the city, my head is spinning and I can't wait to get out of the car.

It's about four, so after checking into our hotel, Rae gives me a quick walking tour of the French Quarter while we still have some daylight. A few blocks and I'm swooning. The buildings are old and charming and colorful, distinctly European in feel. I love the narrow roads, the quaint storefronts, the balconies adorned with hanging plants and beads.

"It's Mardi Gras season," Rae explains. "The parades are starting up next weekend. Trust me, this city will be *crazy*."

We drop into some galleries and antique shops, ogle restaurant menus, and meander around Jackson Square, admiring the cathedral and the work of local artists. After a mouthwatering dinner, I can see why Andre would choose the bustling French Quarter as his home base, especially when Rae mentions the area has tons of gay bars. Whether or not Andre actually frequents them, it's probably the least homophobic area in the state.

We're making our way back toward our hotel when Rae grabs my arm and begs, "Oh, please can we?"

It takes me a few seconds to figure out what she's so excited about, and then I groan. A shop window with an orange neon sign that reads PSYCHIC ADVISER. Is she serious? But it's Rae. Of course she is. The woman checks her horoscope every day.

Ordinarily, I would put my foot down, but after everything I've experienced, I'm curious. Does this so-called psychic actually have an ability, or is it really a scheme, as I've always assumed? And if she *can* see things, how did she learn to harness her ability? If ever there was a time to believe in fortune-tellers, it's here on the dim, lamp-lit streets of the French Quarter.

"Okay," I say. "One condition. You don't give the psychic any hints. No matter what they say, you just nod and go with it. And I get to watch, to make sure you're playing fair."

Rae accepts my terms, and so we walk over to the shop and push open the door. It's just one tiny room with a table and two worn-out red love seats. A young, dark-skinned man slouches on one love seat, legs resting on the table. He looks up from a magazine when we enter and tries to assume a slightly more respectable position, but posture isn't the only thing working against him. He's got a row of earrings in his right ear, purple glitter on his eyelids, and an orange shirt that hugs his long, skinny frame. He looks like he'd rather be at a club, dancing and blowing kisses to straight boys. And he's so young. What does *he* know, psychic or not?

He quickly tucks away his reading material—a costume catalog—and comes to greet us, but not before I see the page of cop outfits he was checking out. Mardi Gras is coming. This week the entire population of New Orleans is probably making a mad dash for the stripper costume of their choice.

Rae seems willing to give him the benefit of the doubt. "Hi!" she says cheerily. "My friend and I would like readings."

"You ladies got lucky," he says. "Most nights my aunt workin' this place, but you got me tonight, and I got twice her gift, not even braggin'. My name is RaJean. Cost you twen'y-five dollas for fifteen minutes. Which a you ladies gone go first?"

I have to admit the flamboyantly gay drawl is pretty cute, but I'm still not sold on his dispensing advice. "We'll go together," I say.

"Betta luck one-on-one," he informs us, "so I'm gettin' pure you, no competin' energies. You *sure* you wan' do togetha?"

Rae hesitates, but I remain firm. "I'm sure."

"'Kay, then." RaJean taps the empty love seat, inviting us to sit down. "Juss gone get centered." Sitting cross-legged, he closes his eyes and extends his hands. He inhales, rolls his wrists around in little circles, lifts his shoulders and drops them back. Finally, he opens his eyes and stares right at me. A creepy stare, like he's reading cue cards behind me.

"I see a man," he tells me. "Tall, dark, and yummy, mm-mm."

Well, that rules out Noah.

"But you . . . you ain't puttin' in the work you need to with him. You takin' him for granted." RaJean shakes a finger in my direction, but he's still looking through me, not at me. "I know he been around a long time, but that don't mean you get to quit workin', understand?"

I almost pity this kid. There has never been a man in my life who stuck around a long time. Even my dad was halfheartedly there at best, his mind always on alcohol, and I put in a *lot* of work with him.

RaJean squints and touches his temple. "I'm feelin' a little girl. A daughta, maybe?"

I nod, poker-faced, like I instructed Rae to do.

No feedback. Just run with whatever he says.

"You wish you got more time with her, but somethin's in the way." He blinks a few times. Slow, purple glitter blinks. "A job. It's wearin' on you, hmm? Well, the good news is, I'm seein' a change." He claps his hands together, grinning. "You got a promotion comin', honey!"

The reading continues, none of it applying to me whatsoever. My eyes wander the old wood floor and the exposed brick wall, embarrassed for him.

Rae, on the other hand, leans forward, glued to his every word—trying to twist it around until it bears some possible relevance to my life, no doubt.

Finally RaJean stops and takes a deep breath. "Well, I hope that helped you some."

I smile and nod, but I'm actually depressed by this. I wanted him to know what he was doing, to make me feel less freakish, but there's nothing mystical going on here. Just a guy out to take our money.

RaJean looks to Rae now, frowns, and closes his eyes. "There's all kinds a darkness 'round you," he murmurs. "You like a foggy night, tryin' to shut me out."

I almost laugh out loud. Rae, shutting someone out? A woman who drops intimate details of her husband's sexual proclivities into casual conversation?

"Oh, honey," RaJean coos, clutching at his own heart. "You hurtin'. You hurtin' *bad*."

Rae looks directly at me then and her face is so sober, so sad, I wonder if this guy sees a part of her that I don't.

"You just lost the love a yo' life now, did'n you? You poor thing. And you think that's it, game ova. But you wrong. You dead wrong." RaJean slaps his thigh for emphasis. "Life has got somethin' in store for you, somethin' *serious*, hear? You got a higher purpose in this world." He cranes his neck forward, peering just beyond Rae's left shoulder. "Well, lookit that! A new love come knockin' at yo' door. Gone sweep you off yo' feet, this one. I'm feelin' March. And don't you worry, 'cause this time it's gone last."

Where does he *get* this stuff? Romance novels? Self-help books?

"Now, I gotta warn you," he continues, "I'm feelin' this shadowy presence. Somebody you thinkin' you wanna trust. A man. He sayin' all the right things, lovin' on you so nice. But you not gettin' the whole story with that one. He ain't who you think. Oh no. Ain't who you think at all."

Seventy-five dollars and a profuse exchange of thank-yous later, we finally extract ourselves from RaJean's psychic clutches. You'd think

Rae's spirits would be dampened by his woefully off-base readings. Instead, she brims with admiration.

"That was amazing," she raves. "It was *so* dead-on!"

I step aside as a cluster of tipsy students brush past us like a giant, brainless amoeba. "Which part? The long-suffering man in my life, or the bit about my daughter?"

Rae stops walking and crosses her arms. "All those things are true, you idiot. For *me*."

She's right, I realize. But I'm not prepared to let RaJean off the hook this easily. "So, what, you think he just mixed us up?"

"He told us not to get our readings done together, didn't he?"

I try to remember what he told Rae. Something about losing the love of her life. Which hardly applies to me, given that Eric and I split up more than two years ago and I'm not sure I even loved him. But.

My throat tightens as I finally understand. Because Keegan was, without question, the love of my life.

"He saw a new love knocking at your door," Rae reminds me, grasping at something positive.

"And he saw a sweet-talking guy I shouldn't trust." I sigh.

"Oh no, hon," she protests, "Noah's the new love, not the sweet-talking guy."

I want to believe her, except RaJean said the new love wouldn't show up until March. As in, I haven't met him yet. I don't want to fall prey to a scam artist barely old enough to purchase alcohol, but what if RaJean is right about Noah?

He ain't who you think. Oh no. Ain't who you think at all.

"I don't care what he said," I tell Rae. "You know I don't believe in that crap." I point to the next cross street. "Isn't that the way to our hotel?"

In some secret part of me, though, I do care. I've been played before, by Eric of all people. There's nothing about Noah I know for sure, only what he's told me. On the other hand, I'm happy. And happiness is such a fleeting, fragile thing, why would I go looking under rocks for something to spoil it?

Maybe happiness is nothing more than the wisdom to remain ignorant.

BY MORNING, I'M EAGER to continue exploring the city. Rae takes me on the St. Charles streetcar and I get a peek at the Garden District, Tulane and Loyola, Audubon Park. It's a sunny seventy degrees, so we hop off the trolley and wander the wealthy neighborhoods, gawking at the sprawling historic homes. The trees and gates are already draped with beads, and I find myself succumbing to the excitement.

"I think I've got to experience the whole Mardi Gras thing," I tell Rae.

"Totally," she agrees. "You won't get New Orleans until you've seen it." She smiles sideways at me. "Bring Noah."

The rest of our day is lovely and leisurely, and it occurs to me that this is the first real traveling I've done since Keegan was born. How many times did I lament the stationary life motherhood imposed on me? How many times did I wish I could pack up a suitcase and get away for a weekend? Suddenly my freedom makes me feel guilty.

I leave the city the next morning so Rae can attend her business meetings. "Tell Mason thank you," I say. "For letting you come early. Tell him it meant a lot to me."

I time the drive back to Chicory, thinking of Neville and Hettie and Andre. When I more or less obey speed limits, it takes just under three hours to get from New Orleans to Evangeline. Someone in a hurry could shave a bunch of time off that, especially in the middle of the night.

With Rae busy and Noah in Texas, I feel unexpectedly lonely. I work awhile, take a long shower, lie in bed and watch a string of mindless TV shows.

Without even trying, I drift over. Recognition, surrender, submergence. All faster this time, because I'm getting a feel for it. Like riding a wave, allowing something murky and powerful to carry me over to the other side. Then I emerge, clear-eyed, blinking away the sun.

Farmland. I'm standing on a long soil path, wedged between two rows of crops. Grassy and thin at the tops, the plants tower over me, obscuring my view of anything else. Their stalks are long and thick and hard like bamboo. Above me, blue skies. A few wispy clouds. I follow the crop line, searching for a way out, but it's just dense plantings as far as the eye can see.

Then, without warning, the field behind me lights up. Fire, hot and hungry, moves toward me in a wave. Smoke billows up as the flames consume the grassy tops of the plants. I run down the dirt path, away from the smoke, but the fire travels with me, flanking me on each side, leaving only the fat stalks in its wake.

Sugarcane, I realize, shielding my nose and mouth from the smoke. This is a controlled burn.

I turn and see a boy in overalls jogging toward me, framed for an instant by the blazing fields. Black. About ten years old. Barefoot.

Suddenly, as if someone has blown out a candle, the fire dies. Orange embers drift to the ground and flicker harmlessly out. We're awash in smoke, dark plumes rising up, lifting chunks of ash into the air. When I pinch my nose, I discover the insides of my nostrils are coated in black dust.

The boy continues confidently toward me, unfazed by smoke or fire. As he gets closer, I notice something wrong with his skin. A bumpy, reddish rash that is especially intense around his cheeks and in the creases of his elbows, though it covers much of his lean body.

He smiles impishly and opens his mouth to display a startling crimson tongue. The unnatural shade of red, coupled with an array of little white bumps, calls to mind a grotesque strawberry.

I had the feva, he says, pointing to his tongue. *Me and my sista, both.*

I take stock of his rash. Is he talking about scarlet fever? Why would anyone in a country with plentiful antibiotics have scarlet fever? I wave away the last of the smoke and draw in a breath of air.

What's your name? I ask, hoping to avoid the investigative work that my dream about Didi Minot required.

Clifford, he tells me, hands on hips.

And your last name?

Don' matta.

If I don't know who you are, I might not be able to help you, I warn him.

You got it all wrong, lady, he laughs. *I'm long gone. Ain't nothin' you can do for me. I'm fixin' to help you.* He holds up an index finger and moves it in a little circle. *Look around yuh.*

The tall stalks of sugarcane have disappeared. Only a couple inches of cut stalks rise out of the soil, giving me a clear view in every direction. Now I can make out a distant line of road, a faraway cluster of rusted white buildings with tall, industrial-looking chimney stacks. I begin walking toward the buildings. They feel important.

I been here a long, long time, Clifford says, scampering to keep up with me. *I seen things.*

Yeah? What have you seen?

You lookin' for him, ain'tcha? I stop in my tracks, and he nods sagely, satisfied that he's got my full attention. *Nobody found him, but you lookin'. Come on, I'll show you the place.*

A coldness spreads through my body, moving inward from my limbs. Everything's slow. He's going to take me to Gabriel. I hunt for a geographic landmark, something I can use later. Apart from the white buildings, though, there's just open land.

Okay, I say. *Let's go.*

Clifford holds out a hand to me. *Gone be dark.*

I lay my palm across his, grasp his fingers, and then everything vanishes. The farmland, the blue skies.

I've lost it.

How could I get so close and walk away with nothing? But it's not nothing, I see now. The boy is still beside me, holding my hand in the dark. Around us, giant, shadowy structures loom. I reach out gingerly with my free hand. Beneath a layer of dust and grime, I feel metal. Machinery, perhaps? I touch the ground. Concrete. We must be inside the buildings with the chimney stacks I saw before. The only light comes from a broken window to the left, something outside shining in. I think I know where we are now, but I don't understand how Gabriel could be here. What about the swamp and the boat?

Clifford? I whisper, squeezing his hand. *Is this right? Are we—*

Some kids come with a dog last night, he says. *Been a lotta years, a lotta animals, but one a they dogs found a piece a him. He drug it in here.*

I can't chicken out now. I'm standing in a room with Gabriel's remains, and I will find them, damn it.

Where is he? I croak. *Show me.*

You holdin' him, Clifford says.

Only then do I realize that it's not Clifford's hand I'm holding at all. It's bone.

I FUMBLE FOR MY PHONE before my eyes are fully open. The lights in the cottage are still on, blindingly bright, and the television plays on mute. I dial Detective Minot's number without bothering to check the time. He'd better answer or I'm driving over there, throwing rocks at his window, setting off every burglar alarm in his neighborhood.

He picks up on the seventh ring with a groggy "Yeah?"

"It's Charlie. I need your help." I can't remember the last time I asked anyone for help, certainly not in the middle of the night, yet Detective Minot doesn't hesitate.

"Tell me how."

I try to get a handle on my shivering. "You know the old sugar mill that the Deveau family owned? The one that closed in the seventies? I need you to take me there."

"The sugar mill," he repeats. "You think we'll find something important?"

"I think we'll find *him*." My stomach clenches as I say the words. "I think we'll find Gabriel."

PART III

chicory, louisiana

FEBRUARY

22.

Sitting in the passenger seat of the Impala, I can't stop shivering. The heater is cranked up and Detective Minot has given me a blanket he normally reserves for shock victims, but I'm still freezing. We're parked in a lot outside the old mill. It's four a.m., pitch-black except for the weak beam of the car's headlights.

"Do you want me to go in alone?" he asks. "Tell me where, I'll go."

But I don't want him to leave. I pull the blanket closer to my body. "Give me a minute."

"I'll take you to my house," Detective Minot says. His voice is calm, but from the way he's gripping the steering wheel, he's losing his patience. "You can stay with Justine. Just tell me what to look for."

I stall for time. "Maybe we should wait until it's light out."

"If you saw the place in the dark, this is what you'll recognize. Which is why I'd prefer to have you with me."

"Don't you need a warrant? I mean, aren't we trespassing?"

He shakes his head. "This land is being leased by Strickland Organics. They've called the police department over here a bunch of times. It's a party spot."

"Yeah, I heard that." Even Deacon knew that much.

"Kids are kids. They'll mess with farm equipment if you give them half a chance." He shrugs. "Anyway, Deenie Strickland is used to officers checking on the place. She's asked us to do it."

I follow the beam of the headlights with my eyes. The graying building in front of us has orange graffiti on its exterior, a broken window, and a cluster of beer bottles on the ground. After thirty years, shouldn't one of these teenagers have seen something by now?

Why me? Why on this particular night? I can't shake the feeling that someone—or something—has orchestrated this all.

"Maybe we won't find anything," I say hopefully.

"You sounded mighty sure on the phone."

"Well, now I'm not."

"You're just scared."

His dismissive tone pisses me off. "I have a *right* to be scared. Maybe you're used to seeing the worst of people, but I'm not. Maybe I don't want to see some poor little boy scattered around the—"

"Shut up and listen to me." In the dark, Detective Minot's face is especially haggard, his eyes wild. "I don't know about God, but I know about you. I know you've got an ability nobody else has got. I'm sorry it scares you, but you need to go in there."

"I don't know," I whimper.

But he's no longer listening to me. "Hey." He turns to me, awed. "Do you see what time it is?"

I glance at the digital clock on the dashboard. Four sixteen.

"That's when Didi died," he murmurs. "Right when you told me. That's your message, do you understand? Four sixteen. From Didi. Now get out of the damn car."

I open the door, put a reluctant foot on the pavement. Detective Minot comes around with two huge flashlights and presents me with one. It's surprisingly heavy, something you could use as a weapon in a pinch. Only moderately comforting when the things you're most terrified of have no flesh or form at all.

My bad feelings only grow as we approach the main building. I don't like the fact that Gabriel didn't come to me himself. Why did this Clifford kid get involved? If he died of scarlet fever, he must have lived in a time before antibiotics. Why suddenly appear to help me? And what he told me is in direct conflict with what Gabriel himself communicated about the swamp and the boat. Something isn't adding up. I tell myself that dead children don't set traps for the living, don't lure them to remote places with evil intentions, but what the hell do I know? Maybe that's exactly what they do.

Detective Minot leaves his headlights on and walks around the perimeter of the building until he finds a door. I'm on his heels, as near as possible without actually stepping on him.

"Does this look familiar?" he asks. "There're a few buildings, but this is the biggest."

"I didn't see it from the outside. I won't know until we're in."

Detective Minot jerks the door open and gestures for me to go first. I shoot him a dirty look. "Hell no."

I follow him in and we sweep our flashlights around the space: high ceilings with metal rafters, piping in every direction, stairs and narrow catwalks, and huge, rusted gears. A large but cramped space that must have housed many workers. I make my way through the building, ducking under pipes, my eyes on the ground. There's rubble, scraps of metal, soda cans, and wrappers. Nothing resembling bone. I'm not even convinced this is the right building until I see a broken window on the far wall, the one we saw from the car. The Impala's headlights shine through from the parking lot, and I remember this window in my dream, the light shining in, its placement relative to my position.

I grab Detective Minot's arm. "See that window?" I drag him over to what feels like the right general area. "Check around here."

We drop to our knees and shine our flashlights in slow lines across the cement floor. The machinery casts odd shadows, making a wadded-up napkin look highly suspicious.

Detective Minot finds something wedged behind a steel post and pulls out a fast-food container. He whips it to the ground in annoyance.

I try to recall exactly what I saw in my vision. I know I was holding bone, but I don't think I saw it, really. I just *knew*, I just *felt* what it was. My mind keeps returning to what Clifford said about a dog dragging a piece of Gabriel in, and I shudder.

Detective Minot is still groping around the floor, totally focused, and I feel a wave of uncertainty. *Are we really in the right place?* I glance back at the window and my stomach lurches. Detective Minot yells, "Holy shit!"

Someone is watching us through the window. A face I know.

Then he's gone, so fast I'd think I were imagining things if Detective Minot hadn't also reacted.

"You saw him," I whisper. My heart is straining against my rib cage. "You saw him, too, right?"

"Saw who?" Detective Minot aims his flashlight at the door. "You saw someone?"

"At the window! Didn't *you*? You screamed."

"Look what turned up under a McDonald's bag."

I can't see well, but the item in the palm of his hand appears to have a tooth.

"Jawbone," he murmurs.

"Oh Jesus." My eyes fill up with tears.

Detective Minot tucks the bone fragment into his pocket and looks over at the window. "Now, are you saying there's someone outside?"

Is my mind playing tricks on me? It must've been.

"I thought . . . I thought I saw a man."

"Let's go look." His hand hovers by his waist, ready to draw his gun, and I realize I'm not the only one who's totally spooked.

We wind back through the building, squeezing past equipment until we make it to the door.

Back in the parking lot, the Impala is exactly as we left it. Detective Minot checks beneath the car and points his light at the backseat but finds no murderous psychos lying in wait.

"We would've heard a car drive up," he says. "I guess someone could be in one of the other buildings. You wanna look?"

"No," I say quickly. "I must've been seeing things. Forget it."

"Maybe you were having one of your visions." He opens the car door for me.

"It was an adult. In the visions, I've only ever seen kids."

"Oh. What did he look like?"

"He looked . . ." Like Noah, I want to say. That expressionless, watchful face looked an awful lot like Noah. But it couldn't be. Noah's in Texas. And why on earth would he be roaming around the sugar mill at night? "It doesn't matter. Let's just go. This place is messing with my head."

We say little as we pull away from the mill, but I'm sure Detective Minot is wondering the same things that I am. Did Gabriel die out here, or was the sugar mill just a dump site? What does the location tell us about Gabriel's killer, and how do the swamp and the boat fit in? Where is the rest of the body? Does the mill hold any other clues? I lean against the car window and watch the stars.

"What will you tell them at the station?"

He's obviously been working this one out in his head. "That I stopped by the mill to make sure no one was getting into trouble and found a bone. That I want an expert to give it a look, tell us if it's human or animal."

"And when it's human? What happens next?"

"There'll be a search. If the Deveaus don't consent, we'll get a warrant."

"You can prove that bone belonged to Gabriel," I say. "A lab could extract the DNA and run the genetic profile against a sample from Hettie." My time at *Cold Crimes* taught me a lot about the sorry state of government-run forensic labs. I'm aware that this process could take months, maybe longer.

Detective Minot is about to say something, then thinks better of it. "We'll see what happens, Charlotte. I'll let you know how it all plays out." He pats my shoulder without looking away from the road. "You came through tonight. Thank you."

We both know I'd never have faced that mill alone, and he was the one who found something, not me.

"Remy," I tell him softly, "you came through tonight, too."

THE SECURITY GUARD at Evangeline is puzzled when I return a little after five a.m. "Didn't think I'd see you again today," he says as he logs me in. "You left so early, I figured you had a flight to catch."

I ignore his unspoken question. Apparently the security personnel, unlike the help, have not been trained to mind their own business. Once inside the gate, I park and hustle back to my cottage. The grounds are especially unsettling this dark morning. He was here once, alive. Playing. Making mischief. And then somebody took him away. Stole him from his bed in the night, brought him to that awful mill, and did who-knows-what unspeakable things before they killed him. He wasn't even three years old. Now he's just bone.

I turn on every light in the cottage, but I'm shaking again, can't stop. I can no longer distinguish between paranoia and well-founded fear.

Where is Noah when I need him, damn it? He's in Texas, I tell myself. *He'll be back tomorrow.*

Unless that was Noah I saw in the window tonight. But why would he lie about going to Texas? Why would he be prowling around the site of Gabriel's body?

You not gettin' the whole story with that one. RaJean's words haunt me. *He ain't who you think.*

I can't be alone right now, I realize. I'll go crazy. As soon as Leeann arrives, I head up to the house. She buys my story about a nightmare and makes me warm milk with honey and vanilla. The steaming mug proves moderately comforting, and when Benny, Bailey, and the big-bellied Paulette all file in for breakfast, the scene is so normal, I can almost forget what I've seen.

Paulette is due March first, just a month away. She no longer walks; she lumbers. I don't know how she manages to clean the house anymore—at that stage of pregnancy, I was too tired to load a plate in the dishwasher.

From her conversation with Leeann, though, it's clear she's more worried about *not* working. "Bailey, she come two weeks early," Paulette says. "Lord knows, we can't afford that again. I'm prayin' every night this baby stay in. We need those paychecks."

Benny nods heavily and Leeann mentions some kind of state assistance program she went on after having her son. I listen to their financial woes, grateful my days of sharing crappy studio apartments with a roommate are over. My mother came from nothing, but my father was raised solidly middle-class, and with a college education, I knew that if I could handle some lean years, I'd eventually move onward and upward. But what opportunities do Paulette and Leeann really have? When Hettie dies and Evangeline goes to the historical association, what will become of them?

I choke down some eggs and let Bailey tell me about her baby brother. She will feed him bottles, she says, but she will *not* share toys because babies break things. She asks why I'm not married. I'm about to navigate the minefield topic of divorce when Jules hurries into the kitchen looking uncharacteristically rumpled.

"I thought I'd give you all fair warning," he says. "Sydney called. She and Brigitte just left New Orleans. This house needs to be spotless when they get here, so use your time wisely."

Leeann looks a little queasy. "They stayin' all week?"

"They'll be visiting their mother indefinitely," Jules says grimly. "You're responsible for weekday meals, as per usual. I suggest you put together a menu before they get here."

Leeann rubs her temples and exhales. The wrath of the twins, particularly Brigitte, is legendary amongst Evangeline's staff. Paulette and Benny are already scraping their plates, trying to hustle Bailey out of the kitchen.

"Paulette." Jules's voice is a warning, but not unkind. "You know she's looking for a reason to get rid of you. Don't give her any."

Paulette nods, and then Jules is gone, presumably covering his own ass before the sisters arrive.

"What was that about?" I ask. "Why would they want to get rid of you?"

She gestures to her belly, tired.

I frown. "You know that's illegal, right? If an employer terminates you because of pregnancy, you could file a lawsuit."

Paulette smiles faintly. "Sure I could."

It is, I realize, one of the dumber things I've uttered. Even if Paulette could afford a lawyer, she'd be up against the bottomless pockets of the Deveau empire. My own middle-class white privilege makes me cringe. I duck out of the kitchen and pass into the foyer, where Jules is reading a piece of mail.

The study door opens and Andre, in a swanky blue bathrobe, peers out. Barring Hugh Hefner, it's the only time I've actually seen a guy in a bathrobe.

"Jules," he calls, "can I see you in the office?"

"Certainly." Jules folds up the letter and heads in. I can hear the door lock behind them.

Despite their outward nonchalance, I have the feeling that things are about to heat up in there. They must've made up. That would explain the wrinkles in Jules's shirt, his less-than-perfect hair. He *is* here awfully early—maybe he never left last night. I'm glad for Andre. He seemed like he needed a pick-me-up.

I leave the house before I hear any telltale sounds from the study. There are, as it turns out, limits to what I want to know about Evangeline's goings-on.

WITH THE BONE now in the hands of local law enforcement, I decide to do a little digging on Noah's mother. I need something to occupy myself with, to keep me from obsessing over the sugar mill, and Violet Johnson has been kicking around in my mind for a while. She was involved with Sean Lauchlin, once worked at Evangeline, and could well have been an accomplice to whatever pulled in Sean's half-million dollars.

As a former Deveau employee, Violet's name must've come up during the Gabriel investigation, so I start with a call to Detective Minot.

"Violet Johnson?" His voice is devoid of recognition. "I think I've seen the name in our files, but I don't think she was ever under investigation. Why? You find something?"

"I heard she might've been involved with Sean Lauchlin. Just . . . covering my bases." I don't want to tell him about Noah just yet, don't want him sniffing around the only remaining Lauchlin for answers. Noah was upset enough when he felt I was violating Hettie's privacy. I can only imagine how aggravated he'd be if I pointed law enforcement in *his* direction and they began dredging up details of his family that he's already told me he doesn't care to know.

I put in a call to the vital records registry and learn that in Louisiana, birth certificates are not public record for one hundred years, death certificates not for fifty. Only a relative could obtain Violet Johnson's records—assuming she *has* records. I don't know if she was born in Louisiana or if she's even really dead. There's no trace of her on the Internet, so I head for the library and spend the remainder of my day perusing microfiches, town archives, even yearbooks from the local high school. Nothing. I'm on my way out, discouraged and increasingly anxious, when my phone vibrates.

"Hey," Noah says. "It's me. Listen, I got some bad news."

I don't like the sound of this.

"One of our big projects just hit some road bumps. I'm gonna need some extra time to sort this out."

"You won't be back tomorrow then?"

"Prob'ly not 'til next week," he concedes.

There is a sizable lump in my throat as I digest this.

"I'm sorry, babe . . . I miss you. How's everything goin'?"

"It's going." I try not to sound as lost as I feel. "But come back soon."

"I will. Promise."

As soon as I hang up, the full weight of this day comes crashing down on me. I came to Chicory to help Gabriel. Was that one measly bone all he wanted from me? Am I done? Maybe the police can put the pieces together now, maybe not. All I can do is wait. But waiting is hard for me, especially with Noah gone. I'm not going to make it through these next days without some support. Who can I turn to?

I want someone who knows where I'm coming from, someone I don't have to explain it all to. I need more than a ten-minute phone call with Grandma will solve. Leeann's too young. She doesn't even know about Keegan. Detective Minot will be tied up in the case, and he's not a warm and fuzzy guy anyway. When I freaked out at the sugar mill this morning, he tried to pawn me off on his wife.

His wife.

Who else is better positioned to understand me? We're grieving mothers. And she knows about the things I've seen. She believes in me.

If I were comfortable reaching out to others, I would not be the woman I am today. I would have more friends. I might still be married. I would most certainly be happier. At this point, though, I'm so far out of my comfort zone, it doesn't sound all that crazy to just dial a number and foist myself upon someone I barely know. To say, *Hi, this is Charlotte Cates. I need someone to talk to, and I'm hoping it's you.*

So I do it. I call Detective Minot's home phone, and she answers. Justine Pinaro. Didi's mother. And she listens. And she tells me, "Please, come right over. I'm so glad you called."

For the first time since Keegan died, I see the only way through this, the only way forward. It's not by hiding, or avoiding, or running away, or keeping others out. It's the long, slow process of inviting them in that will save me. I, who have never let people in, not even my husband, must learn to.

And that's only the second-most terrifying discovery I've made today.

23.

From the moment I step into Justine Pinaro's home, I know I made the right call in coming. The front hall is cluttered with shoes, a jacket tossed on the floor, shopping bags not yet emptied. A table overflows with mail. It reminds me of my house in the weeks after I lost Keegan, and I love Justine fiercely for not cleaning up.

"You know how it is," she says, and I nod. Unlike the last time I saw her, she's not dressed for going out in public. In pajamas and no makeup, she's still a nice-looking woman, but her sheer exhaustion is evident. Dark circles. What Rae would call "I Don't Care Hair."

"I've been meaning to have you over," she tells me apologetically, "but there's been a parade of people running through ever since Didi passed. They mean well, but I get so tired of putting on a good face."

"Don't bother on my account."

She smiles. "I wouldn't have asked you over if I thought I had to."

And it's that easy.

I clear a space on the living room carpet and sit down cross-legged.

We talk about work. We talk about love. We talk about our children, tentatively at first, and then with warmth. For the first time in weeks, I speak my son's name aloud, allow myself the pleasure of my Keegan memories. The day he and Zoey rolled down the slope in our backyard two dozen times before Rae and I noticed they'd been crashing through poison ivy. The time I took him to the park to feed the ducks and an aggressive goose went after him and I hit it and he told everyone for weeks, "Mommy punched a goose." Justine has her own stories. I listen. I laugh. I get to know Didi, the little girl who brought us together.

When I mention that I haven't been sleeping well at Evangeline, she looks scandalized. "Stay here," she says. "I can't believe Remy didn't offer." She glances at a nearby clock. "It's after five. Run and get your things. I'll get the guest room ready."

I tell her I don't want to impose.

Justine rolls her eyes. "You spoke to my comatose daughter, you're helping out my husband, you're lending me an ear in a time of need. How could you impose?"

I'm pretty sure this means I've made a friend.

THE PLAN IS TO GRAB a quick overnight bag at Evangeline, but when I get out of my car, I see Andre outside smoking the last of a fragrant cigar. He's dressed in his version of casual wear: khakis, desert boots, and a blue-checked button-down under a V-neck sweater.

He spots me and smirks.

"Charlotte! You're just in time for dinner." He waves me over. From the look on his face, the family hasn't been notified about the bone yet. "Please. If I have to sit through a meal with just Syd and Bridgie, my head might explode."

I'm not excited by the prospect of some uptight Deveau dinner, but they *are* my hosts, and I can't afford to miss an opportunity to speak with all three. "All right. If you don't think your sisters would mind."

When I enter the dining room with Andre a few minutes later, Sydney looks like she does, in fact, mind.

"You brought company." She unfolds a napkin on her lap, each movement laced with displeasure. "I guess this is a working dinner?"

Andre casts me a knowing smile, as if Sydney's rudeness further proves the need for my presence. He slips his hand under my elbow and pulls out my chair with a flourish. "Kind of you to join us this evening, Charlotte. Evangeline is becoming increasingly geriatric, as you can see. We need more of you pretty young things to keep the place fresh."

Without all the guests and fancy place settings, the long, formal dining table is an odd space to have a meal. Even after Brigitte joins us, we are at less than half the seating capacity. The mostly empty table, combined with Brigitte's determined cheer, feels a bit desperate, as though she is a mother presiding over a birthday party no one has chosen to attend.

"So! Charlotte!" The exclamation points in her voice are a far cry from her sister's frosty reception. "I just spoke with Isaac this morning, and I've been waiting for an update. He says that he is *very* pleased with your work. Tell us all about it." Her hamster cheeks puff out in an expression of delight.

"Give the poor girl a minute to catch her breath before you grill her, Bridgie, I don't want you scaring this one away." Andre pats my hand. "She's a good one."

"Oh! *Well* then." Having decided I am a potential romantic interest for her brother, Brigitte looks both wildly curious and a bit dismayed by his selection. "I think it's only fair to warn you, Charlotte, our brother is *quite* a charmer. But his attention span for relationships has never been a strong point."

"He'd rather be dead than married and so would I," Sydney advises me, clearly pleased with the chance to take a swipe at her sister. "Marriage is an antiquated institution."

Brigitte smiles indulgently at her twin. "Oh, you'll find someone.

Third time's the charm. And Andre would meet the right woman in a heartbeat if he just stopped working once in a while instead of settling for whatever convenient thing drifted his way." She turns to me in wide-eyed apology, as if the remark were unintentional. "I didn't mean you, of course, honey."

"Of course." I fight back the urge to laugh.

How can these two be so obtuse? The facts are staring them in the face. Andre's forty-seven years old, and he's probably never had a serious relationship with a woman. He calls hot young Jules into his office for private meetings *while wearing a bathrobe*, and these two don't know.

Andre, however, is enjoying himself. He uncorks a bottle of wine. "I've had my fun in life, Charlotte," he says with a wink. "But who knows? Maybe I've finally reached a settling-down age."

I think I'm going to throw up in my mouth. Is this why he invited me to dinner? To put on a heterosexual show for his sisters?

Fortunately, dinner arrives before things can get any more bizarre. Leeann and Paulette bring in a water pitcher, butter, a basket of hot rolls, and serving dishes of steaming food, both women exuding professionalism.

"Tilapia, okra, and sweet potatoes," Leeann says. "I hope y'all enjoy you meal."

Sydney waits until they leave and then utters a long sigh. "That okra looks dry."

Brigitte butters a roll, her attention still on me. "I really am anxious to hear about the book. Have you found, I don't know, an *angle*?"

I don't tell her that I've completed chapters—it would only invite scrutiny. "Still primarily fact gathering at this stage," I tell her.

"Any facts that we can help you gather?" Andre asks.

"Yes, actually." I hadn't intended to bring this up, but with all three Deveau siblings present, I'm curious to see their collective reaction.

"Obviously the media portrayal of your family in the wake of Gabriel's disappearance was . . . unflattering."

Andre shrugs as if unflattering and accurate are not mutually exclusive, but Brigitte leaps at this. "Yes," she agrees. "Yes, it was."

I turn to her. "I'm interested in something you said the other day. You mentioned that on the night of your birthday you had nothing to drink but a glass of champagne. I'm wondering why the media reported that you and Sydney were *both* intoxicated and ill that evening."

"They get everything wrong, don't they?" Brigitte says carelessly. "I wasn't sick."

"Really? The police reports also stated that you spent the night ill. Were those wrong, too?" I can scarcely believe what I'm hearing. *Is this woman really arrogant enough to blow up her own alibi after thirty years in the clear?*

"Maybe we told someone I was sick to get them off my back, I don't remember." Brigitte dabs at her eye and removes a stray clump of mascara. "The police were *very* concerned about my movements that night."

"Evidently so is Charlotte," Sydney says acidly. "I told you, Bridgie."

Brigitte remains untroubled by her own dubious alibi. She sits back in her chair and laughs lightly. "It's a sad world, I think, when a sixteen-year-old girl is better off vomiting from alcohol poisoning than sleeping peacefully all night in her own bed. Being the good girl should never be used against someone."

"I'm not trying to use anything against anyone. Just clarifying."

She leans across the table, fluffy blond head tilted in my direction. "People have written some nasty things about us over the years, I'm sure you know that. It truly is an act of faith to open our home like this after the unfortunate relationships we've had with *some* journalists."

I nod politely.

"You probably heard about that *ugly* lawsuit we won years back." Brigitte shakes her head, as if to indicate that winning lawsuits is a distasteful business, but her words could hardly be more pointed. "You've met us, Charlotte. You know we're a loving family with a rich history and a terrible wound in our past. *That's* the story that needs telling. And I trust you with that story." She smiles, her eyes still fixed on me, and I see that Brigitte has more in her arsenal than temper tantrums when it comes to getting what she wants. "It's important that we can trust each other, isn't it?"

I glance at Andre, wondering if he'll weigh in, but he's cutting his tilapia into neat bites, poker-faced. A duck-and-cover maneuver.

"Trust . . . is important," I say.

It's hard to imagine the meal getting any more awkward, but then Paulette appears in the doorway. "Sorry to intarupp," she murmurs, one hand held protectively against her belly, "but they's some policemen at the gate. Security wanna know if they should buzz 'em in."

I stare down at my plate, face burning. Of all the times to come by, the sheriff's department picks *now*?

"What do they want?" Sydney frowns.

"Somethin' 'bout the sugah mill." Paulette's eyes dart around as if waiting for a land mine to go off.

Sydney gives a little snort of irritation. "This is Deenie Strickland's problem. We lease her the land, that doesn't mean it's our job to chase off every frisky teenager."

Brigitte takes a quick sip of wine and stands up. "Send the officers in. I'll handle this." She strides off down the hall.

I push okra around my plate and sneak a peek at Sydney and Andre. Sydney eats her okra with a tragic expression, sighing at each long, green piece she loads onto her fork. Andre, on the other hand, regards me curiously.

"Are you okay?" he asks. "You look a bit jumpy."

"She probably doesn't like the food," Sydney says. "Who can blame her?"

Andre tries, charitably, to engage me in a discussion of New York City restaurants. Although I do my best to respond, I'm straining to hear what's going on in the other room. Brigitte and some officers are talking in the foyer, but I can't make out any words beyond some expressions of dismay on Brigitte's part.

A few minutes later, she returns, visibly shaken. "I think we might need a lawyer," she whispers.

"A lawyer? Why?" Andre delivers the last forkful of fish to his mouth.

"The police found a human bone in the old sugar mill. They want our consent to do a search."

"I'm sorry," Sydney interjects. "They found *what?*"

"A *bone.*" Brigitte presses her hand to her lips as if it's a dirty word.

"When?" Andre's all ears now. "When did they find it?"

She shrugs helplessly. "I don't know. The middle of the night? They said an officer dropped by to make sure there weren't any teenagers hanging around, and he found a bone."

"Found it where?" Andre prompts her. "In the parking lot? In the mill?"

"I don't know!"

"But it belongs to a *person?*" Sydney clutches her wineglass anxiously.

"I guess so. They had some expert from the university look at it today."

"Oh my God," Sydney moans. "And now they're going to search the place?"

"Unless we stop it." Brigitte turns to her brother, the legal brain of the group. "What do you think, Andre? Should I call the lawyer?"

"No," he says. "No, of course not. We want to know what they'll find just as much as they do." He presses his hands to the bridge of his nose, thinking hard. "Did they say how old the bone was?"

Brigitte shakes her head. "You don't think it could be . . ."

Sydney clamps her hand over her mouth. "No, no, no. It *can't* be."

"I don't know," Brigitte wails. "Come talk to them, would you both?"

"Go ahead, Syd. I'll be just a minute." Andre waits for his sisters to leave and then assesses me coolly. "You don't look very surprised." There's nothing friendly in his demeanor now.

"Well . . ." Sometimes I wish I wasn't such a rotten liar.

"You knew about this, didn't you? How did you know?"

"I know somebody at the sheriff's department." Even the truth—albeit a partial truth—sounds lame coming out of my mouth.

"The guard said you were gone this morning from three to five a.m. Where were you?"

Tattletale, I think.

"I was just out." Winner: worst excuse ever.

"You're the one who found the bone, aren't you?" His nostrils flare. "Who's giving you information, and why the hell haven't you shared it with my family?"

I don't know how to answer.

"Are you really a writer or just some FBI plant? Because if you're with the FBI, you've harassed my family more than enough over the years without infiltrating our home and—"

"Whoa!" I exclaim, half-flattered I could come off as badass enough to be a federal agent. "I'm not some secret agent, I just . . . got to know one of the cops in town, okay? We met up early this morning and . . ." Met up at three a.m.? I'm aware of how flimsy this explanation is, and I'm guessing psychic visions won't go over any better, so I grope for something more credible. "Look," I say, "the officer is married and we . . . made a mistake. Please don't go dragging me into it." This is actually the most inspired lie I've ever told. I think of Rae's Third Rule of Lying—admit to something bad, but not as bad as the truth—and I wonder about the legitimacy of my lies of omission.

Andre rubs his forehead like I'm giving him a pain. "You're telling me you went to the sugar mill to have relations with some married man and you accidentally found human remains?"

It sounds vaguely plausible, so I run with it. "Well, yeah."

He sighs. "What are you, fifteen? The *sugar mill*? Get a motel like a grown-up." He leaves the room without looking back. Hopefully that means he's crossed me off the Possible Undercover Agent list, although I'm guessing there will be no more intimate fireside chats.

I slink off, now extra glad I've made alternative sleeping arrangements.

JUSTINE AND I SPEND the night devouring Toll House cookies and watching every terrible reality TV show we can find about New Jersey. Detective Minot returns very late, and if he's taken aback by the sight of me sprawled across his couch in my pajamas, he does a good job hiding it.

"How are things going?" Justine asks, passing him a cookie.

He shrugs. "Progressing. We have a search planned first thing to-morrow. We got a cadaver dog lined up and a forensic anthropologist from the university on call if we find anything."

"A cadaver dog?" I'm surprised. "Can those guys really sniff down something thirty years old?"

"A good one can." Detective Minot lingers in the doorway a mo-ment, and I get the feeling he's debating whether or not to tell me something. "Listen, Charlotte. Don't be disappointed if we don't find anything connected to the kidnapping. You did your part. All anybody could've asked for and more." He sounds so fatalistic. After all we've been through, it irritates me.

"I bet you'll find more than you think," I tell him.

"Maybe so. But thirty years is a long time." He holds up one hand in a halfhearted wave. "Good night, ladies. Got a long day tomorrow."

Before we go to bed, I ask one more thing of Justine: to see Didi's room. She doesn't ask why, just leads me to a strangely familiar pink bedroom. The hospital bed and IV drip are gone, but I recognize the layout and some details from my dream. The ballet-shoes lamp. The shelves of teddy bears. I shiver at my own impossible accuracy.

"I know it's a little babyish for an eleven-year-old," Justine says. "Didi kept wanting to redecorate, but then she'd get sick again and . . . there was never time."

I pick up a few items in the room, hoping to get a better sense of the little girl. I'd like to have something comforting to tell her mother. That I feel a presence, that I'm picking up some happy memory. Instead, the room feels vacant. The girl who lived here is gone.

"It feels so empty, doesn't it?" Justine says as she rearranges a slumping teddy bear. "I keep telling myself she's in heaven. It's the only thing that brings me any comfort. That and prayer."

I say nothing. I like Justine, but we're miles apart on the God issue.

"Your son's in heaven, too, Charlotte," she says, flipping off the light. "He and Didi—they're beyond pain."

I'd like to believe in eternal paradise. I'd like to believe that Keegan is off in the clouds riding a friendly dinosaur, driving a dump truck, eating the frosting off a cupcake. Heaven is a beautiful idea, but everlasting happiness and perfection are about as believable to me as Santa Claus.

Yes, Keegan and Didi are beyond pain. That doesn't mean that I am.

I DON'T WANT TO OVERSTAY my welcome with Justine, so in the morning I head off to the library again. Though more productive than yesterday, I periodically find myself spacing out, thinking about the search. *What will turn up? And will it be enough?*

With the right bones, forensic anthropologists could offer many plausible theories as to how Gabriel died. And if investigators recover bullets, they could even potentially locate the weapon. Beyond that, though, I have trouble envisioning any discoveries that would provide definitive answers about the killer—probably why Detective Minot was so pessimistic last night.

I do know one thing: if the remains of a very young child are discovered on Deveau property—even if investigators can't positively identify the bones as belonging to Gabriel—this case will be catapulted back into relevance. My book will go from bad idea to possible bestseller. There will be a mad scramble in the publishing world to see who can release a Deveau kidnapping book first, and I'll have the head start.

I write until midday, then make a pit stop at Evangeline for lunch. The kitchen is as busy as I've ever seen it. Leeann, Benny, Paulette, and several guys from Evangeline's landscaping service sit around the breakfast nook chatting animatedly as they wolf down their lunches. Even the old dog has joined the gathering; he lingers by Leeann's feet, tail thumping.

The room quiets when they catch sight of me. "Don't worry 'bout Charlie," Leeann reassures them. "She not gonna rat y'all out." She slips the dog some chicken and fills me in. "We just talkin' 'bout what a terror Brigitte's been."

I nod and the conversation resumes, but my eyes are on Paulette.

She's the only one present who doesn't look outraged. She grips the edge of the table, taking deep breaths, eyes half-closed.

"Paulette," I say, concerned she's about to give birth on the kitchen floor, "are you okay?"

"She just havin' some contractions," Benny explains. "False labor, they call it."

"Did you call your doctor?" I ask.

"I'm all right," Paulette insists weakly, looking anything but. "I ain't givin' that woman a reason to say boo."

I make a mental note to keep an eye on Paulette and fix myself a plate at the island. As I scoop some potato salad, I spy Hettie and Andre out in the garden. Even from a distance, Hettie's pale and skeletal, propped up in a wheelchair with several pillows. Her mouth is moving, though. She looks alert. Must be having one of her good days.

But Andre's clearly upset. He shakes his head, puts a hand up as if to silence her, but she continues anyway. His face crumples up. She places a quavering hand on his arm, attempting to soothe him, but he's weeping, wiping away tears with the palm of his hand.

I step away from the window, not wanting to gawk. I remember how Noah gave her the narcissus bulbs a few weeks ago, saying they should be out by Valentine's Day. *Not sure I care to make it that long,* she told him. Valentine's Day is now less than two weeks off, and however ready Hettie may be, Andre seems unprepared to let her go. I don't entirely fault him. Who will be left? His ditzy sisters? A jet-setting niece too busy to visit her dying grandmother?

I scarf down my lunch and head back to my cottage to work, wondering again how Gabriel ended up in the sugar mill. When someone knocks on my door thirty minutes later, my heart does a crazy little dance. *Is it Noah? Is he back after all?* I throw open the door, ready to pounce, and find myself faced with a much less appealing sight.

I thought my last encounter with Andre Deveau was bad. Now he stares despondently at my doorstep, eyes red-rimmed and swollen. Something tells me we're about to plunge to new depths of discomfort.

He lifts his gaze slowly to mine, and for a second I forget that he's approaching fifty years old. His blue eyes are young, almost boyish. And lost.

"Hi," he says, but what I hear is, *I want my mommy.*

24.

Having made it through childhood without any real mother to speak of, I have limited sympathy for grown men with mommy issues. I suppose everyone's entitled to an off day, and coming to terms with your mother's imminent mortality probably constitutes an off day. That doesn't mean I want to dive into Andre's emotional mess.

"Hi," I greet him. "Are you all right?"

He plays it off. "I just came by to apologize for yesterday. I hope I didn't make you feel unwelcome."

Riiiiight, I think. *You came to apologize, never dreaming that your big red eyes would evoke sympathy.* The man is looking for a makeshift therapist, and the fact that he didn't go to Jules says a lot about their relationship. I shouldn't be surprised he picked me, not after I encouraged him to blab for hours about his dysfunctional family last week.

"There's nothing to apologize for," I say. "*I'm* sorry. I wish I could've told you about the bone myself."

"I understand your situation," he says, holding up a hand. "And I didn't intend to dig into your private life. I'm the last person to judge who you have—relations with. I was just having a hard time processing the, uh, discovery of human remains on our property."

I have to crack a smile. "Best excuse I've ever heard for bad behavior. No hard feelings." I wait a few long seconds to see if he leaves, but he's planted himself firmly on my porch. "So . . . ," I begin. "How's your mom?"

"Confused. She goes in and out. Half of what she says is just—fantasy."

I'm not sure what to do from here. Tell him I'm busy? That I've got somewhere to be? Compassion wells up, despite my best efforts to remain aloof. Of the four remaining Deveaus, I like Andre best, and his presence on my doorstep now is a sad reminder: he has nowhere else to go.

"You're welcome to come in," I say.

He shakes his head. "That'll get the rumor mill going. And I'm not . . . like that. I'm not the person my sisters think, believe me."

"You mean a womanizer?" I meet his gaze straight on, done playing along with a lie he shouldn't have to tell. "You're not even close. I can see that."

Andre swallows. "You can see that?"

He wants to talk about it, I think. *He's tired of hiding.*

I go for broke. "Maybe I'm reading things wrong, but I thought you and Jules were . . . good friends. Not that it matters."

He closes his eyes and exhales slowly. "Oh, it matters. Louisiana is not like New York. You don't know what that could do to me professionally. Please tell me you aren't going to—"

"I'm writing about Gabriel, not your love life," I promise. "I hope Jules makes you happy."

"Happy? I wouldn't go that far." He gives me a crooked smile, as if aware how ridiculous he looks. "Anyway, I guess we're even. I know the dark secrets of your love life, now you know mine."

It takes me a second to realize he's referring to my supposed affair with a married cop. I cringe.

Andre looks around at the other cottages. "This isn't a good place to talk. I was going to take the boat out, anyway. You can come with me."

Instantly, my guard goes up. "What boat?"

There's no way I'm getting in that rowboat with him. Or anybody else. Ever.

"The airboat. It's docked out front."

I stare Andre down for a moment, deciding whether or not I trust him. He was eighteen when Gabriel disappeared, and although I don't think he was involved, I don't know he wasn't. As Detective Minot pointed out, he doesn't have a solid alibi for the night Gabriel went missing. And I've just revealed myself to be in possession of information that could, in his view, destroy his career. Is this really a man I want to tour the desolate swamps with? Alone?

"All right," I say slowly, "let me just grab my phone." I duck inside and send Detective Minot what is hopefully not my final text. *Going for boat ride in swamp w/ Andre D. If I don't call you in 2 hrs, send in cavalry. Not kidding.*

GIVEN THE DEVEAU FAMILY'S BANKROLL, I was expecting something a little more glamorous than the four-seat floating hunk of metal we find tied up at Evangeline's dock. With a giant, fanlike apparatus in the back and a front that curves inward like a sled, the boat's not exactly pretty.

Andre chuckles at my skeptical look. "This baby's made for the swamps," he explains. "Flat-bottomed for shallow areas. The propeller and engine are up inside that cage so they don't catch debris. And the seats are raised so we can see whatever's floating by."

"Floating by? Are we looking for something?"

"Stumps, branches, birds, gators, anything we don't want to hit." He squints at me. "You don't get motion sick, do you?"

I shake my head and watch as he steps onto the flimsy vessel. It doesn't capsize, which is at least one point in its favor, but I'm still reluctant to board. "How old is that thing?"

"Couple years," he says. "It's funny, but I never spent any time in the swamps growing up. We were all about the ocean. Then a few years ago, I don't know, I decided it was time to explore my own backyard."

Sydney and Brigitte also mentioned family sailing trips. It didn't seem like an important detail, sailing around the Virgin Islands and chartering yachts in Greece, but maybe it was. The Deveau family is not, by all accounts, comprised of swamp people. Yet whoever took Gabriel out in that rowboat must've been able to navigate the swamps in the dark while hauling around a two-year-old who may or may not have been conscious. That, in my mind, rules out Andre.

Andre opens a metal box at the front of the boat and tosses me a life jacket—another point in his favor. He doesn't take one for himself. Water safety devices must be reserved for the squeamish. I strap myself in and he holds out a hand. "Ready?"

I climb onto the airboat and secure myself in a seat. "Let's go."

He unties the boat from the dock and pushes us away from the shore. After starting up the noisy engine, he settles into the operator's seat in the rear. The boat zips down the bayou at what feels like a dangerously high speed. Once, this would've freaked me out. Now it's exhilarating. I stay on the alert for bad Gabriel vibes, feelings that might signal we're approaching his death site, but nothing comes. It's just a pleasant afternoon on the water.

Though we pass a couple of shacks with rickety docks, this section of the river is largely unpopulated and there aren't any other boats out. After ten minutes or so, Andre eases up a bit. "There's an inlet up here," he yells, and sure enough, the bayou splits off ahead of us. He urges the boat into a sharp turn, and we travel through water that rapidly narrows and becomes more mucky. Then the waterway flares out, and soon it's no longer clear where the shore ends and the water begins. Trees rise up out of green clumps that may be land or floating plants. Andre slows us down, then turns off the engine.

"Well," he says, "it's not the ocean, but it's got its own kind of beauty."

"It's nice," I say, but the truth is I can't see these swamps as anything but a horrible place to die. "Do you take Jules out here?"

"Just once." He laughs, the first lighthearted gesture I've seen from him all day. "He hated the wind in his hair. Doesn't like convertibles, either."

"Somehow that doesn't surprise me."

"He's beautiful, isn't he?" Andre smiles wistfully. *"Oh thou, my lovely boy, who in thy power / Dost hold Time's fickle glass, his sickle, hour."*

I raise my eyebrows.

"Shakespeare," he says, and I remember that book of sonnets I found, wonder exactly how many times he read it. "Look, I understand why you'd think Jules is just some brainless boy toy, but that's not how it is. I care about him." His eyes don't leave the water, but I imagine this admission is a fairly major one for him.

"Well—good. I hear that's more satisfying than brainless boy toys."

"It's certainly more complicated." He steps from the operator's chair and seats himself beside me as if we're old buddies. "I'm forty-seven years old, Charlotte. Too damn old to be sneaking around like some nervous schoolboy, but here I am. I don't know what the answer is." He glances up at the overcast sky. "I tell you, some nights I don't sleep at all."

With the clouds moving in, it's getting chilly. I hug myself, glad for the extra layer the life jacket provides. "I don't sleep so well either," I confess. "But Ambien helps."

Andre smiles. "Jules takes Ambien, too. Myself, I'd rather have a few nightcaps."

We bob along, both caught up in our own thoughts. Unlike the bayou, which moves, wanders, flows slowly to a destination, the swamp is still. But it's a pregnant stillness, like something crouched low, waiting, and I don't like it. As if to confirm my bad feeling, Andre rises slowly to his feet and points at some nearby brush.

"Gator," he says.

I follow the line of his finger and find a bumpy head peeking out near some weeds. The eyes are olive colored, and they don't blink. "God, he's *huge.*"

"Four feet, maybe. Pretty small." He peers admiringly at the creature. "Plucky little bastard. You don't see a lot of gators this time of year. They're sluggish in the cold."

Andre starts up the engine and urges us deeper into the swamp. The rainfall, I'm told, has been decent this winter, so the water isn't quite as low as usual. As we skim across the muddy shallows, I can better appreciate the airboat's ability to seemingly walk on water. With all the random twists and turns we're making, though, I'm increasingly anxious about Andre's ability to navigate us back home.

Eventually he kills the engine again, taking in the view around us as if it's somehow different from the last fifteen minutes of swamp. I try not to fidget, but I've had enough already.

"So." He stretches. "Who's the bad guy?"

"Bad guy?" My mind is on the sugar mill. I'm trying to figure out why someone would've drowned Gabriel in the swamps and then buried him miles away on dry land.

"Your book," Andre presses me. "Not a satisfying story if you've got no one to blame. And pardon my saying so, but at the point you're trying to punch holes in Bridgie's alibi, you must be running pretty low on theories."

I'm embarrassed by my inelegant mishandling of the topic at dinner yesterday. As much as I dislike Brigitte, there's no reason to think she had a hand in Gabriel's disappearance. "I wasn't accusing her, I was just trying to understand—"

Andre chuckles. "A word of advice? Don't piss Bridgie off. She's hardly a criminal mastermind, and she had zero incentive to hurt our brother. But she sure can harbor a grudge."

"So I've seen. She's still bitter about you missing her sweet sixteen party." I hunch forward in my seat, trying to concentrate my warmth in a ball. "How'd you wrangle your way out of attending, anyway?"

"Oh." He yawns. "My relationship with my family was—strained at that point. So I did what I wanted. Hung out with a friend in the city."

"A friend," I repeat. I brush some hair from my eyes, considering how best to approach this. I don't think Andre hurt his brother—I doubt teenage Andre really even thought much about Gabriel one way or another—and I want to give him a chance to explain himself. "Agent Schaffer says that he fabricated your friend for reports," I murmur. "That your father paid him off." I watch his reaction carefully, searching for signs of panic, but Andre looks tired, not rattled.

"Yes, well. My father didn't like the friend I spent the night with. Go figure."

"A man?"

He nods. "From a club. Kyle Komen. I met him that night, but we dated for a couple months after. I guess you could call him my first boyfriend."

"You told your dad about him?"

"Sort of. He read between the lines. He had me tell the officers I'd been with a prostitute, presumably female. Thought it would go better for me that way." A twisted smile plays across his lips. "Funny, right?"

"So your father knew you were gay."

That's a surprise. Somehow Neville was the last family member I expected to be in the know.

"He never acknowledged it, but he knew," Andre says. "Listen, if your friend in the police department needs to check my story, tell him to talk to Kyle Komen, K-O-M-E-N, in Lake Charles." He licks his lips. "I trust this can be handled confidentially."

"Of course." I really want to leave now. Not because I'm having some profound psychic impression, but because I detest the swamp. I've never liked water you can't see the bottom of, and this? It's a watery graveyard for plants and probably animals, a feeding ground for dark, slippery things that feast on decay. Things you can't see. Things that wait for you to die. I breathe in, trying not to reveal my disgust. "You know, you're right about me running low on theories," I tell Andre. "But I've got to come up with something for this book. Any ideas?"

Andre shrugs. "I thought it was done with when they arrested Roi Duchesne. He'd lied to get the job at Evangeline, had a criminal history, and my father had fired him a few weeks earlier. He made sense. And I didn't like him." He stares vacantly at the water, and I think how easy it is to imagine a body in it, a human face just beneath the surface, hair fanning out, eyes wide and unseeing. "Life would be simpler, wouldn't it," he says, "if guilty people were always the ones you disliked."

"It must be awful. Not knowing."

"I think about my brother a lot." Andre's index finger grazes his lips. "Sometimes I think he was the lucky one."

Sensing he's about to drift into the therapy zone with me, I change the subject. "Do you remember a woman named Violet Johnson? She worked for your family when you were about eleven or twelve."

He gives me an apologetic look. "I don't remember much about the help. Apart from Danelle and the Lauchlins, most of them came and went."

"Tell me about the Lauchlins, then. I'm interested in them."

"Interested why?" Andre frowns. "There was surveillance on them for months. There was never any sign they did wrong."

"I take it you were fond of Maddie and Jack."

"Maddie was . . . well, she was my nanny. We kids were her life. Especially Gabriel."

Maddie is not who I'm worried about, of course. "What about Jack?" I ask, toying with the strap of my life jacket. "Were you close to him?"

Andre shakes his head. "I wasn't his kind of boy. He tried to teach me about car engines once. I told him I'd pay people to do that stuff for me when I grew up, so he shouldn't waste our time." He smiles sheepishly. "I was a brat."

I hate to ask, knowing how Noah feels about his grandfather, but I have to. "Did Jack spend much time with Gabriel?"

"Oh, sure. Gabriel followed him around. He liked to watch Jack use tools." He kneels down at the edge of the boat and, with one hand, shoves away some brush. "He was a handful, that kid. Always trying to stick objects into sockets or toss things in the toilet. He'd run away, too. That's why they locked him in at nights."

Keegan went through a similar phase, but I don't let myself dwell on that thought. "Did you know Maddie's son well? Sean?"

Something in Andre's face flickers at the mention of Sean. "I knew him, sure, but not well. He's twelve years older . . ."

"Brigitte had quite the crush on him."

"Did she? I don't remember." His nonchalance doesn't fool me for a second. Danelle Martin was right. Andre had it bad for Sean.

"He was handsome. I've seen pictures."

Andre drums his fingers against the metal frame of the boat, a little flustered by my persistence. "You want to know if I was interested in him? Sure. I was a teenage boy. He was nice to me. Of course I was interested. But nothing ever happened. He was completely straight."

His agitation betrays the depth of his feelings for Sean, but I don't push my luck.

"Was he involved with anyone, do you know?"

"I didn't keep track of his relationships. He was very private."

Neither Danelle nor Andre knew about Violet, then. Maybe Sean and Violet had no relationship at all, and Noah was the product of a fling. He could've been an illegitimate son the Lauchlin family never even acknowledged until Violet died. Unless, of course, she's the mystery woman Sean wanted to flee the country with. Whatever made him want to run away with her might also have made them hide their relationship from others.

"You know Sean disappeared just a few months before your brother," I say. "Don't you find that odd?"

"Disappeared?" Andre frowns. "The story I heard was that he left."

Could he have come back? Conspired with someone to kidnap Gabriel, hoping to build on his half million? Sean could easily have learned from his unwitting parents when Neville and Hettie would be out of town, and the family dog would've known him well enough not to make a fuss. He was a local, likely knew the swamps, and had military training. Gabriel would've trusted him. All he had to do was wait.

"Sean left," I say thoughtfully. "But maybe he didn't go so far."

"We should probably get back," Andre tells me, uninterested in exploring my Sean Lauchlin conspiracy theories. "My niece is joining our family for dinner tonight. Wouldn't want to miss the details of her wild spending spree in Cabo."

Brigitte's daughter is in her early twenties, too young to have been mixed up with Sean or Gabriel, and by all accounts too much like her mother for me to endure. I'm happy to sit this one out.

On the ride home, Andre's in his own world, adeptly retracing our course through the swamp and bayou all the way back to Evangeline. I wish I knew what he was thinking, what potentially useful memories he might hold. So many pieces of the truth out there, and everyone trying to conceal their own little part. Not because they're guilty, necessarily, but because the truth is ugly or uncomfortable or embarrassing.

I understand. I have my own ugly truths to contend with.

I've been on land for about thirty seconds when I feel my phone vibrating. It's Detective Minot. I left him that crazy text and then forgot to call him. Oops.

"Hey." I move away from the dock where Andre is tying up the airboat. "I'm still alive."

"Jesus, Charlotte. Don't send me messages like that. Better yet, don't run off alone with people you think are gonna—" I lose the remainder of his scolding to poor reception.

"Sorry. I was freaking out over nothing."

"I called you three times."

I feel both guilty and relieved that someone in this world is looking out for me. "Thanks. For checking up on me."

"I wasn't just checking up on you," he says. "I have something to tell you. Can you be at City Park in fifteen minutes?"

The search. Oh my God, the search. I glance at my watch. Almost five, and they've been at it since six this morning. Something must've turned up.

"I'll be there in ten."

I find Detective Minot on a bench by the duck pond. The sun hangs low, and the dwindling light casts everything in melancholy shadows. Even the fat, waddling ducks are depressing, reminders of children who will remain suspended in time. Keegan loved feeding ducks, and I'm sure Detective Minot took Didi here when she was small. Was he different before his daughter got sick, I wonder, or has he always been the serious, brooding type? It's hard to picture him as someone's dad, but Justine showed me old photos of him. He looked so normal, carrying little Didi on his shoulders, grinning, smooching his wife. I'm not sure I wanted to see that side of him, to be burdened with knowledge of the man he could've been had he never heard the words "acute lymphocytic leukemia."

I take a seat beside him on the bench. "Well? What's your news?"

He rubs a hand over his stubbly face. "Looks like this whole mess has gotten bigger than the sheriff's department can handle. The Feds are sending over some guys tomorrow."

"Are you serious? The FBI's getting involved?" My eyes widen. "You must've ID'd him, right? They wouldn't care unless it was Gabriel. Did you match the bone?"

"It's not Gabriel," Detective Minot says gently.

I wrap my fingers around the wooden slats of the bench, unable to fully comprehend what he's just said. "But it has to be. You know it has to be."

"No. I never thought it was." His tone is apologetic. "That jawbone we found in the sugar mill didn't belong to a two-year-old. It was too large."

Over on the weedy pond, a pair of ducks begin to squabble. I feel like the air's been knocked from me. "Why didn't you tell me?" I whisper. "Why'd you let me think there was a chance when you knew I'd failed?" All my high hopes, all this faith I had in my "gift," it was all for shit.

"I think there's a reason you led us to that sugar mill," he insists. "It could be part of the puzzle."

I'm still smarting from my mistake, but his department wouldn't have called in the FBI unless this was a big deal. "What happened?"

"Didn't take long with the dog this morning, I'll tell you that. You expect to spend days on this kind of search, but those bones . . . it's like they were begging to be found." He looks a little spooked. "The team's still excavating as we speak, but I think they got the bulk of it."

"Did the forensic anthropologist from the university get a look?"

Detective Minot nods. "He's overseeing the excavation. Today was mostly just bagging fragments they found, but from what I understand, they got a decent portion of the skull and pelvis."

I remember vaguely that these parts are helpful in determining gender. "Male or female?"

"Off the record, very preliminary, he's guessing the victim was an adult Caucasian male."

The wind rustles my hair, sending shivers up and down my back. I can feel there's more. It's like we're in court and Detective Minot is building his case for me, bit by bit.

"Looks like there was a bullet hole in the skull," he says. "They haven't retrieved any casings so far, and we don't know yet if there were multiple shots, or if that was the cause of death, but this guy took a bullet to the back of the head."

"Point-blank?" I'm imagining a mob-style execution.

"Probably not. A handgun, most likely, but we'll have to wait for the report."

"Anything else? Clothes? A wallet?"

"We found a shoe in the same approximate location," he continues. "Size-twelve tenny shoes. A brand called Raceway. I looked them up, and this particular style was sold for just two years: 1980 and '81."

I don't speak, just wait. A greedy duck approaches me, his black eyes glassy and alert as he calls for handouts, but I shoo him away.

"There was one last thing." Detective Minot pauses, gearing up for his smoking gun. "Dog tags."

I'm confused. "There was a dog?"

"No, no. Military dog tags."

"Military . . ." At last it dawns on me. "Oh my God. You think—"

"I saw the name, plain as anything. It's him, Charlotte." The park, the setting sun, the overweight duck strutting around my feet—I see none of it. All I can see is Remy Minot, his look of awe as he tells me in hushed tones that, after nearly thirty years, they've found him. They've found Sean Lauchlin.

25.

There's no evidence that Gabriel's disappearance is related to Sean Lauchlin's murder, but that doesn't stop Detective Minot and me from speculating as we wander the empty park. We pass a couple of sagging picnic tables and a trash can that gives off an unpleasant smell, but no people. Even the ducks have retreated into the long grass at the pond's edge.

"Revenge," I say. "Sean killed Gabriel, and Neville found out. Neville took matters into his own hands and disposed of Sean himself."

"Neville couldn't do that," Detective Minot contends. "Not with local, state, and federal law enforcement agencies breathing down his neck. The minute Gabriel was reported missing, they monitored his every movement."

"Neville hired someone to do it for him."

"That's exactly what law enforcement was looking for when they thought he orchestrated Gabriel's kidnapping—calls and meetings with possible criminals for hire. They found nothing. Anyway, it still wouldn't explain the half million in Sean's bank account." He pauses by an old tree and runs his hand over initials carved in its trunk as if this scar might possess an answer. "You've said there's a sexual-abuse element to this case."

I nod. "I felt it when we went to the swamp."

"My money's on Andre Deveau. He had access to Gabriel and no alibi."

I fill him in on today's boat ride. "You should look into this Kyle Komen guy he claims he was with, but I don't think Andre fits. Someone took the rowboat out and dumped Gabriel in the swamps. I don't think anyone in the Deveau family had the know-how."

"Whoever took the boat put it back. That points to an employee, like Jack Lauchlin."

I'm aware that Daddy Jack's involvement would destroy Noah, but I, too, keep coming back to him. "Jack had access to the boat and to Gabriel," I concede. "And Jack could easily have gotten the key to Gabriel's bedroom from his wife."

Detective Minot breaks from the path and begins pacing. "He's from the area. He would know boats, know the water."

A couple of streetlights flicker on in the distance. I fold my arms tight against my chest. The New Yorker in me wonders how many rapes and muggings have happened in this park after dark. "Okay," I say, "Jack could've killed Gabriel. But what about Sean? You're saying Jack killed his own son too?"

Detective Minot shrugs. "Maybe Sean knew his father was molesting the kid. Sean had a big fight with his parents right before he left in June, right? Maybe he never left at all. Maybe Jack killed him to cover up what he was doing to Gabriel."

"That still doesn't explain the half million in Sean's bank account." I'm relieved to find a flaw in his theory, something to remove Noah's grandfather from the equation.

"The money is a sticking point," Detective Minot agrees.

I concentrate on the money and start down another line of thinking. "Maybe Sean was blackmailing Neville. If Neville was abusing Gabriel, and Sean somehow found out—"

"No," Detective Minot interrupts. "Those payments to Sean's account began before Gabriel was even born."

I revise my theory. "Sean grew up at that house. Maybe Neville molested *him*." I feel a lot better pinning all this evil on a man I've never met, one who has no blood ties to the guy I've been sharing a bed with. Still, I don't find the scenario entirely convincing. Neville displayed no special affinity for children from what I've heard—and would he really be cheating on Hettie with adult women if his real interest lay in young boys?

Detective Minot shares my reservations, but for different reasons. "I could buy the blackmail angle, that Neville killed Sean to shut him up. But it doesn't explain Gabriel. Neville has an alibi for the night of the kidnapping. Which means he would've hired someone, and I'm telling you, investigators couldn't find a damn thing to support that."

I kick at some dead leaves. "Maybe . . . they overlooked something. Someone local Neville might've used for the job."

Detective Minot sinks onto a lopsided picnic table, and I can tell he's close to giving up for the night. "I can see why they focused on Roi Duchesne," he says ruefully. "He sure fit the bill."

"There's no wiggle room in Duchesne's alibi?"

"Nope. At least a dozen people saw him that night at a casino in Alabama."

"If Duchesne did jail time, he might've known the right people," I suggest. "Maybe he was just a middleman. We should talk to him." Detective Minot makes some kind of grunt that I take to be agreement. Finally, I gather the courage to ask the question that's been plaguing me throughout this whole discussion. "Do you know if they've notified Sean Lauchlin's family?"

He shakes his head. "None of what I told you has been released to the public yet. Your lips are sealed, you understand?" He eyes me, sensing there's a reason I'm asking. "I don't think the Lauchlins have any family living. Maddie had a sister in Texas, but I'm pretty sure she's dead."

I can't pretend Noah doesn't exist any longer, can't neatly separate my work from my romantic life. Noah has far more of a right to know about his dad than I do.

"Sean had a son," I say softly. "I know him. We're . . . kind of close."

"A son? You're kidding me." Detective Minot blinks a few times as if trying to orient himself. "How old? And who's the mother? You realize this could have major implications in the investigation."

I cover my face. The last thing I wanted to do was drag Noah into this. His father's murder will be hard enough to process without getting grilled on every little thing Jack and Maddie ever mentioned about his parents. And what if his cherished Nanny and Daddy Jack are involved?

Detective Minot, meanwhile, has his own betrayal to sort through. "Why didn't you tell me about this guy before?" he demands. "I mean, hell, you have a personal connection to the Lauchlins? I would never have shared—"

"Exactly why I didn't tell you."

"Charlotte." His nostrils flare. "I don't care how much this guy means to you. You wait for forensics to make a positive ID. If that information is leaked prematurely, it could compromise the investigation. And I'd lose my job."

I don't want to screw things up for him, and really, silence is the easier course of action here. I can't predict Noah's response. For all I know, he'll show up at the sheriff's department wanting answers and it would be Detective Minot's ass. Carrying around this secret indefinitely, though, makes me sick to my stomach. Sean is his father. All these years Noah thought his dad didn't care . . . but maybe Sean did care.

"Promise me you won't blow this." In the deepening twilight, Detective Minot's watching me closely, searching for signs of resistance. "Give me your word."

"I promise." But I want to cry. Noah trusts me.

"What's the son's name?"

"Noah Lauchlin." I dispense his vital stats dutifully; the sheriff's office will need to notify him once Sean's identification is official. "He was born March 19, 1979. He lives in Sidalie, Texas. Maddie and Jack raised him after his mom died. Her name was Violet Johnson."

"Violet." He searches his memory. "You asked about her the other day."

"She used to work at Evangeline."

"Right. Housekeeper. She only lasted a few months. Didn't part on very good terms."

I try to swallow back the sour taste in my mouth. "Look, I know you'll need to ask Noah questions about his family, but . . . give him time to process the news about his dad, okay?"

"Fine."

We trudge quietly back to the parking lot. In the yellowy light of a streetlamp, Detective Minot watches me step into my car, his face hard even as he ensures my safety. He's angry at me, understandably, and angry at himself for confiding in me. I'm angry with me, too. I'm surrounded by good people who believe in me, and I'm letting them all down.

THE NEXT FEW DAYS pass in a slow, excruciating haze. Over the weekend, several local news outlets cover the discovery of human remains at the old sugar mill. The stories contain nothing about the shoe or the military ID tags found, but all play up the fact that the land is Deveau owned. *This is not the first time the family has been connected to a major criminal investigation*, a reporter reminds viewers. *Nearly thirty years ago, two-year-old Gabriel Deveau was abducted from the family's Chicory home. Despite a highly publicized national search, the kidnapping remains unsolved. No word from authorities on whether the newly discovered remains have any connection to the 1982 case, but Bonnefoi Parish sheriff Jim Pardy says the bones recovered so far appear to belong to an adult.*

The program cuts to a press conference with Sheriff Pardy, a half-bald man who fields the questions of aggressive reporters. He confirms rumors of FBI involvement, explaining that they've been called upon for their superior resources and expertise. Asked about the identity of the victim, Sheriff Pardy declines to comment pending the official reports of forensic experts. He stresses that although the bones were on Deveau land, the family has not been charged with any wrongdoing.

I turn off the TV, head aching, but there's no way to escape an event this big in Chicory. By Monday, Evangeline's staff are all abuzz with the news. At dinner, Leeann talks about nothing else. She and her boyfriend have a bet going. She thinks the murder points to the presence of organized crime in Chicory and gleefully tosses around words like "hit" and "enforcer." Mike thinks it's a sex crime, a rape and murder. The bet strikes me as surprisingly ghoulish.

"What do you win if you're right?" I ask, but she only shrugs.

Even Jules, who stops in to discuss tomorrow's menu with her, can't resist participating in the gossip. "It's probably someone who crossed Neville," he tells us. "He was not a man to mess with."

"Oh no," Leeann protests, "Mr. D. wasn't like that . . . wouldn' kill no one."

"Not in his final years, maybe," Jules says with condescension. "When he was younger, though, he had quite the temper. His own family feared him. And he was a ruthless businessman."

I can guess where Jules is getting all of his information. Does that mean Andre thinks Neville is responsible for the body at the sugar mill, or is that Jules's own conclusion? And does Andre suspect it's Sean Lauchlin they've found? He was certainly guarded when he spoke about Sean with me in the boat.

"Neville's not the only ruthless businessman around," I say, just to see how Jules will react. "You know what they say. Like father, like son."

Jules snorts. "Trust me when I say all of Neville's killer instincts went to his daughters."

For the hundredth time, I wonder about Jules and Andre's relationship. I believed Andre when he said that Jules was more than just his boy toy, and I remember the phone call I overheard in the garden— Jules upset about hiding their relationship. Though I'm sure they have their own brand of intimacy, I also have the distinct impression that Andre knows things, dark and burdensome things he hasn't shared with Jules. But, as I think of Noah and all I haven't told him, I know that doesn't negate Andre's feelings for Jules. It just complicates them.

I don't know about Andre Deveau, but I'm tired of complication, tired of omissions. If I can't tell Noah the truth about his father, I can at least tell him the truth about myself.

On Tuesday morning, Noah calls to say he's en route to Evangeline. I walk around the grounds, brooding, and see Hettie outside in her wheelchair with all three children and a watchful nurse. The twins are engaged in their own conversation while Andre stares into space and Hettie dozes. Do her kids intend to stick around until she dies? Is she that close to the end? Maybe it's time to extricate myself from Evangeline before the family is consumed by her loss. I have enough to pull off the book that Isaac wants, and I don't know how to help Gabriel any further. Do I just . . . go home?

It all depends on Noah, and that scares me.

Hours later, Noah's truck pulls down the drive. He's earlier than expected—he must have driven like a demon to get here.

Don't look too eager.

But he looks excited enough for both of us. "Well, lookit here." He lifts me off my feet in a bear hug. "Got my very own welcomin' committee."

We walk back to his cottage hand in hand. I can't get over how happy he looks.

Do I really make someone this happy? How long can that last?

"How you been?" he asks. "You and Rae have a good time in the city?"

New Orleans feels so long ago.

"Yeah, we had fun."

He punches in the key code to his door and motions for me to go inside. "You okay? You seem like you got somethin' on your mind." I wince as he lifts his shirt and removes the gun and holster from his side. I didn't even realize he was wearing it.

"A lot's been going on here," I tell him. "A body turned up."

"A body?"

"Well. The bones."

"Here?" The lightness in his mood evaporates. "Don't tell me they found Gabriel."

"Not at Evangeline. A few miles away on some land that Hettie owns. And it's not Gabriel."

"Do they know who?" He hesitates before placing his gun in his sock drawer, as if it might not be safe to part with just yet.

I swallow. I omit. I hate myself for it. "The police haven't released that information yet." It's the only true thing I can think of that doesn't break my promise to Detective Minot.

"You look real upset about this, darlin'. Is there somethin'—"

Before I even know what I'm doing, I blurt out another truth. "I dreamed it." This isn't where I meant for this conversation to go, but maybe it's for the best. "I dreamed about the bones, Noah . . . exactly where they were. And then they were really there. It's not the first time, either."

"Wait a minute." He leans back against the counter, and I realize with a sinking feeling that my confession made sense to only one of us. "Was there a body, or did you have a bad dream?"

"There *was* a body. There were bones. It's all over the news, haven't you seen?" I don't have time to clarify, however. Someone is knocking urgently on Noah's door.

I find Benny on the front step, out of breath and all in a panic.

"Benny? What's wrong?" But I already know, can read it on his face. Something more powerful, more important than my dreams of death.

"Baby's comin'," Benny gasps. "You phone workin'? We gotta call an ambulance."

I reach for my keys. Noah and I can talk about bones and premonitions later. "I'll get you guys to the hospital."

"Leeann said we can't move 'er," Benny says in a rush. "The head's comin' out."

I freeze. "Oh my God. Noah!"

He's already sprinting back toward the driveway with his phone. "I'll call an ambulance and wait by security."

Benny and I race back to his cottage, where he leads me past mounds of Bailey's toys and piles of dirty clothes, then over to the bed. Paulette lies back, bare from the waist down. Panting. Legs spread. Sure enough, a strip of baby head is visible between her legs.

My heart lurches.

Leeann stands at the foot of the bed looking surprisingly composed. "Don't you worry, Paulie," she croons. "We gonna help this li'l boy get born. You almost there. Next contraction, you give it all you got."

Paulette acknowledges her with a moan.

EMS will never make it in time. I check my phone for a signal, hoping to search "emergency birth," but no luck. I rack my brain for everything I know about childbirth, but it's not much. I was in a hospital when I had Keegan, under anesthesia, surrounded by trained professionals who could respond to any emergency. What do I know about delivering babies?

Leeann, meanwhile, doles out instructions, the growing thickness of her Cajun accent the only sign of her anxiety. "Benny, you help 'er sit up," she says. "Baby'll come out easier if she not flat on 'er back. Get right behind 'er."

Benny hops obediently onto the bed and eases Paulette into an upright position.

"Now hold 'is hand, honey," Leann tells her. "And when it's time to push, you squeeze dat hand like you mean to break it."

"Do you have *any* idea what you're doing?" I hiss.

"I'm the oldest of six," she says. "My mama had fast labors. Won't be the first baby I seen born in a bed."

"What if something goes wrong?" Paulette could start hemorrhaging. The cord could get wrapped around her son's neck. And what if he's not breathing? I can more or less remember how to do CPR on adults and children, but the rules are different for infants.

"It's gone be fine," Leeann says resolutely. "A body knows what to do."

Paulette lets out a long, guttural roar. A contraction. She squeezes Benny's hand and bears down with all the force she can muster. Her face is damp and contorted, her eyes in another world.

I try not to look at the blood.

"You doin' fine, Paulette," Leeann says. "This is it, yeah. Time for you baby join da world."

When Paulette closes her eyes, I can feel her resolve, her need to eliminate all stimuli except the sensation of this baby. I grab a clean towel, getting ready.

"I see 'im!" Benny breathes. "He comin'!"

I see him coming, too.

Leeann reaches for the slick, hairy head straining to get out. The baby is close. So close. Leeann is there, fingers on his gooey head, trying to ease him out without tearing his mother. There's a brief rest period, then another round of contractions. Can this baby fit? It seems impossible. He's big. Too big. Except he's moving, descending, millimeter by millimeter, brought forth by his mother's sheer strength of will.

Paulette bellows, and then Leeann finds herself with a full head in her cupped hands. There's blood and mess everywhere as she slides this brand-new creature out and wraps him in the towel I provide. The umbilical cord is gray and gelatinous, but Leeann tells me not to cut it yet.

"He look all right?" Benny calls from the bed.

I study the baby. He has that sort of swollen, waterlogged look that newborns get, but I'm pretty sure that's normal. Leeann uses the towel to remove any lingering muck from his nose and mouth. He offers a long, high-pitched cry in response. Definitely breathing.

"He's perfect," I tell Benny, my eyes welling up. "Congratulations."

Paulette's slumped back in bed like the victim of a violent crime, but she perks up somewhat when her husband lays her teeny son against her chest. She lifts up her shirt to nurse him, while Leeann covers the stained bedsheets with fresh towels.

"You still got the aftabirth," she reminds Paulette. "You get that pushin' feelin', you just let it out nice 'n' easy."

She's on top of things, Leeann. Twenty-three years old, but so together, so unafraid.

I move slowly away from the bed, dizzy.

Within minutes, emergency responders descend upon the scene. As

Leeann gives them a breathless account of the birth, I drift away, no longer sure I'm inhabiting my own body. There's something about Paulette, how fully she experienced every excruciating moment, how present she was in her body, that makes me doubt my own physical existence. How could anyone ever think life would be easy when it comes so hard?

Outside, it hits me. The miracle of this beautiful baby. The permanence of my own loss. I crouch down by an oak tree and vomit. Even when there's nothing left, I keep retching.

Then there's a hand on my shoulder, Noah brushing the hair out of my face. I realize that I'm crying, noisy choking sobs I can't stop. He tries to rub my back, but I shrug him off.

"It's okay," he tells me. "Darlin', it's okay."

But it's not. My baby is dead, and that will never be okay. I spit on the ground one last time and rise to my feet. "You don't understand."

"Shhh." Noah engulfs me in a hug I can't escape. "You don't have to explain. I get it." His mouth is against my ear, almost whispering. "You miss him. Of course you miss him."

I wriggle free and stare. "Who? Who are you talking about?"

"Your son." The compassion in his face says it all.

I take a step backward and stumble on one of the oak tree's massive roots. "How do you know about my son? Have you been checking up on me?" The idea angers me, even if I've been poking around his own family more than I care to admit. "It was Rae, wasn't it? Rae and her big fat mouth. So this is what you guys were talking about the other day."

"You could've told me," he says, leaving Rae out of it. "Why didn't you tell me?"

I wipe snot from my face and brush away tears with the back of my hand. My stomach is still shaky, my mind swirling, and I can't process any of this. A baby was born, and a little boy died. *My* little boy died, but a baby was born even so. I saw a child enter this world, I heard his tiny cries. Just like *my* baby. Where is *my* baby?

I feel light-headed. "I need to be alone now."

He reaches for me, making some objection, but I ignore him. I hurry back to my guest cottage and bolt the door. Plant myself in bed, face-first. When he knocks, I don't answer.

THE LIGHT CHANGES. My lavender room turns purple-gray as the sun shifts. The outside sounds eventually dwindle away. Noah knocks on my door again, calls to me, but I stay put, not yet ready to talk Keegan.

I think about the day my son was born. He came five days after his due date, and the delay sent me into a nervous, impatient frenzy. I wished they would induce me, hold him to a schedule. When the contractions finally began, they took me by surprise. Labor hurt. A lot. I hadn't expected it to hurt so much, not when so many women endured it, going back for seconds or thirds. Eventually the epidural did its magic, and in the end there was a baby in my arms. He was pink and puffy and a little grumpy about his eviction from my womb, but he was mine.

No one told me then, *He's yours, for four years. He's yours, but not for long.* I am not by nature an optimistic or hopeful person, but when I held my child, I believed absolutely in the future. His future.

I think about calling Justine. How can you pray to a God, I want to ask, who is so unfair? How can you look in Didi's empty bedroom and see any reason, any purpose? It isn't a rhetorical question—I really want to know the answer. Justine told me that prayer gives her comfort, but I can't imagine seeking solace from the being who orchestrated my misery. God's the one doling out the suffering, if you believe in Him. How do people pray without getting pissed off?

I roll over in bed and stare up at the ceiling. Take several deep breaths. Feel my anger subsiding. I think about breaking out the old Deveau Bible, searching for answers in its pages, but who am I kidding? Those stories sound ridiculous to me. Instead, I go through the box of Andre's things and take out his book of Shakespearean sonnets. I could use something beautiful right now.

I flip through the pages, pausing at a few that he bookmarked with strips of lined paper. I breeze past a few poems about the peaks and valleys of love, then stop when I reach Sonnet 126. I recognize the opening line: *Oh thou, my lovely boy.* It's the Shakespeare Andre quoted in the boat. He must've read this book many times. As I close the book, I notice again the message on the title page. *For Andre on his 18th birthday. Hope you enjoy these as much as I did.—Sean.*

A birthday gift from Noah's father. Interesting. I lift the book to my face, studying Sean's chicken-scratch letters, and something slides from between two pages in the back.

A torn sheet of lined notebook paper, folded in half. But this isn't another bookmark. It's a letter. The writing, made by a blue ballpoint pen that was running out of ink, matches Sean's messy handwriting. I read through it quickly once, then slowly a second time, my breath catching in my throat as I start to fully grasp the implications.

So here I am, finally. Done with the army, a free man. You've got to know by now how crazy I am about you. It's time to make a decision about who you are. I can't watch you compromise yourself every damn day and say nothing. I think about you all the time and I want a life with you. It won't be the life you're used to, but it could be better. You can't live under Neville's thumb forever, him never knowing who you really are. There is so much more possible. I know being a Deveau means you're afraid of the tabloids, but if we leave the country, they'll leave us alone. I don't care what people think when they see us. If we

don't fit with their ideas of love, that's their problem, not ours. Be
strong and take what you want. With or without you, I'm leaving
tonight. You know where to find me.

Love you.
Sean

My mind reels. Sean Lauchlin. And Andre. This is big.

So here I am, finally. Done with the army, a free man. It must have been
written in June when he got out, during that final visit to see Maddie
and Jack. *With or without you, I'm leaving tonight.* Could it have been his
final day at Evangeline? The fight with his parents now makes sense.
Maddie and Jack would've lost it when they learned what their son was
up to. Andre was only eighteen years old, a full twelve years younger
than Sean. And he was their employer's son. Maddie had raised him
like her own. Add in the homosexual element, and you have the full
trifecta of Lauchlin parental horror.

So what next? I can't confront Andre and make an enemy of the
only Deveau who seems to like me. Detective Minot isn't assigned to
the Sean Lauchlin case, and I can't turn the letter in to police without
revealing that I know the identity of the bones recently found. I'll have
to wait until they release the name. I still don't know how any of this
ties in to Gabriel—if at all—but one thing is clear.

This letter contains a motive for murder.

26.

I can't disregard the impact this letter could have on Noah. Discovering that your father tried to run off with a teenage boy—and was likely killed for it—would disturb anyone. I still don't know who killed Sean, however, or where Maddie and Jack stood in all this, which makes it easier to justify not telling Noah yet. Too many questions remain to burden him with partial truths.

Instead, I photocopy the letter and leave it in Detective Minot's mailbox with a note. He risked his career to share classified information about Sean Lauchlin with me, an act of faith I repaid by neglecting to mention my relationship with Lauchlin's son. Hopefully this letter will help make amends. Maybe together we can get some answers.

With everything that's been going on, I'm glad when the pace at Evangeline seems to slow. Operations plod along without Paulette. Hettie seems to have plateaued for the time being, not improving but not worsening. I finish a chapter while Noah irons out the details of some local subcontractors he's hiring. Each morning when I wake up and see him sprawled beside me, I think he belongs there. And yet, I never talk about the future with him. Our time together is running out, but we don't say a word. We root ourselves firmly in the present.

It's different now. Not bad, but different. He knows about Keegan. I didn't think I could mention my child to anyone without dissolving into a weeping, emotional mess, but as I found with Justine Pinaro, there's relief, maybe even pleasure, in remembering Keegan out loud. Noah doesn't say much. He squeezes my hand or smiles. Mostly, he listens. He'll never understand my loss, of course, never love anything as much I loved my son. Though he's too well mannered to bring it up, I haven't forgotten that this man walked away from ten years of marriage precisely to avoid parenthood. He's not a Kid Person.

On Friday, Detective Minot calls. He skips any polite greetings. "That letter," he says, "you found it in a book?"

I stand up from the kitchen table, where I've been hammering dutifully away on my laptop. "Andre's book," I inform him. "In a box of Andre's stuff from high school."

"That fits with the time Sean went missing." He pauses. "You think Neville found out Sean was involved with his son?"

"I don't know. But if he found Sean and Andre running off together, he wouldn't have been too happy."

"Neither would Sean's parents," Detective Minot muses. "Maddie was a pretty devout Catholic."

I pop open a can of Pringles, both hungry and intrigued. Might items belonging to the Lauchlins have gotten mixed up with Deveau family junk? Those Bible passages about sexual sin could've been Maddie's. "That relationship would've upset a lot of people, not just Neville," I acknowledge. "But it's a starting point. Anything else going on?"

He sighs. "I tracked down Kyle Komen. The guy Andre said he was with the night Gabriel went missing."

"Did his story check out?"

"All signs say yes." Detective Minot doesn't sound happy about removing Andre from his suspect list. "Komen was surprised to see me. Said he hadn't heard from Andre in a good twenty-five years. But he was very definite about being with Andre that night. August fourteenth is Komen's birthday. He said he was out celebrating with friends when he met Andre."

I wolf down some chips and try not to crunch directly into the phone. I wish I'd been there to meet Kyle Komen. I have so many questions about young Andre. "Did he say anything else?"

"Just that the kidnapping put a lot of stress on Andre. Komen said they dated a few months. He described Andre as a screwed-up rich kid. Said you couldn't help but feel sorry for him."

"You believe him?"

"I looked Komen up," Detective Minot says. "He seems okay. His birthday really is August fourteenth."

"So why'd they split up?"

"Apparently Andre was always paranoid about someone seeing them together. He never wanted to go out in public."

Funny. Andre's current boyfriend has similar complaints.

"He sounds legit," I concede, forcing myself to put away the Pringles. I'm not usually a junk-food type, but Louisiana has aroused salt and sugar cravings I never knew I had.

"There's one other thing worth checking out," Detective Minot tells me. "Roi Duchesne just turned up."

He sounds less enthusiastic about this news than I feel. I don't care if Duchesne was cleared of any wrongdoing in Gabriel's kidnapping. A sketchy ex-con groundskeeper still might have heard things, might have noticed someone with an unhealthy interest in the toddler. And he might have known Sean Lauchlin. "He turned up where?"

"Right here in Chicory. Got pulled over for running a red light a couple days ago. I did some asking around. He's been working under the table as a bartender at the Cajun Canteen."

I dimly recall seeing a divey place by that name not far from the highway. "Did you talk to him?"

"Not yet. The guy has served time, so he's not gonna cozy up with law enforcement." Detective Minot sounds discouraged at the prospect of another uncooperative witness. "Still working out a strategy. There's gotta be something in it for him."

"I could help. I could visit the bar."

"No," he says. "Hell no. Cajun Canteen is for lowlifes. It's not your scene. I mean that. And Roi's bad news. You stay away from that guy, okay?"

"Hey, if you don't want my help, I won't help you." I'm hoping he doesn't realize the verbal gymnastics I'm employing. Meeting Roi would help *me*, and I'm not about to walk away from a chance to speak with him, even if it means braving a seedy bar for a night.

Detective Minot accepts my words at face value. "I'll let you know if anything comes of it," he assures me. "Just one more thing, Charlotte." His voice becomes gruff, almost fatherly. "This guy of yours? Noah Lauchlin? He could be a great guy. But that doesn't mean his family is."

"I know."

"And if he's not a great guy? Trust me. I'll find out."

I grin. I'm pretty sure that when cops go background-checking your boyfriend, you're family.

THE CAJUN CANTEEN is small and smoky, with flickering neon signs that advertise various brands of beer. Its reddish-orange lighting imbues patrons with a sickly, sunburned quality that makes the drunk look drunker. Given Detective Minot's strenuous warnings, I expected the place to be rough-and-tumble, and the half-dozen customers on this Monday night are about what I imagined: men with craggy, hard-drinking faces, one burly, one built, one skinny with a rodent face and squinty eyes, all nursing their alcoholic beverage of choice. What I didn't anticipate was the complete absence of women.

I've tried to dress like I belong: tight jeans and a boob-hugging T-shirt, makeup that does not scream high-class. It's not my clothing that does me in, though—it's the very fact of my gender. All eyes slither over me, the only female in the room. I feel them forming judgments about the kind of woman who would come here alone at ten o'clock on a weeknight. Meeting someone? Hoping to meet someone? Hooking? I have half a mind to run for the door, but when I glance behind the bar, I see him. Roi Duchesne, counting a stack of bills. Not tens and twenties, but hundreds.

This can't be a good sign.

I take a seat at the empty bar, still contemplating flight. Behind me, the men are scattered around a few tables, and I know without looking that they're watching me.

"Hey, pretty lady," someone calls. "Where you come from?"

Alcohol-themed establishments have never been my scene. I don't know the rules, don't know how to walk the line between bitchy and encouraging, so I nod in his general direction without answering the question.

Roi finishes counting his money and stuffs half in his pocket and half behind the bar. I've seen the mug shots from his arrest all those years ago. He was twenty-four, sullen and sleazy-sexy in that bad-boy, I-probably-beat-my-girlfriend way. Although he's put on weight over the years and grayed, he's still surprisingly fit and not unattractive, if you like tattoos. One thing I'm fairly sure of: his stack of cash did not come from the proceeds of this crappy little bar.

Detective Minot was right. I shouldn't have come here.

"What can I getcha?" Roi asks, his face impassive.

I can't leave without having a drink, so I tilt my head to the side and play with a lock of hair, summoning all my feminine charms for this man. "Umm . . . is a Corona Light too girly?"

He cracks a half smile. "Nah, sounds about right."

He pulls a Corona from the cooler, pops the cap, and shoves a lime wedge down the bottle's narrow neck.

"Let me get that for you, baby," the rat-faced guy across the room offers when Roi hands me my beer.

"No thanks. Always buy my own alcohol." I don't bother looking at Rat Face or trying to sweeten the rejection. I didn't intend to spend my night fending off local creepers, but I'm realizing now that may be un-avoidable. All the more reason to get friendly with Roi. Protection.

I lean toward him, ready to establish a cover story. "You didn't see a redhead in here before, did you? I'm supposed to meet a girlfriend."

Roi assures me I'm the only lady who's been in tonight. Translation: the women of Chicory have the good sense to avoid this place. I bring up Detective Minot's contact info on my phone and send him a quick text. *At Cajun Canteen. It's sketchy, all right.*

"Nice tat." I point to the image of a snake half-coiled around Roi's neck. "Who did your ink?"

"Guy in Biloxi."

"You from there?"

He shakes his head. "I was a trucker for a while. Passed through." He pauses, almost reluctant to make conversation with me. Some bar-tender. "Where *you* from?"

"New York, originally. I'm down here working for the Deveaus." I roll my eyes. "Rich people whining. We all need more of *that* in our life, right?"

He doesn't bite.

Fortunately, a grizzled man with a potbelly does. "Roi knows all 'bout the Deveaus, don'tcha, Roi?" he chuckles.

"Oh yeah?" I take a sip of my Corona, one elbow on the bar. "What kinda dirt do *you* have on them, 'cause I could tell you stories that'll make your head spin."

Roi scowls, clearly annoyed at somebody sharing his business. "Used to work for 'em. Long, long time ago."

"You probably worked for Neville, right? I heard he was all right. But I'm stuck with Hettie, who's gone loony, and her daughters, who are just bitches. And Andre . . . God, he's . . ." I trail off and let Roi fill in his adjective of choice.

"Fruity," he says, and I gather that Andre's teenage attempts to appear straight were not as successful as his adult efforts.

My phone dings as a text comes in from Detective Minot. *WHAT IS WRONG WITH YOU?? I told you to stay out of that place. Coming to get you NOW.* I put my phone down and let out a long, put-upon sigh. "My friend's running late. She always does this to me."

"You friend cute like you, or she da ugly one?" the grizzled guy asks.

"Cuter," I say. "Way cuter."

"Aw, now, I don' buy dat. You got some nice curves, honey, you do."

I don't know what to say, don't know how to steer clear of these guys. When I don't respond, Rat Face stands up and yells from his table. "Hey! Where's you manners, New York? The man paid you a compliment!"

"Settle down there, Neg," Roi says with a slow, measured smile that frightens me every bit as much as the unruly drunk guy. "You gonna scare her away." He turns to me, suddenly more friendly, and I realize uneasily that he's decided he wants me around. "What kinda business you got with the Deveaus, sweetheart?"

"I'm a writer," I tell him, then inwardly curse my honesty. "For a ladies' magazine," I add, hoping that sounds less highbrow. "I write about clothes and hair and makeup."

"They don't have enough clothes 'n' makeup in New York?" From the skeptical expression on Roi's face, I'm striking out.

"I just . . . thought this would be a fun story, you know?" I need an in, and I need one fast. "My aunt used to work for the Deveaus. Maybe you knew her. Violet Johnson." It's the first name that pops into my head, and it must be a good one because Roi leans his head back and breaks into a low, rumbling laugh.

"Violet Johnson?" He chuckles. "Well, shit . . . Violet. Sure."

From his smile, I wonder if he slept with her. Danelle did mention something about Violet knowing a lot of men. Or maybe Violet was involved in some kind of criminal activity with Roi. Drugs? But I don't see how that would tie in to Gabriel.

Roi looks me up and down as if searching for a family resemblance. "Your aunt, huh? She was a little spitfire, Violet was. Forgot she worked for the Deveaus." He scratches his unshaven chin, a faint smile still playing on his lips. "She was workin' at the old Piggly Wiggly when I knew 'er. Never could keep a job, that girl. What she up to these days?"

"We're not in touch much . . ." I'm struck by his assumption that Violet is alive. If she really died in a car accident when Noah was a baby, wouldn't Roi have heard about it? "When's the last time you saw her?"

"Aw, we were just kids. I was, oh, twen'y, maybe. You tell her I said hi."

I want to ask more about Violet, but don't want to arouse his suspicions, not when he's just warming up to me. "That's cool you knew my aunt," I say. "And you worked for the Deveaus, too? They're driving me freaking crazy. How'd you deal?"

"Kept to maself." He runs his thumb along the snake tattoo. "Did'n get too near Andre or Hettie. I know trouble when I see it." He says nothing about getting fired or his six weeks in custody, and the other men seem to be too involved in their own conversations now to chime in.

"You think Andre's trouble? So far he seems like the best one."

"'Cause you're a lady," Roi says. "He don' give a hoot about ladies."

"Oh yeah? Was he into *you*?"

He bristles at the idea of being another man's crush object. "I don' care what family he from, he'da laid a finger on me or looked at me wrong, I woulda beat the crap outta that kid and he knew it." He whips out a dishrag and begins scrubbing the bar top. "Hettie was the one to watch."

Funny what comes out when a guy feels his manhood has been insulted. "Hettie? No kidding?"

He scrubs a little harder. "Oh yeah. Like a bitch in heat. If I'da smiled at her, she'da jumped my bones."

I remember what Danelle told me about the night Neville hit his wife. Hettie said if he wanted to continue on with his whores, then fine, but the least he could do was find her a nice pool boy. Roi would've made a hunky pool boy, all right, if that's really what she was after. But somehow I doubt it. Hettie was depressed, isolated, profoundly lonely. Some hothead who spoke only in monosyllables would not have filled that void. Roi's ego strikes me as far too inflated to provide an accurate version of events, but I encourage him to continue anyway. "Wow, so Hettie was a slut?"

"Woulda been . . . if I gave her half a chance. She was a liar, too. Squirrelin' money away from her husband."

Now *this* is getting interesting. "No way! How do you know?"

Roi licks his lips. "She convinced Neville there to give 'er a monthly allowance, see?"

I nod, trying not to puke at the paternalism of a wife begging for a monthly allowance.

"Well, I heard 'er tellin' him the stuff she needed it for. Shoppin' trips, a horse, a party she was gonna throw. But it was crap. She never did the stuff she was talkin' 'bout."

"Whoa. Was it a lot of money?"

"She got more in a month than I made in a year back then," Roi confirms, his lip curling at the injustice of it. "'Bout twelve thousand dollars."

Now I know how Sean Lauchlin ended up with his abnormally large bank account—though I don't know *why*. I'm about to drop Sean's name, to see what reaction that gets from Roi, when one of the men speaks up from the back of the room. "You got company, Roi."

In the doorway of the bar, a very agitated Detective Minot stands staring daggers at me. I'm a little annoyed he couldn't have waited five more minutes instead of interrupting right as I was getting answers, but he's in no mood for complaints.

"Get. In. The car," he says through clenched teeth. *"Now."*

Rat Face lets out a long, low whistle. "Yuh lady been out lookin' for a good time, huh? She didn' tell us she married."

Once again, all eyes are on me, but this time the gazes are hostile, not hungry, as if waiting to see that I get what's coming to me. I've pushed my luck as far as it will go tonight. I toss a ten-dollar bill on the bar top and scramble to join Detective Minot at the door.

Before we make it outside, Rat Face intercepts him, gives Detective Minot a consoling punch on the shoulder. "Cheatin' bitches," he says, jerking his thumb at me. "We all got one."

ONLY WHEN WE'RE WALKING BACK to my car does it truly sink in. The danger I just put myself in. My lack of a solid exit strategy. The rear lot I'm parked in is poorly lit and secluded from view—exactly the kind of place a woman should never be wandering alone at night—and a shady-looking guy with a ponytail hangs around a nearby Dumpster. I don't know who or what he's waiting for, and I'm pretty sure I'm happier not knowing. There's no denying that without Detective Minot to escort me out, I could've found myself in a tight spot.

I owe him one.

"Before I drive myself home," he says tersely, "I'd like a word with you."

He's still fuming as he climbs into the passenger side of my Prius, so I swallow my pride and allow him a good five minutes of vitriol. I nod at his accusations of unparalleled stupidity, concur that I demonstrated a reckless approach to personal safety, and am appropriately ashamed when he points out the selfishness of my actions, which required him to leave his distraught wife late at night on some ill-advised extraction mission. By the time he gets to *Don't you ever pull this kind of dumb-ass stunt again*, though, a small grin has found its way to my face.

"What the hell are you so smug about?" he demands.

"Nothing," I say. "Continue, please. My personal flaws are obviously much more interesting to you than learning who funded Sean Lauchlin's bank account."

Detective Minot doesn't exactly look pleased, but he ends his rain of insults. "Whatever you found out, it still doesn't excuse your behavior tonight," he says huffily. "But go on. Let's hear it."

I tell him what Roi said about Hettie squirreling money away. "Twelve thousand dollars. The exact amount deposited in Sean's account each month." I adjust the climate settings in the car and wait for his excitement, his praise for a job well done.

I receive only a thoughtful grunt. "Go hit the drive-through across the street," he instructs me. "You're buying me french fries."

At another time or place, the request might seem odd, but french fries make a certain kind of sense right now. And milk shakes. Louisiana brain food.

Obediently, I drive over to the Carl's Jr. and pull up behind a car full of teenagers. A greasy stoner type in the backseat hangs his head out the window like a dog as his friends shout various food items into the speaker.

"So Sean was blackmailing Hettie," Detective Minot muses as the teenagers continue with their lengthy order. "But why?"

"Maybe he threatened to tell people Andre was gay."

He shakes his head. "Not with that love letter you found. I mean, Sean was gay, too. It sounded like they had a relationship. How could he blackmail Hettie over that? He had a lot to lose himself, getting busy with a kid who was barely legal."

"True." I watch the stoner boy sway from side to side, eyes half closed, while the rest of his car argues about the number of Cokes they need. "What if it wasn't blackmail? What if she was paying him for something?"

Detective Minot looks doubtful. "Information? Or drugs, maybe. Sean *did* talk about running off to Mexico."

"Did you look into Violet Johnson yet?" I ask. "The woman Sean had a son with? Roi said he knew her. Maybe Sean and Roi and Violet were all part of—I don't know—a drug ring. Maybe they sold to Hettie."

He shakes his head again. "No one's ever mentioned Hettie behaving unusually. There's no way she could cover up a drug addiction that was costing her that kind of money. And she certainly had no financial incentive to deal."

The car of teenagers pulls up to the drive-through window, allowing us to place our order through the crackling speaker. With my window down, I can smell traces of marijuana emanating from the kids' vehicle. Detective Minot either fails to notice or chooses to ignore it. I think about Roi's wad of cash, the large bills, certain that he's involved in something a lot heavier than the sale and distribution of marijuana. Detective Minot is right. It's hard to picture Hettie ever associating with those guys.

I search for something else that might be worth twelve grand a month to her but come up empty. Hettie wasn't a gambler, and pool-boy remark notwithstanding, if she was going to pay that kind of money for sex, there had to be better options than her son's boyfriend.

"What if Hettie knew about Andre and Sean's relationship?" I flounder along, trying to talk myself into a reasonable hypothesis. "Hettie could've given Sean the money to—I don't know. Help him and Andre."

"She gave Sean money for three years," Detective Minot reminds me. "Andre was only fifteen when Sean opened that account."

I'm more than a little icked out by the thought of a fifteen-year-old and twenty-seven-year-old embarking on a forbidden romance, regardless of their genders. "So maybe she paid Sean to stay away. Maybe she wanted to avoid a scandal."

I try to picture it from Hettie's perspective. Her son was in love with Sean. Had she gone to police and accused Sean of being a sexual predator, she would've jeopardized her relationship with Andre forever. He would've been questioned extensively by police, and who knows how cooperative he'd have been? Even if the press couldn't legally mention Andre by name, word would get around. The fact that he'd been a willing participant would eventually emerge. Hettie probably thought she could wait it out. Send Andre back to school, wave Sean back to his army job. Paying Sean off might make sense if she felt that she was protecting not just her child but the whole family from unwanted scrutiny and embarrassment.

But twelve thousand a month is, as Roi pointed out, a lot of money. If she later learned that Sean was violating the terms of their agreement, she would be understandably angry. The question is *how* angry.

Detective Minot has drawn similar conclusions. "She must've caught them. Three years trying to keep them apart, and there they are."

"And then Sean ends up dead and buried." I exhale. "On her land."

The drive-through cashier is waving me on, I realize, so I pull forward and collect our food, too preoccupied to feel guilt about what I'm about to ingest.

Whether Hettie killed Sean herself or finally turned to Neville for some help, I don't know. But I need to talk to Noah about this. As soon as the authorities positively identify his father's body, I have to tell him everything that I know.

I park the car and take a noisy sip of milk shake. Detective Minot makes quick work of his fries, his anger with me dissipating with each bite. "I can believe Hettie paid to keep Sean and Andre apart," he says with a frown. "I could even believe that she killed him. But there's still one thing I don't understand."

"I know." I finish his thought for him. "How the hell does this relate to Gabriel?"

VALENTINE'S DAY falls a week before Fat Tuesday. I don't intend to make a big deal of it, but Noah has a surprise for me: he's scored coveted hotel reservations for the coming weekend in downtown New Orleans. The idea of experiencing party-happy New Orleans on its wildest days of the year wouldn't always have appealed to me, but I now find myself surprisingly cool with the idea of reckless, joyful sin before Lent. I'm ready for Mardi Gras.

"It's three nights," Noah says. "We'll leave Saturday mornin'. Think you can plan somethin' for us?"

Can I? What a ridiculous question. *Noah, meet Charlotte's incredibly compulsive research and organizational skills.* I spend my week alternating between writing sessions and Mardi Gras planning. I trace parade routes and traffic detours, print out maps, research parking, and piece together an itinerary. By Friday afternoon, I'm bubbling over, eager to dazzle Noah with my scheduling masterpiece.

As evening falls and Noah still hasn't come by, my impatience turns to concern. It's seven p.m. Where *is* he? The estate is all but empty. No one works late the weekend before Fat Tuesday; even I know that. I call him, but his phone is turned off. On a scouting run, I see his truck parked up by the house. He must have gone to visit Hettie.

I duck in through the empty kitchen, thinking I might pop in to see how she's doing and maybe even bring up Sean Lauchlin. It's a good time to snoop. Apart from a nurse and security guard, the help has gone and won't be back until Wednesday—a reprieve courtesy of Sydney and Brigitte, who decided they could afford to be generous while out of town anyway. Except for the blazing lights of the foyer, the lower level of the house is dark. Noah must be upstairs.

"Charlotte!"

At the sound of my name, I nearly wet myself. I spin around and, through the open door to the study, can barely make out the figure of Andre in one of the armchairs. I assumed he'd returned to New Orleans with his sisters, but apparently not. He leans forward, drink in hand, and smiles, oblivious to the fact that he looks rather deranged lounging around in the dark. And he's wearing that ridiculous bathrobe again.

I put a hand over my racing heart and catch my breath. "Hi. I didn't see you there."

He flips on a little light on the table beside him. "Better? Come, sit."

Actually, the last thing I want to do right now is listen to Andre's tales of upper-crust angst. Had I realized he was still here, I might've thought twice before embarking on my Noah search. There's no way around it now, though. He's seen me. I step into his office but don't sit down. Maybe he'll take the hint.

"You haven't been around the house lately," Andre observes. "What have you been up to?"

"Just working on the book."

"Naturally." He takes a vigorous gulp of whatever he's drinking. "I heard you helped deliver Paulette's baby the other day."

"That was all Leeann." Just thinking about the birth and that perfect, tiny boy gives me a lump in my throat. Paulette has been staying with her sister since her son was born, so I haven't had the chance to see him again, but I think about him often. "It was pretty intense," I tell Andre. "I'm just glad she and the baby are all right."

Andre scarcely hears me. He looks flushed, a little sweaty. I wonder how much he's had to drink. "Let me fix you something. You told me you like Shirley Temples, so I got some grenadine."

"Some other time. Thanks, though." I glance over in the direction of the staircase, but still no sign of Noah.

"Is something wrong?" His brow furrows.

"I'm just—looking for Noah. I think he may have gone up to visit your mother."

"You mean the landscaper? I didn't realize you two were friends." There's something nasty in his face now, and it's plain as day: Andre hates Noah. Hates him.

Admitting an alliance with Noah could be a profound misstep. And I want to know why Andre is gunning for him, if only to warn Noah. "I don't know him that well," I say slowly. "He was supposed to give me a ride somewhere."

Andre wags a finger at me. "I don't know who that man is, but he's a lying, manipulative son of a bitch. If I see him in this house again, I'll—"

"You'll do what?" Jules appears in the office doorway, his smile mocking. Perhaps he's the reason Andre chose to stay at Evangeline for the weekend. "What will you do, Andre? Please tell."

Andre looks flustered. "I thought you'd gone. It's late."

"I'm reviewing last year's books so I can pass them on to the accountant. I figured I'd spend the night here."

Andre's flush deepens. He wipes his forehead with the back of his hand but makes no comment. Why is he so ill at ease? I already know about their relationship.

Jules's eyes pass quickly around the room. "Have you seen my pills? I thought I left them on the desk last night. It might be nice to actually sleep for once." He casts Andre a long look, but Andre doesn't dare meet his gaze.

"Sorry. Haven't seen them."

Either Jules knows I'm privy to their relationship and isn't trying to be discreet about it, or he's deliberately flaunting their involvement to piss off Andre. I don't know if they've been fighting or if Jules is just in one of his notorious moods, but there's a tension in the room I can't quite pinpoint.

Andre clears his throat. "Perhaps you'd like a drink, Jules? Some tequila? You're the only one who drinks the stuff." He turns to me. "Jules is quite the bartender. Tequila Collins, Tequila Sour, Tequila Sunrise, Tequila Manhattan . . . you name it, he makes it. With tequila."

Jules yawns. "The last thing in the world I want to do tonight is watch you drink yourself into oblivion, Andre. God knows I've seen that enough times."

"You're hardly a teetotaler yourself, my friend."

"I'm not your friend," Jules says softly. "I'm many things to you, but I am not your friend."

Andre glances at his liquor stash and then at Jules. His desire to flee whatever weirdness exists between them outweighs his desire to drink. "On that note," he says, "I'm going to my room. Good night, Charlotte. We'll chat tomorrow. And I'll make you that Shirley Temple."

Finally. A chance to extricate myself. I'm ready to bolt, but before I can make my getaway, Noah comes down the staircase.

Andre's face clouds over, and I know we're in for more drama. "Were you talking to my mother?" he demands.

Oh no. It's on.

Noah's mind is elsewhere. He glances at Andre with mild distaste, the kind of look you might give an insect that ventured into your home, but he doesn't acknowledge Andre's question. I can see how this would rub Andre the wrong way.

"My sisters have explicitly told you to stay away from her," Andre says, moving into Noah's path. "Any conversations about your project should be with Mr. Sicard."

Andre's the taller of the two, but Noah is obviously stronger. I doubt this fact is lost on either one as Noah clenches his fists and says, barely able to maintain civility, "It wasn't a business conversation, it was personal."

"Personal?" Andre puffs up. "We're done with this charade. Whatever lies you've been telling my mother end here. There is *nothing* personal about your relationship with my family." He's halfway up the staircase when he delivers the final cowardly blow. "Jules. Please handle this."

And Jules does. He swoops in with his chiseled jaw and manicured fingers and swiftly disposes of Noah. "I'm afraid the family has elected to cancel your contract," he states. "Step into the office, and I'll write you a check for services rendered."

"You can't cancel my contract." I've never seen Noah's face turn this particular shade of pink. "That contract is with Hettie. She's the one who signed it, not you."

Jules doesn't look up from the check he's writing. "Given Hettie's condition, that contract will never hold up in court. Especially with its highly unusual terms." He shakes his head. "Unlimited funding for your project even in the event of Hettie's death? It looks . . . how shall I put this? Greedy."

"Those are the terms she chose."

"I can't imagine a woman on her deathbed is competent to make any important financial decisions. She's in a vulnerable position. Fortunately, as the estate manager I have power of attorney." Jules tears off a check and holds it out to Noah with a pleasant smile. "That should cover your time and expenses. If you disagree, you are of course free to take it up with us in court. Now I'll have to ask you to leave the premises. Please pack your belongings. I'll tell security to expect you in half an hour."

Noah looks poised to punch him in the face, and while part of me would enjoy the vicarious thrill of a Jules beat-down, I understand that standing idly by is not the noble, caring thing to do.

"He isn't worth it," I whisper, nudging Noah toward the door. "Come on. Let's get you out of here."

Jules follows us to the door, and there's a lightness in his step that makes it clear he's enjoying this. He slips the check into my hand as I leave. "Your friend will want this later," he says, smirking. "Trust me."

BACK AT HIS COTTAGE, Noah storms around pulling clothes out of drawers and cramming toiletries into a suitcase. I've never seen him like this before, so I stay out of his way. I'm freaking out, too. Everything has changed. He's leaving Evangeline. Noah and I can exist as a couple now only through actual effort, conscious choice. And we have less than half an hour to make this decision.

It doesn't take long to empty his place. He travels light. Wallet, watch, loose change, a handful of condoms purchased weeks ago—he distributes these items quickly amongst his pockets. The last thing he takes is his handgun. I'm uncomfortable with his toting that thing around any day, but knowing that he's packing when he's this angry scares me.

Even scarier: he's said nothing about us. In fact, I'm not convinced he's thought about me at all. Is he leaving, then? Just—going back to

Texas? Is this it? I find myself panicky at the thought. It's too soon. And with no notice. I'm not good with good-byes.

"You better pack a bag, too," Noah says, prompting another internal freak-out.

Does he think I'm going to just run off with him? Where would we go? This decision is too big to make so quickly; doesn't he know that? I stand, mouth agape, as he regards me impatiently. "Would you come on? I'm not goin' to miss out on Mardi Gras just 'cause Hettie's kid has a bug up his ass."

Oh. Our trip. Right. Relief, disappointment, and dread all mix together in a confounding fashion. We're in a holding pattern, for now.

"Okay," I say, but then hesitate. He's halfway out the door and I don't trust his grim look of purpose. "Noah?" I jog after him. "Where are you going?"

"Back to the house," he says. "I left my phone up there."

This might be one of the worst ideas I've ever heard. "I'll go," I volunteer. "You don't want to deal with those two again."

But he brushes by me. "I don't give a shit about them. I want my phone."

Please don't let Andre and Jules see him, I think as he strides off into the night. *Let them be holed up in Andre's bedroom or rendezvousing in the study.*

I don't know exactly how long he's gone, but it's too long. I start running through every awful scenario in my mind. If Noah lays a hand on Andre or Jules, he'll be arrested for assault. And we're in Louisiana. I'm fairly sure that if he does something threatening on Andre's property, Andre can shoot him with impunity. I gather some clothing, but our Mardi Gras vacation no longer excites me.

When Noah does finally return, he seems moody, not fired up. He's silent, barely noticing me as I drag my suitcase up to his truck and climb into the passenger seat. I don't know what he's thinking about as we take our leave with security, but when I look back at the immense house, I feel oblivion. I can never come back here with him. I feel the huge, gaping uncertainties of the future.

This is what we're left with: four final days of carefree abandon. And then, Ash Wednesday. Lent. Forty days of self-denial, a time to reflect upon one's past transgressions and repent. Even in New Orleans, the fun can't last forever. I glance at Noah in the driver's seat. His hands grip the wheel tightly; he stares straight ahead.

Maybe, I think, *the end is here already. Maybe the fun is already over.*

WE SPEND THE NIGHT at a local motel. There's no romance, just fast food, an uneventful check-in, the television flashing in a dark room. Noah remains quiet. I don't know how to lift the dark cloud around him, so I don't try. We go to bed early, although neither of us really sleeps. He tosses and turns, getting up occasionally and stalking around the little room. Despite several signs prohibiting smoking, he opens a window and goes through a half-dozen cigarettes. I can't tell if he's angry or upset or simply worried about what his next step will be. It's unnerving. What am I supposed to do? Reassure him? Give him space? I'm not any good with feelings. Not my own, not anyone else's.

Around one a.m., I bring him a glass of water. It's a move from my grandmother's playbook: ply distressed person with liquid while avoiding discussion of actual problem.

"Thanks." He stands shirtless by the window, staring out at the parking lot. But he drinks the water. A good sign.

I sit cross-legged on the floor beside him and wait. When he finally does speak, it's not what I'm expecting.

"Why do you like me?"

I don't know what to say. I like how he makes me feel—calm, comfortable, present in the moment—but does that sound too self-absorbed? And I like how easygoing he is, polite and pleasant to others, rarely ruffled by the little things—but given his current mood, that seems like the wrong quality to praise. And I like him physically, but that's superficial.

"I like you because—you're good," I stammer.

My answer seems to depress him. "You don't even know me."

A fair point. A month together does not constitute a high degree of knowing.

"Well, you're better than *I* am," I tell him.

He presses his forehead to the window. "There's so many lies in my life, I don't even know who I am at the bottom of it all."

Whose lies? But he must mean Maddie and Jack, all the things about his past that they left out or twisted around. I wait for him to elaborate, but instead he climbs back in bed. Buries himself in covers. Turns his back to me and sleeps. Or pretends to.

His warm body beside me fails to calm me down. For the first time, being together is not enough. For the first time, I realize with a pang, I feel lonely.

APPARENTLY NOAH IS MUCH BETTER at willing himself out of a funk than I am, because by morning, he is relentlessly cheerful. I try to reconcile the man singing in the shower with the brooding stranger of last night but can't. We don't discuss the loss of his job or his ensuing existential torment. I'm curious, naturally, but his happiness seems so precarious. It's easier to chatter about the drive to New Orleans, which parades to see, which restaurants to try. Considering how much time I now spend delving into the secret lives of strangers, I'm remarkably willing to avoid issues of any depth in my relationships.

About forty minutes out of Chicory, conversation lags and Noah begins messing with the radio. He breezes past a country station but stops on a song I find even more disturbing.

"Really? Christian rock?" For a New Yorker who spends a lot of time around atheists and Jews, unabashed Jesus love is sort of startling. Even my grandmother, an occasionally practicing Catholic, has always felt that religion, like kissing or farting, should be conducted as discreetly as possible.

Noah smiles, a bit sheepish, his thumbs resting on the wheel. "Just like the sound of it, I guess." For a moment we listen to the lyrics, delivered by a gravelly-voiced man in a somewhat melodic shout.

Despite the pain, I keep believing.
Despite the hurt, I keep my faith.
I pray that you'll forgive my weakness
And hold me in your eternal embrace.

"Forgiveness and unconditional love," Noah says. "Who doesn't want some a that?"

"You don't want God," I say, shaking my head. "You want a mom."

His smile vanishes. "Yeah, I want a mom. A mom and a dad, doesn't everyone? A kid deserves to know his parents." He switches off the radio. "Forget it. You wouldn't understand."

"Are you obsessing about your parents again?" I ask. "They don't have to define you, Noah. I don't think they matter as much—"

"They don't matter? You *would* say that. You pretty much chased away your kid's father. You didn't think he mattered, although maybe you shoulda asked your kid what he thought."

After everything I've told him about my divorce, this interpretation of events shocks me. "Eric *cheated* on me."

Noah's voice is flat. "He mighta been a shitty husband, but that didn't make him a shitty dad."

I'm a fighter by nature, but his accusation cuts too deep for me to defend against. To blast my parenting decisions when Keegan is gone, when I can never right my wrongs, can only stew in my own regret—this is cruelty I did not think Noah capable of. I fall into a stunned silence.

The miles go by, long and wordless, before Noah finally apologizes. "I shouldn'a said that," he says. "I'm just . . . feelin' a little raw."

I nod mutely, although it doesn't make me feel much better. I know he's in a lousy mood, but that doesn't mean he wasn't being honest. Doesn't mean he's wrong.

ONCE IN THE CITY, I'm relieved to have organizational details to attend to. Disposing of the car proves a bit of a fiasco, but soon Noah and I are wandering the downtown area. Traffic more or less flows along Canal Street, although some of the side streets are blocked off. We trudge along for a mile or two until we hit a parade route.

Spectators line the empty streets, many camped out on lawn chairs, downing beers. Vendors hawk jester hats, glow necklaces, and lemonade. I've always pictured Mardi Gras as a sort of *Girls Gone Wild*, drunken college girls flashing their breasts, so I'm surprised by the number of families, the children perched on ladders for better viewing. We keep walking, taking it in, until we hear the tinny strains of a marching band approaching. A police vehicle rounds the corner, its siren chirping once to alert the crowd.

I don't remember attending a parade as a kid, but I can see the magic of it when the floats pass by strewing goodies. Beads, stuffed animals, and plastic cups soar into the crowd. Noah manages to catch a couple of strings of beads for us and we slip them on, hoping to blend in. The excitement of the floats is tempered by public figures driving by in cars, the occasional police officer on a motorcycle, and high school girls in skintight uniforms dancing with batons. All those swirling hips and shaking rumps remind me of Zoey's dance recital, and I miss her suddenly, and Rae, too. And Keegan. Of course I miss Keegan.

I retreat from the street's edge and lean against the iron fence in someone's front yard. Noah joins me, eyes still on the floats.

"Whatta ya think?"

"Keegan would've loved this."

He puts an arm around me, but I don't want his comfort. Sometimes discomfort is deserved. Noah was right about Eric, much as it pains me to admit it. I should've offered Eric shared custody. He might have refused it, might have moved to Chicago regardless, but I owed Keegan a chance, at least. A chance for a more involved father.

Beside me, Noah bobs along to the thumping stereo of another approaching float, oblivious to my regret. A few more days, and he'll be gone. I know the drill. Everything, both good and bad, comes with an expiration date.

BY SUNDAY NIGHT, we're starting to feel like Mardi Gras veterans. We've seen four parades, each a little different. The night parades are more dramatic, floats lit up in the dark, robed men on foot bearing flambeaus—big, fiery torches that cast an eerie orange light on onlookers.

Noah drinks, but he seems to pace himself. If he's tipsy, I can't tell. He gets a little overly competitive when he tries to catch beads, but he seems to be having fun, relaxing. He hugs me, nuzzles the top of my head. From the outside, we look like a couple with a future, not two people who will say their good-byes in less than forty-eight hours.

Back at our hotel room, he's all over me: He leads me out to the balcony, kisses my neck, tries to slip a hand up my shirt. I push him off.

It's too loud, too public, with all the music, yelling, cars, and other hotel guests partying on their balconies. On our left, a guy attempts to pee onto the street below. Not, in my book, a recipe for romance.

Noah laughs. "Aw, come on. That doesn't put you in the mood?"

I head back into our room and lie down. Maybe he's drunk after all. Or else his good manners have been a front this whole time, and now that we're basically over, he's throwing all ceremony to the wind.

IN THE MORNING, I order an extravagant breakfast, which room service sets up on the balcony. Noah remains in bed, snoring, while I work my way through eggs, bacon, sausage, biscuits and gravy, coffee, and a slice of king cake, a traditional Mardi Gras dessert. I'm pouring another coffee when Noah joins me outside.

"Someone's hungry, huh?" His eyes are a little puffy, but he doesn't appear to be feeling the aftereffects of excessive alcohol consumption. After years of living with an alcoholic, I notice these things. Noah takes the one remaining piece of toast and slathers it with jelly. "Whatcha got planned for today?"

Suddenly I can't bear the thought of seeing another parade, pretending to feel a joy that I no longer feel. "I don't know. Whatever."

"You don't seem too happy."

I peer over the edge of the balcony. We're ten stories up, and though I've never been afraid of heights, I'm overwhelmed for a few flickering seconds. "It just . . . stresses me out," I say.

He comes up behind me, slips his arms around my waist. "What does?"

"Not knowing what's coming." I can't take my eyes off the distant ground. "We're going back to Chicory tomorrow and . . . I don't know what comes next."

"I've been tryin' not to think on it." He lays his face on my shoulder, so I can't see his expression. "I'm still sortin' out what's happened."

I have to ask him, have to know and make my peace with it. "Once I'm back at Evangeline, what'll you do? Where will you go?"

His arms tighten around my waist. "Gotta settle some things. But home . . . I guess."

"It'll be weird staying there without you."

"Yeah. I thought we had more time."

"Maybe I'll go home, too. I've done all I can there and I have everything that I need." I close my eyes. "I'll miss you, though."

"Yeah?" He runs his thumb slowly up my arm. "Maybe we could go somewhere. Travel around. Drop outta life for a while."

My chest aches at the thought, but why drag out our fling any longer? Could I ever really enjoy my time with him when I knew it had to end? And, while I'd love to postpone the inevitable return to reality, there are responsibilities and ties I can't ignore. "I have to see my grandmother. She's old. And she's all I have left. If something happened and I wasn't there . . ."

"No, no, you're right. You should be with her." He pauses before asking a question too loaded to be casual no matter the delivery. "You think she'd like me?"

I whirl around and get a good look at his face. "Why? You want to come with me?"

"I dunno." He's embarrassed. "You said she didn't like your ex. I bet he'd look great next to some Texas hick, huh?"

I try to imagine what Grandma would say about Noah. She didn't like Eric because he was too wishy-washy and always seemed a little scared of her. But my grandmother's ideal man is Gary Cooper in *High Noon*. She is no stranger to the allure of a man in cowboy boots. And I've already seen what a way Noah has with elderly ladies.

"Actually, I think you guys would get along." It's a giant, crazy leap, but what the hell. "Do you want to meet her?"

"Do *you* want a visitor?" His eyes search mine. "See where things go?"

It's funny. When I first saw Noah at that awful dinner party, I found him memorable mainly for his poor choice of wardrobe. Now, in the glowy light of a New Orleans morning, I see someone grounded, good-natured, and considerate. Someone strong. Someone sexy. That first night, I reached for him almost intuitively, as if my body knew something my mind didn't. This time it's my mouth, answering him even before I know what I'll say.

"Come to Connecticut," I say. "Please."

27.

People have never been a reliable source of happiness in my life. They die, they lie, they disappear. And yet here I am, setting aside my well-earned cynicism, preparing to introduce Noah to my grandmother. Why run deeper and deeper into a relationship that can only end badly? Is it stupidity? Masochism? An elaborate distraction tactic to avoid dealing with Keegan's death? D, all of the above? Whatever's going on with me, I'm not ready to walk away from Noah. I want to be with him.

On our last full day in the city, the day before Mardi Gras, I surrender to that desire, however ill advised. I enjoy myself. I imagine happy days ahead.

We meander about the bead-draped city, eat sausage from questionable food carts, pocket shiny doubloons from various krewes, dance each time a marching band passes. At dinner, we plan our trip north like two giddy kids. I know that Noah's running away, trying to hide from the past, but so am I. If it's escapism, we're both guilty. For now, we take pleasure in making decisions that are concrete and immediate. Drive together or separately? If together, what do we do with Noah's truck? Once in Stamford, where do we stay? My house has tenants for another six weeks, and we don't want to impose upon my grandmother. Do we find a motel? The plodding details keep us from facing bigger questions.

Now that I can see what's coming—at least in the short term—I want to leave Louisiana as soon as possible, to put Evangeline and its phantom child behind us. Noah, though, needs a couple of days. He has loose ends to tie up in Chicory, he tells me.

We leave New Orleans on the morning of Fat Tuesday, too tired of partying to make it through the day's festivities. I'm ready to get back, to say my good-byes. I'm ready to move forward.

As we approach the entrance to Evangeline, I get a bad feeling. The security gate is open, and there's a Bonnefoi Parish police cruiser parked near the guard shack. Noah stops the truck, frowning. He's said little for the last couple of hours. Almost as soon as we left New Orleans, his black mood seemed to return.

"Uh-oh," I say. "What do you think that's all about?"

He shakes his head. "I dunno. But I can't exactly go in there and find out. They probably got me on some list."

He's right. There's no sense stirring up more trouble with Jules and Andre. "I'll get out here," I say. "Are you going to be okay? Where are you off to the next couple of days, anyway?"

"I'll be around. Just—gotta take care of some things." He glances uneasily at the police vehicle.

I grab my suitcase out of the back and give him a quick kiss on the cheek. "I'll call you Thursday morning. We'll figure out a place to meet."

As he drives off, I evaluate the scene before me. Did the sheriff's department officially identify Sean Lauchlin? I thought the FBI had taken over the investigation. I take a few steps and realize the front pocket of my suitcase isn't fully zipped. When I bend down to fix it, I see why. Noah's phone. He must've run out of room in his duffel bag and shoved it in with my things. I sigh. This will make it much harder to reach him on Thursday.

At the security gate, an officer steps from his car to intercept me. I realize I look a bit peculiar showing up on foot. "Hi . . ." I try a tentative smile. "Can I go in?"

"Who are you?"

"Charlotte Cates. I'm staying in one of the cottages."

Immediately, he lightens up. "Oh, Miss Cates. Detective Minot said to keep an eye out for you."

"Is he here?"

"In the house." He pulls a walkie-talkie from its holster. "Go ahead. I'll let him know you're comin'."

There are two other units parked by the house, plus Detective Minot's familiar white Impala. This seems like a fairly major police response, especially for Mardi Gras day. What the hell happened?

Detective Minot appears on the front steps and nods when he sees me. "I've been looking for you. We've gotta talk." He jogs down the steps and gestures for me to walk with him. "Trouble follows you around, huh?" he observes.

"What's going on in there?" I ask, anxiety mounting.

"Looks like an overdose." He doesn't sound especially impressed. Maybe Chicory gets a lot of overdoses around Mardi Gras. "Jules Sicard. The estate manager."

"Oh my God. Jules?! Is he dead?"

Detective Minot leads me toward the dock in front where the airboat was tied the other day, keeping one eye on the house as he speaks. "He's in the ICU over at St. Mary's. Last I heard, he's in some kind of coma. Hettie's nurse found him this morning in the study, lying in his own vomit."

"What did he OD on?"

"A mixture of tequila and sleeping pills."

The tequila doesn't surprise me. But sleeping pills? My eyes widen. "You mean Ambien." When Jules complained about his missing pills on Friday night, I never dreamed they would kill him just days later. Anyone who's been prescribed sleep meds knows the risk of combining them with alcohol. And Jules is not stupid. "Did he do it on purpose?"

"Probably." Detective Minot leans back against a tree trunk, the dappled light of the leaves playing across his face. "Sicard had a prescription for the pills, but he must've taken a handful. Looks like he drank at least a half-dozen tequila sunrises. But we still have to rule out foul play."

I remember mixing tequila sunrises for my father before he started drinking everything straight up: one part tequila, two parts orange juice, and a generous splash of grenadine. They were his prettiest drink. I liked stirring them, watching the red of the grenadine swirl up through the amber tequila and orange juice like an actual sunrise. That may have been the last thing Jules saw as he washed down his pills with drink after hypnotic drink.

"That's horrible," I murmur.

Detective Minot looks tired. "Yeah, well. Our homicide unit spends more time investigating suicides and attempted suicides than actual murders. Turns out people usually hate themselves more than each other."

"I didn't think Jules was the type."

"Some people are good at hiding their problems." He shrugs.

The front door of Evangeline swings open, and a small man in glasses steps outside and approaches Detective Minot, a cardboard box of bagged items in his arms. Must be from the crime scene unit. The two exchange a brief series of gestures, and then the man waves, loads up his vehicle, and leaves.

Something occurs to me, something very sad. "Has anyone told Andre Deveau?"

Detective Minot nods. "He's at the hospital. Word is he lost it when he found out. Got completely hysterical. My buddy Blake said they had half a mind to put him on suicide watch, too. Helluva way to get outed." He shifts gears. "So listen. I've got to talk to you. This boyfriend of yours."

"*That's* why you've been looking for me?"

"Yeah," he says. "Noah Lauchlin."

The fact that Detective Minot finds Noah a more pressing topic of conversation than someone nearly offing himself concerns me. "What about him?"

"Was that L-A-U-C-H-L-I-N?"

"Yes . . ."

"Born March 1979 to Violet Johnson, and he's a resident of Texas."

"That's right."

"So I've got some Noah Laughlins, L-A-U-G-H-L-I-N," he tells me. "But none of them in their early thirties."

"I just told you, it's with a C."

"That's what I've been looking for," Detective Minot says. "And I'm coming up empty. You know why that might be?" He sounds suspicious, like I purposely led him astray.

"Um . . . I don't know what state he was born in. Look for records out of state?"

"I did," he says grimly. "I've searched the whole United States. There's no Noah Lauchlin born March 19, 1979."

A cold breeze ruffles my hair and stings my eyes. Could I be mistaken? But I'm not, I know I'm not. I remember birthdays, and he told me March 19. And he told me he was thirty-two years old. I would remember that, for sure. A gnawing worry gathers in the pit of my stomach.

"I don't know what to tell you," I say. "He lives in Texas, and he told me that was his birthday. Did you look for his mother? Violet Johnson?"

"Oh, I found Violet Johnson," Detective Minot confirms. "Died in 2007. Gave birth in Natchitoches, May of '79."

I'm at a loss. "Maybe the records are off?"

"The baby was stillborn," he says softly. "I don't know who this guy is, Charlotte, but Noah Lauchlin doesn't exist."

HOURS AFTER PARTING WAYS with Detective Minot, I sit staring at Noah's phone. I've run through the contacts list a dozen times, hoping it might provide answers about the phone's owner. No such luck. The entries are all one uninformative word, like HANSEN, RJ, and, worryingly, WORM. For a business owner, this seems strange. Shouldn't he have a long roster of employees and customers? I check the area codes and discover that most, like his, are Texas-based. That much of his story appears to be true.

I don't know what to make of all this. Did he intentionally leave the phone behind so I couldn't contact him? Will he be back for me on Thursday, or has he been planning to disappear all along? Maybe the vague issues he had to attend to were just an excuse to bring me back to Evangeline and get rid of me. Where has he gone?

"A family like the Deveaus, they're gonna attract a lot of gold diggers," Detective Minot told me after breaking the bad news. "Anybody could get taken in by one of those creeps, don't feel bad."

But Noah? *My* Noah?

The sinking feeling in my stomach is not one of surprise but inevitability. Haven't I known all along that this man was too good to be true? I remember the fortune-teller in New Orleans, his warnings of a sweet-talking man. *He ain't who you think,* RaJean cautioned us. *Ain't who you think at all.*

Jules spelled it out the night he fired Noah. Noah—or whoever he really is—is after Hettie's money. Jules could see it. Andre could see it. But I couldn't.

He was smart, I'll give him that. He claimed to be the grandson of two people Hettie loved dearly, both of whom were dead. His so-called father had been safely missing for thirty years, and he cast another dead woman with connections to Evangeline as his mother. No wonder he showed no interest in learning about Violet when I brought it up. She was just a name to him, a convenient stranger. Of *course* I haven't found a relationship between Sean Lauchlin and Violet Johnson—there wasn't any.

Hettie is a vulnerable target. Noah appeared precisely when she was diagnosed with terminal cancer, showering her with the attention her own children didn't provide. Somehow, he coaxed her into signing a contract that offered him almost unlimited funding and no oversight. He probably doesn't even have a landscaping company. For all I know, he's just some guy who picked up a few things mowing lawns and faked his way through the rest. The icing on the cake? His being almost the same age as her lost son. He had to know, psychologically, how that would affect Hettie. With the dark eyes and dark hair, he probably even bore a passing resemblance to Gabriel, cementing the connection in Hettie's mind, unconsciously or not. I remember when Noah and I visited Hettie that rainy night, how she called him Gabriel. I thought she was senile, but perhaps Noah himself planted the idea in her mind.

And where do I fall in all of this? Am I a side note? An enjoyable little fling he deceived right along with everyone else? I'm filled with self-disgust for buying Noah's bullshit, and yet part of me can't believe that's what it was. Not all of it. That night in the hotel room, when he asked me why I liked him, he must've been wrestling with his conscience. He must've cared.

You don't even know me, he said, in what may have been our only truthful moment together. *There's so many lies in my life, I don't even know who I am at the bottom of it all.*

I thought the lies he was talking about were someone else's, not his own.

There were red flags, moments when I doubted him but ultimately looked the other way. They flow in again now like a tsunami. Cristina Paredes, Noah's lovely "business associate." Is she in on the scam? Is she his girlfriend, as I originally suspected? He could be a liar *and* a cheater. And there was the day he stole that photograph of Sean and Maddie from the library. I thought it was a token of his father, but perhaps it was to show Hettie, to "prove" his bogus identity, his fabricated parentage. He certainly did his homework on me, uncovering the son I never told him about. That trip he supposedly took to Texas could've been another lie. Maybe that *was* Noah I saw in the window of the sugar mill.

One way or another, Noah charmed his way into Evangeline, won Hettie's affection, and gained access to her bankroll. And no one stopped him. Until, of course, Jules stepped in. And look where he ended up.

I start to panic. Could Noah have had a hand in Jules's overdose? Andre said Jules was the only one who ever drank tequila. If somehow Noah knew that, it wouldn't have been hard to crush up a bottle of sleeping pills, mix it in with the tequila, and wait for the lethal combination to do its work. He had the opportunity when he went back to the house to get his phone. If he went to get his phone at all.

Did I fall for not just a con man but a killer?

. . .

THE NIGHT, as if I don't have enough on my mind, I see Gabriel. I'm not even asleep, but as I lie in bed paging through a book, I feel a pull. It's not the pull of exhaustion; this is something new, an insistent tugging from somewhere behind my eyes. I don't resist. I sink into the blankets and give myself up to that now-familiar weightless feeling.

Darkness.

Thin, stiff carpeting against my knees and bare feet.

A small window frames a slice of night sky: moon hanging over a busy road. Headlights, streetlights, a traffic light blinking from yellow to red—all cast a glowing square upon the floor beside me. Inside the square, a boy kneels, his hands pressed together in prayer. My heart leaps as I recognize the shaggy head.

Jo-Jo?

He looks up, liquid brown eyes bright and full of yearning. When his lips part, I see the chipped front tooth.

You comin' for me? he asks. *You gone find me soon?*

I have one final chance to get this right.

I've been looking for you, I tell him. *But I don't know where to go. I went to the big white house where you used to live. Do you remember that house?*

He nods, lower lip quavering, and his body slips into shadow. *He made me go.*

Who? I lean close to him. *The man who took you?*

He's a bad guy.

I'm not sure what to ask, how to get more than vague, childlike replies from him. His communication skills are admittedly better than those of your average two-year-old, but without a name, a place, what good is this conversation? *Where are you now, honey?* I say. *Where can I find you?*

I'm with the bad guy, he whispers, eyes huge. *He wanna keep me foreva.*

I don't know what this means, but it's quite possibly the most terrifying thing I've ever heard. Serial killers often keep trophies that remind them of their victims. Is some sicko hanging on to Gabriel's remains? Does that mean his killer is alive?

What's his name? I ask. *You need to tell me who the bad guy is.*

He hesitates. *You gone get him? You gone make him go away?*

I'll do everything I can, I promise. I know he hurt you.

He said don't tell. He said he gone kill Mommy.

I know. I don't tell him that his mother is old now and about to die anyway; it probably wouldn't make a lot of sense to a kid on the spirit plane. *We won't let him hurt your mom. But you've got to tell me his name.*

As if in reply, the little boy lies down and stretches out flat on his back. He stares upward, unblinking, and I see the light around us lift to gray, feel the walls melt away and the worn carpet go wooden beneath us. A quick, sweeping glance around, and I know where we are. The creepy dock by the boat launch. I peer over the side and see the familiar dark water of the swamp. But something's off. There are bubbles. Dozens upon dozens of bubbles rise up, and then something neon orange shoots to the surface, bobbing there. Then another. And another.

Goldfish, I realize, unnerved. Not real ones. The crackers.

I turn away from the eerie ring of floating Goldfish crackers and look back at the dock, where Gabriel lies splayed, unmoving.

Are you in the water? I ask. *You want me to look for you in the water? It's too big. You have to tell me where.*

His dark eyes search mine, and I watch the hope in his gaze flicker out. He turns on his side and curls up as if preparing to go to sleep. I feel him fading on me.

Stay with me, Gabriel. You've got to tell me more. Who's the bad guy? Gabriel? Who's the bad guy?

But even a two-year-old can sense my weakness. I couldn't save my own child. How could I save him? Save his mother? The dock, the swamp, the bobbing Goldfish crackers, and the little boy all grow fuzzy. He's given up on me. I stand up, the only clear form left in a world that is starting to resemble a weird, smudgy piece of expressionist art.

Why? I beg him. *Why don't you tell me?*

I love my mommy, he says simply.

28.

I t's time to leave Chicory, to admit defeat. Because I've been defeated. Thoroughly. The child I came to help has lost his faith in me. I have no idea who killed Gabriel Deveau *or* Sean Lauchlin or why. And I'm nursing a pretty bruised—if not broken—heart, having been stupid enough to fall for a charming liar, at best, or at worst, a murderer. How can I trust my judgment about *anything* after a mistake this severe?

I'm heading for a breakdown. Fast.

I push cornflakes around my bowl and logically assess the mess that is my life. It's Wednesday morning. I'm supposed to reconnect with Noah tomorrow. I still don't know if he intentionally left his phone with me or genuinely forgot it. I don't know if he'll ditch me or show up looking for me. And I don't know if I want to see him again. Part of me wants to tell him off, to feel empowered by my anger and not victimized by my hurt. Another part says, *Walk away. The only thing you have left is your dignity, girl.* And what if he did try to kill Jules? He could be dangerous.

In the end, I find myself sitting with a bowl of soggy cereal and an abundance of self-loathing. Whether or not Noah turns up tomorrow, I need to return to Stamford. To see Grandma, to put my house on the market, to finish the book somehow. To start my lonely new life, instead of postponing it here in Louisiana limbo.

I soon discover I'm not the only one having a bad day. In the kitchen, Leeann waves an oven mitt over a pan of smoky corn bread. She holds one hand to her head and looks ready to cry. It's the day after Mardi Gras, so I assume she's suffering from the usual postparty affliction.

"Hangover?"

She shakes her head miserably. "I got no excuse. Just did'n grease the pan."

"Don't worry about it. Sydney and Brigitte aren't back yet. No one will care."

"I know, I . . ." She takes a deep breath, but her voice wavers anyway. "I had a rough few days at home, is all."

"I think the last few days have been rough on everybody."

Her eyes fill up with tears. "I can't even believe it about Jules. I shoulda seen through it, that whole attitude. I shoulda seen him hurtin'."

"They don't know exactly what happened," I say. "Maybe Jules didn't mean to . . ."

She gives me a long look. "I heard 'e took a lotta pills. I don't think it was an accident."

I don't think it was an accident either, but I'm not about to share my theory with Leeann. Not when all I have to go on is a hunch. Not when I want so badly to be wrong. I change the subject. "Listen, I wanted to tell you . . . I'm leaving Evangeline tomorrow."

"What?! No! You mean, like, foreva?"

"I've finished my research."

"Oh, Charlie, how can you leave now? I'm gone miss you. It's gone be so quiet."

"You'll just have to start planning that trip to New York you've been dreaming about."

"Shoot, if I didn't have the li'l man, I'd be there in a heartbeat." She manages a wobbly smile. "But I guess I know someone else who's gone miss you. How's Noah takin' it?"

Evidently Jules's possible suicide attempt has eclipsed the news of Noah's firing. "He took it fine," I say, unable to look her in the eyes. "The family canceled his project. So he's going home, and I'm going home." I shrug and try to look like this is no big deal, like I wasn't planning to introduce him to my family just twenty-four hours ago, like he's not a liar and a fraud and maybe even responsible for Jules's near death.

"You two seemed so sweet togetha," Leeann says wistfully. "I thought maybe things was gone work out." The old rust-colored dog wanders into the room, a welcome diversion. Leeann looks thoughtfully at her ruined batch of corn bread. "Come see, *chien*," she calls, and the dog trots over obediently. She sets down the pan and he digs in, his tongue and nose carving their way eagerly through the crumbs. Leeann scratches his ears while he gorges himself. "Always got one fan, don't I? You a good boy." She turns to me. "Neva met a betta dog. You shoulda seen him with Jo-Jo. Had the patience of a saint."

For a second, just a second, time stops. My heart stops. My blood freezes in my veins. "Jo-Jo?" I repeat.

"Jonah," she says, making kissy faces at the dog. "Ma son."

I lived in the big white house. I had a doggie.

Oh. God.

"Leeann," I croak. "You said you used to live in one of the cottages, right?"

She grimaces. "A few months, yeah. Then we got floodin' from a storm, and our cottage was full up with mud. They spent all last spring remodelin'." She takes the pan away from the dog and begins soaking it in the sink. "Lucky for us, Hettie had a sweet spot for Jonah and let us stay in the house. But I was so glad to leave. I swear, meetin' Mike and movin' in with 'im was the best thing ever happened to us."

Mike.

He made me go, Jo-Jo said when I mentioned the big white house. And Mike did, in his way, by inviting Leeann—and her son—to share a home with him.

Where can I find you? I asked the boy in last night's dream.

I'm with the bad guy, Jo-Jo said, and my mind turned to the macabre, imagined some serial killer fetishist who was hanging on to his remains. But it was simpler than that, much simpler. It's so obvious now, so clear what's been going on.

Mike, who watches her son every day. Mike, who, according to Leeann, loves her baby like his own. Mike, who saw the young, vulnerable, unwed mother of a toddler and made a terrible, evil calculation.

I might puke.

How could I have been so utterly blind? This isn't the first time I saw something *before* it happened. I dreamed about Zoey's injury in advance, and Didi's death. Why did I assume that I was seeing a child from the past? Why, when Jo-Jo was so close, did I overlook him again and again? I knew Leeann had a son. She talks about him all the time. I knew he was three years old. I knew she left him with Mike all day, just the two of them, and that her son called her once at work, sobbing, begging her to come home. I knew about this little boy, and not once, as a friendly gesture, did I ever ask his name.

Because I was jealous. I didn't want to hear about her child, not when I'd lost mine.

No wonder Jo-Jo gave up on me last night. He saw me for what I was. Clueless. Selfish. Too caught up in my own sadness to help anyone.

"Where is Jonah?" I ask faintly. "Right now, where is he?"

"With Mike," Leeann says, searching through the pantry. "I think they goin' fishin' today."

"Fishing? Like, on a boat?" It gets worse and worse.

"Yeah, Mike's got a motorboat for swampin'. Jonah said he didn't wanna go, but Mike was so keen on it. He tries, Mike really does, but it's hard these days. Ma baby's goin' through a mama phase where he cries any time I'm not holdin' 'im."

Her ignorance leaves me breathless, although it's not so surprising, really. Faced with two explanations, the clingy child versus the sexually abusive boyfriend, what would most people prefer to believe? Sometimes, to stay sane, you let yourself trust the shiny surface instead of digging for the darkness beneath. And I'm hardly one to cast stones at someone who has grossly misjudged a lover or failed to see her child was in danger. There's just one more question, one last piece to fall in place.

"Leeann, this might sound weird, but does Jonah have a chipped tooth?"

Please say no, I think. *If he hasn't chipped his tooth yet, maybe there's time. Maybe I can stop it.*

Leeann peers at me, mouth hanging open. "He broke 'is front tooth yestaday ridin' 'is bike. You givin' me the frissons, Charlie. How'd you know that?"

I cover my face with my hands. Despair is setting in. I'm too late. Too damn late. "We need to find him. We need to find your son right away."

"Why? Why you lookin' like that?" She's getting panicky now.

"What's Mike's last name?" I need to tell Detective Minot who we're looking for.

"Findley. Mike Findley." She wrings her hands. "What's goin' on?"

"I want you to call him. Call him and tell him there's an emergency. Tell him you need Jonah home right away."

"His phone won't work in the swamp."

"Try."

"That look on you face—you think somethin' bad gonna happen, don't you?"

"Where were they going fishing?" I persist. "Do you have any idea where Mike might've taken him?"

She shakes her head, big-eyed. It doesn't matter. Because I know where to find them. I've known all along.

THANK GOD Detective Minot answers his phone. I can't imagine trying to explain this situation to a 911 dispatcher. "Hey." I'm almost breathless. "You remember the boat launch I took you to? The one near Deveau property?"

"Sure. You find something?"

I jog along the gravel path toward my car. "Get every boat you can out there, Remy. There's a three-year-old boy, Jonah Landry, who's in danger."

Detective Minot exhales deeply. "Please tell me you've got more than a hunch to go on. I can't launch some large-scale Water Patrol search if you don't have—"

"He's with a man named Mike Findley. And I think Mike's going to kill him." I'm fully prepared to fabricate some story about a kidnapping if necessary, but Detective Minot jumps to conclusions without any deliberate deception on my part.

"Oh, Jesus. Findley took the kid?" From his voice, the name is not unknown to him. "I knew that pervert couldn't keep his hands to his damn self. I've been waiting five years to nail the piece of shit."

I climb into the driver's seat of my car. "This is your chance."

"We'll get him," he promises me. "I'll move on this fast as I can. Just . . . stay out of it now, okay? Findley was arrested before when a kid came forward. The state felt we didn't have enough to prosecute and dropped charges, but Findley's not going to forget that. He's not going to leave witnesses this time. You don't want to mess with one of these creeps when they get cornered, Charlotte."

I make a noncommittal noise and hang up. I remember how long it took the ambulance to arrive when Paulette was having her baby, and I can't imagine Water Patrol will move any faster. I'd be out there in a heartbeat if I knew how to help, yet despite my hustle to the car, there's little I can *do* at the boat launch. Assuming Mike has already got them in the water, I'm helpless. Land-bound. I could try to take Andre's air-boat, but I have no idea how to operate the thing, and it's docked in front of the house, anyway. I've got no idea how the waterways connect, if at all.

I feel sick to my stomach. It's like Keegan all over again. I realize something's wrong only when it's too late. By the time help comes, Jonah will be gone. Mike will undoubtedly have some story prepared about a terrible fishing accident. And Jonah will never have the chance to speak against him, to reveal the awful things Mike did. There is nothing I can do to stop this.

Unless.

There's a piece that I've been forgetting. The boat. That spooky old rowboat in the carriage house.

Leeann said Mike had a motorboat, and that makes sense. There's no way he took Jonah out in that rowboat, no way he'd have access to—or even knowledge of—that item. And yet, when I touched the wooden boat that night, I had a clear vision.

I'm pushing the boat into the water. Trying to hold it steady.

I'm peering over the side. Searching. Searching.

Water. Murky. Plunging deep. Deeper.

What if this, like my dream of Jonah, was not a vision of the past but of the future? Before, I was convinced that boat was an instrument of Gabriel Deveau's death. What if it could be the only way to save Jonah Landry's life?

I take off running for the carriage house, praying that Jonah is still alive to save.

29.

The sky is a misty gray when I pull up to the boat launch. The threat of rain only strengthens my conviction that Mike's intentions are pure evil—who would take a small child fishing in this weather? No people, no boats in sight, but I do observe a beat-up station wagon parked nearby with a hitch on the back. That's got to be them. Thank goodness I left Leeann back in the kitchen. I don't know what I'll find here, but it could be something no mother should ever have to see.

I step from the car, expecting a barrage of nasty sensations to strike as they have before, but there's nothing. Nothing but my own rising dread. The air sits thick and heavy in my lungs, making it hard to breathe. Am I too late? What now? I've got nothing to aid me except memories of what I've already experienced.

I jog over to the station wagon and peer inside, hoping for some clue about where Mike might have gone. There's a car seat in the back littered with orange crumbs and Goldfish crackers. I shudder, remembering my vision, and check the front seat. No telltale maps, but on the passenger side of the car, I spot fishing tackle. Which means by the time they got out of this vehicle, Mike was no longer telling Jonah they were going on a fishing trip.

Jonah must've been conscious on the drive over—he was eating Goldfish, evidently. Did he sense something bad coming, or was he used to bad things happening every time he was alone with his mother's boyfriend? I remember the first time I came here. Even before I'd seen Evangeline, this terrible place drew me in, showed me its secrets. I felt what Jonah must've felt, a crack to the back of the head, panic, no air. I told Detective Minot that he drowned, that his abductor threw him into the water while he was still living. If I'm right, Jonah might not be dead yet. He could still be out there, on that boat.

Leeann once told me her son saw angels. If ever there was a time for heavenly intervention, I think, it's now. I run back over to my Prius. The old Deveau rowboat protrudes from the back, too large to fit properly into the trunk and backseat. I'm not sure this thing is even seaworthy, but it's my only option. Heaving the front of the vessel onto my back, I drag the boat to the launch area. Every step is a struggle, but I don't care. Leeann's child is out there. Adrenaline is giving me the extra push I need. I run back for the oars and strap on a life jacket, pausing for just a second to peer out at the dark, motionless water of the swamp. I shiver.

Nowhere left for me to go but in.

ROWING IS HARDER than I thought. The boat wobbles precariously when I get in, and even after I've righted her, she seems to have a mind of her own—a sign, no doubt, that I'm completely incompetent at steering. Branches, half-submerged in the relatively shallow swamp water, scratch at the sides of the boat as I slip by. It's unnervingly quiet, nothing but the occasional bird and the gentle *shhh* of parting water. I recognize this place, the brown water and swirls of green scum. I know the dead leaves, the eerie gray light, the rotted branches curling like fingers. I dreamed it.

I catch a flash of movement in some weeds. My heart pounds, expecting the worst: a small boy bobbing facedown. Instead, I see watchful green eyes peering up at me, a bumpy snout. The only time in my life I will ever be relieved to see an alligator.

About fifty yards out from the launch area, I have choices to make. The swampy water funnels into different channels, narrower pathways broken up by oddly jutting fingers of shoreline and islands of weeds and bowing trees. Where do I go? I'm at a loss. Why, oh why, must my intuition fail me now? Have I really endured these disturbing visitations for nothing? I stop rowing and listen. The silence, I realize, is more than just creepy. Mike's in a motorboat. If he were nearby, I would hear him. Unless he's shut off the motor.

Think this through. Why would he stop?

He could've stopped to throw Jonah in the water, of course. I've been here a good fifteen or twenty minutes without hearing a motor, though, and throwing a child overboard shouldn't take that long. He'd want to get away as quickly as possible, wouldn't he? If Mike is like most pedophiles, he's a coward, too weak-willed to resist his own urges, equipped with an endless propensity for self-justification. Detective Minot said he's had a previous run-in with the law. I suspect Mike's getting rid of Jonah as a practical matter, afraid the boy will expose him.

Maybe he's trying to weigh down Jonah's body. That could take twenty minutes. I quickly dismiss the idea, however. A body that's been deliberately weighed down would discredit any stories of an accidental drowning. He wouldn't be that dumb, would he?

I'm starting to despair. Mike's boat must be out here, just beyond my hearing, and if I can't even hear his motor, how can I possibly find the right spot?

There's one more possibility, one that gives me hope. Maybe Mike heard someone coming, another boat. Maybe he killed the motor to avoid detection.

Water Patrol has to be on the alert by now. Maybe they're out there, searching, and Mike is hiding, waiting for his chance to dispose of this child. I look around. Plenty of places to hide in the swamp. With all the trees and brush, it wouldn't be hard to duck down a little waterway and wait for someone to pass by.

I take a few strokes with the oars, and suddenly, without warning, the hairs on the back of my neck begin to rise. There, floating in the water beside my boat, is a single orange Goldfish cracker. Soggy but not yet totally dissolved.

It's you, I think. *He cut the motor when he heard YOU.*

We're not far from the boat launch—he could've heard my car pull up. He's probably been listening all along, listening to me struggle with the boat, listening to me curse as I tried to row. He's waiting me out. He's close.

It's just me and Mike.

You will NOT be afraid, I tell myself. *Look who he chose to prey upon. A three-year-old. A young mother. Mike Findley is no big, bad man—he's completely chickenshit. But you, Charlie, you are not.*

The thick air gathers around me, warm and damp on my neck, like breath. I smell death, living matter decomposing in the turbid, stagnant water, and yet the swamp itself feels very much alive. Alive and watchful. Predatory. The quiet scares the hell out of me.

"Mike Findley, you sonnuvabitch, I'm coming for you!" In this desolate landscape, my voice is both startling and small. Even if I found Mike, what could one woman in a wobbly rowboat really do? But it's all I have left: strong words to camouflage my weakness. *"I know what you've done, you sick bastard! I know what you've done!"*

Fear can clear your head, focus you, enable you to act decisively and intelligently. Or it can make you stupid. When I hear something near a cluster of moss-draped trees off to my right—a rustling, then scraping sounds—I know that fear has made Mike stupid. I know I have a chance. I row toward the sounds, heaving my body into each stroke until my muscles burn.

There's a splash, and even in the seconds before I hear the rumble of a motor starting, I know it's Jonah. Jonah is in the water.

I row. Through the gloomy, humid air. Past tree roots, swamp grass, and branches. I collide with a log and the rowboat bounces off to the side, costing me precious seconds as I fight to get back on course.

From around the curve of trees, a boat zips out, engine roaring. The man at the helm turns to get a look at me, and in the seconds that our eyes lock, I forget to breathe. *This is what evil looks like.* A husky, pale-faced man with a shock of red hair. Jeans and an orange puffer vest. Not ugly, not handsome, not memorable in any way. A man you'd smile at politely in the grocery store and never think of again.

This is what evil looks like, and he's staring right at you.

His hand moves down toward the throttle in a quick, jerky motion, accelerating. *He's going to hit you.* He has speed on his side, and power. I can't possibly escape.

But I'm wrong. Instead of bearing down on me, the motorboat loops away, shoots deep into the belly of the swamps. Mike casts me a backward glance over his shoulder, and then he's gone, a coward through and through.

I let him flee. Don't waste any time or headspace on him. Instead, my eyes trace his path backward, trying to pinpoint the area he came from. I have to get to Jonah.

I row. Row, though my shoulder blades are on fire, my triceps leaden. Row, although I can't see where I'm going. No sign of where Jonah went in. I've read plenty of pool safety brochures in my day, and

I know how quickly a child can drown. And that's in clear water without all this muck, not to mention gators. Time is not on my side.

"Jonah!" I think I'm in approximately the right location. The water doesn't look deep, but when I dip a paddle in, it doesn't touch bottom. Deep enough to kill a three-year-old.

My determination is rapidly giving way to panic. He has to be here. Has to be. But the branches, the leaves, the floating scum all conceal what lies beneath the surface.

"Jonah!" I call again.

Then, about twenty feet away, I spot something. A flash of white. His shirt.

Without thinking, I'm in the water. Have to get to him. The water's murky, and the cold shocks my system, but it's the *things* that get to me. Strange shapes and textures brush against me as I swim toward that white beacon. Something rough claws my leg. Branch? Gator? I don't stop to find out.

Grab the shirt. Just grab the shirt.

My hand closes around the sopping fabric, and I feel the weight of a small child's body straining against me. Thank goodness I'm wearing the life jacket. I grope frantically for the rest of him. Leg, torso, fingers, hair. I yank his dark head to the surface. Air. He needs air.

His eyes are closed, his body limp. I can't do anything for him out here in the water, and even if I could get us both back in the boat somehow—unlikely—the bottom of the rowboat is curved, not flat. Too shaky, too unstable for me to attempt any rescue measures. We've got to make it back to the dock.

I lean backward and let myself float. Slide my arms under his armpits and tilt him back against my chest, careful to keep his head out of the water. All I can think about as I start to swim are those first aid and CPR classes I took when Keegan was a baby. *You're so paranoid,* Eric said. *You always expect the worst.* And he was right. I expected the worst, and I tried to prepare for it. I imagined my son choking, drowning, ingesting poisonous substances, and I learned the ways to save him. In the end, I got the worst: a disaster I did not anticipate, an outcome I could not have changed.

But I can change this one. I can still change this.

Swim. Keep Jonah's face up. Don't let him swallow more water.

I can see the dock and the boat launch now, although still no sign of Water Patrol or the sheriff's department. I swim. It's no easier than paddling the rowboat but more instinctive. I try to ignore the unseen objects I'm scraping past, but adrenaline surges freshly through me each time my legs bump something large. God, I hope Andre was right when he said that gators are sluggish this time of year.

Swim. You can make it. You're not so far away. Keep swimming.

Eventually, my feet touch the concrete bottom of the boat launch. I drag Jonah out of the water and lay him out on the dock, flat on his back, like my last vision of him. His eyes are still closed, his skin cold.

"Jonah? Jonah, wake up!" I tap his shoulder, swamp water dripping from my face to his. "Cough, baby! Cough it up!"

He doesn't move. Only the water moves. Trickles from his hair, his clothes, his tiny cheeks. Pools around his body, staining the wooden slats of the dock. This is bad. Very, very bad. He's unconscious and doesn't seem to be breathing. No choice. I've got to do chest compressions. I peel up his T-shirt, my fingers fumbling with the wet fabric, and press my hand to the center of his scrawny chest.

One two three four five . . .

Thirty chest compressions delivered in rapid succession. I hope I didn't break any of his ribs. Know that it might not matter if I did.

I tilt his head back, trying to clear his airway. *Am I doing this right?* There's no time to doubt myself. Brain damage can occur after just four minutes without oxygen, and it's been much longer than four minutes. I scan for signs that he's breathing. No rising chest. When I place a hand near his mouth and nose, no breath. I press my hands to his neck, attempting to check his circulation. My fingers are so frozen, so numb from my swim, I can't feel anything. I grope his chest, searching for a heartbeat. Again, nothing.

Please help me. I don't know who it is I'm looking to, what force I think can intervene here. I just know that I can't do this alone. *Help me save this little boy. I can't let him die. I won't let him die.*

I pinch Jonah's nose. Cover his mouth with mine. Administer a couple rescue breaths. His chest rises as I breathe air into his lungs, but he doesn't resume breathing. I feel his neck for a pulse and get none.

Chest compressions, again. Two more rescue breaths. Another round of compressions.

What else can I do? This is all I have to give. My breath. My hands. My will to keep trying. Because this is someone's little boy, somebody's child, and I will *not* let Leeann suffer as I've suffered, I will not let a twenty-three-year-old girl, already so grossly betrayed, lose more than she has lost.

I. Will. Not.

The entirety of my being now lies in Jonah's small rib cage rising at my breaths, his pale chest depressing and expanding beneath the flat of my hand. Over and over, I count. I press. I breathe. Over and over. And still, that boy lying on the dock doesn't wake up.

I don't notice the cars pulling up, an airboat launching, a pair of EMTs rushing to my side. I only know they're pulling me away from him. I start yelling. Nonsensically yelling, swatting at people, somehow convinced their expertise is not enough, that only I can bring this boy back to life.

"You did all you could do," Detective Minot tells me, and I wonder where he came from, why he seems to be restraining me. Or maybe that's a blanket he's trying to wrap around me. I guess I'm still wet.

And very cold. "It's out of your hands now, Charlotte. It's out of your hands."

One of the EMTs covers Jonah's nose and mouth with a plastic device, squeezing air through a bulb, while the other, a woman, performs chest compressions. They're more efficient than I was, fifteen chest compressions for every two breaths, but they're no more successful. Detective Minot tries to steer me away from the dock, but I won't budge. If Jonah's gone, I have to know.

"We're going to find Mike Findley," Detective Minot says, as if that could make things better. "I promise you, we'll find him. He's not getting away with this one. He will spend the rest of his miserable life—"

He stops. Stares. So do I. Because Jonah has begun to vomit.

The medic kneeling by the boy's chest reaches for his carotid. "We've got a pulse!"

Minutes later, in a miracle that seems far greater than walking on water or multiplying fish and bread, Jonah Landry opens his eyes. He doesn't sit up, just takes in the scene around him with a foggy, confused look. Swamp drool dribbles from his lower lip onto his chin. He blinks a few times, and then his dark, solemn gaze meets mine.

"You came," he says.

I take a few steps toward him. "Jonah? Honey? Do you know who I am?"

"Yeah," he says. "You're my angel."

30.

How to explain this?

I'm at the sheriff's department, working on my official statement. After everything that's happened, I just want to catch my breath, let it sink in that I've found Jo-Jo, that he's alive. The sheriff's department has its own ideas, however, and here I am, almost eight o'clock now, sitting in a cold, white room with paper, a pen, and a can of Sprite. I'm supposed to write down everything I witnessed this evening, recall the events while they're still fresh in my mind.

It's not the statement I'm struggling with, but the questions that will inevitably follow. Why did I suspect Mike? How did I know where to go? *It came to me in a dream* seems an inadequate explanation, although people in these parts might be better prepared to accept that than I am. They believe in angels. They believe in the helping hand of God.

As I piece together a terse account of spotting Mike in the boat, I can't stop thinking of Jonah and Leeann. I thought *I* had trust issues. How will either one of them ever trust men again? Can Leeann's faith remain strong when she learns the truth about this man she thought she loved?

The door opens. For a second, I worry that it's an officer coming to admonish me for spacing out, but no. It's Detective Minot.

"They got him," he says. "Just got the call from Water Patrol."

"Oh, thank God." That's one good piece of news for Leeann. At least she won't have to wonder where Mike is at night. "He'll be convicted, right?"

He nods. "Jonah's physical exam was fairly conclusive. And we've got your account. Findley should get life in prison." In a grim way, Detective Minot sounds pleased.

"Poor Leeann," I murmur. "This will destroy her."

"The mother?" Detective Minot's mouth twists in scorn. "Please. She left her son alone with that bastard over and over. It was her job to protect her kid from perverts and she invited one into her home."

Maybe, if I didn't know Leeann, I would agree with him. But I *do* know her. "She's twenty-three years old," I say quietly. "She thought she'd found her Prince Charming. Don't put this on her."

"Look, we'll do everything we can to help her and her son. There are support groups. Therapy. It'll be a long, ugly road, but she'll make it. So will the kid."

I lay my arms on the table and stare down at them. "I'm going to have to testify, aren't I?"

"Maybe. But this stuff can take years. He could take a deal, plead guilty. It might never even go to trial." He peers at me, his haggard face softening. "You've been through a lot today. How you feeling?"

"Stupid."

He raises an eyebrow. "How's that?"

"I was wrong." I stare down at my half-completed written statement. "Everything I told you about Gabriel was wrong. I'm so sorry, Remy."

"What are you talking about?" He sits down across from me. "You saved that boy's life."

"If I wasn't so stupid, I wouldn't have had to. I had the information

I needed staring me in the face from day one, and I didn't put it together. Who knows how many times Mike got his hands on Jonah that I could've prevented." My stomach turns at the thought.

"Jonah's alive because of you." Detective Minot leans across the table and studies me with intense blue eyes. "You can't excuse his mom and then tell me you blame yourself."

"You don't have to be nice. We both know that I've been wasting your time."

"You kidding me? Nobody would've known what happened to Sean Lauchlin if you hadn't taken me to the sugar mill."

"You still don't know what happened to Sean Lauchlin," I point out. "They'll probably never solve that case."

"Fine." Detective Minot stands up. "If you want to sit around feeling guilty, go ahead. But I want you to know, this is why I joined the force. To help people. To get the bad guy. Knowing you and going through all this—it hasn't been a waste of time for me," he says. "It's been an honor."

He's gone before I can thank him, hug him, tell him the privilege was mine. Before I can tell him what an amazing and good man he is. There's a lump in my throat when I think about leaving Chicory and never seeing Remy or Leeann again, but I take a sip of Sprite and press forward. I'll find a way to express my gratitude to him later. Right now, I have to finish writing this damn statement.

JUSTINE CALLS as I'm packing early the next morning. She's heard that I'm leaving today and wants to take me for a farewell breakfast. We meet at Crawdaddy's, exchange quick hugs, and sit in a booth by the window. After ordering us a stack of pancakes and receiving the requisite coffee, Justine raises her mug in a toast.

"To Charlotte. For keeping the little boys of Chicory safe."

"Thank your husband," I tell her. "Thank Water Patrol. I'm not the one who caught Mike."

"I'm thanking *you*," she insists. "You knew where to go and when. Remy said you did CPR on that child, kept him going 'til the paramedics got there." She reaches across the Formica table and puts a hand on mine. "God did right when He picked you, honey."

I look around the diner at all the patrons. A whiskery man in a sweatshirt and hat. A woman reading the newspaper. A bearded father trying to ignore his squabbling twin daughters, who seem to be disputing ownership of a My Little Pony. Am I any different from these people? I want to tell Justine she's wrong, that I'm not an instrument of God, just some woman plagued with bad dreams. The truth is, though, I'm no longer certain. Is there some omniscient Creator orchestrating everything? Probably not. But Jonah Landry still recognized me out there on the dock. He'd seen me before. His angel.

Our gangly waiter arrives and presents us with an obscene pile of pancakes. "On the house," he says. "The owner's not in today, ma'am, but if he were, I know he'd be givin' you a whole lot more than pancakes. That was his grandbaby you helped yesterday."

Justine smiles as he leaves our table. "Guess I'm not the only one who thinks you've done good."

The kindness in Justine's voice makes me unexpectedly sad. "Thanks," I say.

"For what?" She saws off a hunk of pancake and takes a bite.

"For making me feel like I'm special and not a freak. You take my crazy dreams in stride."

"A freak? No." She shakes her head. "Prophetic dreams are nothing new. Look at the Old Testament. You know the story of Joseph and what he did for Egypt, don't you?"

"Sort of." I don't have the heart to tell her that my knowledge is limited to what I can recall from a *Joseph and the Amazing Technicolor Dreamcoat* revival.

She gives me a quick recap. "The Pharaoh, his baker, and his cupbearer all had prophetic dreams. They just needed Joseph to help interpret them."

"I wish I'd had a Joseph to walk me through mine," I tell her. "My interpretive powers haven't been the best." Her mention of the Bible reminds me of something I've been meaning to ask about: the story that was bookmarked in the Deveau Bible. "Justine, you must know the whole Judgment of Solomon story."

She nods. "The two mothers fighting over a baby. Solomon offers to cut the baby in half."

I wince. "That's the one. What does that story mean to you? Is there some—I don't know—special biblical message?"

She stops eating and dabs her mouth with a napkin. "It's funny you're asking. I thought about that story a lot when Didi was sick."

"Why?"

Justine exhales deeply, and I know things are about to get heavy. "Once the cancer spread and we knew she couldn't beat it, we had to decide. Continue with treatment and try to extend her life a little, or stop. Let her go." She swallows. "I kept thinking about that story, how the child's true mother was willing to give up her baby to protect him." She folds her hands on the edge of the table. "I knew I couldn't protect Didi from dying. But I could protect her from pain. If I gave her up to God, I could save her some pain. It seemed like . . . that's what a true mother would do." She wipes her eyes, embarrassed. "Sorry."

"Don't be. That makes a lot of sense."

She shrugs. "I guess I'm always going to wonder if it was the right call. Who knows, maybe if she'd gone through more treatments . . . I mean, miracles happen."

I know this line of thinking, this road to self-blame. "No," I tell her firmly. "Didi told me the exact minute she'd pass away. That was her time, Justine, and she knew it." I remember that bald head, Didi's bone-thin body, her look of exhaustion, and I believe absolutely in Remy and Justine's decision. "It's what she wanted," I say.

She picks up her fork and nudges a limp piece of pancake. "She was eleven years old. I shouldn't have had to make a choice like that."

And she's right. It's not fair that an eleven-year-old girl should spend years of her short life in and out of hospitals, wondering if she'll make it to her next birthday. Not fair that her parents, good people and re-spected public servants, should lose their only child when others much less worthy never do. Not fair that Justine's lifetime of church involve-ment and prayer should yield the same result as my lifetime of sinful skepticism.

Justine Pinaro may be a woman of God, but I realize from the tor-ment on her face that even *she* wrestles with doubt. Her faith does not insulate her from anger or from grief any more than it has shielded her from death. I can hate myself enough to believe I deserve my misery, but Justine? She does not deserve this, and the utter lack of justice or reason at work depresses me deeply. I stare out the window, watching the traffic thicken as we hit the worst of rush hour, watching the mad scramble to get to work, earn a living, press forward no matter who or what we've lost.

Whatever Jonah may think, I know I'm a poor excuse for an angel.

BACK AT EVANGELINE, I find myself dragging. My bags are packed, the car is loaded, and I've sent Sydney and Brigitte—still in New Orleans—a polite e-mail thanking them for their hospitality. I don't know why I'm lingering in my guest cottage, drifting from the sink to the bed to the table and back again. *The drive back will help clear your head,* I promise myself. And I'll get to see Grandma soon—even if I won't be bringing Noah home to meet her.

I try to put Noah from my mind but can't. He's another one of Evangeline's ghosts to me now, as vital and as absent as Gabriel or Neville or the Lauchlins. Why did I let myself get in so deep? Just one more mystery I'll never solve.

I take one last look around the cottage, do a quick sweep for forgotten objects. The only personal items remaining are the boxes of Deveau junk, and though I'm tempted to take something, I want a clean break from Evangeline. Still, I can't resist fishing the old Bible from the drawer one last time. Thinking of my conversation with Justine, I flip to the Judgment of Solomon. Before, I read the story as a lesson on justice and wisdom. Upon another read, though, I can see where Justine was coming from. Solomon's wisdom lies in understanding a mother's innate drive to sacrifice herself for the safety and well-being of her child. If this Bible was owned by Hettie or Maddie Lauchlin—both mothers—perhaps that resonated.

I think about what Justine said. *The child's true mother was willing to give up her baby to protect him.* If Maddie attempted to protect her son from harm, she was wildly unsuccessful—Sean spent nearly three decades buried in an unmarked grave. And there's no evidence Maddie ever made a conscious decision to give Sean up to ensure his safety, not unless she killed him in some bizarre religious attempt to save his soul from the perils of homosexuality. A weak theory, at best. Which brings me back to Hettie.

Okay. The Judgment of Solomon, and that handwritten page of biblical quotes. Where's the connection? Initially, all the biblical excerpts about sexual immorality, temptation, lust, and sin look pretty forbidding, but at the end is a cause for hope: *Love bears all things, believes all things, hopes all things, endures all things.* And there's another hopeful concluding thought. *Above all, keep loving one another earnestly, since love covers a multitude of sins.*

Did Hettie love the sinner but hate the sin? Maybe she was willing to give up Andre to protect him. From Neville's crushing disapproval. From the life of faking it that she'd resigned herself to. Maybe she gave Andre her blessing to go with Sean.

Then what went wrong? How did Sean end up dead? And why the years of monthly payments to him? I'm on the wrong path, missing something. Something about Gabriel. Hettie had two sons, after all, and Gabriel was the one she lost.

The child's true mother was willing to give up her baby to protect him.

Which baby was she protecting, and from what?

A wild hunch begins to form, not in my brain but in my chest. I unearth the book of sonnets from its box and remove Sean's letter. As I skim through the contents, my suspicions take shape, grow in weight. *You can't live under Neville's thumb forever,* Sean says, and later acknowledges that *being a Deveau means you're afraid of the tabloids.* He refuses to accept others' disapproval as a reason to be apart. *I don't care what people think when they see us,* he states. *If we don't fit with their ideas of love, that's their problem, not ours.*

Now I understand, and it changes everything.

I have assumed that the letter found in Andre's book was meant for Andre, and I'll wager he was the one to *find* it, the one who pressed it between pages of Shakespeare. But the letter was not *for* him. It was for the other Deveau who lived in fear of Neville.

Hettie.

"Damn."

Sean and Hettie. How did I miss this? Roi Duchesne's assessment of Hettie wasn't so far off the mark, after all.

Mind racing, I work through the implications of their affair. That

Bible must have belonged to Hettie. It wasn't Andre's sexual offenses she wrestled with but her own. For a time, though, love won out. Love covered a multitude of sins. A relationship would explain the money she'd been giving Sean. They must have been planning to run away together, stashing money until the time was right. Three years spent building their bank account, and the payments started when she was just a few months pregnant with Gabriel.

"Shit, shit, *shit*." That baby wasn't Neville's.

According to Danelle Martin, Neville threatened to kill his wife if she ever took a lover. Threatened her and hit her, years before Gabriel was born, and probably years before her affair with Sean began. Hettie would not have forgotten that threat. She must have feared Neville every time she and Sean were together—what her husband might do not just to her, but to her child.

I don't know what happened in August of 1982, but Sean had been missing since June, probably dead, and Hettie must have thought her youngest son was in grave danger. So, like a true mother, she gave up her child to protect him. Gave him to the one person who loved him almost as much as she did, a woman who'd helped to raise him from the very beginning: Maddie Lauchlin. His grandmother.

No wonder Hettie was uninterested in helping Detective Minot with his investigation. She knew what had happened. She knew where her son was. I sink down to the floor, legs too weak to carry me when the realization hits.

Gabriel Deveau is alive. Gabriel Deveau is Noah.

31.

I have many burning questions for Hettie, but one above all others can't wait. I sprint up Evangeline's grand staircase and burst into her bedroom without so much as a knock.

"Does he know? Does he know who he is?"

Propped up on a pile of carefully arranged pillows, Hettie observes my breathless entrance with clear, unsurprised eyes. Her skin hangs from her skull like a ghostly, milky-blue fabric. She doesn't have long. Still, I'm convinced she recognizes me. Understands exactly what I'm saying, and why.

Her redheaded nurse, who has been rocking out with his iPod, rises quickly from his chair. He plucks out his earbuds and moves to escort me out, but Hettie turns, tortoiselike, and waves him from the room with a feeble hand. I've had my concerns about her mental state—still do—but I know she is, at this moment, perfectly lucid. Why else would she demand privacy? She knows what I'm about to accuse her of.

"You're still here," Hettie murmurs. "I thought you would have gone with him."

The curtains are pulled back today, and the brightly lit room is less tomblike than I've seen it. On a table by her bed, I recognize the pot of paperwhite narcissus that Noah brought weeks ago, now in full flower. I stand at the foot of her bed, awash in sunshine, wishing I could simultaneously interrogate her and dash off in search of Noah.

"Did you tell him that he's your son?"

"He doesn't believe me." She looks so fragile lying there in a flowered nightgown, fingers grasping the rail of her hospital bed. It's hard to believe that she sustained such an incredible lie all these years. "I waited too long, and now he doesn't believe me."

"When did you tell him?" I can't blame Noah for having secrets, not when I have so many of my own, but I want to know how long he's been carrying this around. If he didn't find it credible, why keep it from me?

"I told him the other night," Hettie says vaguely. "He said he had to leave the house, that he wasn't welcome anymore. I told him, 'Darling, you're always welcome in my home, you're my child.' I tried to explain to him." She closes her eyes. "He just looked at me like I was some crazy woman."

She's talking about last Friday, I realize, when Andre and Jules fired him. I thought Noah was reeling from the loss of his job, and I'm sure he was at first. But after he went to the house to get his phone, he became brooding and withdrawn—so much so, I thought perhaps he'd tried to poison Jules. Now I understand. He must've gone to say his good-byes to Hettie and received an earful. Though he wasn't quite prepared to believe her, the first seeds of doubt were planted.

There's so many lies in my life, he said, *I don't even know who I am at the bottom of it all.* But he did know. Part of him knew that Hettie wasn't speaking to him from a senile cloud. If anything, her foggy mind made her more honest, unable to continue the deception she'd perpetrated for thirty years.

"He doesn't think you're crazy," I tell her slowly. "He *wishes* you were."

"He asked me for proof this morning," she says. "I have nothing but my word, and you know what that's worth."

"He was here this morning?" I'm dubious. "Noah? I mean, Gabriel?"

"He was here and then left. Didn't you come with him?"

"No." I'm hurt that he didn't come to see me, although I'm beginning to understand the magnitude of what he's processing.

Hettie fingers the lace collar of her nightgown. "He was so distant. He kept asking about some woman who used to work here, then he left."

"Violet Johnson," I murmur. "He thinks that's his mother."

She stares at the edge of her sheet. "Of course. I'd forgotten her name."

"Tell me how you did it." I drag a footstool with a tasseled mauve cushion over to the bed and sit beside her. "The FBI had their eye on Maddie and Jack for months after the kidnapping. Where was Gabriel all that time?"

I'm expecting some evasion, but Hettie is surprisingly forthright. "Maddie had a sister in Texas," she replies. "Ran a little day care from her home. She took him for a while."

"Nobody ever looked at her?" This seems incredible, given the scrutiny Maddie and Jack were under.

"Oh, the FBI came 'round to ask about Maddie a couple times, asking questions. Gabriel was right there, playing with the other kids. But they never realized." She smiles faintly at their ineptitude.

I'm less amused. "The FBI didn't recognize the kid they were searching for when he was right in front of them?"

"She'd cut off most his hair and dyed it blond. I expect he looked different."

Hiding in plain sight. Given the attention this case received, I'm sort of disappointed in the simplicity of the plan. "So eventually Maddie and Jack came to get him, and that was it? They raised him?"

"They changed his name," Hettie says. "They dropped off the grid and raised him as Noah Palmer."

"Palmer," I repeat. "Is that what he goes by? Noah Palmer?" I rack my brain for times that Noah explicitly told me his last name was Lauchlin but find none. I always just assumed it, because of his father and his grandparents. A different surname would explain why Detective Minot couldn't find records of him.

"Noah Palmer," Hettie confirms. "When he got older and wanted to know why his last name was different than theirs, Maddie just blamed it on reporters, said she didn't want him mixed up in all the Deveau kidnapping press."

"But how did you . . ." I can't believe the scope of what they pulled off. "I mean, he's a business owner. He files taxes. Legally, Noah Palmer exists, right?"

"Oh, yes." She smiles. "It took years, but I helped Maddie and Jack get papers for him."

It must be nice being rich and connected. "And Violet Johnson? How did her name end up on the birth certificate?"

"She worked for us years earlier," Hettie explains. "We had her Social Security number, her birth date. She was about the right age."

"And Neville never knew?"

She shudders. "Lord, no. He knew I kept in touch with Maddie and Jack, but he didn't know . . . what we'd done. Nobody did. Not even Gabriel." With great effort, Hettie rises from her cluster of pillows and leans toward me. "They told him his mama was dead. Sometimes I wished I was."

I can't stop thinking of little Noah, living in Texas with a great-aunt he barely knew, suddenly cut off from his entire former life. It was hard enough for Keegan when his father left, and he still had me, the house, all his normal routines. But Noah lost everything. Not three years old, and he lost everyone and everything.

"Have you told him about Sean? Have you told him his father is dead?"

For the first time I sense a reluctance to answer. "Andre told me you were asking about Sean," Hettie says. "He's been worrying over it."

Andre must have known, all along, who those bones at the sugar mill belonged to. How did he get involved in this mess, anyway? He was only eighteen. Surely Hettie wouldn't have intentionally dragged him into this. Did he somehow stumble upon Sean's letter and work it out for himself?

"I'm not here to make trouble for you all," I say.

"I know. You wouldn't hurt Gabriel." She's so persuaded of the bond between Noah and me. Has he talked about me or has she just drawn her own wild conclusions? "I'm glad he's picked a smart woman. I was never one. Neville wouldn't have married me if I was." She studies me. "You haven't told my son everything, have you?"

"It's not mine to tell."

"You're a smart woman," she says again.

I'm not interested in her compliments. "They found Sean. They found where he was buried."

She sinks back into the hospital bed. "Andre told me," she says. "I knew he would turn up one day. I guess in some ways it's a relief." I still can't tell if she herself buried him.

"The FBI will want to speak to you."

"They already have. Some men came asking about Sean the other day."

"What did you tell them?"

She frowns. "I didn't tell them a thing. I pretended I didn't understand the questions, didn't know who they were talking about. The nurses told them that I've been suffering from dementia, and they left me alone. Of course, they've been pestering Andre and my girls ever since."

I wonder if the twins are in on this, too. Probably not. Sydney and Brigitte are the ones inviting nosy authors into the home. They don't seem to realize all their family has to hide.

Although she's avoided the issue of Sean's death thus far, I'm convinced something in Hettie wants to talk. Wants to unburden herself, to explain.

"Why?" I ask, intentionally leaving the question open-ended. "Why did you do it?"

She presses her fingers to her lips and finally offers me an answer. "I was so alone," she whispers. "That's not an excuse, I know. But I thought—maybe it would save me."

I don't know if she's offering her reason for the affair or the murder. Either way, I'm curious.

"I always knew Sean had a little crush on me," she goes on. "Neville and I used to laugh about it, back when he was a kid. He was so young. Sixteen, maybe? I was eleven years older than him. I never thought of him that way, believe me."

"When did you start to . . . ?" I don't want to sound indelicate.

Hettie shifts around in bed, wincing at each movement, and for a few guilty seconds I'm reminded that she's dying. She's in pain. The humane thing would be to call in the nurse and ask for meds, but I can't bring myself to cloud her clear mind with drugs.

"It was my thirty-ninth birthday," she says. "Neville was in Atlanta with a woman. He thought I didn't know, but I did." Her breathing catches, and for a horrible second I think it'll all end there, that final breath, but she fights through it, determined to get the story out. "The kids were away at school. And they forgot, Neville and the kids, they all forgot about my birthday. But Sean, he was on leave, visiting his parents—and he remembered. He said, 'How's it going, birthday girl?'" She shakes her head, and her ragged breathing eases somewhat. "The littlest kindness. That was all I needed."

I lean against the rail of her hospital bed, half-wanting to touch her, empathizing with her loneliness in spite of myself. I can smell the flowers on her bedside table, their perfume thick and cloying. "Did you love him?"

She fixes her tired gaze on me. "Oh, honey. Love or desperation, what's the difference? He was something to look forward to." Her face crumples a little, remembering. "He had such big plans for us. It wasn't right, and I never thought it was. I just didn't know how to stop."

"I found one of his letters," I tell her. "He was asking you to run away with him." |

She smiles a little. "He started that as soon as he found out I was pregnant. He wanted me to take Gabriel and just leave. Start a family, the three of us. I knew it was more complicated than that, and I had three other children to think of. But we'd put aside some money every month, talk about how it was going to be, how we'd run off to Mexico where Neville couldn't find us." Hettie presses her cheek to the pillow, sad now. "Maddie and Jack used that money later to raise Gabriel."

"Sean's parents knew about the affair, then?"

"Oh, yes. Poor Maddie got stuck covering for us plenty of times. We scared her to death."

I see now why Maddie and Jack were so against their son's mystery woman—and how helpless they must have been to do anything. On the one hand, Maddie had the luxury of raising her beloved grand-child. On the other, Neville's temper was widely known. Maddie had to have felt the danger her son was in. But what could she do? Refuse to help the pair, and risk Neville's wrath?

"Did you consider going to Mexico?" Running away doesn't strike me as the perfect solution, but years of sneaking around seem worse.

Hettie considers this. "It never seemed real to me," she admits. "It was nice to talk about. Made me feel like . . . I had a choice. But it never seemed real."

"Did Sean threaten to tell Neville?"

"No," she says. "Sean wasn't like that. He wanted me to leave for love, not fear. In the end, he told me to choose, now or never. And I was a coward. I chose never."

"And that was in June, two months before Gabriel disappeared?"

"Yes."

There's just one gaping hole. If she didn't try to leave Neville, and Sean didn't spill the beans . . .

"How did Sean end up dead?"

I'm met with silence.

Nothing but her breathing. Ugly, shallow gulps for air, followed by a long, moaning sigh. "Because he came back," she says. "The night he was going to leave. He came back to the house and tried to take Gabriel."

"So you killed him?"

Hettie won't look at me. She turns her head away. "God will judge me," she says dully. "I've lived for thirty years knowing that. Believe me, I don't ever forget."

"But I don't understand—"

She holds up a trembling hand, warding me off. "Please. It was a horrible thing, and I'd undo it if I could. But don't you understand? I had to protect my son. Let it be."

You fool. Did you really think you could reclaim your lost son without also accepting responsibility for what happened to his father? But killing Sean isn't the worst of her crimes, not in my book.

"How could you do it?" I ask. "Just—give your child away?"

"He's safe," she says simply. "When he was with me, I always had to worry. What if Neville found out? What if—I don't know—there was a blood test and it came out that Gabriel wasn't his? My husband might've killed him. Killed us both."

The child's true mother was willing to give up her baby to protect him.

Privately, I wonder how much of Hettie's decision was fueled by self-interest versus motherly sacrifice, but I keep my thoughts to myself.

Hettie senses she hasn't won me over. "I did the right thing," she insists. "Look at him. He's safe and he's happy. You've seen my children. Andre and the girls, do they seem happy to you?" She answers her own question. "No. Nothing's enough for them. But Gabriel . . . he's different. Comfortable in his skin."

She has a point, but I'm not sure I find it powerful enough to justify her entire betrayal, the hell she put her husband through.

Hettie's face softens. "You love my son, don't you?"

"I think so." I feel myself flushing as I remember the horrible things I suspected Noah of just an hour before.

"He wouldn't be the man you love if he had stayed."

That one thing I do believe. Suddenly she's gasping for air again, her face twisting up in agony. I can't do this to her any longer.

"I'll send the nurse in," I tell her. "You look like you could use some painkillers."

"Wait." Her voice is raspy and pathetic. "Tell Gabriel to come back. Tell him to forgive me. Please. I don't want to be alone."

The selfishness of this request infuriates me. She has no regard for Noah's feelings in any of this, no thought for how completely she has damaged his sense of self. I thought my own mother took the cake in the Shitty Mom department, but I'm starting to think Hettie wins. At least when my mother left, she stayed away instead of luring me back under false pretenses. The whole garden project was obviously a sham from the get-go, one Hettie concocted to draw her son back to Evangeline. And even now that she's revealed the truth to Noah, she's cherry-picking facts. She wants all the warm fuzzies of motherhood minus any culpability for what happened to Sean.

I'm not inclined to plead her case with Noah no matter how she begs, but one indisputable fact renders the point moot anyway.

"Sorry." I don't look back, don't let her see the hurt on my face. "I can't tell him anything when I don't know where he is."

32.

I want to find him. Of course I do. I stand in Evangeline's grand foyer, trying to plan my next move. I can only imagine what Noah must be feeling. Here he's facing what may be the most devastating news of his life—that his mother did not die but willingly gave him up, that his grandparents lied, that the person he believed himself to be is a fabrication—and he's facing it alone. And he still doesn't have the whole story. He doesn't know that his father is dead. That Hettie is responsible.

If I'm to believe Hettie's version of events, then the man Noah thought abandoned him died trying to get him back. But there are problems with that story. Detective Minot said Sean was shot at least once from behind, a bullet in the back of his skull. There's no way she shot him inside the house—the forensics team would've discovered traces of blood during the search for Gabriel. Did Hettie really have time to run into the study, retrieve one of Neville's guns from the safe, and run outside to shoot him? A gun screams premeditation, not "Oh my gosh, this guy is running off with my kid." I try to envision the scene, her pleading with Sean to leave their son behind, Sean's refusal. Surely Gabriel would've showed signs of emotional trauma if he'd witnessed someone getting shot, yet no one reported any changes in his behavior that summer. And if Hettie killed Sean to keep him from taking Gabriel, why was she suddenly willing to part with her child in August, ready to foist him off on Maddie and Jack?

This isn't adding up.

I pace the foyer, idly glancing at the stiff artwork. How strange that Noah, so easygoing and casual, spent his first years living amidst all this stylish formality. Noah, in his jeans and cowboy boots, was once a longish-haired toddler in polo shirts and boat shoes.

Hettie's right. He wouldn't be the man he is if she hadn't given him up. And I'm pretty sure I want to be with that man, if only I can track him down.

I don't know what Noah's been up to in the forty-eight hours since he dropped me off at Evangeline, but I no longer believe it had anything to do with his landscaping work. If I were Noah, grappling with the disturbing possibility that I might not be the person I've always thought, what would I do? Investigate. Research. Look for holes in the story that Maddie and Jack told all these years. Locate whatever information I could on Violet Johnson. If Hettie's telling the truth, and he came to her this morning asking for proof of his identity, then he probably hasn't found any answers. Which means he hasn't found anything to disprove her claims, either.

So where might he be? Hunting down Violet's birth certificate at the Department of Vital Records? Scouring every ancestry site on the Internet? Or perhaps he's retreated into his own mental man cave to work through it all. He could've gone back to Texas.

Without me.

I can only guess how the timing of Hettie's confession impacted Noah's dealings with me. Frankly, I don't know how he made it through our Mardi Gras trip with something like that kicking around his brain. Denial, I suppose. The trip was probably a welcome distraction. Maybe the whole Run Away with Charlie plan was just a way to avoid a truth he wasn't yet ready for. If that's the case, so be it. But I have a right to hear it from him.

I remind myself that he knows where I am. Hettie must have smoothed things over with security if he came by this morning. I just need to wait. *When he wants to see you, he'll come.*

And if he doesn't?

I stop in front of the study. The door is shut, but police tape no longer blocks off the room. The crime scene unit must have finished their work yesterday. I'm glad that Noah no longer appears responsible for Jules's overdose, but I do feel a twinge of sadness about the suicide attempt. Mostly on behalf of Andre, whose open anguish following the incident has invited widespread speculation about their relationship.

Was Jules acting out of despair or spite? I wonder. Punishing Andre for some real or imagined crime? Maybe Jules was sick of being kept at arm's length, pretending to be what he was not. I imagine him downing a string of tequila sunrises, his bottle of Ambien dissolved into the liquor, anticipating Andre's torment with bleak satisfaction.

"You're still here."

Speak of the devil. I turn and find an unshaven and disheveled Andre standing by the front door. He's wearing a long, rumpled coat and exquisite leather gloves that were probably custom-made in Italy. I suspect he's been with Jules all night at the hospital, keeping a bedside vigil.

"I heard you were leaving," he says. "Glad I caught you."

He looks awful. I wonder how long it's been since he's showered. "How's Jules?" I ask.

He shrugs. "Not alive, not dead. The same." He regards me with bloodshot eyes. "Were you really going to leave without saying good-bye?"

The short answer: yes. Andre hasn't been a factor in my plans. "I didn't want to bother you. I figured you had enough on your plate right now."

He laughs, a thin, mirthless sound. "Yes, I'd say my plate's full. Very full." He takes a few steps closer, scrutinizing me. It occurs to me that I, too, probably look like hell. "What are you doing in the house? No one's around but my mother."

"I know." I'm too distraught to lie, and he looks like he has a pretty good idea of what I've been up to. "I just spoke with her."

"About what? You know she's not supposed to be receiving visitors." His voice is shrill and accusatory.

I'd like to cut him some slack—this can't be an easy time for him— but I no longer trust Andre. However candid he may have appeared, he's been holding out on me, trying to feel out how much I know and reporting back to his mother. Every interaction we've had has been a careful dance, me trying to draw out the truth and him deflecting, misdirecting. He once accused me of being an undercover FBI agent, and maybe that was the real Andre. Paranoid.

"I just—wanted to thank your mother for hosting me." I can't quite meet his eyes. Hopefully we can avoid a scene; he looks ready to detonate. "We chatted a bit."

"What did she tell you?" From the tone of his voice, he's having none of it.

I give up. "Everything, I guess." I sigh. "Pretty much everything."

Andre runs his hand through his hair and begins pacing the foyer. "I knew she would." He shakes his head bitterly. "What does *she* care? She's got nothing left to lose."

I almost ask him what *he* thinks he has to lose, but at this point, all I want is to find Noah. "It's not worth getting mad over, Andre. I'd already worked most of it out for myself."

"Oh?" He jams his hands into his coat pockets. "How's that?"

"I found the letter Sean wrote your mother. From the day he died."

The blood leaves his face. He knows *exactly* what letter I'm talking about. "Where did—have you told anyone?"

"No," I tell him. "And I have no desire to."

"Where's the letter now?" Andre presses me.

From his look of agitation, I'm onto something. "It's back in the guest cottage," I say slowly.

"Then we'll go get it. I want it back."

I wonder what horse Andre has in this race. He's clearly alarmed by his mother's telling me the truth, and he's threatened by the content of Sean's letter. But what is he so afraid of? Bad press for the family and its hotel business? I've always had the sense that he tended to the business out of duty, not love. Does he think some prosecutor will throw obstruction-of-justice charges at him thirty years after the fact? I'm no lawyer, but I thought the statute of limitations expired on everything except murder. Does Andre's guilt run deeper than I've been led to believe?

I reevaluate. Maybe Hettie *didn't* tell me everything. She accepted blame for Sean's death—*God will judge me,* she said—but she never actually confessed to killing him. Maybe she didn't. She told me plainly that she had to protect her son. *Which* son?

From its contents, I mistakenly assumed Sean's letter was meant for Andre, not Hettie. Could Andre have made the same mistake? He had, by his own admission, a crush on Sean. Even if Sean gave him the book of sonnets quite innocently, the gesture could have been misconstrued as romantic. And to later find that letter . . . I imagine him reading Sean's words, thrilled at the idea that someone reciprocated his feelings, that someone saw who he was and accepted him. If he was unaware of Hettie and Sean's relationship, it would've been so easy to read those words and see what he wanted to see: Sean inviting him to escape Neville and start a new life. And Andre might've found this a much more attractive proposition than Hettie did.

I look at the trim, gray-haired man before me. He's wild-eyed and wrecked, totally desperate to bury any voices from his past—he has enough to contend with in his present. It's easy to envision him as a teenager, caught between a burning need for parental approval and the fantasy of leaving it all behind. He was young. In love. Of course he would've chosen Sean.

"Did you go to meet him that night?" I ask softly. It's starting to make sense now. Why Andre's running scared. Why Hettie blames herself. "Did you get Sean's letter and then go to meet him?"

Andre squeezes his eyes shut and takes a few deep breaths, as if practicing some anxiety management technique. "I just want it back," he says. "It's not yours. You have no right to it."

"It's not yours either," I say. "You know that letter was for your mother."

He clutches his stomach like he might throw up. "Thirty years," he whispers, "and suddenly she can't keep her damn mouth shut."

"I take it you didn't know they were involved until that night."

He shakes his head, mute.

"Was she with him? Did you find them together?"

"No." He slumps back against the wall. "She never got the letter. He was waiting for her at the sugar mill, but I showed up instead." He still hasn't removed his coat and gloves. There's something pathetic in the way he hovers around the foyer, like a stranger lingering in someone else's home.

"Where'd you get the gun?"

"It was my father's. He was home that night, that's why I brought the gun. I thought . . . if he found out, if he tried to stop me from going . . ." His blue eyes fill with tears, but he's smiling. A painful smile. "It's funny, isn't it? I was willing to leave everything for him."

"So you showed up, ready to go, and what? He told you he was in love with your mother?"

Andre glances at the staircase. "My mother's nurse," he says in a low voice. "Can she hear all this?"

"It's that red-haired guy's shift," I tell him. "He can't hear a damn thing with his iPod always in, I promise you."

"Okay." Andre swallows, resolved, I guess, to finally come out with it. "It was late. My parents had gone to bed. I waited outside the house in my car. Had my suitcases packed and everything. The gun was in my pocket, just in case."

"In case your dad showed up."

Even indoors, wearing a coat, Andre seems cold. He hugs himself, shivering. "Sean came out of the house carrying Gabriel and started to drive away. I was confused, but I followed him to the sugar mill in my car."

So this part of Hettie's story was accurate: Sean returned for his child. He didn't want to leave Noah behind.

"When I got out of the car, he seemed . . . strange. I asked if he was taking Gabriel, and he said yes. I asked why, and he told me to go home. 'I got your letter,' I said. 'I'm going with you.'"

"So he told you the truth." I can almost understand where Andre was coming from when he killed Sean. I can *almost* excuse it.

"He told me the truth. That he'd been fucking my mother for years. That Gabriel was his."

"And you shot him?"

Andre stares straight ahead, trancelike, as he walks me through it. "I stood there in front of his car. Crying. Gabriel was still asleep in the backseat. Sean told me to get out of his way, but I didn't move. I couldn't, I just . . . I'd pinned all my hopes to him. There was nowhere else to go. I asked if he would take me anyway." He drags a hand across his forehead. "I didn't mean anything by it. It was clear by that point, any feelings—they were all in my head. But I wanted to get away so badly."

"He wouldn't take you?"

"He said . . ." Andre chokes on the words. "He said, 'Did you really think I was a faggot like you?'" He closes his eyes. "He started walking to his car, and that's when I took out the gun. I don't know why. I don't know."

"You were only eighteen, Andre."

"Eighteen," he echoes. "Legally, an adult. What could I do? There was no one to go to except my mother. She was all I had." He takes a few listless steps down the hallway. "She helped me clean up. She helped me bury him." He wipes his eyes. "I don't know who she was covering for, me or herself. Part of me wanted to go to the police, but I didn't want to go to prison. Can you imagine what they'd do to me in prison?"

"You would've had a good case," I murmur. "You were under extreme emotional duress. You'd just learned that your mother was being unfaithful to your father."

"That's still manslaughter," he says, "best case. Up to forty years in Louisiana." He stares at the floor. "Everything would've come out at trial. You think I would've had a chance once the jury found out I was gay? And God knows what my father would've done to my mother."

"She wasn't just protecting *you* all these years," I observe. "You've been protecting each other."

"Yes. So now you know." He smiles wanly at me. "This is what you wanted, isn't it? Answers? A tearful confession?"

Something about the way he says it makes me ashamed. What *did* I hope to accomplish here? Justice? Andre is not the purely evil villain I've been looking for. He was a frightened kid, and bringing all of this to light now, when Sean's been dead so long, does little more than punish the innocent. Namely, Noah. He's the only innocent one in this whole dirty story.

"What are you going to do?" he murmurs.

"Nothing," I tell him. "It was a long time ago." I don't know if I'm being honest or trying to placate a man who has just confessed to murder. Should I tell Detective Minot about this? Would legal punishment really be worse than the mental anguish Andre has already suffered? Perhaps silence is best. Either way, the choice should not be mine to make.

"I'll make it worth your while." Andre's gotten hold of himself again. "Tell me how much. I'll get my checkbook. Name the amount, and we'll settle this." He opens the study door and marches inside.

"I don't want your money," I protest, but he rummages through his desk nonetheless, searching.

"A million dollars. How does that sound?" He shuffles through some papers. "That was what I asked for in the ransom note."

"*You* wrote the ransom note?"

He plucks a key from the back of the drawer and inspects it for a moment. "I told my mother the night Sean died that it was him or me. That she could send me off to jail if she wanted, but I wasn't going to watch her dupe my father every day, pretending Gabriel was his. After that night, the kid was poison. Every time we looked at him, all we could think of was Sean."

The idea of anyone viewing a two-year-old as poison sickens me, but I'm not done with my questions. "What about Maddie and Jack?" They participated in this whole elaborate cover-up, after all. "Did they know you killed their son?"

"You think Maddie was surprised?" Andre flashes me another one of his jaded, not-really-amused smiles. "Only that it was me who did it. She'd been telling Sean for years that my father would kill him. She knew he was playing with fire every time he touched my mother." Andre sees this blame-the-victim stance doesn't sit well with me. "It could've been worse for Nanny and Daddy Jack," he says defensively. "They got what they wanted in the end."

"You mean Gabriel."

Finally, he devotes a thought to his brother. "I don't know what be-came of that poor son of a bitch, but he's probably had a better time of things than I have."

Wow. He really doesn't know.

I know from various chats with Noah that Hettie spent years culti-vating a relationship with him through cards, little gifts, a handful of visits. When he was nineteen, she gave him money to start his own business. On her deathbed, she found a way to bring him back to Evangeline. All that contact, yet no one ever found out who Noah re-ally was. Not Noah, and not Andre, her co-conspirator in just about everything else. I have to admire, if not respect, the woman's ability to dissemble.

"I bet your brother turned out okay," I say.

Andre has already abandoned all thoughts of Gabriel, however. He stands by the desk, staring at the key in his hand. The gears in his head are turning. "You really don't want money?"

I shake my head. "I wanted to know what happened to Gabriel. Now I do." I back away from the study, ready to put all the distance I can between myself and Evangeline. "I should go, Andre. The past is past, I understand that. Let's leave it there."

"Wait." He holds out the key to me. "You're in this deep with us, you might as well know everything. There's one last thing you should see."

Part of me wants to leave. I have the answers I need. If this family prefers to live with all these lies, I have no business interfering. Maddie and Jack struck their dirty bargain years ago, absolving Andre and Het-tie of their son's death in return for their grandchild. If they could for-give, or at least move on, it seems ridiculous for me to make waves now. And yet, as Andre offers this small metallic object to me, I can't help wondering what I'm missing.

What's left for him to show me? What final piece of the puzzle remains?

I enter the study gingerly. He points to the bottom right-hand drawer of the desk: a keyhole. He presses his gloved hand firmly into mine and deposits the key.

"Go ahead. Open it."

I unlock the drawer, already regretting the decision. My stomach tenses up into a hard knot. "This isn't going to be—gross, is it?"

"No," he promises with a dry laugh. "Just open it."

I pull open the drawer and discover a small silver revolver lying on a green cloth. This is actually better than I anticipated. It's not a tooth, at least, or human hair.

"Is that the gun that killed Sean?"

"No," Andre replies, and in one quick, smooth motion, he picks it up, presses it to my neck. "This is the gun that's going to kill *you*."

I've never been held at gunpoint before, but the experience is not what I imagined.

I don't get hysterical. Don't scream, don't beg for my life. My mind is surprisingly clear, surprisingly logical, as if sharpened by my fear. I tell myself not to piss him off. That no one will hear me if I yell, and even if I do, it'll be too late. He could've shot me already, but he hasn't. I want to see what his next move will be.

If he were a stranger, I might take my chances with a struggle. But I know Andre's secrets. He's on the edge right now, unstable, his mother terminally ill and his boyfriend teetering between life and death. If I'm calm, maybe I can defuse this. But I've got to keep him talking.

"Andre," I say in a steady voice, "don't make this mistake again." The butt of the revolver pushes my chin up so I can't see his face. "Killing me will create a lot more problems for you than it will solve, you know that."

"*Not* killing you is what got me into this mess," Andre retorts. "I should have dealt with you when you started asking questions about Sean. I told my mother this was coming."

It sounds like Andre has been contemplating how to rid himself of the Charlotte problem for a while. His awkward attempts to be my friend were not pathetic, I now realize, but strategic. Friends close, enemies closer. My palms begin to sweat.

"I'm not your enemy," I say. But even I can hear the lameness of this approach. "I got in over my head, and all I want to do is go home."

"Right. Home." He doesn't have to tell me; I know now we're well past the point of my walking away. His weight shifts behind me as he considers his next step. "You said Sean's letter was in the guesthouse. Is that true?"

"Yeah."

"Good. Let's go for a little walk."

He repositions the gun so it's no longer tilted up toward my head, but directly at my neck. This seems worse. A well-aimed shot through the chin would kill someone instantly, but a hole through the neck? Would I bleed out? Choke to death on my own blood? I don't want to end that way.

As he steers me out of the study and toward the kitchen, I run a quick mental calculation. From the rear of the house, what are the chances that the guard at the gate or the person monitoring cameras in the carriage house could hear me if I screamed? More to the point, what are the chances they could help? Slim to none. By the time someone arrived to help, I'd be dead, and Andre would be free to tell whatever convenient story he liked.

But there are cameras. He wouldn't shoot me on camera. There must be some gesture I can make to get the attention of Zeke, or who-ever's watching the cameras today, some universal sign that I'm in a hostage situation.

I rack my brain for ideas, my calm rapidly devolving into panic as Andre pushes me through the kitchen. He nudges me out the French doors, his hand on my left shoulder to ensure that I don't make a sud-den break for it. When he catches me looking hopefully at a camera on the perimeter of the house, he makes a little *tsk, tsk, tsk* sound.

"I'm afraid the camera system is down today." His breath is warm on my ear. "I had to send Zeke into town to see about repairs."

This could happen, I think. *I could die. He's really going to do this.* Be-cause Andre's not behaving rashly. He's not a guy who needs to be talked down from the ledge. He has planned this carefully. Somehow he's disabled the security system and cleared Evangeline of anyone who might interfere with his plans. He's wearing gloves so that his fin-gerprints will never turn up on that revolver. He had me unlock that drawer myself, so the only prints on that key will be my own. What's he aiming for? Another supposed suicide right on the heels of the Jules incident would strain credulity. Maybe he'll pretend that I attacked him, claim self-defense.

"When we get to the cottage, enter the door code and walk straight in," he instructs me. "I'll be right behind you. Do you know where the letter is?"

Of course I do. It's on the bed where I left it, folded in the book of Shakespearean sonnets. But I won't tell Andre that. There might be something in the cottage that I could use as a weapon. A knife. Or something heavy I could strike him in the head with.

"I don't—remember where I put it," I stammer. "I might've left it in the kitchen."

I could tell him that he's wasting his time, that Detective Minot al-ready has a copy of the letter, but it might well be the only thing Andre's keeping me alive for. I'm not sure why he's so fixated on it. Sean's words and their implications are not as obviously damning as Andre's guilty conscience seems to think, but as long as *he* believes it's evidence against him, I've got leverage. Sort of.

Now, if I can just find the right moment—a distraction, maybe, to break his focus—then I can make my escape. Or die trying. Because I'd rather get shot several times in the back than bleed out my neck. I think.

"You're very quiet," Andre remarks. "I thought you'd try to talk your way out of this."

I trudge along the path, increasingly doubtful I can avoid taking a bullet, wondering what type of wound gives me the best chance of survival. "It sounds like you've made up your mind what's going to happen."

"You know, I didn't want it to be like this, Charlotte." I still can't see Andre's face, but there's something genuinely regretful in his voice. Fat lot of comfort that gives me. "You've given me no options. You could've left us alone, but you didn't. What am I supposed to do? Turn myself in? After everything my mother and I have sacrificed?" He shakes his head. "I made one mistake, and I hate myself for it every day. I never wanted to hurt anyone."

"Then don't."

"It's too late. You've screwed up my life past the point of no return."

That seems like an unfair overstatement. "Me? What did I do?"

"You helped them find Sean. I don't know how, but you did. Now I've got the FBI up my ass, and Jules might as well be dead because of you. The one person who made me happy, gone."

He's starting to sound totally delusional now. "You think I'm to blame for Jules's overdose? That doesn't even make sense."

"Oh no? Who do you think all that Ambien was for?"

I stop walking. It never occurred to me that Andre was the one slipping drugs into the booze. And it certainly never occurred to me that said drugs were intended for *me*.

"But I don't even drink tequila."

"No." He pushes me forward with his free hand. "You drink Shirley Temples. With grenadine."

Grenadine. Of course. The sickly sweet cherry flavor would help to mask the bitterness of all that Ambien. And if you mix grenadine with tequila and orange juice, you have yourself a tequila sunrise—the drink that nearly did Jules in. So Jules didn't have a death wish. He had a drunk wish, and he had the misfortune of using a bottle that his boyfriend had laced with sleeping pills. A bottle meant for me.

"It should've been easy," Andre says. "You had a prescription for Ambien, and I found out about you, about your son. Of course you'd be depressed. Nobody would've questioned it when they found you."

He's right. Even Detective Minot might've bought the idea of my offing myself, knowing how much I miss Keegan.

"If you'd just sat down with me last Friday," Andre laments, "if you had just joined me for a drink. You could've saved us both a world of pain. Jules, too."

"But I didn't," I say. "And no one will believe it's a suicide now. Not after Jules."

"No," Andre agrees. "It'll be harder this way, for both of us."

I want to ask what he means by that, but I have a feeling I already know. He's got that gun, and he's got a boat. I may have saved Jonah from a watery grave only to end up in one myself.

We're at the cottage now. He steps back, revolver still trained on my neck, while I punch in the door code. I sneak in a sideways glance and finally get a look at his face: a little green as he contemplates the next phase of his plan.

"This is going to be a mess," he murmurs, like I might actually feel sorry for him.

The keypad blinks and the door opens. I'm running out of time. I need to make a move or it's game over. We enter the cottage, and I note that Andre leaves the door half open behind us. Not that I could get by him. But maybe if I knocked him over, somehow caused him to lose his footing?

I try to distract him. "They'll find my car, you know. You'll have a lot of explaining to do." I could dash into the bathroom. There's a lock on the door but no window, no way out. Still, it might buy me some time.

"I can get rid of the car." Andre's eyes fall on the boxes of family junk, scanning for Sean's letter. "They all think you're leaving today. I'll tell them you did. They'll believe me."

I can't disagree. It would take days for anyone to realize I was missing, and weeks before police would take a missing-person report seriously. A lot could happen to a woman driving alone from Chicory to Stamford. How hard would anyone really look at Andre?

"The letter," Andre reminds me impatiently. "I want the letter."

"I'm trying to remember where I put it."

His eyes narrow, suspicious now, and he closes the distance between us, holds the revolver to my temple. "Don't screw with me. Is it here or not?"

"It's here somewhere, I just . . ."

No time left for hesitation. I have to act, however wrongly. I glance down at the floor, ready to slip my ankle behind his and try to knock him off balance. But before I can position myself correctly, attack him with what little I have, something freezes me in my tracks.

"Put that gun on the ground and your hands in the air."

Never, I think, has a Texas twang sounded so beautiful.

Andre's head jerks over toward the door to see who's speaking, but he doesn't release his grip on me. I can't see much with the revolver pressed to my head, but from my peripheral vision, I can make out the familiar slope of Noah's broad shoulders, his square jaw. And, in his outstretched hands, the nine-millimeter I always feared. I wonder if this moment will alter my views on gun control.

Whatever happens, at least I know he came back for me.

"Maybe you didn't hear me the first time," Noah tells Andre. "You put down your gun or I shoot you. First the kneecaps, then your stomach. Then any other place I can think of that'll hurt like hell."

I twist just enough to get a glimpse of Andre's face. He doesn't look angry or defeated, just confused. "Aren't you the gardener?" he asks, somewhat absurdly. "What are you doing on my property? I fired you."

Noah ignores the question. "I'm gonna count to three. One way or another, you're gonna drop your damn weapon."

"Don't tell me what to do." Andre's voice rises. "This isn't any of your business. Just—leave."

"One," says Noah. "Two."

"Stop! Stop counting at me! Who the hell do you think you are?"

"I'm your fuckin' *brother*."

One word, but for Andre Deveau, more frightening than any firearm. I can feel the instant he puts it all together: the sharp intake of breath, Andre's arm going limp. The revolver drags lightly across my cheek, then dangles at his side. I disentangle myself and scurry over to Noah, blood pumping so hard I think every vessel in my body might burst.

"No," Andre says softly. "My mother wouldn't do that. She promised."

"Promised what?" Noah counters, his gun still leveled at Andre. "Promised not to contact me? To leave me and my grandparents alone? To never tell me who I am? Believe me, I'd be a whole lot happier if she'd kept her promise."

"But she said . . . she said you were here to landscape the garden." There is something profoundly sad about Andre's desire to believe Hettie, even now.

"Our mother is a liar."

I wince at the words "our mother." So does Andre.

"Jesus," he says. "Oh, Jesus. You even look like him a little." He seems to have forgotten about the weapon in his hand, but Noah, I see, has not. "So . . . Maddie and Jack, they raised you?"

"Yeah."

"And you were happy?"

"Sure. They couldn't have loved me more."

The man who held a gun to my head seconds earlier begins to cry. Big, ugly, choking sobs. "I thought she chose *me*," he says. "I thought she sent you away because she loved me more." He sinks down to his knees, still weeping. "Look at my life. Look. She knew what she was doing. She knew you were the lucky one."

That's all the reunion that Noah will get. Andre stares at the revolver in his hand and makes his decision. He knows that it's over. He will leave on his own terms. I look away, hand covering my mouth. Even though I know what's coming, my body recoils at the sound of the gunshot. There's a thud, and then silence.

Noah hustles me out of the cottage, shielding my eyes with one hand. I'm grateful to him. I don't need to see the particular horrors of what I know to be true.

Andre Deveau is dead.

PART IV

stamford, connecticut

MARCH

33.

On a chill Wednesday in early March, I park my Prius in the lot outside my grandmother's assisted-living facility and prepare myself for our reunion. It hasn't been so long since I left—scarcely more than two months—but I feel unexpectedly emotional about my return. Part of it is grief, moving through the spaces that Keegan once occupied, but a larger part of it is gratitude. I'm grateful that my grandmother is here, that I have someone to come back to.

"We goin' inside or what?" In the passenger seat, Noah is starting to fidget.

"Yeah, let's go."

The lights and tacky holiday decorations are long gone, but otherwise it's all pretty close to what I left: bare trees, a slate-gray sky, bone-chilling wind. Spring, though, isn't so far off. A recent thaw has left the ground a soggy mess, turned mounds of snow to mud. Noah discovers this the hard way when he tries to cut across a strip of mulch and sinks two inches into the ground.

"Damn it." He stares down at his soiled boots. "I'm gonna ruin your gramma's carpet. Helluva first impression."

I smile. "You're nervous."

"Yeah," he admits, "kinda."

"After everything you've been through the last few weeks, you're worried what my little grandmother thinks?" I punch his arm playfully.

He isn't feeling lighthearted. "You haven't told her yet," he says. "You were in a lotta danger, and you didn't even tell her. I just hope she doesn't blame me."

I roll my eyes but don't reply. We've had variations on this conversation throughout the drive up. I don't think an eighty-seven-year-old woman needs to know about her only grandchild prowling around at night for the bones of murdered people, or chasing sexual predators into remote swamp regions, or getting held at gunpoint. Noah disagrees.

"Don't keep secrets, Charlie," he urges me. "Not from your family."

I can understand where he's coming from. His life, after all, has been built upon secrets. He's watched members of his family collapse under their weight.

LESS THAN A WEEK AGO, Noah and I went to Hettie's funeral. Her passing was a peaceful one, preceded by days of unconsciousness. Unlike the private burial Brigitte had arranged for Andre a few days earlier, Hettie's service was widely attended. Amidst the many prominent guests who filed into the church that morning, Noah and I were an unremarkable pair. Noah sat in the back looking uncomfortable in his suit while the priest waxed poetic about Hettie's many philanthropic contributions, her admirable devotion to her family. No one would've guessed that the broad-shouldered man with big, callused hands was her son.

The real star of Hettie's funeral, as it turned out, was Andre. His name, uttered in hushed tones, was on the lips of almost everyone present, although whether his death constituted a tragedy or a family

disgrace was debated. Despite his sisters' attempts to keep the circumstances of his death a secret, a few tantalizing details had inevitably
leaked. Tabloids jumped all over the story: DEVEAU CEO DEAD IN GAY SUI-
CIDE PACT. Gossip columnists chronicled Andre's long, forbidden affair
with Jules Sicard—more handsome than ever in the photographs—and
speculated that, ultimately, the star-crossed lovers had chosen to die
together rather than face a world that would not accept them. There
was no mention of Noah or me, just that Andre's body "was discovered by two employees of the estate." Sean Lauchlin's name was also
conspicuously absent, though there was a tangential reference to the
remains recently discovered on Deveau property.

In the end, I suppose, Andre got his way. The family secrets he fought
so hard to conceal remain buried.

In her death, Hettie acknowledged her youngest child in a way she
never had while living. If Noah preferred to sever all his painful ties to
the Deveau clan, Hettie had other plans. According to her legal documents, Noah will inherit a quarter of the family fortune. What a hard-
working Texas landscaper will do with that kind of wealth is anyone's
guess; he's too shell-shocked right now to really process such a life-
altering change in finances. For the present, he seems more concerned
with the fate of Evangeline, which, as per Hettie's promise, has been
gifted to the Louisiana Historical Association. Knowing that his work
on the estate has served its intended purpose—that, despite her other
lies, on this Hettie spoke true—seems to bring Noah a measure of
comfort nothing else can provide.

Naturally, Sydney and Brigitte have not received any of this news
with enthusiasm. Though I'm sure the twins would've liked to attribute
the upsetting contents of their mother's will to an unsound mind, the
documents had been drawn up more than a year ago, before Hettie's
cancer diagnosis. In these pages, Hettie never identified Noah as her
own, but she did write of her abiding fondness for "the son of my much

beloved friend Sean Lauchlin." Neither Sydney nor Brigitte knew quite what to make of that until I gave them a copy of Sean's letter. As far as I know, they never did piece together their brother's paternity, but I think the revelation of Hettie's infidelity, coupled with the official identification of Sean Lauchlin's body, led both sisters to suspect their father's involvement in his murder. That suits Noah just fine, as it keeps them from asking any inconvenient questions about the past. Murderers are not good for the family brand.

It's been easier for me. Nobody apart from Detective Minot knows the extent of my involvement. The only real consequence for me was a jubilant call from my editor, received just hours after news of Andre's death hit the media. "Finish the book!" Isaac exclaimed, breathless. "I don't care if it's a piece of shit, just finish it. You're sitting on a gold mine."

I told Noah about the conversation later, having already decided to abandon the project. To my surprise, he asked to read my manuscript. He studied it intensely for hours and then, when he was done, turned to me with sad, dark eyes that made me want to crawl under a rock.

"I didn't know a lotta that stuff," he said quietly. "You've learned all about 'em, haven't you?"

"I'll throw it away," I told him. "It doesn't matter now."

But he shook his head, suddenly adamant. "If it's not you writin' it, it'll be someone else. At least you knew some of 'em. At least you care. Write an end for it. Just . . . leave me out of the story, would you?"

So I've continued, for his sake, with a book I can no longer be objective about. I've tried to use some of our travel time to write, to cobble together a narrative we can all live with. All my old notions of journalism—truth, accuracy, accountability—now seem so foolishly black and white when the facts in this case hurt no one so much as the innocent. Instead, I build off the official story, spin a more sensitive version of the gay suicide pact. Although my feelings about Andre are complicated following our final encounter, I try to make him a sympathetic figure. I include stories from Danelle Martin and Kyle Komen, Andre's first boyfriend. I write about how Neville convinced Andre to pretend he was with a prostitute on the night of Gabriel's disappearance. I paint a sad little portrait of homophobia and self-loathing in one of the South's oldest, finest families, but I sidestep Sean Lauchlin. I leave the fate of Gabriel Deveau unresolved.

WHATEVER ANXIETIES Noah may have nursed about my grandmother prove unfounded within half an hour of our showing up at her door. She's been expecting him, but my briefing over the phone was short on details. At first, she's skeptical. She inspects Noah for signs of unworthiness, tests his manners, studies his body language, questions him closely and evaluates his answers. Unlike Eric, who was always a little terrified of my grandmother, Noah is unfazed. He met Carmen as a teenager, after all, and had to earn the approval of two brothers, a handful of male cousins, and an overprotective Catholic father who didn't trust white guys. He can handle Grandma, and he does. Before I even know what's happened, she's been Officially Charmed, reduced to coquettish smiles and other mystifying forms of elderly flirtation.

"Well, Charlotte," she beams, "I can see why you extended your trip. What nice scenery they have in Louisiana."

In no time, she is plying him with pound cake, giggling at his stupid but good-natured jokes, tasking him with the repair of her broken dishwasher. The woman who was always civil yet cool to my ex-husband can't get enough of the man she refers to as my "cowboy friend." She dismisses his plans to stay in a hotel, insisting she has room for us both on her pull-out couch. If Noah is relieved and pleased by the warm welcome, I'm a little alarmed by it. Where is Grandma's New England reserve? Who is this bright-eyed old gal inhabiting my grandmother's body?

"I'm just happy to see you," she says when I ask about it. "And to see you like *this*." She looks over at the kitchen, where Noah is tinkering with her dishwasher. "I was afraid you were running away from the world down there and instead—well, it looks like you've found it again."

In the end, I can only be happy for her blessing, which matters, I sense, very deeply to Noah. With Andre and Hettie gone, he's lost the only family he might've ever hoped to claim as his own. And he *wants* family. He *wants* some old lady fussing over him, insisting he have another slice of cake. I suppose if he were really desperate, Sydney and Brigitte are living relations, but in addition to being unbearable, they still don't know the true origin and fate of their missing brother.

"They can handle thinkin' Neville was a killer and Hettie was unfaithful," he told me before we left Evangeline. "But knowin' their baby brother turned out a gardener? I don't think so." His real fear, of course, was that they would expose him to the press in a play for publicity. "I'm Noah Palmer," he said. "I don't want people breathin' down my neck, callin' me Gabriel."

I don't blame him for disavowing his awful sisters but can't help feeling guilty that he's traded in his ex-wife's huge and exuberant extended family for just my grandmother and me. Can we really be enough? As the afternoon wears on and it's clear their little love fest will only deepen, I come to a decision. Noah is right. Grandma deserves more than the sanitized-for-her-protection story I've been feeding her about my time in Chicory. In her eighty-seven years, she has lost her husband, son, and great-grandson. For years, she lived with her own spooky premonitions. The woman can handle the darker sides of life.

After dinner, I sit her down and tell her the whole story, more or less, while Noah listens and interjects. I've had ample time to fill him in on my side of things, but it still gets to him, my visions of Jonah, Didi, and Clifford. It's not that he doesn't believe in what I've seen—it's that he believes too much. If I told him there was a child ghost standing by his side, I have the feeling he would shoot ten feet into the air like an old Looney Tunes character. Grandma, for her part, shows little reaction beyond the occasional headshake, pursed lips, and widening eyes. It's reassuring. Displays of raw emotion are not in her nature.

When I get to the part about searching the sugar mill at night, it's Noah who gets edgy, jiggling his leg and gripping the bottom of his chair.

"I can't believe you found my father," he murmurs. "And he was *there* with you. He was lookin' through that window watchin' you." He shakes his head, spooked.

I can't deny the face I saw at the precise moment Detective Minot located the piece of Sean Lauchlin's jawbone, but I'm not ready to concede any ghostly sightings. "I might've imagined it," I say. "I thought it was *you*."

"No," Noah says definitely. "That was my father. He knew you were gonna find him. He knew you'd put it all together and tell me what happened. That he didn't bail on me."

My grandmother, who has been quietly absorbing everything from her high-backed wooden chair, seems to agree. "You went down there to find Gabriel Deveau, Charlotte, and you did," she says when I've concluded my story. "Some things are meant to be."

Noah clears his throat. "I hope you'll forgive me, ma'am, for not keepin' a better eye on her. When I think of how things coulda turned out . . ."

"A person could drive themself crazy thinking of how things might've turned out," Grandma says. "And I'm certainly not one to talk about keeping an eye on Charlotte. I let her parents do the job, and quite frankly, they didn't."

This is not the turn I expected this conversation to take. "That wasn't your fault, Grandma," I say. "My mother didn't stick around long enough to do much damage, anyway."

She avoids my eyes, addresses Noah like I'm not there. "I love my son, but I know he wasn't much better. He drank away her childhood, and I didn't stop it. She was fourteen years old when I got her, almost all grown up. That's fourteen years I didn't keep an eye on her."

I've never heard my grandmother express guilt or regret over my upbringing before. Something about her unexpected humility makes me squirm.

She stands slowly, still not looking at me, and places a veiny blue hand on Noah's shoulder. "The fact that Charlie is sitting here in my living room instead of floating around some godforsaken swamp— well, I've got you to thank. So I'd say you've kept an eye on her. I'd say you've done just fine."

Neither Noah nor I know what to say. Her words feel like a kind of blessing, a sign that she approves not just of him but of us, and they make our relationship that much more official. My grandmother doesn't give us time to ponder it too deeply, however.

"Come on." She opens the hall closet. "Let's get you two some sheets and make up that sofa."

I'm GROGGY, almost but not quite asleep, when I feel a hand on my shoulder, shaking me. Without opening my eyes, I assume it's Noah. "You still awake?" I mumble. The couch is uncomfortable, but it's not like Noah to wake up in the middle of the night; ordinarily, he could sleep through a marching band.

"Mommy?"

I bolt up in the foldaway bed.

That little voice is unmistakable.

And there he is. Keegan. Standing beside me with the same expectant, slightly impatient look he always wore when he woke me. His hair is tousled and he wears the Batman pajamas Grandma bought him last Christmas. They were getting too snug, I remember, but he loved them, wouldn't let me give them away.

He reaches over and tugs on my hand. His touch is solid. Unbelievably solid. "Mommy," he says again.

He looks so familiar, so unchanged, I wonder if I've dreamed it all, the long and terrible autumn, this whole twisted, eventful winter. But no. Here I am in my grandmother's house, Noah asleep face-first in the pillow beside me.

"Hey, baby." I can barely get the words out. "I'm so happy to see you." I scoop him up into the bed with us. It's already pretty crowded in the foldaway, but I make space for him anyway, curving my body to his. He snuggles against me. "Oh, sweetie." I press my face to his hair and marvel at his curls, their shampoo scent, the way they tickle my nose. "I've missed you so much." I'm choking up now, overwhelmed.

"Don't be sad." He pats my head the same awkward way he used to pet dogs and cats.

"I can't help it. I really, really miss you, Kee." He's warm in my arms, and a little wriggly. Every inch the boy that I remember.

"I'm right here, Mom."

"I know. But you're going to leave again, aren't you? You won't stay with me. You just came to . . . what? Make me feel better for a little while?" I trace his precious little ears, his pointy chin.

He shakes me off. "I came to tell you a secret."

"Yeah? What kind of secret?"

Joy—sweet and unadulterated—lights up his face. "I have a little sister!"

I guess I shouldn't be surprised that Eric and Melissa decided to have a baby, but I am. Surprised and maybe a little angry. *It's not fair. Why does he deserve another chance?*

"Congratulations," I say with some difficulty. "That means you're a big brother, huh? What's her name?"

"I don't know," he says. "What are you going to name her?"

"Me? Honey, I don't get to decide—" But I realize then what he's telling me.

I've had only one period since Keegan died. When I stopped menstruating after his death, the doctor told me not to worry. It was stress related, she said, not uncommon. Eventually I should resume having them normally. And I did have a period, one period, just after Christmas. Which means, assuming my body *did* somehow get back on schedule, I would've ovulated fourteen days later. Right around the time I met Noah.

Oh. My God.

"Mom," Keegan tells me, "my little sister is growing in your belly."

It's both the best news and the worst news I could imagine. I have nowhere to live and no job, and Noah does not want a child. I don't want to be with a man who isn't ready and ecstatic to be a father. Having a baby will mean the end of us.

But.

It's a baby. A daughter.

No matter how ill-timed, how crazy or inconvenient her arrival, she will be my child. The joy of that will get me through all the rest.

I hug Keegan tightly to me. He's the only one who can share in my happiness. "Thank you," I murmur. "I didn't know."

"That's how come I had to tell you."

I nod. "It's . . . a surprise. A really good surprise." Something terrifying occurs to me. "Keegan, what about her brain? Will she be like you? Will she . . ." I can't even finish the question.

He nestles his head on my shoulder and yawns. "She'll be okay," he assures me. "She won't get sick."

He's so matter-of-fact, so devoid of blame, yet I still can't shake the guilt. "I'm sorry I couldn't help you, baby. I'm sorry I didn't see something was wrong." I swallow. "I wish that I'd . . . paid better attention."

"I had to leave, Mommy."

"No. It was my job to keep you here. To keep you safe. And I didn't."

He sighs, like I'm missing the whole point of everything. "If I didn't leave," he explains patiently, "then you wouldn't grow my little sister."

Is that how it works? I want to ask. Is the universe really this unfair? To lead you on a circuitous path to one child, it takes away another? What a crock. Had anyone given me a choice, I would've chosen Keegan. I would've chosen him a thousand times over. I would've kept my crappy job and stumbled through my lonely single-mom existence until the end of time if only he could've stayed. No matter what Keegan says, I'm not convinced there's a master plan in any of this. As far as I can tell, life is pure chance, with good events and bad falling randomly upon us. Do the why and how even make a difference? I have to live in this world regardless.

"Kee?" Suddenly I feel sleepy, too exhausted to contemplate any of this.

His head shifts against my shoulder as he looks up at me. "What, Mommy?"

"What was the last thing I said to you?" It's always bothered me. I've reviewed the day he died in my mind a thousand times, but I can never remember our final moment together. "When I dropped you off at school, what was the last thing I said?"

He rolls his eyes. "What you *always* say. You said, 'Have a good day, Kee, I love you.'"

Something in me relaxes. It shouldn't matter, not after everything, but it does. "Good," I say. "I hope you never forget. I love you so much. Always."

Even now, my love is unremarkable to him, maybe even a little embarrassing. His mother will forever be something he can take for granted, and I'm glad. "I know, Mommy," he says. "I *know*."

WHEN I WAKE UP, my son is gone. There's a hollow space in my arms where I held him. I should feel loss, emptiness, devastation, all the emotions I've been wrestling with since he died. Instead, I feel calm. A sense of peace has fallen over me, wrapped me in its warmth like a soft, protective blanket.

He was here, I think. *He was really here.*

I could've been dreaming. There's no proof that I wasn't. All I have to go on is this feeling of comfort, and yet somehow that's enough. I believe in something impossible. For the first time in my life, I have faith. Not in some omnipotent creator or the weird workings of the universe, but in my son. I believe in my son.

It's still dark out. Not quite six a.m., according to my phone. Beside me, Noah snores loudly despite the pillow covering his head. I slip from bed, away from his warmth, and press my face to the window, gazing down at the parking lot. The cars sparkle beneath the streetlights, covered in a thin layer of frost. Spring will be here soon, then summer. Come autumn, I will have a baby girl.

I stand by the window for a long time, watch the rising light. A pair of birds skitter across the branches of a tree and fly away. An early riser begins to scrape the frost from his windshield in long, laborious strokes. From the couch, I hear Noah rustling around.

"Whatcha see out there?" he asks.

He looks bizarrely content for someone who spent the night on a foldaway bed in the house of an eighty-seven-year-old woman. But he's never asked for much. This whole trip he's just seemed glad to have a place to go.

"You okay?" He squints at me. "You look all spooky."

I don't reply. For as little time as he's known me, he reads me pretty well.

"You had one of those dreams, didn't you?" He leans forward, fascinated, but also creeped out. "What did you see?"

I hesitate. There's only one key part of my Keegan encounter that I should share, but I don't know how he'll react. "I need to tell you something."

He's lost his family, I think. *Maybe he'll change his mind. Maybe he'll want the baby.*

"That doesn't sound good," he says.

I don't draw it out. "I think I'm pregnant."

"What do you . . . but *how?*" He blinks a few times. "By *who?*"

This is worse than I was expecting. "Did you really just ask me that?"

He's too busy trying to wrap his brain around my pregnancy to apologize.

"Wait, so . . . you're gonna have a baby? *My* baby?"

"Yeah."

"I don't get it." He climbs out of bed looking more befuddled than distraught. "You said you don't get a period. I didn't think you could *have* kids. And we've been safe. After the first time, we've always used—" He stops. "You think it was the first time?"

"I'm guessing."

"Jesus. So that would make you . . . uh . . ." His math skills fail him. "How far along?"

"About eleven weeks. It's a girl."

"A girl." He rubs his eyes like he might be dreaming. "This is crazy. You're sure?"

"Pretty sure." I remove all the pillows from the bed, peel off the sheets, and begin folding up the couch. It's easier not to look at him. "Listen, you've been very up-front with me about the kids thing, and this was more my mistake than yours. I have no expectations here. If you want out—"

"Out? Out of what?"

"Of us. Of being a dad. I know this wasn't part of your plan."

"Well, no, but . . ." His voice gets very, very quiet. "Are you tellin' me *you* want out? That you don't want this baby?"

I stop fussing with the couch. "I want this baby more than anything."

"Well, good." He looks tremendously relieved. "Me too."

Now it's my turn to be confused. "I thought you and Carmen split up because you *didn't* want kids."

His face asks how I got such an absurd notion in my head. "No, we split up 'cause I *did*."

I'm at a loss for words.

"I didn't *always* want kids," he explains. "When Carmen and I got together, neither one of us did. I was kinda a party boy, I guess, and she never liked little 'uns. But then my granddaddy got sick, and I dunno. Somethin' was missin'. I realized I didn't want it to be just her and me forever."

"You changed your mind," I say softly, recalling now the conversation we had the night we met. He said he and Carmen used to be on the same page about children, but he changed his mind. Not knowing him, I'd assumed he was one of those guys who fear responsibility, who put off their wife's requests for a baby with an *I'm not ready yet*. But that's not Noah. Of course it's not.

Noah flops down on the reassembled couch and massages his temples. "I thought you knew where I stood on this. Remember when I asked how you felt about kids, and you got all weird on me, just totally shut me down?"

I nod, dazed; it was right before Rae came to visit.

"I didn't get why you were actin' so funny until Rae told me about Keegan."

Of course. The little chat they had in the garden. Why would I ever underestimate Rae's big mouth? Noah, however, is clearly grateful to her.

"She said I shouldn't give up on you," he tells me. "That you were a great mom. She said you loved kids."

Listening to Noah speak, I suddenly have the odd feeling that Keegan is with me. The curly head, the Batman pajamas—they're close, if only I knew how to see. "I do," I say. "I do love kids."

"I didn't mean for it to go like this," Noah says. "I wanted to give you some time. To grieve, you know? I thought, when you were ready, we could see a doctor. And even if we couldn't have a kid together, we could maybe adopt. But I thought it could work."

It could work. It could actually work. I hear sounds of my grandmother moving around her bedroom, louder than necessary, as if warning us she can hear. This isn't the most private place to have this conversation, I realize, but I can't imagine putting it off.

"You really want to do this?"

"I'm not pretendin' it's gonna be easy," he acknowledges. "We got a lot to do before this little lady comes. I hope you weren't lookin' for a big weddin'."

"Wedding?" I raise my eyebrows.

He acts like this is no big thing. "Well, sure, we gotta get married."

"We've got two divorces between us, Noah, and the ink on your papers is still wet. We're not getting married."

"Yes. We are." He meets my gaze straight on, and from the way his jaw is set, I know I've met my match in stubborn. "Nobody's gonna look at me and think I'm not committed to the mother of my child."

"Sorry you feel that way," I tell him evenly, "but I don't give a crap what people think. I'm done with marriage. And I'm certainly not going to get strong-armed into it just because I'm pregnant. What century do you Texans live in, anyway?"

He takes a deep breath, drawing on some deep reserve of calm that is probably available only because my grandmother is in the other room. "We're not gonna argue about this now," he says. "We got plenty other decisions to make."

"Such as?"

"Well, to start, we gotta find somewhere to live. Carmen got the house, and my place isn't right for raisin' a family." He rubs his chin, thinking it over. "We can spend a couple more days here, but we should probably get back and start house-huntin'."

"Get back where? You think I'm going to raise my kid in Texas?" This will be an even bigger sticking point than marriage.

"You'll like Sidalie," he promises me. "The schools are good. We can get a big house, big yard—"

"*I'm not living in Texas.* How can you expect me to just . . . drop everything . . ."

"Honey, that's where I work. I gotta oversee my company."

I call bullshit. "You just inherited a quarter of the Deveau fortune. Don't tell me you have to work."

"I happen to love my job," he begins, and then decides this line of reasoning will get him nowhere. "Just come to Sidalie with me. Give it a chance. You'll like it, I know you'll like it."

"It doesn't matter if I like it or not, it's in *Texas*! Are you *listening* to me? Texas is out." I don't know if my blind resistance to the Lone Star State is a result of hormones, a fear of change, or what, but even I can hear now that I sound a little nuts.

"You can't rule out an entire state you've never been to," Noah says in a tone that indicates some experience dealing with unreasonable females. "You should at least visit. The weather is better, the real estate is more affordable."

I'm about to launch a spirited defense of the Northeast, but suddenly in the middle of what seems to be a Very Important Debate, I can't help myself. I break into a huge, stupid grin. I start to laugh. It's too amazing, too miraculous for me to get angry. Where will we live? Should we get married? *These* are our issues. This moment is too good to waste on petty squabbling. Because what were the chances? After abandonment, betrayal, a pair of failed marriages, and personal losses too great to enumerate, Noah and I have survived. We're semifunctional human beings. We're expecting a baby. And we're together. One way or another, we'll have to iron out the details. But right now, how can I be anything but happy?

Irritation flashes across Noah's face as he realizes that I'm not absorbing any of his pro-Sidalie talking points. "Charlie? Why you smilin'? I don't find this funny." His reproof only broadens my smirk. He already sounds so fatherly.

"Babe," he says, trying again. "Please. Stay with me on this. We're talkin' about our future. We're talkin' about our daughter."

"I know." My whole body seems to tingle at the words "our daughter," so wonderful and strange to my ears. I reach out and weave my fingers through his, feel him relax slightly at my touch. "That's why I'm smiling."

Acknowledgments

Anyone interested in Louisiana's historic plantation homes can learn much from the knowledgeable guides at Oak Alley Plantation in Vacherie and Shadows-on-the-Teche in New Iberia. They answered several questions for me as I got started with the writing process. Visiting a currently occupied and somewhat modernized plantation home, on the other hand, seemed a tall order. I am fortunate that former governor Mike Foster and his wife, Alice, generously open Oaklawn Manor, their family estate in Franklin, to the public. On both my visits, guide Mary Edwards provided chatty and colorful tours, which proved immensely helpful in the writing of this novel.

My appreciation goes to Rosaleigh Young, Deborah Hoff, and Carolyn Wise, who each offered thoughtful commentary on various drafts. Over and over again, Ellen Madigan and Todd Moore gave me the child-free writing time I needed in the homestretch—I am so grateful for their friendship. For nurturing my interest in writing from an early age and comparing my mediocre fifth-grade stories to the classics, I owe my father, John, a thank-you as well.

Above all, my profound gratitude goes to Spencer Wise, who read each chapter as I wrote it, happily accompanied me on several research trips, and pushed me to put my work out in the world when I was tempted to hide it in a drawer. I have wanted to be a writer since I was six years old. Spencer, you were the wind in my sails that brought me here.